D0807084

HOMEFRONT HORRORS

FRIGHTS AWAY FROM THE FRONT LINES

1914–1918

Edited by
JESS NEVINS

DOVER PUBLICATIONS, INC.
Mineola, New York

Bibliographical Note

Homefront Horrors: Frights Away From the Front Lines, 1914–1918, first published by Dover Publications, Inc., in 2016, is a new anthology of seventeen stories reprinted from standard sources.

Jess Nevins has selected and edited the stories, and provided the Introduction and the biographical notes that precede each story.

Sensitive readers should be forewarned that the text in places contains cultural references characteristic of the era, which may be deemed offensive by modern standards.

International Standard Book Number

ISBN-13: 978-0-486-80907-6
ISBN-10: 0-486-80907-2

Manufactured in the United States by RR Donnelley
80907201   2016
www.doverpublications.com

Contents

INTRODUCTION:
NEGLECTED MASTERS

No ONE WOULD ever call World War One a pleasant war. Millions of soldiers died from artillery, machine guns, trench warfare, and disease; millions more civilians were killed as a result of the war. The scars the war left on those who experienced it never faded.

British civilians on the homefront had it relatively easy compared to French, German, and Belgian civilians, who were more directly touched by the war. Yet the British homefront during the war had its own particular unpleasantries—food rationing, aerial bombing by the Germans, and strikes by discontented workers primary among them. The British homefront culture thrived, with huge increases in the circulation of magazines and attendance at music halls, but the effects of the war were felt everywhere.

Yet one would never know there was a war being fought judging by the horror stories which were published during the time. With one or two exceptions, like Arthur Machen's "The Bowmen" (1914), authors of horror fiction refrained from using the war as a setting, as a theme, or even referring to it, if only in passing.

This is indeed curious, especially compared to other literary genres and other media, which incorporated the war into stories and films at about the rate one would expect for such a major contemporary event.

It may be that the topic of the war was seen as too serious, the threat of the Germans too ominous, for it to be fodder for something as trite and meaningless as horror stories. (Although this was a time before horror stories were condemned to inhabit a literary ghetto; note how many of the stories in this collection appeared in hardcover collections or mainstream magazines, rather than the lower-class story papers. Horror stories were treated by writers and readers as seriously as stories in the mainstream). Conversely, perhaps writers were determined to give the public—who were after all preoccupied with all the horribleness of the war—truly escapist literature, stories which would take the readers away from their current, dreadful realities.

Or perhaps it was as simple as the writers not wanting to limit themselves to writing about the war when there were so many other things and people who inspired them and their stories. Algernon Blackwood had his Egyptian trip on his mind when he wrote "The Wings of Horus;" Thomas Burke was thinking of his beloved Limehouse during the writing of "The Bird;" Stacy Aumonier's "Old Fags" deals with the "new poor" of London; Sir Hugh Clifford calls on his experience in Malaysia in "The Ghoul."

Whatever the case, the horror stories which British civilians got to read avoided the war, and instead concentrated on doing what the writers did best: frightening the reader. In this, they were highly successful. The war years, 1914–1918, lie in the middle of the golden age of horror fiction, that roughly forty-year span from 1900 to 1940 when a large number of extremely talented men and women were turning out a great amount of high-quality stories of terror, horror, and the supernatural weird. 1918, in fact, was very nearly the century anniversary of the modern horror genre. Mary Shelley published *Frankenstein* in 1818, but that was both a Gothic novel and the first science fiction novel. It was in 1819 when John Polidori published "The Vampyre," both the first modern vampire story and in a very real sense the first modern horror story.

The difference between science fiction and horror is that what followed *Frankenstein* was several decades of intermittent science fiction short stories and novels. Therefore, it wasn't until the 1880s, and especially the 1890s, with H.G. Wells and the other major British and American science fiction authors of that decade, that science fiction truly came of age. Conversely, high-quality horror fiction began comparatively quickly after "The Vampyre," with Walter Scott's "Wandering Willie's Tale" (1825) and then the work of J. Sheridan Le Fanu in the 1830s. In mid-century a craze for ghost stories and haunted house stories gripped British writers and readers, with numerous excellent stories following over the next few decades, so that by the turn of the century—when science fiction was only coming of age, when the first professional mystery writers were starting to make their mark, when Western/frontier fiction was still in its infancy—horror fiction had several decades of solid work on its resume.

Yet none of that could have prepared readers for what was to follow. There were horror stories of note in the 1890s—Charlotte Perkins Gilman's "The Yellow Wallpaper" (1892), Ambrose Bierce's "The Damned Thing" (1893), Arthur Machen's "The Great God Pan" (1894)—but the flood of memorable and even classic stories that began in the early 1900s was unprecedented. Vernon Lee, Mary Wilkins

Freeman, F. Marion Crawford, William Hope Hodgson . . . the list goes on, writers whose work retains its power to move and chill us, stories which have aged very little, if at all, and which any fan interested in supernatural fiction should read if they want to understand how the genre developed as it did.

In fact, the numbers of superbly talented authors and classic stories which appeared during the 1900–1940 period were so great that numerous authors and stories were—perhaps inevitably—overshadowed and forgotten about by later fans and readers. Which brings us, by roundabout fashion, to the authors and stories included in this anthology. Algernon Blackwood and Lord Dunsany are still remembered and in print, but the same cannot be said of Stacy Aumonier or Clemence Dane or Phyllis Bottome, despite the general excellence of their work. "An Episode of Cathedral History" and "Thirteen at Table" have been reprinted within the last twenty years, if not in widely available books, but not so "The King Waits" or "Powers of the Air" or "The Liqueur Glass," all stories once acclaimed and anthologized. Like many other authors and stories of the time, most of the inclusions in this anthology are forgotten gems by neglected masters, and I hope that, once you finish reading *Homefront Horrors*, you will be inspired to seek out more work by these authors, whether online or in used bookstores.

JESS NEVINS

HOMEFRONT
HORRORS

THE WINGS OF HORUS

Algernon Blackwood
(1869–1951)

*Algernon Blackwood should be familiar to readers of this anthology. He was famous during his lifetime for his pantheistic fantasies (*The Centaur *(1911),* Pan's Garden *(1912)) and his children's books (*Jimbo *(1909),* Sambo and Snitch *(1927)) as well as his radio broadcasts, in which he told radio-formatted versions of his best stories. Since his death he has become known as one of the best writers of supernatural fiction of his day, author of classics like "The Willows" (1907), "The Wendigo" (1910), and the landmark occult detective collection* John Silence—Physician Extraordinary *(1908).*

Blackwood's life makes for a good story, though not as frightening as his horror stories: hardships as a young man in Canada and New York City; travels through remote sections of northern Canada, the Caucasus mountains, and down the Danube; several years' experiences with the occult group The Hermetic Order of the Golden Dawn; a broken heart when his "soul mate" married someone else; work as an intelligence agent and Red Cross volunteer during World War One; and eventual success and stability in his sixties in his radio career.

"The Wings of Horus" comes from Blackwood's Egyptian phase, from his time spent there in 1914, although it was not published until his Day And Night Stories *(1917). Blackwood was much inspired by Egyptian culture and philosophy, and wrote a number of stories while there. "The Wings of Horus" is generally regarded as the best of the bunch, and one of Blackwood's best overall, what Blackwood biographer Mike Ashley calls "both a beautiful love story and an awesome story of power and belief."*

BINOVITCH HAD THE bird in him somewhere: in his features, certainly, with his piercing eye and hawk-like nose; in his movements, with his quick way of flitting, hopping, darting; in the way he perched on the edge of a chair; in the manner he pecked at his food; in his twittering, high-pitched voice as well; and, above all, in his mind. He skimmed all subjects and picked their heart out neatly, as a bird skims lawn or air to snatch its prey. He had the bird's-eye view of everything. He loved birds and understood them instinctively; could imitate their whistling notes with astonishing accuracy. Their one quality he had not was poise and balance. He was a nervous little man; he was neurasthenic. And he was in Egypt by doctor's orders.

Such imaginative, unnecessary ideas he had! Such uncommon beliefs!

"The old Egyptians," he said laughingly, yet with a touch of solemn conviction in his manner, "were a great people. Their consciousness was different from ours. The bird idea, for instance, conveyed a sense of deity to them—of bird deity, that is: they had sacred birds—hawks, ibis, and so forth—and worshiped them." And he put his tongue out as though to say with challenge, "Ha, ha!"

"They also worshiped cats and crocodiles and cows," grinned Palazov. Binovitch seemed to dart across the table at his adversary. His eyes flashed; his nose pecked the air. Almost one could imagine the beating of his angry wings.

"Because everything alive," he half screamed, "was a symbol of some spiritual power to them. Your mind is as literal as a dictionary and as incoherent. Pages of ink without connected meaning! Verb always in the infinitive! If you were an old Egyptian, you—you—" he flashed and spluttered, his tongue shot out again, his keen eyes blazed—"you might take all those words and spin them into a great interpretation of life, a cosmic romance, as they did. Instead, you get the bitter, dead taste of ink in your mouth, and spit it over us like that"—he made a quick movement of his whole body as a bird that shakes itself—"in empty phrases."

Khilkof ordered another bottle of champagne, while Vera, his sister, said half nervously, "Let's go for a drive; it's moonlight." There was enthusiasm at once. Another of the party called the head-waiter and told him to pack food and drink in baskets. It was only eleven o'clock. They would drive out into the desert, have a meal at two in the morning, tell stories, sing, and see the dawn.

It was in one of those cosmopolitan hotels in Egypt which attract the ordinary tourists as well as those who are doing a "cure," and all these Russians were ill with one thing or another. All were ordered out for their health, and all were the despair of their doctors. They were as unmanageable as a bazaar and as incoherent. Excess and bed were their routine. They lived, but none of them got better. Equally, none of them got angry. They talked in this strange personal way without a shred of malice or offense. The English, French, and Germans in the hotel watched them with remote amazement, referring to them as "that Russian lot." Their energy was elemental. They never stopped. They merely disappeared when the pace became too fast, then reappeared again after a day or two, and resumed their "living" as before. Binovitch, despite his neurasthenia, was the life of the party. He was also a special patient of Dr. Plitzinger, the famous psychiatrist, who took a peculiar interest in his case. It was not surprising. Binovitch was a man of unusual ability and of genuine, deep culture. But there was something more about him that stimulated curiosity. There was this striking originality. He said and did surprising things.

"I could fly if I wanted to," he said once when the airmen came to astonish the natives with their biplanes over the desert, "but without all that machinery and noise. It's only a question of believing and understanding—"

"Show us!" they cried. "Let's see you fly!"

"He's got it! He's off again! One of his impossible moments."

These occasions when Binovitch let himself go always proved wildly entertaining. He said monstrously incredible things as though he really did believe them. They loved his madness, for it gave them new sensations.

"It's only levitation, after all, this flying," he exclaimed, shooting out his tongue between the words, as his habit was when excited; "and what is levitation but a power of the air? None of you can hang an orange in space for a second, with all your scientific knowledge; but the moon is always levitated perfectly. And the stars. D'you think they swing on wires? What raised the enormous stones of ancient Egypt? D'you really believe it was heaped-up sand and ropes and clumsy leverage and all our weary and laborious mechanical contrivances? Bah! It was levitation. It was the powers of the air. Believe in those powers, and gravity becomes a mere nursery trick—true where it is, but true nowhere else. To know the fourth dimension is to step out of a locked room and appear instantly on the roof or in another country altogether. To know the powers of the air, similarly, is to annihilate what you call weight—and fly."

"Show us, show us!" they cried, roaring with delighted laughter.

"It's a question of belief," he repeated, his tongue appearing and disappearing like a pointed shadow. "It's in the heart; the power of the air gets into your whole being. Why should I show you? Why should I ask my deity to persuade your scoffing little minds by any miracle? For it *is* deity, I tell you, and nothing else. I *know* it. Follow one idea like that, as I follow my bird idea,—follow it with the impetus and undeviating concentration of a projectile,—and you arrive at power. You know deity—the bird idea of deity, that is. *They* knew that. The old Egyptians knew it."

"Oh, show us, show us!" they shouted impatiently, wearied of his nonsense-talk. "Get up and fly! Levitate yourself, as they did! Become a star!"

Binovitch turned suddenly very pale, and an odd light shone in his keen brown eyes. He rose slowly from the edge of the chair where he was perched. Something about him changed. There was silence instantly.

"I *will* show you," he said calmly, to their intense amazement; "not to convince your disbelief, but to prove it to myself. For the powers of the air are with me here. I believe. And Horus, great falcon-headed symbol, is my patron god."

The suppressed energy in his voice and manner was indescribable. There was a sense of lifting, upheaving power about him. He raised his arms; his face turned upward; he inflated his lungs with a deep, long breath, and his voice broke into a kind of singing cry, half-prayer, half-chant:

> "O Horus,
> Bright-eyed deity of wind,
> Feather my soul[1]
> Through earth's thick air,
> To know thy awful swiftness—"

He broke off suddenly. He climbed lightly and swiftly upon the nearest table—it was in a deserted card-room, after a game in which he had lost more pounds than there are days in the year—and leaped into the air. He hovered a second, spread his arms and legs in space, appeared to float a moment, then buckled, rushed down and forward, and dropped in a heap upon the floor, while every one roared with laughter.

But the laughter died out quickly, for there was something in his wild performance that was peculiar and unusual. It was uncanny, not quite natural. His body had seemed, as with Mordkin and Nijinski, literally to hang upon the air a moment. For a second he gave the distressing impression of overcoming gravity. There was a touch in it of that faint horror which appalls by its very vagueness. He picked himself up unhurt, and his face was as grave as a portrait in the academy, but with a new expression in it that everybody noticed with this strange, half-shocked amazement. And it was this expression that extinguished the claps of laughter as wind that takes away the sound of bells. Like many ugly men, he was an inimitable actor, and his facial repertory was endless and incredible. But this was neither acting nor clever manipulation of expressive features. There was something in his curious Russian

---

1. The Russian is untranslatable. The phrase means, "Give my life wings."

physiognomy that made the heart beat slower. And that was why the laughter died away so suddenly.

"You ought to have flown farther," cried someone. It expressed what all had felt.

"Icarus didn't drink champagne," another replied, with a laugh; but nobody laughed with him.

"You went too near to Vera," said Palazov, "and passion melted the wax." But his face twitched oddly as he said it. There was something he did not understand, and so heartily disliked.

The strange expression on the features deepened. It was arresting in a disagreeable, almost in a horrible, way. The talk stopped dead; all stared; there was a feeling of dismay in everybody's heart, yet unexplained. Some lowered their eyes, or else looked stupidly elsewhere; but the women of the party felt a kind of fascination. Vera, in particular, could not move her sight away. The joking reference to his passionate admiration for her passed unnoticed. There was a general and individual sense of shock. And a chorus of whispers rose instantly:

"Look at Binovitch! What's happened to his face?"

"He's changed—he's changing!"

"God! Why he looks like a—bird!"

But no one laughed. Instead, they chose the names of birds—hawk, eagle, even owl. The figure of a man leaning against the edge of the door, watching them closely, they did not notice. He had been passing down the corridor, had looked in unobserved, and then had paused. He had seen the whole performance. He watched Binovitch narrowly, now with calm, discerning eyes. It was Dr. Plitzinger, the great psychiatrist.

For Binovitch had picked himself up from the floor in a way that was oddly self-possessed, and precluded the least possibility of the ludicrous. He looked neither foolish nor abashed. He looked surprised, but also he looked half angry and half frightened. As some one had said, he "ought to have flown farther." That was the incredible impression his acrobatics had produced—incredible, yet somehow actual. This uncanny idea prevailed, as at a séance where nothing genuine is expected to happen, and something genuine, after all, does happen. There was no pretense in this: Binovitch had flown.

And now he stood there, white in the face—with terror and with anger white. He looked extraordinary, this little, neurasthenic Russian, but he looked at the same time half terrific. Another thing, not commonly experienced by men, was in him, breaking out of him, affecting directly the minds of his companions. His mouth opened; blood and fury shone in his blazing eyes; his tongue shot out like an ant-eater's, though even in that the comic had no place. His arms were spread like flapping wings, and his voice rose dreadfully:

"He failed me, he failed me!" he tried to bellow. "Horus, my falcon-headed deity, my power of the air, deserted me! Hell take him! Hell burn his wings and blast his piercing sight! Hell scorch him into dust for his false prophecies! I curse him, I curse Horus!"

The voice that should have roared across the silent room emitted, instead, this high-pitched, bird-like scream. The added touch of sound, the reality it lent, was ghastly. Yet it was marvelously done and acted. The entire thing was a bit of instantaneous inspiration—his voice, his words, his gestures, his whole wild appearance. Only—here was the reality that caused the sense of shock—the expression on his altered features was genuine. That was not assumed. There was something new and alien in him, something cold and difficult to human life, something alert and swift and cruel, of another element than earth. A strange, rapacious grandeur had leaped upon the struggling features. The face looked hawk-like.

And he came forward suddenly and sharply toward Vera, whose fixed, staring eyes had never once ceased watching him with a kind of anxious and devouring pain in them. She was both drawn and beaten back. Binovitch advanced on tiptoe. No doubt he still was acting, still pretending this mad nonsense that he worshiped Horus, the falcon-headed deity of forgotten days, and that Horus had failed him in his hour of need; but somehow there was just a hint of too much reality in the way he moved and looked. The girl, a little creature, with fluffy golden hair, opened her lips; her cigarette fell to the floor; she shrank back; she looked for a moment like some smaller, colored bird trying to escape from a great pursuing hawk; she screamed. Binovitch, his arms wide, his bird-like face thrust forward, had swooped upon her. He leaped. Almost he caught her.

No one could say exactly what happened. Play, become suddenly and unexpectedly too real, confuses the emotions. The change of key was swift. From fun to terror is a dislocating jolt upon the mind. Some one—it was Khilkof, the brother—upset a chair; everybody spoke at once; everybody stood up. An unaccountable feeling of disaster was in the air, as with those drinkers' quarrels that blaze out from nothing, and end in a pistol-shot and death, no one able to explain clearly how it came about. It was the silent, watching figure in the doorway who saved the situation. Before any one had noticed his approach, there he

was among the group, laughing, talking, applauding—between Binovitch and Vera. He was vigorously patting his patient on the back, and
his voice rose easily above the general clamor. He was a strong, quiet
personality; even in his laughter there was authority. And his laughter
now was the only sound in the room, as though by his mere presence
peace and harmony were restored. Confidence came with him. The
noise subsided; Vera was in her chair again. Khilkof poured out a glass
of wine for the great man.

"The Czar!" said Plitzinger, sipping his champagne, while all stood
up, delighted with his compliment and tact. "And to your opening
night with the Russian ballet," he added quickly a second toast, "or to
your first performance at the Moscow Theatre des Arts!" Smiling significantly, he glanced at Binovitch; he clinked glasses with him. Their
arms were already linked, but it was Palazov who noticed that the doctor's fingers seemed rather tight upon the creased black coat. All drank,
looking with laughter, yet with a touch of respect toward Binovitch,
who stood there dwarfed beside the stalwart German, and suddenly as
meek and subdued as any mole. Apparently the abrupt change of key
had taken his mind successfully off something else.

"Of course—'The Fire-Bird,'" exclaimed the little man, mentioning
the famous Russian ballet. "The very thing!" he exclaimed. "For *us*,"
he added, looking with devouring eyes at Vera. He was greatly pleased.
He began talking vociferously about dancing and the rationale of dancing. They told him he was an undiscovered master. He was delighted.
He winked at Vera and touched her glass again with his. "We'll make
our debut together," he cried. "We'll begin at Covent Garden in London. I'll design the dresses and the posters—'The Hawk and the Dove!'
Magnifique! I in dark gray, and you in blue and gold! Ah, dancing, you
know, is sacred. The little self is lost, absorbed. It is ecstasy, it is divine.
And dancing in air—the passion of the birds and stars—ah! they are the
movements of the gods. You know deity that way—by living it."

He went on and on. His entire being had shifted with a leap upon
this new subject. The idea of realizing divinity by dancing it absorbed
him. The party discussed it with him as though nothing else existed in
the world, all sitting now and talking eagerly together. Vera took the
cigarette he offered her, lighting it from his own; their fingers touched;
he was as harmless and normal as a retired diplomat in a drawing-room.
But it was Plitzinger whose subtle maneuvering had accomplished the
change so cleverly, and it was Plitzinger who presently suggested a
game of billiards, and led him off, full now of a fresh enthusiasm for

cannons, balls, and pockets, into another room. They departed arm in arm, laughing and talking together.

Their departure, it seemed, made no great difference. Vera's eyes watched him out of sight, then turned to listen to Baron Minski, who was describing with gusto how he caught wolves alive for coursing purposes. The speed and power of the wolf, he said, was impossible to realize; the force of their awful leap, the strength of their teeth, which could bite through metal stirrup-fastenings. He showed a scar on his arm and another on his lip. He was telling truth, and everybody listened with deep interest. The narrative lasted perhaps ten minutes or more, when Minski abruptly stopped. He had come to an end; he looked about him; he saw his glass, and emptied it. There was a general pause. Another subject did not at once present itself. Sighs were heard; several fidgeted; fresh cigarettes were lighted. But there was no sign of boredom, for where one or two Russians are gathered together there is always life. They produce gaiety and enthusiasm as wind produces waves. Like great children, they plunge whole-heartedly into whatever interest presents itself at the moment. There is a kind of uncouth gamboling in their way of taking life. It seems as if they are always fighting that deep, underlying, national sadness which creeps into their very blood.

"Midnight!" then exclaimed Palazov, abruptly, looking at his watch; and the others fell instantly to talking about that watch, admiring it and asking questions. For the moment that very ordinary timepiece became the center of observation. Palazov mentioned the price. "It never stops," he said proudly, "not even under water." He looked up at everybody, challenging admiration. And he told how, at a country house, he made a bet that he would swim to a certain island in the lake, and won the bet. He and a girl were the winners, but as it was a horse they had bet, he got nothing out of it for himself, giving the horse to her. It was a genuine grievance in him. One felt he could have cried as he spoke of it. "But the watch went all the time," he said delightedly, holding the gun-metal object in his hand to show, "and I was twelve minutes in the water with my clothes on."

Yet this fragmentary talk was nothing but pretense. The sound of clicking billiard-balls was audible from the room at the end of the corridor. There was another pause. The pause, however, was intentional. It was not vacuity of mind or absence of ideas that caused it. There was another subject, an unfinished subject that each member of the group was still considering. Only no one cared to begin about it till at last, unable to resist the strain any longer, Palazov turned to Khilkof, who was saying he would take a "whisky-soda," as the champagne was too sweet, and whispered something beneath his breath; whereupon Khilkof, forgetting his drink, glanced at his sister, shrugged his shoulders, and made a curious grimace. "He's all right now,"—his reply was just audible,—"he's with Plitzinger." He cocked his head sidewise to indicate that the clicking of the billiard-balls still was going on.

The subject was out: all turned their heads; voices hummed and buzzed; questions were asked and answered or half answered; eyebrows were raised, shoulders shrugged, hands spread out expressively. There came into the atmosphere a feeling of presentiment, of mystery, of things half understood; primitive, buried instinct stirred a little, the kind of racial dread of vague emotions that might gain the upper hand if encouraged. They shrank from looking something in the face, while yet this unwelcome influence drew closer round them all. They discussed Binovitch and his astonishing performance. Pretty little Vera listened with large and troubled eyes, though saying nothing. The Arab waiter had put out the lights in the corridor, and only a cluster burned now above their heads, leaving their faces in shadow. In the distance the clicking of the billiard-balls still continued.

"It was not play; it was real," exclaimed Minski, vehemently. "I can catch wolves," he blurted; "but birds—ugh!—and human birds!" He was half inarticulate. He had witnessed something he could not understand, and it had touched instinctive terror in him. "It was the way he leaped that put the wolf first into my mind, only it was not a wolf at all." The others agreed and disagreed. "It was play at first, but it was reality at the end," another whispered; "and it was no animal he mimicked, but a bird of prey at that!"

Vera thrilled. In the Russian woman hides that touch of savagery which loves to be caught, mastered, swept helplessly away, captured utterly and deliciously by the one strong enough to do it thoroughly. She left her chair and sat down beside an older woman in the party, who took her arm quietly at once. Her little face wore a perplexed expression, mournful, yet somehow wild. It was clear that Binovitch was not indifferent to her.

"It's become an *idée fixe* with him," this older woman said. "The bird idea lives in his mind. He lives it in his imagination. Ever since that time at Edfu, when he pretended to worship the great stone falcons outside the temple,—the Horus figures,—he's been full of it." She stopped. The way Binovitch had behaved at Edfu was better left unmentioned at the moment, perhaps. A slight shiver ran round the

listening group, each one waiting for some one else to focus their emotion, and so explain it by saying the convincing thing. Only no one
ventured. Then Vera abruptly gave a little jump.

"Hark!" she exclaimed, in a staccato whisper, speaking for the first
time. She sat bolt upright. She was listening. "Hark!" she repeated.
"There it is again, but nearer than before. It's coming closer. I hear
it." She trembled. Her voice, her manner, above all her great staring
eyes, startled everybody. No one spoke for several seconds; all listened. The clicking of the billiard-balls had ceased. The halls and corridors lay in darkness, and gloom was over the big hotel. Everybody
else was in bed.

"Hear what?" asked the older woman, soothingly, yet with a perceptible quaver in her voice, too. She was aware that the girl's arm shook
upon her own.

"Do you not hear it, too?" the girl whispered.

All listened without speaking. All watched her paling face. Something wonderful, yet half terrible, seemed in the air about them. There
was a dull murmur, audible, faint, remote, its direction hard to tell. It
had come suddenly from nowhere. They shivered. That strange racial
thrill again passed into the group, unwelcome, unexplained. It was
aboriginal; it belonged to the unconscious primitive mind, half childish,
half terrifying.

"*What* do you hear?" her brother asked angrily—the irritable anger
of nervous fear.

"When he came at me," she answered very low, "I heard it first. I
hear it now again. He's coming."

And at that minute, out of the dark mouth of the corridor, emerged
two human figures, Plitzinger and Binovitch. Their game was over;
they were going up to bed. They passed the open door of the card-
room. But Binovitch was being half dragged, half restrained, for he was
apparently attempting to run down the passage with flying, dancing
leaps. He bounded. It was like a huge bird trying to rise for flight, while
his companion kept him down by force upon the earth. As they
entered the strip of light, Plitzinger changed his own position, placing
himself swiftly between his companion and the group in the dark corner of the room. He hurried Binovitch along as though he sheltered
him from view. They passed into the shadows down the passage. They
disappeared. And every one looked significantly, questioningly, at his
neighbor, though at first saying no word. It seemed a curious distur-
bance of the air had followed them.

Vera was the first to open her lips. "You heard it then," she said breathlessly, her face whiter than the ceiling.

"Damn!" exclaimed her brother, furiously. "It was wind against the outside walls—wind in the desert. The sand is driving."

Vera looked at him. She shrank closer against the side of the older woman, whose arm was tight about her.

"It was not wind," she whispered simply. She paused. All waited uneasily for the completion of her sentence. They stared into her face like peasants who expected a miracle.

"Wings," she whispered. "It was the sound of enormous wings."

And at four o'clock in the morning, when they all returned exhausted from their excursion into the desert, little Binovitch was sleeping soundly and peacefully in his bed. They passed his door on tiptoe. But he did not hear them. He was dreaming. His spirit was at Edfu, experiencing with that ancient deity who was master of all flying life those strange enjoyments upon which his troubled heart was passionately set. Safe with that mighty falcon whose powers his lips had scorned a few hours before, his soul, released in vivid dream, went sweetly flying. It was amazing, it was gorgeous. He skimmed the Nile at lightning speed. Dashing down headlong from the height of the great Pyramid, he chased with faultless accuracy a little dove that sought vainly to hide from his terrific pursuit beneath the palm-trees. For what he loved must worship where he worshiped, and the majesty of those tremendous effigies had fired his imagination to the creative point where expression was imperative.

Then suddenly, at the very moment of delicious capture, the dream turned horrible, becoming awful with the nightmare touch. The sky lost all its blue and sunshine. Far, far below him the little dove enticed him into nameless depths, so that he flew faster and faster, yet never fast enough to overtake it. Behind him came a great thing down the air, black, hovering, with gigantic wings outstretched. It had terrific eyes, and the beating of its feathers stole his wind away. It followed him, crowding space. He was aware of a colossal beak, curved like a scimitar and pointed wickedly like a tooth of iron. He dropped. He faltered. He tried to scream.

Through empty space he fell, caught by the neck. The huge falcon was upon him. The talons were in his heart. And in sleep he remembered then that he had cursed. He recalled his reckless language. The curse of the ignorant is meaningless; that of the worshiper is real. This attack was on his soul. He had invoked it. He realized next, with a touch of ghastly horror, that the dove he chased was, after all, the bait that had lured him purposely to destruction, and awoke with a suffocating terror upon him, and his entire body bathed in icy perspiration. Outside the open window he heard a sound of wings retreating with powerful strokes into the surrounding darkness of the sky.

The nightmare made its impression upon Binovitch's impressionable and dramatic temperament. It aggravated his tendencies. He related it next day to Mme. de Drühn, the friend of Vera, telling it with that somewhat boisterous laughter some minds use to disguise less kind emotions. But he received no encouragement. The mood of the previous night was not recoverable; it was already ancient history. Russians never make the banal mistake of repeating a sensation till it is exhausted; they hurry on to novelties. Life flashes and rushes with them, never standing still for exposures before the cameras of their minds. Mme. de Drühn, however, took the trouble to mention the matter to Plitzinger, for Plitzinger, like Freud of Vienna, held that dreams revealed subconscious tendencies which sooner or later must betray themselves in action.

"Thank you for telling me," he smiled politely, "but I have already heard it from him." He watched her eyes a moment, really examining her soul. "Binovitch, you see," he continued, apparently satisfied with what he saw, "I regard as that rare phenomenon—a genius without an outlet. His spirit, intensely creative, finds no adequate expression. His power of production is enormous and prolific; yet he accomplishes nothing." He paused an instant. "Binovitch, therefore, is in danger of poisoning—himself." He looked steadily into her face, as a man who weighs how much he may confide. "Now," he continued, "*if* we can find an outlet for him, a field wherein his bursting imaginative genius can produce results—above all, *visible* results,"—he shrugged his shoulders,—"the man is saved. Otherwise"—he looked extraordinarily impressive—"there is bound to be sooner or later—"

"Madness?" she asked very quietly.

"An explosion, let us say," he replied gravely. "For instance, take this Horus obsession of his, quite wrong archaeologically though it is. *Au fond* it is megalomania of a most unusual kind. His passionate interest, his love, his worship of birds, wholesome enough in itself, finds no satisfying outlet. A man who *really* loves birds neither keeps them in cages nor shoots them nor stuffs them. What, then, can he do? The commonplace bird-lover observes them through glasses, studies their habits, then writes a book about them. But a man like Binovitch, overflowing with this intense creative power of mind and imagination, is not content with that. He wants to know them from within. He wants to feel what they feel, to live their life. He wants to *become* them. You follow me? Not quite. Well, he seeks to be identified with the object of his sacred, passionate admiration. All genius seeks to know the thing itself from its own point of view. It desires union. That tendency, unrecognized by himself, perhaps, and therefore subconscious, hides in his very soul." He paused a moment. "And the sudden sight of those majestic figures at Edfu—that crystallization of his *idée fixe* in granite— took hold of this excess in him, so to speak—and is now focusing it toward some definite act. Binovitch sometimes—feels himself a bird! You noticed what occurred last night?"

She nodded; a slight shiver passed over her.

"A most curious performance," she murmured; "an exhibition I never want to see again."

"The most curious part," replied the doctor, coolly, "was its truth."

"Its truth!" she exclaimed beneath her breath. She was frightened by something in his voice and by the uncommon gravity in his eyes. It seemed to arrest her intelligence. She felt upon the edge of things beyond her. "You mean that Binovitch did for a moment—hang—in the air?" The other verb, the right one, she could not bring herself to use.

The great man's face was enigmatical. He talked to her sympathy, perhaps, rather than to her mind. "Real genius," he said smilingly, "is as rare as talent, even great talent, is common. It means that the personality, if only for one second, becomes everything; becomes the universe; becomes the soul of the world. It gets the flash. It is identified with the universal life. Being everything and everywhere, all is possible to it—in that second of vivid realization. It can brood with the crystal, grow with the plant, leap with the animal, fly with the bird: genius unifies all three. That is the meaning of 'creative.' It is faith. Knowing it, you can pass through fire and not be burned, walk on water and not sink, move a mountain, fly. Because you are fire, water, earth, air. Genius, you see, is madness in the magnificent sense of being superhuman. Binovitch has it."

He broke off abruptly, seeing he was not understood. Some great enthusiasm in him he deliberately suppressed.

"The point is," he resumed, speaking more carefully, "that we must try to lead this passionate constructive genius of the man into some human channel that will absorb it, and therefore render it harmless."

"He loves Vera," the woman said, bewildered, yet seizing this point correctly.

"But would he marry her?" asked Plitzinger at once.

"He is already married."

The doctor looked steadily at her a moment, hesitating whether he should utter all his thought.

"In that case," he said slowly after a pause, "it is better he or she should leave."

His tone and manner were exceedingly impressive.

"You mean there's danger?" she asked.

"I mean, rather," he replied earnestly, "that this great creative flood in him, so curiously focused now upon his Horus-falcon-bird idea, may result in some act of violence—"

"Which would be madness," she said, looking hard at him.

"Which would be disastrous," he corrected her. And then he added slowly, "Because in the mental moment of immense creation he might overlook material laws."

The costume ball two nights later was a great success. Palazov was a Bedouin, and Khilkof an Apache; Mme. de Drühn wore a national head-dress; Minski looked almost natural as *Don Quixote*; and the entire Russian "set" was cleverly, if somewhat extravagantly, dressed. But Binovitch and Vera were the most successful of all the two hundred dancers who took part. Another figure, a big man dressed as a Pierrot, also claimed exceptional attention, for though the costume was commonplace enough, there was something of dignity in his appearance that drew the eyes of all upon him. But he wore a mask, and his identity was not discoverable.

It was Binovitch and Vera, however, who must have won the prize, if prize there had been, for they not only looked their parts, but acted them as well. The former in his dark gray feathered tunic, and his falcon mask, complete even to the brown hooked beak and tufted talons, looked fierce and splendid. The disguise was so admirable, yet so entirely natural, that it was uncommonly seductive. Vera, in blue and gold, a charming head-dress of a dove upon her loosened hair, and a pair of little dove-pale wings fluttering from her shoulders, her tiny twinkling feet and slender ankles well visible, too, was equally successful and admired. Her large and timid eyes, her flitting movements, her light and dainty way of dancing—all added touches that made the picture perfect.

How Binovitch contrived his dress remained a mystery, for the layers of wings upon his back were real; the large black kites that haunt the Nile, soaring in their hundreds over Cairo and the bleak Mokattam Hills, had furnished them. He had procured them none knew how.

They measured four feet across from tip to tip; they swished and rustled as he swept along; they were true falcons' wings. He danced with Nautch-girls and Egyptian princesses and Rumanian Gipsies; he danced well, with beauty, grace, and lightness. But with Vera he did not dance at all; with her he simply flew. A kind of passionate abandon was in him as he skimmed the floor with her in a way that made everybody turn to watch them. They seemed to leave the ground together. It was delightful, an amazing sight; but it was peculiar. The strangeness of it was on many lips. Somehow its queer extravagance communicated itself to the entire ball-room. They became the center of observation. There were whispers.

"There's that extraordinary bird-man! Look! He goes by like a hawk. And he's always after that dove-girl. How marvelously he does it! It's rather awful. Who is he? I don't envy *her.*"

People stood aside when he rushed past. They got out of his way. He seemed forever pursuing Vera, even when dancing with another partner. Word passed from mouth to mouth. A kind of telepathic interest was established everywhere. It was a shade too real sometimes, something unduly earnest in the chasing wildness, something unpleasant. There was even alarm.

"It's rowdy; I'd rather not see it; it's quite disgraceful," was heard. "*I* think it's horrible; you can see she's terrified."

And once there was a little scene, trivial enough, yet betraying this reality that many noticed and disliked. Binovitch came up to claim a dance, program clutched in his great tufted claws, and at the same moment the big Pierrot appeared abruptly round the corner with a similar claim. Those who saw it assert he had been waiting, and came on purpose, and that there was something protective and authoritative in his bearing. The misunderstanding was ordinary enough,—both men had written her name against the dance,—but "No. 13, Tango" also included the supper interval, and neither Hawk nor Pierrot would give way. They were very obstinate. Both men wanted her. It was awkward.

"The Dove shall decide between us," smiled the Hawk, politely, yet his taloned fingers working nervously. Pierrot, however, more experienced in the ways of dealing with women, or more bold, said suavely:

"I am ready to abide by her decision,—" his voice poorly cloaked this aggravating authority, as though he had the right to her,—"only I engaged this dance before his Majesty Horus appeared upon the scene at all, and therefore it is clear that Pierrot has the right of way."

At once, with a masterful air, he took her off. There was no with-standing him. He meant to have her and he got her. She yielded meekly. They vanished among the maze of colored dancers, leaving the Hawk, disconsolate and vanquished, amid the titters of the onlookers. His swiftness, as against this steady power, was of no avail.

It was then that the singular phenomenon was witnessed first. Those who saw it affirm that he changed absolutely into the part he played. It was dreadful; it was wicked. A frightened whisper ran about the rooms and corridors:

"An extraordinary thing is in the air!"

Some shrank away, while others flocked to see. There were those who swore that a curious, rushing sound was audible, the atmosphere visibly disturbed and shaken; that a shadow fell upon the spot the couple had vacated; that a cry was heard, a high, wild, searching cry: "Horus! brightest deity of wind," it began, then died away. One man was positive that the windows had been opened and that something had flown in. It was the obvious explanation. The thing spread horri-bly. As in a fire-panic, there was consternation and excitement. Confu-sion caught the feet of all the dancers. The music fumbled and lost time. The leading pair of tango-dancers halted and looked round. It seemed that everybody pressed back, hiding, shuffling, eager to see, yet more eager not to be seen, as though something dangerous, hostile, terrible, had broken loose. In rows against the wall they stood. For a great space had made itself in the middle of the ballroom, and into this empty space appeared suddenly the Pierrot and the Dove.

It was like a challenge. A sound of applause, half voices, half clapping of gloved hands, was heard. The couple danced exquisitely into the arena. All stared. There was an impression that a set piece had been prepared, and that this was its beginning. The music again took heart. Pierrot was strong and dignified, no whit nonplussed by this abrupt publicity. The Dove, though faltering, was deliciously obedient. They danced together like a single outline. She was captured utterly. And to the man who needed her the sight was naturally agonizing—the pro-tective way the Pierrot held her, the right and strength of it, the mas-tery, the complete possession.

"He's got her!" some one breathed too loud, uttering the thought of all. "Good thing it's not the Hawk!"

And, to the absolute amazement of the throng, this sight was then apparent. A figure dropped through space. That high, shrill cry again was heard:

"Feather my soul . . . to know thy awful swiftness!"

Its singing loveliness touched the heart, its appealing, passionate sweetness was marvelous, as from the gallery this figure of a man, dressed as a strong, dark bird, shot down with splendid grace and ease. The feathers swept; the wings spread out as sails that take the wind. Like a hawk that darts with unerring power and aim upon its prey, this thing of mighty wings rushed down into the empty space where the two danced. Observed by all, he entered, swooping beautifully, stretching his wings like any eagle. He dropped. He fixed his point of landing with consummate skill close beside the astonished dancers.

It happened with such swiftness it brought the dazzle and blindness as when lightning strikes. People in different parts of the room saw different details; a few saw nothing at all after the first startling shock, closing their eyes, or holding their arms before their faces as in self-protection. The touch of panic fear caught the room. The nameless thing that all the evening had been vaguely felt was come. It had suddenly materialized.

For this incredible thing occurred in the full blaze of light upon the open floor. Binovitch, grown in some sense formidable, opened his dark, big wings about the girl. The long gray feathers moved, causing powerful drafts of wind that made a rushing sound. An aspect of the terrible was in him, like an emanation. The great beaked head was poised to strike, the tufted claws were raised like fingers that shut and opened, and the whole presentiment of his amazing figure focused in an attitude of attack that was magnificent and terrible. No one who saw it doubted. Yet there were those who swore that it was not Binovitch at all, but that another outline, monstrous and shadowy, towered above him, draping his lesser proportions with two colossal wings of darkness. That some touch of strange divinity lay in it may be claimed, however confused the wild descriptions afterward. For many lowered their heads and bowed their shoulders. There was awe. There was also terror. The onlookers swayed as though some power passed over them through the air.

A sound of wings was certainly in the room.

Then some one screamed; a shriek broke high and clear; and emotion, ordinary, human emotion, unaccustomed to terrific things, swept loose. The Hawk and Vera flew. Beaten back against the wall as by a stroke of whirlwind, the Pierrot staggered. He watched them go. Out of the lighted room they flew, out of the crowded human atmosphere, out of the heat and artificial light, the walled-in, airless halls that were a cage. All this they left behind. They seemed things of wind and air, made free happily of another element. Earth held them not. Toward the open night they raced with this extraordinary lightness as of birds, down the long corridor and on to the southern terrace, where great colored curtains were hung suspended from the columns. A moment they were visible. Then the fringe of one huge curtain, lifted by the wind, showed their dark outline for a second against the starry sky. There was a cry, a leap. The curtain flapped again and closed. They vanished. And into the ball-room swept the cold draft of night air from the desert.

But three figures instantly were close upon their heels. The throng of half-dazed, half-stupefied onlookers, it seemed, projected them as though by some explosive force. The general mass held back, but, like projectiles, these three flung themselves after the fugitives down the corridor at high speed—the Apache, *Don Quixote*, and, last of them, the Pierrot. For Khilkof, the brother, and Baron Minski, the man who caught wolves alive, had been for some time keenly on the watch, while Dr. Plitzinger, reading the symptoms clearly, never far away, had been faithfully observant of every movement. His mask tossed aside, the great psychiatrist was now recognized by all. They reached the parapet just as the curtain flapped back heavily into place; the next second all three were out of sight behind it. Khilkof was first, however, urged forward at frantic speed by the warning words the doctor had whispered as they ran. Some thirty yards beyond the terrace was the brink of the crumbling cliff on which the great hotel was built, and there was a drop of sixty feet to the desert floor below. Only a low stone wall marked the edge.

Accounts varied. Khilkof, it seems, arrived in time—in the nick of time—to seize his sister, virtually hovering on the brink. He heard the loose stones strike the sand below. There was no struggle, though it appears she did not thank him for his interference at first. In a sense she was beside—outside—herself. And he did a characteristic thing: he not only brought her back into the ball-room, but he danced her back. It was admirable. Nothing could have calmed the general excitement better. The pair of them danced in together as though nothing was amiss. Accustomed to the strenuous practice of his Cossack regiment, this young cavalry officer's muscles were equal to the semi-dead weight in his arms. At most the onlookers thought her tired, perhaps. Confidence was restored,—such is the psychology of a crowd,—and in the middle of a thrilling Viennese waltz, he easily smuggled her out of the room, administered brandy, and got her up to bed. The absence of the Hawk, meanwhile, was hardly noticed; comments were made and then forgotten; it was Vera in whom the strange, anxious sympathy had centered. And, with her obvious safety, the moment of primitive, childish panic passed away. *Don Quixote*, too, was presently seen dancing gaily as though nothing untoward had happened; supper intervened; the incident was over; it had melted into the general wildness of the evening's irresponsibility. The fact that Pierrot did not appear again was noticed by no single person.

But Dr. Plitzinger was otherwise engaged, his heart and mind and soul all deeply exercised. A death-certificate is not always made out quite so simply as the public thinks. That Binovitch had died of suffocation in his swift descent through merely sixty feet of air was not conceivable; yet that his body lay so neatly placed upon the desert after such a fall was stranger still. It was not crumpled, it was not torn; no single bone was broken, no muscle wrenched; there was no bruise. There was no indenture in the sand. The figure lay sidewise as though in sleep, no sign of violence visible anywhere, the dark wings folded as a great bird folds them when it creeps away to die in loneliness. Beneath the Horus mask the face was smiling. It seemed he had floated into death upon the element he loved. And only Vera saw the enormous wings that, hovering invitingly above the dark abyss, bore him so softly into another world. Plitzinger, that is, saw them, too, but he said firmly that they belonged to the big black falcons that haunt the Mokattam Hills and roost upon these ridges, close beside the hotel, at night. Both he and Vera, however, agreed on one thing: the high, sharp cry in the air above them, wild and plaintive, was certainly the black kite's cry—the note of the falcon that passionately seeks its mate. It was the pause of a second, when she stood to listen, that made her rescue possible. A moment later and she, too, would have flown to death with Binovitch.

LAURA

Saki
(1870–1916)

H.H. Munro, who wrote under the pseudonym "Saki," had a traumatic early life, losing his mother when he was only two years old and being sent from Burma to England, where strict aunts and a grandmother raised him in a puritanical fashion (his father was in the Anglo-Indian civil service). This early experience marked Munro, and gave him a loathing for petty authority which shows up in many of his stories.

Munro worked in Burma as a policeman, but ill health forced him to return to London, where he worked as a journalist for a number of newspapers while beginning to write the contes cruel *he became best known for. His career took him abroad as a foreign correspondent in Russia, the Balkans, and Paris. When World War One began he enlisted in the British Army, and was killed in combat in France in 1916.*

Saki is perhaps best known for his contes cruel, *those stories of the maliciousness of fate which hover on the border between fantasy and horror. Classics like "Sredni Vashtar" (1911), "The Open Window" (1911), and "The Music on the Hill" (1911) are witty, sharp, and compact, delivering the maximum effect with a minimum of words. "Laura," which first appeared in* Beasts and Super-Beasts *(1914), is one of Saki's most famous stories; less cruel than mischievous, it still has Saki's sardonic viciousness, which never grows old.*

"YOU ARE NOT really dying, are you?" asked Amanda.

"I have the doctor's permission to live till Tuesday," said Laura.

"But to-day is Saturday; this is serious!" gasped Amanda.

"I don't know about it being serious; it is certainly Saturday," said Laura.

"Death is always serious," said Amanda.

"I never said I was going to die. I am presumably going to leave off being Laura, but I shall go on being something. An animal of some kind, I suppose. You see, when one hasn't been very good in the life one has just lived, one reincarnates in some lower organism. And I haven't been very good, when one comes to think of it. I've been petty and mean and vindictive and all that sort of thing when circumstances have seemed to warrant it."

"Circumstances never warrant that sort of thing," said Amanda hastily.

"If you don't mind my saying so," observed Laura, "Egbert is a circumstance that would warrant any amount of that sort of thing. You're married to him—that's different; you've sworn to love, honour, and endure him: I haven't."

"I don't see what's wrong with Egbert," protested Amanda.

"Oh, I daresay the wrongness has been on my part," admitted Laura dispassionately; "he has merely been the extenuating circumstance. He made a thin, peevish kind of fuss, for instance, when I took the collie puppies from the farm out for a run the other day."

"They chased his young broods of speckled Sussex and drove two sitting hens off their nests, besides running all over the flower beds. You know how devoted he is to his poultry and garden."

"Anyhow, he needn't have gone on about it for the entire evening and then have said, 'Let's say no more about it' just when I was beginning to enjoy the discussion. That's where one of my petty vindictive revenges came in," added Laura with an unrepentant chuckle; "I turned the entire family of speckled Sussex into his seedling shed the day after the puppy episode."

"How could you?" exclaimed Amanda.

"It came quite easy," said Laura; "two of the hens pretended to be laying at the time, but I was firm."

"And we thought it was an accident!"

"You see," resumed Laura, "I really have some grounds for supposing that my next incarnation will be in a lower organism. I shall be an animal of some kind. On the other hand, I haven't been a bad sort in my way, so I think I may count on being a nice animal, something elegant and lively, with a love of fun. An otter, perhaps."

"I can't imagine you as an otter," said Amanda.

"Well, I don't suppose you can imagine me as an angel, if it comes to that," said Laura.

Amanda was silent. She couldn't.

"Personally I think an otter life would be rather enjoyable," continued Laura; "salmon to eat all the year round, and the satisfaction of being able to fetch the trout in their own homes without having to wait for hours till they condescend to rise to the fly you've been dangling before them; and an elegant svelte figure—"

"Think of the otter hounds," interposed Amanda; "how dreadful to be hunted and harried and finally worried to death!"

"Rather fun with half the neighbourhood looking on, and anyhow not worse than this Saturday-to-Tuesday business of dying by inches; and then I should go on into something else. If I had been a moderately good otter I suppose I should get back into human shape of some sort;

probably something rather primitive—a little brown, unclothed Nubian boy, I should think."

"I wish you would be serious," sighed Amanda; "you really ought to be if you're only going to live till Tuesday."

As a matter of fact Laura died on Monday.

"So dreadfully upsetting," Amanda complained to her uncle-in-law, Sir Lulworth Quayne. "I've asked quite a lot of people down for golf and fishing, and the rhododendrons are just looking their best."

"Laura always was inconsiderate," said Sir Lulworth; "she was born during Goodwood week, with an Ambassador staying in the house who hated babies."

"She had the maddest kind of ideas," said Amanda; "do you know if there was any insanity in her family?"

"Insanity? No, I never heard of any. Her father lives in West Kensington, but I believe he's sane on all other subjects."

"She had an idea that she was going to be reincarnated as an otter," said Amanda.

"One meets with those ideas of reincarnation so frequently, even in the West," said Sir Lulworth, "that one can hardly set them down as being mad. And Laura was such an unaccountable person in this life that I should not like to lay down definite rules as to what she might be doing in an after state."

"You think she really might have passed into some animal form?" asked Amanda. She was one of those who shape their opinions rather readily from the standpoint of those around them.

Just then Egbert entered the breakfast-room, wearing an air of bereavement that Laura's demise would have been insufficient, in itself, to account for.

"Four of my speckled Sussex have been killed," he exclaimed; "the very four that were to go to the show on Friday. One of them was dragged away and eaten right in the middle of that new carnation bed that I've been to such trouble and expense over. My best flower bed and my best fowls singled out for destruction; it almost seems as if the brute that did the deed had special knowledge how to be as devastating as possible in a short space of time."

"Was it a fox, do you think?" asked Amanda.

"Sounds more like a polecat," said Sir Lulworth.

"No," said Egbert, "there were marks of webbed feet all over the place, and we followed the tracks down to the stream at the bottom of the garden; evidently an otter."

Amanda looked quickly and furtively across at Sir Lulworth.

Egbert was too agitated to eat any breakfast, and went out to super-intend the strengthening of the poultry yard defences.

"I think she might at least have waited till the funeral was over," said Amanda in a scandalised voice.

"It's her own funeral, you know," said Sir Lulworth; "it's a nice point in etiquette how far one ought to show respect to one's own mortal remains."

Disregard for mortuary convention was carried to further lengths next day; during the absence of the family at the funeral ceremony the remaining survivors of the speckled Sussex were massacred. The marauder's line of retreat seemed to have embraced most of the flower beds on the lawn, but the strawberry beds in the lower garden had also suffered.

"I shall get the otter hounds to come here at the earliest possible moment," said Egbert savagely.

"On no account! You can't dream of such a thing!" exclaimed Amanda. "I mean, it wouldn't do, so soon after a funeral in the house."

"It's a case of necessity," said Egbert; "once an otter takes to that sort of thing it won't stop."

"Perhaps it will go elsewhere now there are no more fowls left," suggested Amanda.

"One would think you wanted to shield the beast," said Egbert.

"There's been so little water in the stream lately," objected Amanda; "it seems hardly sporting to hunt an animal when it has so little chance of taking refuge anywhere."

"Good gracious!" fumed Egbert, "I'm not thinking about sport. I want to have the animal killed as soon as possible."

Even Amanda's opposition weakened when, during church time on the following Sunday, the otter made its way into the house, raided half a salmon from the larder and worried it into scaly fragments on the Persian rug in Egbert's studio.

"We shall have it hiding under our beds and biting pieces out of our feet before long," said Egbert, and from what Amanda knew of this particular otter she felt that the possibility was not a remote one.

On the evening preceding the day fixed for the hunt Amanda spent a solitary hour walking by the banks of the stream, making what she imagined to be hound noises. It was charitably supposed by those who overheard her performance, that she was practising for farmyard imita-tions at the forth-coming village entertainment.

It was her friend and neighbour, Aurora Burret, who brought her news of the day's sport.

"Pity you weren't out; we had quite a good day. We found it at once, in the pool just below your garden."

"Did you—kill?" asked Amanda.

"Rather. A fine she-otter. Your husband got rather badly bitten in trying to 'tail it.' Poor beast, I felt quite sorry for it, it had such a human look in its eyes when it was killed. You'll call me silly, but do you know who the look reminded me of? My dear woman, what is the matter?"

When Amanda had recovered to a certain extent from her attack of nervous prostration Egbert took her to the Nile Valley to recuperate. Change of scene speedily brought about the desired recovery of health and mental balance. The escapades of an adventurous otter in search of a variation of diet were viewed in their proper light. Amanda's normally placid temperament reasserted itself. Even a hurricane of shouted curses, coming from her husband's dressing-room, in her husband's voice, but hardly in his usual vocabulary, failed to disturb her serenity as she made a leisurely toilet one evening in a Cairo hotel.

"What is the matter? What has happened?" she asked in amused curiosity.

"The little beast has thrown all my clean shirts into the bath! Wait till I catch you, you little—"

"What little beast?" asked Amanda, suppressing a desire to laugh; Egbert's language was so hopelessly inadequate to express his outraged feelings.

"A little beast of a naked brown Nubian boy," spluttered Egbert.

And now Amanda is seriously ill.

THE PLACE OF PAIN

M. P. Shiel
(1865–1947)

Matthew Phipps Shiell—he went by "Shiel" as a pen-name—was born on the island of Montserrat and was of Irish-Caribbean descent. He moved to England when he was twenty and began a lifetime of writing, in a wide range of commercial genres. His Decadent supernatural fiction, including his "Prince Zaleski" detective stories and his Poe-esque "Vaila" (1896), is still fondly remembered by connoisseurs, while his science fiction, including his post-apocalyptic The Purple Cloud *(1901), is among the most striking and memorable science fiction of the time. A lack of commercial success and consequent money troubles forced Shiel to take on more commercial work, and he unsuccessfully churned out romances and plays and radical political and religious work during the last thirty years of his life.*

Shiel's reputation is now mixed. There is the lingering scandal from the revelation of his imprisonment in 1914 for "indecently assaulting and carnally knowing" his twelve-year-old stepdaughter, an imprisonment which at the time he told everyone was for fraud. There are also the overtly racist politics of some of his future war novels, such as The Yellow Danger *(1898) and* The Dragon *(1913). Viewed on balance, Shiel's personal reputation is dire, but his reputation as a writer remains mostly positive.*

"The Place of Pain," written before his term in jail, is one of Shiel's more significant short stories. It combines science fiction and horror in a way not usually seen in the British science fiction of the era, as well as avoids the stylistic excesses of his more Decadent work, delivering instead a stripped-down piece that nicely hints at more than it reveals.

THOUGH MY THEME is about the place of evil, and about how the Rev. Thomas Podd saw it, it is rather a case of evil in heaven; for I think British Columbia very like heaven, or like what I shall like my heaven to be, if ever I arrive so high—one mass of mountains, with mirrors of water mixed up with them, torrents and forests, and roaring Rhones.

It was at Small Forks that it happened, where I went to pass a fortnight—and stayed five years; and how the place changed and developed in that short time is really incredible, for at first Small Forks was the distributing center of only three mining-camps, and I am sure that not one quarter of the district's two million tons of ore of today was then thought of.

At the so-called Scatchereen lode, three miles from the lake, there was no copper smelter, but not one silver-led mine within fifty miles,

27

and no brewery, no machine-shop, no brick plant. Nor had Harper Falls as yet been thought of as a source of power.

It was Harper Falls that proved to be the undoing of Pastor Thomas Podd, as you are to hear; and I alone have known that it was so, and why it was so.

I think I saw Podd in my very first week at Small Forks—one evening on the Embankment.

(You may know that Small Forks runs along the shore of an arm of Lake Sakoonay, embowered in bush at the foot of its mountain—really very like a nook in Paradise, to my mind).

Podd that evening was walking with another parson on the Embankment, and the effect of him upon me was the raising of a smile, my eye at that time being unaccustomed to the sight of black men in parsons collars and frocks. But Podd was rather brown than black—a meager little man of fifty, with prominent cheek bones, hollow cheeks, a scraggy rag of beard, a cocky carriage, and a forehead really intellectual, though his eyes did strike me as rather wild and scatterbrained.

He was a man of established standing in all Small Forks, where a colony of some forty colored persons worked at the lumber-mills. To these Podd preached in a corrugated chapel at the top of Peel Street.

He held prayer-meetings on Monday nights, and one Monday night, when I had been in Small Forks a month or so, I stopped into his conventicler, on coming home from a tramp, and heard the praying—or, rather, the demanding for those darkies banged the pew-backs and shook them irritably.

When it was over and I was going out, I felt a tap on my back, and it was the reverend gentleman, who had raced after the stranger. Out he pops his pompous paw, and then, with a smile, asked if I was "thinking of joining us." I was not doing that, but I said that I had been "interested," and left him.

Soon after this he called to see me, and twice in three months he had tea with me—in the hope of a convert, perhaps. He did not succeed in this, but he did succeed in interesting me.

The man had several sciences at his finger-ends; I discovered that he had a genuine passion for Nature; and I gathered—from himself, or from others, I can't now remember—that it was his habit ever and anon to cut himself off from humankind, so as to lose himself for a few days in that maze of mountains in which the Sakoonay district towers toward the moon.

No pressure of business, no consideration or care, could keep Podd tame and quiet in Small Forks when this call of the wild enticed him off. It seems to have been long a known thing about the town, this trick of his character, and to have been condoned and pardoned as part of the man. He had been born within forty miles of Small Forks, and seemed to me to know Columbia as a farmer knows his two-acre meadow.

Well, some two weeks after that second visit of his to me the news suddenly reached me that something had gone wrong in the Rev. Thomas Podd's head—could not help reaching me, for the thing was the gossip and laugh of the district far outside Small Forks.

It appears that late on the Saturday evening the reverend gentleman had come home from one of his vast tramps and truant interviews with Nature; then, on the Sunday morning, he had entered the meeting-house scandalously late, and had reeled with the feet of some moon-struck creature into the pulpit—without his coat! without his collar! his braces hanging down!—and then, leaning his two elbows on the pulpit Bible, he had looked steadily, mockingly, at his flock of black sheep, and had proceeded to jeer and sneer at them.

He had called them frankly a pack of apes, a band of black and bab-bling babies, said that he could pity them from his heart, they were so benighted, so lost in darkness; that what they knew in their wooly nuts was just nothing; that no one knew, save him, Podd; that he alone of men knew what he knew, and had seen what he had seen. . . .

Well, he had been so much respected for his intellectual parts, his eloquence, his apparent sincerity as a Christian man, that his congrega-tion seem to have taken this gracelessness with a great deal of toleration, hoping perhaps that it might be only an aberration which would pass; but when the revered gentleman immediately afterwards took himself off anew into his mountains, to disappear for weeks—no one knew where—this was too much. So when he came back at last, it was to see another dark parson filling his place.

From that moment his social degeneration was rapid. He abandoned himself to poverty and tatters. His wife and two daughters shook the dust of him from off their shoes, and left Small Forks—to find a liveli-hood for themselves somewhere, I suppose. But Podd remained, or, at any rate, was often to be met in Small Forks, when he condescended to descend from his lofty walks.

Once I saw him intoxicated on the Embankment, his braces down, his hat in tatters—though I am certain that he never became a drunkard. Anyway, the thin veneer of respectability came off him like wet paint, and he slipped happily back into savagery. On what he lived I don't know.

I met him one afternoon by the new shipbuilding yard which the Canadian Pacific Railway was running up half a mile out of Small Forks. He sat there on a pile of axed pine-trunks lying by the roadside, his chest and one shin showing through his rags, his eyes gloating on the sky, in which a daylight moon was swooning; but, on catching sight of me, he showed his fine rows of teeth, crying out flippantly in French: "*Ah, monsieur, ça va bien?*"—in French, because Negroes are given to a species of frivolity in speech which expresses itself in that way.

I stopped to speak to him, asking "What has it been all about, Podd—the sudden collapse from sanctity to naughtiness?"

"And, now you are asking something!" he answered flippantly, with a wink at me.

I saw that he had become woefully emaciated and saffron, his cheek-bones seeming to be near appearing through their sere skin, and his eyes had in them the fire of a man living a life of some continual exaltation or excitement.

I wished, if I could, to help him; and I said, "Something must have gone wrong inside or out; better make a clean breast of it, and then something may be done."

He suddenly became fretful, saying, "Oh, you all think like a balmy lot of silly little babies fumbling in the dark!"

"That is so," I answered, "but since you are wise, why not tell us the secret, and then we shall all be wise?"

"I tell you what"—shaking his head up and down, his lips turned down—"I doubt if some of them could stand the sight; turn their hairs white!"

"Which sight?" I asked.

"The sight of Hell!" he sighed, throwing up his hands a little.

After a little silence I said, "Now that's rot, Podd."

"Yes, sure to be, Sir, since you say so," he answered quietly in a dejected way. "That, of course, is what they said to Galileo when he told them that this globe moves."

With as grave a face as I could maintain, I looked at him, asking, "Have you seen Hell, Podd?"

"I may have," he answered; and he added, "And so have you, by the way. You have probably seen it since you started out on this walk you are taking, and haven't known."

"Well it can't be very terrible, can it," I said, "if one can see it and not know? But is Hell in Small Forks? For I'm straight from there."

At this he threw up his head with a rather bitter laugh saying, "Yes, that's beautiful, that the ignorant should make game of those who know, and the worse be judges of the better! But, then, that's how it generally is." And now, all at once, whatever blood he had rushed into his face, and he pointed upward: "You see that world there?"

"The moon?" I said, looking up.

"The souls in that place live in pain," I heard him murmur, his chin suddenly sunken to his chest.

"So there are people on the moon, Podd?" I asked. "Surely you know that there is no air there? Or do you mean to imply that the moon is Hell?"

He looked up, smiling. "My goodness, you'd give a lot to know, wouldn't you from the first, and I'll make you a business proposition, as it's you. You agree to give me three dollars a week so long as I live, and when I'm dying I'll tell you what I know, and how, teaching you the whole trick. Or I'll put it in writing in a sealed envelope, which you shall have on my death."

"Dear me," I said, "what a pity I can't afford it!"

"You can afford it well enough," was his answer, "but the truth is that you don't believe a word of what I say: you think I'm moonstruck. And so I am, a bit! By Heaven, that's true enough!"

He sighed and was silent some time, looking at the moon in a most abstracted manner, apparently forgetting my presence.

But presently he went on to say, "Still, a spec., you might risk it. The payments wouldn't be for long, for I've developed consumption, You see—the curse of us colored folks—had a hemorrhage only yesterday. And then, as a charity, you might, for I'm mostly hungry—my own fault; but I couldn't keep on gassing to those poor fools, after seeing what I have seen. If you won't give me the three dollars a week, give me one."

Well, to this I consented—not, of course, in any expectation of ever hearing any "secret," but I saw that the man had become quite unworldly, unfit to earn his living. I considered him more or less insane—still consider so, though I am convinced now that he was not nearly so insane as I conceived: so I promised him that he might draw a weekly dollar from my bank while I was in Small Forks.

Sometimes Podd drew his dollar, but often he did not, though he was aware that arrears would not be paid, if he failed to present himself any week. And so it went on for over four years, during which he became more and more emaciated, and a savage.

Meantime, Small Forks and the Sakoonay district had ceased to laugh at the name of Podd, as at a stale joke, and the fact of his rags and degradation had become a local institution, like the Mounted Police or the sawdust mill—too familiar a thing in the eye to excite any kind of emotion in the mind.

But at the end of those four years Small Forks, like one man, rose against Podd.

It happened in this way: at that date the Sakoonay district was sending an annual cut of some four hundred million feet of lumber to the Prairie Provinces; the mining and smelter companies had increased to four—big concerns, treating three to four thousand tons of ore a day; in which consideration of things all through the district had arisen the cry: "Electricity! Electricity!"

Hence the appearance in Small Forks of the Provincial Mineralogist with a pondering and responsible forehead; hence his report to the Columbian Government that Harper Falls were capable of developing 97,000 horse-power; hence a simmering of interest through the district; and hence the decision of the Small Forks Town Council to inaugurate a municipal power-plant at Harper Falls.

But Podd objected!

He thought—this is what I found out afterwards—that Harper Falls were his; and he did not wish to have them messed with, or people coming anywhere near them.

However, he said nothing; the new works were commenced—so far as the accumulation of material was concerned; and the first hint of a hitch in the business was given one midnight at the beginning of May—a night I'll ever remember—when the class of the municipality's material was burnt to cinders.

The blaze made a fine display five miles out of Small Forks, and I witnessed it in the thick of a great crowd of the townspeople.

It was assumed that the thing had been deliberately done by someone, since there was no other explanation. But the mystery as to who had done it!—for there was no one to suspect. And, like a spider whose web has been torn, the municipality started once more to collect materials for the plant.

Then, at the end of June, occurred the second blaze.

But this time there were night-watchmen with open eyes, and one of them deposed that he believed he had seen Podd suspiciously near the scene of the mischief.

The town was very irritated about it, since the power-plant was expected to do great things for everybody.

At any rate, when Podd was captured and questioned, he did not exactly deny it.

"It might have been I," was his answer; and "what if it was I?"

And this answer was a proof to me that he was innocent, for I took it to be actuated by vanity or insanity. The authorities must have thought so, too, for the man was dismissed as a ninny.

The town, however, was indignant of his dismissal; and three days later I came upon him in the midst of a crowd, from which I doubt that he could have come out alive, but for me, for he was now nothing but a bundle of bones, lighted up by two eyes. Indeed, my interference was rather plucky of me, for there present was a North-West policeman lending his countenance to the hustling of the poor outcast, a real-estate agent, the sawdust-mill manager, reeking of turpentine, and others, whose place it was to have interfered. Anyhow, I howled a little speech, pledging myself that the man was innocent; and my éclat as a Briton, perhaps, helped me to get him gasping out of their grasp.

When he found himself alone with me on the road outside the town, down he suddenly knelt, and, grasping my legs, began to sob to me in a paroxysm of gratitude.

"You have been everything to me—you, a stranger, God reward you—I have not long to live, but you shall know what I know, and see what I have seen."

"Podd," I said, "you have heard me pledge my word that you are innocent. Let me hear from you this instant that it was not you who committed these outrages."

With the coolest insolence he stood up, looked in my face, and said, "Of course I committed them. Who else?"

I had to laugh. But I sternly observed, "Well, but you confess yourself a felon, that's all."

"Look here," he answered, "let's not quarrel. We see from different standpoints—let's not quarrel. What I say is, that during the few weeks or months I have to live, no plant is going to be set up at Harper Falls—afterwards, yes. You don't know what I know about the Falls. They are the eye of this world; that's it—the eye of this world. But you shall know and see"—he looked up at the westering quarter-moon, thought a little, and continued: "Meet me here at nine on Friday night. You've done a lot for me."

The man's manner was so convincing, that I undertook to meet him, though some minutes afterwards I laughed at myself for being so impressed by his pratings.

Anyway, two nights thence, at nine, I met Podd, and we began a tramp and climb of some seven miles which I shall ever remember.

If I could but give some vaguest impression of that bewitched adventure, I should begin to think well of my power of expression; but the reality of it would still be far from pictured.

That little dying Podd had still the foot of a goat, and we climbed spots which, but for his aid, I could scarcely have negotiated—ghostly gullies, woods of spruce and dreary old cedar droning, the crags of Garroway Pass, where a throng of torrents awes one's ear, and tarns asleep in the dark of forests of larch, of hemlock, of white and yellow pine.

We were struggling upward through a gullock of Garroway Pass when Podd stopped short; and when I groped for him—for one could see nothing there—I discovered him with his forehead leant against the crag.

To my question, "Anything wrong?" he answered, "Wait a little—there's blood in my mouth."

And he added, "I think I am going to have a hemorrhage."

"We had better go back," I said.

But he presently brightened up, saying, "It will be all right. Come." We stumbled on.

Half an hour afterwards we came out upon a platform about eight hundred yards square, surrounded by cliffs of pine on three sides. A torrent dropped down the back cliff, ran over most of the platform in a rather broad river, lacerated by rocks, and dropped frothing in a cataract over the front of the platform.

"Here we are," Podd said, seating himself on a rock, dropping his forehead to his knees.

"Podd, you are in trouble," I said, standing over him.

He made no answer, but presently raised himself with an effort, to look at the moon with eyes that were themselves like moons—the satellite, about half-full, then waxing; and now in her setting quadrant.

"Now, look you," Podd said with pantings and tremblings, so that I had to bend down to hear him in that row of the waters, "I have brought you here because I love you a lot. You are about to see things that no mortal's eye but mine ever wept salt water at—"

As he uttered those words, I, for the first time, with a kind of shock, realized that I was really about to see something boundless, for I could no longer doubt that those pantings had the accent of truth; in fact, I suddenly knew that they were true, and my heart began to beat faster.

"But how will you take the sight?" he went on. "Am I really doing you a service? You see the effect it has had on me—to think that what made us—our own—should bring forth such bitterness! No, you shan't see it all, not the worst bit: I'll stop the view there. You see that fall rushing down at our feet? I have the power, by placing a certain rock in a certain position in this river, to change that mass of froth into a mass of glass—two masses of glass—immense lenses, double-convex. Discovered it by accident one night five years since—night of my life. No, I am not well tonight. But never mind. You go down the face of the rock at the side here—easy going—till you come to the cave. Go into the cave; then climb by the notches which you'll find in the wall, till you come to a ledge, one edge of which is about two feet behind the inner eyepiece. The moon should begin to come within your view within four minutes from now; and I give you a five-minutes' sight— no more. You'll see her some three hundred yards from you tearing across your brain like ten trillion trains. But never you tell any man what you see on her. Go, go! Not very well tonight."

He stood up with an effort so painful, that I said to him, "But are you going into the river, Podd, and trembling like that already? Why not show me how to place the rock for you?"

"No," he muttered, "you shan't know; you shan't! It's all right; I'll manage; you go. Keep moving your eye at first till you get the focus-length. There's a lot of prismatic and spherical aberration, iridescent fringes, and the yellow line of the spectrum of sodium bothers every-where—the object-glass is so big and so thin, that it hardly seems at all to decompose light. Never mind, you'll see well—upside down, of course—dioptric-telescopic images. Go, go; don't waste time; I'll man-age with the stone. And you must always say—I paid you back—full measure—for all your love."

At every third word of all this his breast gave up a gasp, and his eyes were most wild with excitement or the fever of disease. He pushed and led me to the spot where I was to descend. And "There she comes," his tongue stuttered, with a nod at the moon, as he flew from me, while I went feeling my way with my feet, the cataract at my right, down a cliff-side that was nearly perpendicular, but so rugged and shrub-grown, that the descent was easy.

When I was six feet down I lifted my chin to the ledge, and saw Podd stopping within some bush at the foot of the platform-cliff to my left, where he had evidently hidden the talisman-rock; and I saw him lift the rock, and go tottering under its weight to the river.

But the thought came to me that it was hardly quite fair to spy upon him, and when he was still some yards from the river I went on down—a long way—until I came to the floor of a cave in the cliff face, a pretty roomy cavern, fretted with spray from the cataract in front of it.

I went in and climbed to the ledge, as he had said; and there in the dark I lay waiting, wet through, and, I must confess, trembling, hearing my heart knocking upon my ribs through that solemn oratory of the torrent dropping in froth in front of me. And presently through the froth I thought I saw a luminous something that must have been the moon, moving by me.

But the transformation of the froth into the lenses which I awaited did not come.

At last I lifted my voice to howl, "Hurry up, Podd!"—though I doubted if he could hear.

Anyway, no answer reached my ear, and I waited on.

It must have been twenty minutes, before I decided to climb down; I then scrambled out, clambered up again, disgusted and angry, though I don't think that I ever believed that Podd had willfully made a fool of me. I thought that he had somehow failed to place the rock.

But when I got to the top I saw that the poor man was dead.

He lay with his feet in the river, his body on the bank, his rock clasped in his arms. The weight had proved too much for him: on the rock was blood from his lungs.

Two days later I buried him up there with my own hands by his river's brink, within the noise of the song of his waterfall, his stupendous telescope—his "eye of this world."

And then for three months, day after day, I was endeavouring in that solitude up there so to place the rock in the river as to transform the froths of the waterfall into frothless water. But I never managed. The secret is buried with the one man whom destiny intended, maybe for centuries to come, to know what paths are trodden, and what tapestries are wrought, on another orb.

THE THREE SISTERS

W. W. Jacobs
(1863–1943)

Some writers, luckily or not, become known for one story, to the point that the rest of their work is completely obscured. Few now recall that Daniel Keyes wrote anything besides "Flowers for Algernon," or Jerome Bixby wrote numerous stories besides "It's a Good Life," or that Walter Miller had a career beyond A Canticle for Leibowitz. *W. W. Jacobs is one of the unfortunate writers who falls into this category. Everyone knows "The Monkey's Paw." Few know any of his many other stories or novels.*

Jacobs was a postal clerk for twenty years before leaving the postal service in 1899 to become a full-time writer. His horror stories, like "The Monkey's Paw" (1902), "The Toll House" (1909), and "The Three Sisters," which first appeared in Night Watches *(1914), were comparatively few. The majority of what he wrote was humorous, nautical, or a combination of the two; British literary expert Michael Sadleir said that Jacobs "wrote stories of three kinds; describing the misadventures of sailor-men ashore; celebrating the artful dodger of a slow-witted village; and tales of the macabre." Most of his post-World War One career was spent adapting his short stories for the stage.*

"The Three Sisters" is perhaps typical of Jacobs' horror work, in that it combines a carefully drawn, realistic setting with mounting terror, lacking only his trademark humor.

THIRTY YEARS AGO on a wet autumn evening the household of Mallett's Lodge was gathered round the death-bed of Ursula Mallow, the eldest of the three sisters who inhabited it. The dingy moth-eaten curtains of the old wooden bedstead were drawn apart, the light of a smoking oil-lamp falling upon the hopeless countenance of the dying woman as she turned her dull eyes upon her sisters. The room was in silence except for an occasional sob from the youngest sister, Eunice. Outside the rain fell steadily over the steaming marshes.

"Nothing is to be changed, Tabitha," gasped Ursula to the other sister, who bore a striking likeness to her although her expression was harder and colder; "this room is to be locked up and never opened."

"Very well," said Tabitha brusquely, "though I don't see how it can matter to you then."

"It does matter," said her sister with startling energy. "How do you know, how do I know that I may not sometimes visit it? I have lived in

37

this house so long I am certain that I shall see it again. I will come back. Come back to watch over you both and see that no harm befalls you."

"You are talking wildly," said Tabitha, by no means moved at her sister's solicitude for her welfare. "Your mind is wandering; you know that I have no faith in such things."

Ursula sighed, and beckoning to Eunice, who was weeping silently at the bedside, placed her feeble arms around her neck and kissed her.

"Do not weep, dear," she said feebly. "Perhaps it is best so. A lonely woman's life is scarce worth living. We have no hopes, no aspirations; other women have had happy husbands and children, but we in this forgotten place have grown old together. I go first, but you must soon follow."

Tabitha, comfortably conscious of only forty years and an iron frame, shrugged her shoulders and smiled grimly.

"I go first," repeated Ursula in a new and strange voice as her heavy eyes slowly closed, "but I will come for each of you in turn, when your lease of life runs out. At that moment I will be with you to lead your steps whither I now go."

As she spoke the flickering lamp went out suddenly as though extinguished by a rapid hand, and the room was left in utter darkness. A strange suffocating noise issued from the bed, and when the trembling women had relighted the lamp, all that was left of Ursula Mallow was ready for the grave.

That night the survivors passed together. The dead woman had been a firm believer in the existence of that shadowy borderland which is said to form an unhallowed link between the living and the dead, and even the stolid Tabitha, slightly unnerved by the events of the night, was not free from certain apprehensions that she might have been right.

With the bright morning their fears disappeared. The sun stole in at the window, and seeing the poor earth-worn face on the pillow so touched it and glorified it that only its goodness and weakness were seen, and the beholders came to wonder how they could ever have felt any dread of aught so calm and peaceful. A day or two passed, and the body was transferred to a massive coffin long regarded as the finest piece of work of its kind ever turned out of the village carpenter's workshop. Then a slow and melancholy cortege headed by four bearers wound its solemn way across the marshes to the family vault in the grey old church, and all that was left of Ursula was placed by the father and mother who had taken that self-same journey some thirty years before.

To Eunice as they toiled slowly home the day seemed strange and Sabbath-like, the flat prospect of marsh wilder and more forlorn than usual, the roar of the sea more depressing. Tabitha had no such fancies. The bulk of the dead woman's property had been left to Eunice, and her avaricious soul was sorely troubled and her proper sisterly feelings of regret for the deceased sadly interfered with in consequence.

"What are you going to do with all that money, Eunice?" she asked as they sat at their quiet tea.

"I shall leave it as it stands," said Eunice slowly. "We have both got sufficient to live upon, and I shall devote the income from it to supporting some beds in a children's hospital."

"If Ursula had wished it to go to a hospital," said Tabitha in her deep tones, "she would have left the money to it herself. I wonder you do not respect her wishes more."

"What else can I do with it then?" inquired Eunice.

"Save it," said the other with gleaming eyes, "save it."

Eunice shook her head.

"No," said she, "it shall go to the sick children, but the principal I will not touch, and if I die before you it shall become yours and you can do what you like with it."

"Very well," said Tabitha, smothering her anger by a strong effort; "I don't believe that was what Ursula meant you to do with it, and I don't believe she will rest quietly in the grave while you squander the money she stored so carefully."

"What do you mean?" asked Eunice with pale lips. "You are trying to frighten me; I thought that you did not believe in such things."

Tabitha made no answer, and to avoid the anxious inquiring gaze of her sister, drew her chair to the fire, and folding her gaunt arms, composed herself for a nap.

For some time life went on quietly in the old house. The room of the dead woman, in accordance with her last desire, was kept firmly locked, its dirty windows forming a strange contrast to the prim cleanliness of the others. Tabitha, never very talkative, became more taciturn than ever, and stalked about the house and the neglected garden like an unquiet spirit, her brow roughened into the deep wrinkles suggestive of much thought. As the winter came on, bringing with it the long dark evenings, the old house became more lonely than ever, and an air of mystery and dread seemed to hang over it and brood in its empty rooms and dark corridors. The deep silence of night was broken by strange noises for which neither the wind nor the rats could be held accountable. Old Martha, seated in her distant kitchen, heard strange sounds upon the stairs, and once, upon hurrying to them, fancied that she saw a dark figure squatting upon the landing, though a subsequent search with candle and spectacles failed to discover anything. Eunice was disturbed by several vague incidents, and, as she suffered from a complaint of the heart, rendered very ill by them. Even Tabitha admitted a strangeness about the house, but, confident in her piety and virtue, took no heed of it, her mind being fully employed in another direction.

Since the death of her sister all restraint upon her was removed, and she yielded herself up entirely to the stern and hard rules enforced by avarice upon its devotees. Her housekeeping expenses were kept rigidly separate from those of Eunice and her food limited to the coarsest dishes, while in the matter of clothes, the old servant was by far the better dressed. Seated alone in her bedroom this uncouth, hard-featured creature revelled in her possessions, grudging even the expense of the candle-end which enabled her to behold them. So completely did this passion change her that both Eunice and Martha became afraid of her, and lay awake in their beds night after night trembling at the chinking of the coins at her unholy vigils.

One day Eunice ventured to remonstrate. "Why don't you bank your money, Tabitha?" she said; "it is surely not safe to keep such large sums in such a lonely house."

"Large sums!" repeated the exasperated Tabitha, "large sums! what nonsense is this? You know well that I have barely sufficient to keep me."

"It's a great temptation to housebreakers," said her sister, not pressing the point. "I made sure last night that I heard somebody in the house."

"Did you?" said Tabitha, grasping her arm, a horrible look on her face. "So did I. I thought they went to Ursula's room, and I got out of bed and went on the stairs to listen."

"Well?" said Eunice faintly, fascinated by the look on her sister's face.

"There was something there," said Tabitha slowly. "I'll swear it, for I stood on the landing by her door and listened; something scuffling on the floor round and round the room. At first I thought it was the cat, but when I went up there this morning the door was still locked, and the cat was in the kitchen."

"Oh, let us leave this dreadful house," moaned Eunice.

"What!" said her sister grimly; "afraid of poor Ursula? Why should you be? Your own sister who nursed you when you were a babe, and who perhaps even now comes and watches over your slumbers."

"Oh!" said Eunice, pressing her hand to her side, "if I saw her I should die. I should think that she had come for me as she said she would. O God! have mercy on me, I am dying."

She reeled as she spoke, and before Tabitha could save her, sank senseless to the floor.

"Get some water," cried Tabitha, as old Martha came hurrying up the stairs, "Eunice has fainted."

The old woman, with a timid glance at her, retired, reappearing shortly afterwards with the water, with which she proceeded to restore her much-loved mistress to her senses. Tabitha, as soon as this was accomplished, stalked off to her room, leaving her sister and Martha sitting drearily enough in the small parlour, watching the fire and conversing in whispers.

It was clear to the old servant that this state of things could not last much longer, and she repeatedly urged her mistress to leave a house so lonely and so mysterious. To her great delight Eunice at length consented, despite the fierce opposition of her sister, and at the mere idea of leaving gained greatly in health and spirits. A small but comfortable house was hired in Morville, and arrangements made for a speedy change.

It was the last night in the old house, and all the wild spirits of the marshes, the wind and the sea seemed to have joined forces for one supreme effort. When the wind dropped, as it did at brief intervals, the sea was heard moaning on the distant beach, strangely mingled with the desolate warning of the bell-buoy as it rocked to the waves. Then the wind rose again, and the noise of the sea was lost in the fierce gusts which, finding no obstacle on the open marshes, swept with their full fury upon the house by the creek. The strange voices of the air shrieked in its chimneys, windows rattled, doors slammed, and even, the very curtains seemed to live and move.

Eunice was in bed, awake. A small nightlight in a saucer of oil shed a sickly glare upon the worm-eaten old furniture, distorting the most innocent articles into ghastly shapes. A wilder gust than usual almost deprived her of the protection afforded by that poor light, and she lay listening fearfully to the creakings and other noises on the stairs, bitterly regretting that she had not asked Martha to sleep with her. But it was not too late even now. She slipped hastily to the floor, crossed to the huge wardrobe, and was in the very act of taking her dressing-gown from its peg when an unmistakable footfall was heard on the stairs. The robe dropped from her shaking fingers, and with a quickly beating heart she regained her bed.

The sounds ceased and a deep silence followed, which she herself was unable to break although she strove hard to do so. A wild gust of wind shook the windows and nearly extinguished the light, and when its flame had regained its accustomed steadiness she saw that the door was slowly opening, while the huge shadow of a hand blotted the papered wall. Still her tongue refused its office. The door flew open with a crash, a cloaked figure entered and, throwing aside its coverings, she saw with a horror past all expression the napkin-bound face of the dead Ursula smiling terribly at her. In her last extremity she raised her faded eyes above for succour, and then as the figure noiselessly advanced and laid its cold hand upon her brow, the soul of Eunice Mallow left its body with a wild shriek and made its way to the Eternal.

Martha, roused by the cry, and shivering with dread, rushed to the door and gazed in terror at the figure which stood leaning over the bedside. As she watched, it slowly removed the cowl and the napkin and exposed the fell face of Tabitha, so strangely contorted between fear and triumph that she hardly recognized it.

"Who's there?" cried Tabitha in a terrible voice as she saw the old woman's shadow on the wall.

"I thought I heard a cry," said Martha, entering. "Did anybody call?"

"Yes, Eunice," said the other, regarding her closely. "I, too, heard the cry, and hurried to her. What makes her so strange? Is she in a trance?"

"Ay," said the old woman, falling on her knees by the bed and sobbing bitterly, "the trance of death. Ah, my dear, my poor lonely girl, that this should be the end of it! She has died of fright," said the old woman, pointing to the eyes, which even yet retained their horror. "She has seen something devilish."

Tabitha's gaze fell. "She has always suffered with her heart," she muttered; "the night has frightened her; it frightened me."

She stood upright by the foot of the bed as Martha drew the sheet over the face of the dead woman.

"First Ursula, then Eunice," said Tabitha, drawing a deep breath. "I can't stay here. I'll dress and wait for the morning."

She left the room as she spoke, and with bent head proceeded to her own. Martha remained by the bedside, and gently closing the staring eyes, fell on her knees, and prayed long and earnestly for the departed soul. Overcome with grief and fear she remained with bowed head until a sudden sharp cry from Tabitha brought her to her feet.

"Well," said the old woman, going to the door.

"Where are you?" cried Tabitha, somewhat reassured by her voice.

"In Miss Eunice's bedroom. Do you want anything?"

"Come down at once. Quick! I am unwell."

Her voice rose suddenly to a scream. "Quick! For God's sake! Quick, or I shall go mad. There is some strange woman in the house."

The old woman stumbled hastily down the dark stairs. "What is the matter?" she cried, entering the room. "Who is it? What do you mean?"

"I saw it," said Tabitha, grasping her convulsively by the shoulder. "I was coming to you when I saw the figure of a woman in front of me going up the stairs. Is it—can it be Ursula come for the soul of Eunice, as she said she would?"

"Or for yours?" said Martha, the words coming from her in some odd fashion, despite herself.

Tabitha, with a ghastly look, fell cowering by her side, clutching tremulously at her clothes. "Light the lamps," she cried hysterically. "Light a fire, make a noise; oh, this dreadful darkness! Will it never be day!"

"Soon, soon," said Martha, overcoming her repugnance and trying to pacify her. "When the day comes you will laugh at these fears."

"I murdered her," screamed the miserable woman, "I killed her with fright. Why did she not give me the money? 'Twas no use to her. Ah! Look there!"

Martha, with a horrible fear, followed her glance to the door, but saw nothing.

"It's Ursula," said Tabitha from between her teeth. "Keep her off! Keep her off!"

The old woman, who by some unknown sense seemed to feel the presence of a third person in the room, moved a step forward and stood before her. As she did so Tabitha waved her arms as though to free herself from the touch of a detaining hand, half rose to her feet, and without a word fell dead before her.

At this the old woman's courage forsook her, and with a great cry she rushed from the room, eager to escape from this house of death and mystery. The bolts of the great door were stiff with age, and strange voices seemed to ring in her ears as she strove wildly to unfasten them. Her brain whirled. She thought that the dead in their distant rooms called to her, and that a devil stood on the step outside laughing and holding the door against her. Then with a supreme effort she flung it open, and heedless of her night-clothes passed into the bitter night. The path across the marshes was lost in the darkness, but she found it; the planks over the ditches slippery and narrow, but she crossed them in safety, until at last, her feet bleeding and her breath coming in great gasps, she entered the village and sank down more dead than alive on a cottage doorstep.

AN EPISODE OF CATHEDRAL HISTORY

M. R. James
(1862–1936)

James' reputation within horror fiction remains the same as it has been for a century: as one of two or three of the greatest ghost story writers ever. The stories within Ghost Stories of an Antiquary *(1904) and* More Ghost Stories of an Antiquary *(1911) are classics and amongst the most influential of their time. James used modern settings and characters, rather than those drawn from the Gothics, and lightly incorporated his vast scholarly knowledge into the stories, not only modernizing the ghost story but creating the genre of the "antiquarian ghost story."*

James was a scholar by trade, gaining his degree at Cambridge and then working as a provost at King's College. His scholarly work, including The Apocalypse in Art *(1931), his description of a number of library catalogues, his translation of* The New Testament Apocrypha, *and his 1917 edition of "Two Lives of St. Aethelbert, King and Martyr," remain authoritative and well-used by scholars and students.*

But among literateurs he is still best known as the premier ghost story writer of his time. "An Episode of Cathedral History," first published in The Cambridge Review *in June, 1914, is in some ways typical of his work: excellently told, about unwise triflers who, against all advice, uncover a buried tomb in an old location, leading to unpleasant consequences.*

THERE WAS ONCE a learned gentleman who was deputed to examine and report upon the archives of the Cathedral of Southminster. The examination of these records demanded a very considerable expenditure of time: hence it became advisable for him to engage lodgings in the city: for though the Cathedral body were profuse in their offers of hospitality, Mr. Lake felt that he would prefer to be master of his day. This was recognized as reasonable. The Dean eventually wrote advising Mr. Lake, if he were not already suited, to communicate with Mr. Worby, the principal Verger, who occupied a house convenient to the church and was prepared to take in a quiet lodger for three or four weeks. Such an arrangement was precisely what Mr. Lake desired. Terms were easily agreed upon, and early in December, like another Mr. Datchery (as he remarked to himself), the investigator found himself in the occupation of a very comfortable room in an ancient and "cathedraly" house.

One so familiar with the customs of Cathedral churches, and treated with such obvious consideration by the Dean and Chapter of this Cathedral in particular, could not fail to command the respect of the Head Verger. Mr. Worby even acquiesced in certain modifications of statements he had been accustomed to offer for years to parties of visitors. Mr. Lake, on his part, found the Verger a very cheery companion, and took advantage of any occasion that presented itself for enjoying his conversation when the day's work was over.

One evening, about nine o'clock, Mr. Worby knocked at his lodger's door. "I've occasion," he said, "to go across to the Cathedral, Mr. Lake, and I think I made you a promise when I did so next I would give you the opportunity to see what it looks like at night time. It's quite fine and dry outside, if you care to come."

"To be sure I will; very much obliged to you, Mr. Worby, for thinking of it, but let me get my coat."

"Here it is, Sir, and I've another lantern here that you'll find advisable for the steps, as there's no moon."

"Anyone might think we were Jasper and Durdles, over again, mightn't they?" said Lake, as they crossed the close, for he had ascertained that the Verger had read *Edwin Drood*.

"Well, so they might," said Mr. Worby, with a short laugh, "though I don't know whether we ought to take it as a compliment. Odd ways, I often think, they had at that Cathedral, don't it seem so to you, sir? Full choral matins at seven o'clock in the morning all the year round. Wouldn't suit our boys' voices nowadays, and I think there's one or two of the men would be applying for a rise if the Chapter was to bring it in—particular the altos."

They were now at the south-west door. As Mr. Worby was unlocking it, Lake said, "Did you ever find anybody locked in here by accident?"

"Twice I did. One was a drunk sailor; however he got in I don't know. I s'pose he went to sleep in the service, but by the time I got to him he was praying fit to bring the roof in. Lor'! what a noise that man did make! said it was the first time he'd been inside a church for ten years, and blest if ever he'd try it again. The other was an old sheep: them boys it was, up to their games. That was the last time they tried it on, though. There, sir, now you see what we look like; our late Dean used now and again to bring parties in, but he preferred a moonlight night, and there was a piece of verse he'd coat to 'em, relating to a Scotch cathedral, I understand; but I don't know; I almost think the effect's better when it's all dark-like. Seems to add to the size and heighth. Now if you won't mind stopping somewhere in the nave while I go up into the choir where my business lays, you'll see what I mean."

Accordingly Lake waited, leaning against a pillar, and watched the light wavering along the length of the church, and up the steps into the choir, until it was intercepted by some screen or other furniture, which only allowed the reflection to be seen on the piers and roof. Not many minutes had passed before Worby reappeared at the door of the choir and by waving his lantern signalled to Lake to rejoin him.

"I suppose it is Worby, and not a substitute," thought Lake to himself, as he walked up the nave. There was, in fact, nothing untoward. Worby showed him the papers which he had come to fetch out of the Dean's stall, and asked him what he thought of the spectacle: Lake agreed that it was well worth seeing. "I suppose," he said, as they walked towards the altar-steps together, "that you're too much used to going about here at night to feel nervous—but you must get a start every now and then, don't you, when a book falls down or a door swings to?"

"No, Mr. Lake, I can't say I think much about noises, not nowadays: I'm much more afraid of finding an escape of gas or a burst in the stove pipes than anything else. Still there have been times, years ago. Did you notice that plain altar-tomb there—fifteenth century we say it is, I don't know if you agree to that? Well, if you didn't look at it, just come back and give it a glance, if you'd be so good." It was on the north side of the choir, and rather awkwardly placed: only about three feet from the enclosing stone screen. Quite plain, as the Verger had said, but for some ordinary stone panelling. A metal cross of some size on the northern side (that next to the screen) was the solitary feature of any interest.

Lake agreed that it was not earlier than the Perpendicular period: "but," he said, "unless it's the tomb of some remarkable person, you'll forgive me for saying that. I don't think it's particularly noteworthy."

"Well, I can't say as it is the tomb of anybody noted in 'istory,'" said Worby, who had a dry smile on his face, "for we don't own any record whatsoever of who it was put up to. For all that, if you've half in hour to spare, Sir, when we get back to the house, Mr. Lake, I could tell you a tale about that tomb. I won't begin on it now; it strikes cold here, and we don't want to be dawdling about all night."

"Of course I should like to hear it immensely."

"Very well, Sir, you shall. Now if I might put a question to you," he went on, as they passed down the choir aisle, "in our little local guide—and not only there, but in the little book on our Cathedral in

the series—you'll find it stated that this portion of the building was
erected previous to the twelfth century. Now of course I should be glad
enough to take that view, but—mind the step, sir—but, I put it to
you—does the lay of the stone 'ere in this portion of the wall (which
he tapped with his key), does it to your eye carry the flavour of what
you might call Saxon masonry? No, I thought not; no more it does to
me: now, if you'll believe me, I've said as much to those men—one's
the librarian of our Free Libry here, and the other came down from
London on purpose—fifty times, if I have once, but I might just as well
have talked to that bit of stonework. But there it is, I suppose every
one's got their opinions."

The discussion of this peculiar trait of human nature occupied Mr.
Worby almost up to the moment when he and Lake re-entered the
former's house. The condition of the fire in Lake's sitting-room led to
a suggestion from Mr. Worby that they should finish the evening in his
own parlour. We find them accordingly settled there some short time
afterwards.

Mr. Worby made his story a long one, and I will not undertake to
tell it wholly in his own words, or in his own order. Lake committed
the substance of it to paper immediately after hearing it, together with
some few passages of the narrative which had fixed themselves verbatim
in his mind; I shall probably find it expedient to condense Lake's record
to some extent.

Mr. Worby was born, it appeared, about the year 1828. His father
before him had been connected with the Cathedral, and likewise his
grandfather. One or both had been choristers, and in later life both had
done work as mason and carpenter respectively about the fabric. Worby
himself, though possessed, as he frankly acknowledged, of an indifferent
voice, had been drafted into the choir at about ten years of age.

It was in 1840 that the wave of the Gothic revival smote the Cathedral of Southminster. "There was a lot of lovely stuff went then, Sir,"
said Worby, with a sigh. "My father couldn't hardly believe it when he
got his orders to clear out the choir. There was a new dean just come
in—Dean Burscough it was—and my father had been 'prenticed to a
good firm of joiners in the city, and knew what good work was when
he saw it. Crool it was, he used to say: all that beautiful wainscot oak,
as good as the day it was put up, and garlands-like of foliage and fruit,
and lovely old gilding work on the coats of arms and the organ pipes.
All went to the timber yard—every bit except some little pieces
worked up in the Lady Chapel, and 'ere in this overmantel. Well—I

may be mistook, but I say our choir never looked as well since. Still there was a lot found out about the history of the church, and no doubt but what it did stand in need of repair. There was very few winters passed but what we'd lose a pinnicle." Mr. Lake expressed his concurrence with Worby's views of restoration, but owns to a fear about this point lest the story proper should never be reached. Possibly this was perceptible in his manner.

Worby hastened to reassure him, "Not but what I could carry on about that topic for hours at a time, and do when I see my opportunity. But Dean Burscough he was very set on the Gothic period, and nothing would serve him but everything must be made agreeable to that. And one morning after service he appointed for my father to meet him in the choir, and he came back after he'd taken off his robes in the vestry, and he'd got a roll of paper with him, and the verger that was then brought in a table, and they begun spreading it out on the table with prayer books to keep it down, and my father helped 'em, and he saw it was a picture of the inside of a choir in a Cathedral; and the Dean—he was a quick-spoken gentleman—he says, 'Well, Worby, what do you think of that?' 'Why,' says my father, 'I don't think I 'ave the pleasure of knowing that view. Would that be Hereford Cathedral, Mr. Dean?' 'No, Worby,' says the Dean, 'that's Southminster Cathedral as we hope to see it before many years.' 'Indeed, Sir,' says my father and that was all he did say—leastways to the Dean—but he used to tell me he felt really faint in himself when he looked round our choir as I can remember it, comfortable, and furnished-like, and then see this nasty little dry picter, as he called it, drawn out by some London architect. Well, there I am again. But you'll see what I mean if you look at this old view."

Worby reached down a framed print from the wall. "Well, the long and the short of it was that the Dean he handed over to my father a copy of an order of the Chapter that he was to clear out every bit of the choir—make a clean sweep—ready for the new work that was being designed up in town, and he was to put it in hand as soon as ever he could get the breakers together. Now then, Sir, if you look at that view, you'll see where the pulpit used to stand—that's what I want you to notice, if you please." It was, indeed, easily seen; an unusually large structure of timber with a domed sounding-board, standing at the east end of the stalls on the north side of the choir, facing the bishop's throne. Worby proceeded to explain that during the alterations, services were held in the nave, the member of the choir being thereby disappointed of

an anticipated holiday, and the organist in particular incurring the suspicion of having wilfully damaged the mechanism of the temporary organ
that was hired at considerable expense from London.

The work of demolition began with the choir screen and organ loft,
and proceeded gradually east-wards, disclosing, as Worby said, many
interesting features of older work. While this was going on, the mem-
bers of the Chapter were, naturally, in and about the choir a great deal,
and it soon became apparent to the elder Worby—who could not help
overhearing some of their talk—that, on the part of the senior Canons
especially, there must have been a good deal of disagreement before the
policy now being carried out had been adopted. Some were of opinion
that they should catch their deaths of cold in the return-stalls, unpro-
tected by a screen from the draughts in the nave: others objected to
being exposed to the view of persons in the choir aisles, especially, they
said, during the sermons, when they found it helpful to listen in a pos-
ture which was liable to misconstruction. The strongest opposition,
however, came from the oldest of the body, who up to the last moment
objected to the removal of the pulpit. "You ought not to touch it, Mr.
Dean," he said with great emphasis one morning, when the two were
standing before it: "you don't know what mischief you may do." "Mischief? it's not a work of any particular merit, Canon." "Don't call me
Canon," said the old man with great asperity, "that is, for thirty years
I've been known as Dr. Ayloff, and I shall be obliged, Mr. Dean, if you
would kindly humour me in that matter. And as to the pulpit (which
I've preached from for thirty years, though I don't insist on that), all I'll
say is, I know you're doing wrong in moving it." "But what sense
could there be, my dear Doctor, in leaving it where it is, when we're
fitting up the rest of the choir in a totally different style? What reason
could be given—apart from the look of the thing?" "Reason! Reason!"
said old Dr. Ayloff; "if you young men—if I may say so without any
disrespect, Mr. Dean—if you'd only listen to reason a little, and not be
always asking for it, we should get on better. But there, I've said my
say." The old gentleman hobbled off, and as it proved, never entered
the Cathedral again. The season—it was a hot summer—turned sickly
on a sudden, Dr. Ayloff was one of the first to go, with some affection
of the muscles of the thorax, which took him painfully at night. And at
many services the number of choir-men and boys was very thin.

Meanwhile the pulpit had been done away with. In fact, the
sounding-board (part of which still exists as a table in a summer-house
in the palace garden) was taken down within an hour or two of Dr.

Ayloff's protest. The removal of the base—not effected without considerable trouble—disclosed to view, greatly to the exultation of the restoring party, an altar-tomb—the tomb, of course, to which Worby had attracted Lake's attention that same evening. Much fruitless research was expended in attempts to identify the occupant; from that day to this he has never had a name put to him. The structure had been most carefully boxed in under the pulpit-base, so that such slight ornament as it possessed was not defaced; only on the north side of it there was what looked like an injury; a gap between two of the slabs composing the side. It might be two or three inches across. Palmer, the mason, was directed to fill it up in a week's time, when he came to do some other small jobs near that part of the choir.

The season was undoubtedly a very trying one. Whether the church was built on a site that had once been a marsh, as was suggested, or for whatever reason, the residents in its immediate neighbourhood had, many of them, but little enjoyment of the exquisite sunny days and the calm nights of August and September. To several of the older people—Dr. Ayloff, among others, as we have seen—the summer proved downright fatal, but even among the younger, few escaped either a sojourn in bed for a matter of weeks, or at the least, a brooding sense of oppression, accompanied by hateful nightmares. Gradually there formulated itself a suspicion—which grew into a conviction—that the alterations in the Cathedral had something to say in the matter. The widow of a former old verger, a pensioner of the Chapter of Southminster, was visited by dreams, which she retailed to her friends, of a shape that slipped out of the little door of the south transept as the dark fell in, and flitted—taking a fresh direction every night—about the Close, disappearing for a while in house after house, and finally emerging again when the night sky was paling. She could see nothing of it, she said, but that it was a moving form: only she had an impression that when it returned to the church, as it seemed to do in the end of the dream, it turned its head: and then, she could not tell why, but she thought it had red eyes. Worby remembered hearing the old lady tell this dream at a tea-party in the house of the chapter clerk. Its recurrence might, perhaps, he said, be taken as a symptom of approaching illness; at any rate before the end of September the old lady was in her grave.

The interest excited by the restoration of this great church was not confined to its own county. One day that summer an F.S.A., of some celebrity, visited the place. His business was to write an account of the discoveries that had been made, for the Society of Antiquaries, and his wife, who accompanied him, was to make a series of illustrative draw-ings for his report. In the morning she employed herself in making a general sketch of the choir; in the afternoon she devoted herself to details. She first drew the newly-exposed altar-tomb, and when that was finished, she called her husband's attention to a beautiful piece of diaper-ornament on the screen just behind it, which had, like the tomb itself, been completely concealed by the pulpit. Of course, he said, an illustration of that must be made; so she seated herself on the tomb and began a careful drawing which occupied her till dusk.

Her husband had by this time finished his work of measuring and description, and they agreed that it was time to be getting back to their hotel. "You may as well brush my skirt, Frank," said the lady, "it must have got covered with dust, I'm sure." He obeyed dutifully; but, after a moment, he said, "I don't know whether you value this dress particu-larly, my dear, but I'm inclined to think it's seen its best days. There's a great bit of it gone." "Gone? Where?" said she. "I don't know where it's gone, but it's off at the bottom edge behind here." She pulled it hastily into sight, and was horrified to find a jagged tear extending some way into the substance of the stuff; very much, she said, as if a dog had rent it away. The dress was, in any case, hopelessly spoilt, to her great vexation, and though they looked everywhere, the missing piece could not be found. There were many ways, they concluded, in which the injury might have come about, for the choir was full of old bits of woodwork with nails sticking out of them. Finally, they could only suppose that one of these had caused the mischief, and that the work-men, who had been about all day, had carried off the particular piece with the fragment of dress still attached to it.

It was about this time, Worby thought, that his little dog began to wear an anxious expression when the hour for it to be put into the shed in the back yard approached. (For his mother had ordained that it must not sleep in the house.) One evening, he said, when he was just going to pick it up and carry it out, it looked at him "like a Christian, and waved its 'and, I was going to say—well, you know 'ow they do carry on sometimes, and the end of it was I put it under my coat, and 'uddled it upstairs—and I'm afraid I as good as deceived my poor mother on the subject. After that the dog acted very artful with 'iding itself under the bed for half an hour or more before bed-time came, and we worked it so as my mother never found out what we'd done." Of course Worby was glad of its company anyhow, but more particularly when the nui-sance that is still remembered in Southminster as "the crying" set in.

"Night after night," said Worby, "that dog seemed to know it was coming; he'd creep out, he would, and snuggle into the bed and cuddle right up to me shivering, and when the crying come he'd be like a wild thing, shoving his head under my arm, and I was fully near as bad. Six or seven times we'd hear it, not more, and when he'd dror out his 'ed again I'd know it was over for that night. What was it like, sir? Well, I never heard but one thing that seemed to hit it off. I happened to be playing about in the Close, and there was two of the Canons met and said 'Good morning' one to another. 'Sleep well last night?' says one—it was Mr. Henslow that one, and Mr. Lyall was the other. 'Can't say I did,' says Mr. Lyall, 'rather too much of Isaiah 34:14 for me.' '34:14,' says Mr. Henslow, 'what's that?' 'You call yourself a Bible reader!' says Mr. Lyall. (Mr. Henslow, you must know, he was one of what used to be termed Simeon's lot—pretty much what we should call the Evangelical party.) 'You go and look it up.' I wanted to know what he was getting at myself, and so off I ran home and got out my own Bible, and there it was: 'the satyr shall cry to his fellow.' Well, I thought, is that what we've been listening to these past nights? and I tell you it made me look over my shoulder a time or two. Of course I'd asked my father and mother about what it could be before that, but they both said it was most likely cats: but they spoke very short, and I could see they was troubled. My word! that was a noise— 'ungry-like, as if it was calling after someone that wouldn't come. If ever you felt you wanted company, it would be when you was waiting for it to begin again. I believe two or three nights there was men put on to watch in different parts of the Close; but they all used to get together in one corner, the nearest they could to the High Street, and nothing came of it.

"Well, the next thing was this. Me and another of the boys—he's in business in the city now as a grocer, like his father before him—we'd gone up in the choir after morning service was over, and we heard old Palmer the mason bellowing to some of his men. So we went up nearer, because we knew he was a rusty old chap and there might be some fun going. It appears Palmer 'd told this man to stop up the chink in that old tomb. Well, there was this man keeping on saying he'd done it the best he could, and there was Palmer carrying on like all possessed about it. 'Call that making a job of it?' he says. 'If you had your rights you'd get the sack for this. What do you suppose I pay you your wages for? What do you suppose I'm going to say to the Dean and Chapter when they come round, as come they may do any time, and see where you've been bungling about covering the 'ole place with mess and plaster and Lord knows what?' 'Well, master, I done the best I could,' says the man; 'I don't know no more than what you do 'ow it come to fall out this way. I tamped it right in the 'ole,' he says, 'and now it's fell out,' he says, 'I never see.'

"'Fell out?' says old Palmer, 'why it's nowhere near the place. Blowed out, you mean'; and he picked up a bit of plaster, and so did I, that was laying up against the screen, three or four feet off, and not dry yet; and old Palmer he looked at it curious-like, and then he turned round on me and he says, 'Now then, you boys, have you been up to some of your games here?' 'No,' I says, 'I haven't, Mr. Palmer; there's none of us been about here till just this minute'; and while I was talking the other boy, Evans, he got looking in through the chink, and I heard him draw in his breath, and he came away sharp and up to us, and says he, 'I believe there's something in there. I saw something shiny.' 'What! I dare say!' says old Palmer; 'well, I ain't got time to stop about there. You, William, you go off and get some more stuff and make a job of it this time; if not, there'll be trouble in my yard,' he says.

"So the man he went off, and Palmer too, and us boys stopped behind, and I says to Evans, 'Did you really see anything in there?' 'Yes,' he says, 'I did indeed.' So then I says, 'Let's shove something in and stir it up.' And we tried several of the bits of wood that was laying about, but they were all too big. Then Evans he had a sheet of music he'd brought with him, an anthem or a service, I forget which it was now, and he rolled it up small and shoved it in the chink; two or three times he did it, and nothing happened. 'Give it me, boy,' I said, and I had a try. No, nothing happened. Then, I don't know why I thought of it, I'm sure, but I stooped down just opposite the chink and put my two fingers in my mouth and whistled—you know the way—and at that I seemed to think I heard something stirring, and I says to Evans, 'Come away,' I says; 'I don't like this.' 'Oh, rot,' he says, 'give me that roll,' and he took it and shoved it in. And I don't think ever I see anyone go so pale as he did. 'I say, Worby,' he says, 'it's caught, or else someone's got hold of it.' 'Pull it out or leave it,' I says. 'Come and let's get off.' So he gave a good pull, and it came away. Leastways most of it did, but the end was gone. Torn off it was, and Evans looked at it for a second and then he gave a sort of a croak and let it drop, and we both made off out of there as quick as ever we could. When we got outside Evans says to me, 'Did you see the end of that paper?' 'No,' I says, 'only it was torn.' 'Yes, it was,' he says, 'but it was wet too, and black!' Well, partly because of the fright we had, and partly because that music was wanted in a day or two, and we knew there'd be a set-out about it with the organist, we didn't say nothing to anyone else, and I suppose the workmen they swept up the bit that was left along with the rest of the rubbish. But Evans, if you were to ask him this very day about it, he'd stick to it he saw that paper wet and black at the end where it was torn."

After that the boys gave the choir a wide berth, so that Worby was not sure what was the result of the mason's renewed mending of the tomb. Only he made out from fragments of conversation dropped by the workmen passing through the choir that some difficulty had been met with, and that the governor—Mr. Palmer to wit—had tried his own hand at the job. A little later, he happened to see Mr. Palmer himself knocking at the door of the Deanery and being admitted by the butler. A day or so after that, he gathered from a remark his father let fall at breakfast that something a little out of the common was to be done in the Cathedral after morning service on the morrow. "And I'd just as soon it was to-day," his father added; "I don't see the use of running risks." "'Father,' I says, 'what are you going to do in the Cathedral to-morrow?' And he turned on me as savage as I ever see him—he was a wonderful good-tempered man as a general thing, my poor father was. 'My lad,' he says, 'I'll trouble you not to go picking up your elders' and betters' talk: it's not manners and it's not straight. What I'm going to do or not going to do in the Cathedral to-morrow is none of your business: and if I catch sight of you hanging about the place to-morrow after your work's done, I'll send you home with a flea in your ear. Now you mind that.' Of course I said I was very sorry and that, and equally of course I went off and laid my plans with Evans. We knew there was a stair up in the corner of the transept which you can get up to the triforium, and in them days the door to it was pretty well always open, and even if it wasn't we knew the key usually laid under a bit of matting hard by. So we made up our minds we'd be putting away music and that, next morning while the rest of the boys was clearing off, and then slip up the stairs and watch from the triforium if there was any signs of work going on.

"Well, that same night I dropped off asleep as sound as a boy does, and all of a sudden the dog woke me up, coming into the bed, and thought I, now we're going to get it sharp, for he seemed more frightened than usual. After about five minutes sure enough came this cry. I can't give you no idea what it was like; and so near too—nearer than I'd heard it yet—and a funny thing, Mr. Lake, you know what a place this Close is for in echo, and particular if you stand this side of it. Well, this crying never made no sign of an echo at all. But, as I said, it was dreadful near this night; and on the top of the start I got with hearing it, I got another fright; for I heard something rustling outside in the passage. Now to be sure I thought I was done; but I noticed the dog seemed to perk up a bit, and next there was someone whispered outside the door, and I very near laughed out loud, for I knew it was my father and mother that had got out of bed with the noise. 'Whatever is it?' says my mother. 'Hush! I don't know,' says my father, excited-like, 'don't disturb the boy. I hope he didn't hear nothing.'

"So, me knowing they were just outside, it made me bolder, and I slipped out of bed across to my little window—giving on the Close—but the dog he bored right down to the bottom of the bed—and I looked out. First go off I couldn't see anything. Then right down in the shadow under a buttress I made out what I shall always say was two spots of red—a dull red it was—nothing like a lamp or a fire, but just so as you could pick 'em out of the black shadow. I hadn't but just sighted 'em when it seemed we wasn't the only people that had been disturbed, because I see a window in a house on the left-hand side become lighted up, and the light moving. I just turned my head to make sure of it, and then looked back into the shadow for those two red things, and they were gone, and for all I peered about and stared, there was not a sign more of them. Then come my last fright that night—something come against my bare leg—but that was all right: that was my little dog had come out of bed, and prancing about making a great to-do, only holding his tongue, and me seeing he was quite in spirits again, I took him back to bed and we slept the night out!

"Next morning I made out to tell my mother I'd had the dog in my room, and I was surprised, after all she'd said about it before, how quiet she took it. 'Did you?' she says. 'Well, by good rights you ought to go without your breakfast for doing such a thing behind my back: but I don't know as there's any great harm done, only another time you ask my permission, do you hear?' A bit after that I said something to my father about having heard the cats again. 'Cats?' he says; and he looked over at my poor mother, and she coughed and he says, 'Oh! ah! yes, cats. I believe I heard 'em myself.'

"That was a funny morning altogether: nothing seemed to go right. The organist he stopped in bed, and the minor Canon he forgot it was the 19th day and waited for the Venite; and after a bit the deputy he set off playing the chant for evensong, which was a minor; and then the

Decani boys were laughing so much they couldn't sing, and when it came to the anthem the solo boy he got took with the giggles, and made out his nose was bleeding, and shoved the book at me what hadn't practised the verse and wasn't much of a singer if I had known it. Well, things was rougher, you see, fifty years ago, and I got a nip from the counter-tenor behind me that I remembered.

"So we got through somehow, and neither the men nor the boys weren't by way of waiting to see whether the Canon in residence—Mr. Henslow it was—would come to the vestries and fine 'em, but I don't believe he did: for one thing I fancy he'd read the wrong lesson for the first time in his life, and knew it. Anyhow, Evans and me didn't find no difficulty in slipping up the stairs as I told you, and when we got up we laid ourselves down flat on our stomachs where we could just stretch our heads out over the old tomb, and we hadn't but just done so when we heard the verger that was then, first shutting the iron porch-gates and locking the south-west door, and then the transept door, so we knew there was something up, and they meant to keep the public out for a bit.

"Next thing was, the Dean and the Canon come in by their door on the north, and then I see my father, and old Palmer, and a couple of their best men, and Palmer stood a talking for a bit with the Dean in the middle of the choir. He had a coil of rope and the men had crows. All of 'em looked a bit nervous. So there they stood talking, and at last I heard the Dean say, 'Well, I've no time to waste, Palmer. If you think this'll satisfy Southminster people, I'll permit it to be done; but I must say this, that never in the whole course of my life have I heard such arrant nonsense from a practical man as I have from you. Don't you agree with me, Henslow?' As far as I could hear Mr. Henslow said something like 'Oh well! we're told, aren't we, Mr. Dean, not to judge others?' And the Dean he gave a kind of sniff, and walked straight up to the tomb, and took his stand behind it with his back to the screen, and the others they come edging up rather gingerly. Henslow, he stopped on the south side and scratched on his chin, he did. Then the Dean spoke up: 'Palmer,' he says, 'which can you do easiest, get the slab off the top, or shift one of the side slabs?'

"Old Palmer and his men they pottered about a bit looking round the edge of the top slab and sounding the sides on the south and east and west and everywhere but the north. Henslow said something about it being better to have a try at the south side, because there was more light and more room to move about in. Then my father who'd been watching of them, went round to the north side, and knelt down and felt of the slab by the chink, and he got up and dusted his knees and says to the Dean: 'Beg pardon, Mr. Dean, but I think if Mr. Palmer'll try this here slab he'll find it'll come out easy enough. Seems to me one of the men could prise it out with his crow by means of this chink.' 'Ah! thank you, Worby,' says the Dean; 'that's a good suggestion. Palmer, let one of your men do that, will you?'

"So the man come round, and put his bar in and bore on it, and just that minute when they were all bending over, and we boys got our heads well over the edge of the triforium, there come a most fearful crash down at the west end of the choir, as if a whole stick of big timber had fallen down a flight of stairs. Well, you can't expect me to tell you everything that happened all in a minute. Of course there was a terrible commotion. I heard the slab fall out, and the crowbar on the floor, and I heard the Dean say, 'Good God!'

"When I looked down again I saw the Dean tumbled over on the floor, the men was making off down the choir, Henslow was just going to help the Dean up, Palmer was going to stop the men (as he said afterwards) and my father was sitting on the altar step with his face in his hands. The Dean he was very cross. 'I wish to goodness you'd look where you're coming to, Henslow,' he says. 'Why you should all take to your heels when a stick of wood tumbles down I cannot imagine'; and all Henslow could do, explaining he was right away on the other side of the tomb, would not satisfy him.

"Then Palmer came back and reported there was nothing to account for this noise and nothing seemingly fallen down, and when the Dean finished feeling of himself they gathered round—except my father, he sat where he was—and someone lighted up a bit of candle and they looked into the tomb. 'Nothing there,' says the Dean, 'what did I tell you? Stay! here's something. What's this? a bit of music paper, and a piece of torn stuff—part of a dress it looks like. Both quite modern—no interest whatever. Another time perhaps you'll take the advice of an educated man'—or something like that, and off he went, limping a bit, and out through the north door, only as he went he called back angry to Palmer for leaving the door standing open. Palmer called out, 'Very sorry, Sir,' but he shrugged his shoulders, and Henslow says, 'I fancy Mr. Dean's mistaken. I closed the door behind me, but he's a little upset.' Then Palmer says, 'Why, where's Worby?' and they saw him sitting on the step and went up to him. He was recovering himself, it seemed, and wiping his forehead, and Palmer helped him up on to his legs, as I was glad to see.

"They were too far off for me to hear what they said, but my father pointed to the north door in the aisle, and Palmer and Henslow both of them looked very surprised and scared. After a bit, my father and Henslow went out of the church, and the others made what haste they could to put the slab back and plaster it in. And about as the clock struck twelve the Cathedral was opened again and us boys made the best of our way home.

"I was in a great taking to know what it was had given my poor father such a turn, and when I got in and found him sitting in his chair taking a glass of spirits, and my mother standing looking anxious at him, I couldn't keep from bursting out and making confession where I'd been. But he didn't seem to take on, not in the way of losing his temper. 'You was there, was you? Well, did you see it?' 'I see everything, father,' I said, 'except when the noise came.' 'Did you see what it was knocked the Dean over?' he says, 'that what come out of the monument? You didn't? Well, that's a mercy.' 'Why, what was it, father?' I said. 'Come, you must have seen it,' he says. 'Didn't you see? A thing like a man, all over hair, and two great eyes to it?'

"Well, that was all I could get out of him that time, and later on he seemed as if he was ashamed of being so frightened, and he used to put me off when I asked him about it. But years after, when I was got to be a grown man, we had more talk now and again on the matter, and he always said the same thing. 'Black it was,' he'd say, 'and a mass of hair, and two legs, and the light caught on its eyes.'

"Well, that's the tale of that tomb, Mr. Lake; it's one we don't tell to our visitors, and I should be obliged to you not to make any use of it till I'm out of the way. I doubt Mr. Evans'll feel the same as I do, if you ask him."

This proved to be the case. But over twenty years have passed by, and the grass is growing over both Worby and Evans; so Mr. Lake felt no difficulty about communicating his notes—taken in 1890—to me. He accompanied them with a sketch of the tomb and a copy of the short inscription on the metal cross which was affixed at the expense of Dr. Lyall to the centre of the northern side. It was from the Vulgate of Isaiah xxxiv., and consisted merely of the three words—

IBI CUBAVIT LAMIA.

THE PAVILION

E. Nesbit
(1858–1924)

Edith Nesbit considered herself a poet first and a commercial writer second. She wrote poetry throughout her life, and took it considerably seriously, as she did her politics—she was an active lecturer and writer on socialism during the 1880s. But her unhappy marriage and the failure of her husband's business led her to become a commercial writer, and it is there that she gained her greatest fame.

Nesbit, writing as "E. Nesbit," created modern children's literature in her "Bastable," "Psammead," and "House of Arden" series, in addition to her other stories, novels, and collections for children—40 novels and collections in all by herself, as many again in collaboration with others. Before Nesbit, secondary worlds (fictional universes) were the mode for children's books, but as her biographer Julia Briggs said, Nesbit wrote about "the tough truths to be won from encounters with things-as-they-are, previously the province of adult novels."

Less well-known now are Nesbit's adult novels and short story collections, a number of which were horror stories. "The Pavilion," which first appeared in The Strand *(Nov. 15, 1915), was one of Nesbit's last works, but has the delicacy, ambiguity, and edge of earlier classics like "From the Dead" (1893) and "The Five Senses" (1909).*

THERE WAS NEVER a moment's doubt in her own mind. So she said afterwards. And everyone agreed that she had concealed her feelings with true womanly discretion. Her friend and confidant, Amelia Davenant, was at any rate completely deceived. Amelia was one of those featureless blondes who seem born to be overlooked. She adored her beautiful friend, and never, from first to last, could see any fault in her, except, perhaps, on the evening when the real things of the story happened. And even in that matter she owned at the time that it was only that her darling Ernestine did not understand.

Ernestine was a prettyish girl with the airs, so irresistible and misleading, of a beauty; most people said that she was beautiful, and she certainly managed, with extraordinary success, to produce the illusion of beauty. Quite a number of plainish girls achieve that effect nowadays. The freedom of modern dress and coiffure and the increasing confidence in herself which the modern girl experiences, aid her in fostering the illusion; but in the sixties, when everyone wore much the same sort of bonnet, when your choice in coiffure was limited to bandeaux or ringlets, and the crinoline was your only wear, something very like genius was needed to deceive the world in the matter of your personal charms. Ernestine had that genius; hers was the smiling, ringleted, dark-haired, dark-eyed, sparkling type.

Amelia had blonde bandeaux and kind appealing blue eyes, rather too small and rather too dull; her hands and ears were beautiful, and she kept them out of sight as much as possible. In our times the blonde hair would have been puffed out to make a frame for the forehead, a little too high; a certain shade of blue and a certain shade of boldness would have made her eyes effective. And the beautiful hands would have learned that flowerlike droop of the wrist so justly and so universally admired. But as it was, Amelia was very nearly plain, and in her secret emotional self-communings told herself that she was ugly. It was she who, at the age of fourteen, composed the remarkable poem beginning:

> I know that I am ugly: did I make
> The face that is the laugh and jest of all?

and goes on, after disclaiming any personal responsibility for the face, to entreat the kind earth to "cover it away from mocking eyes," and to "let the daisies blossom where it lies."

Amelia did not want to die, and her face was not the laugh and jest, or indeed the special interest, of anyone. All that was poetic licence. Amelia had read perhaps a little too much poetry of the type of '*Quand je suis morte, mes amies, plantez un saule au cimetière*'; but really life was a very good thing to Amelia, especially when she had a new dress and someone paid her a compliment. But she went on writing verses extolling the advantages of The Tomb, and grovelling metrically at the feet of One who was Another's until that summer, when she was nineteen, and went to stay with Ernestine at Doricourt. Then her Muse took flight, scared, perhaps, by the possibility, suddenly and threateningly presented, of being asked to inspire verse about the real things of life.

At any rate, Amelia ceased to write poetry about the time when she and Ernestine and Ernestine's aunt went on a visit to Doricourt, where Frederick Powell lived with his aunt. It was not one of those hurried motor-fed excursions which we have now, and call weekends, but a long leisurely visit, when all the friends of the static aunt called on the dynamic aunt, and both returned the calls with much state, a big barouche and a pair of fat horses. There were croquet parties and archery parties and little dances, all pleasant informal little gaieties arranged without ceremony among people who lived within driving distance of each other and knew each other's tastes and incomes and family history as well as they knew their own. The habit of importing huge droves of strangers from distant counties for brief harrying raids did not then obtain. There was instead a wide and constant circle of peasant people with an unflagging stream of gaiety, mild indeed, but delightful to unjaded palates.

And at Doricourt life was delightful even on the days when there was no party. It was perhaps more delightful to Ernestine than to her friend, but even so, the one least pleased was Ernestine's aunt.

"I do think," she said to the other aunt whose name was Julia—"I daresay it is not so to you, being accustomed to Mr. W. Frederick, of course, from his childhood, but I always find gentlemen in the house so unsettling, especially young gentlemen, and when there are young ladies also. One is always on the *qui vive* for excitement."

"Of course," said Aunt Julia, with the air of a woman of the world, "living as you and dear Ernestine do, with only females in the house . . ."

"We hang up an old coat and hat of my brother's on the hat stand in the hall," Aunt Emmeline protested.

". . . The presence of gentlemen in the house must be a little unsettling. For myself, I am inured to it. Frederick has so many friends. Mr. Thesiger, perhaps, the greatest. I believe him to be a most worthy young man, but peculiar." She leaned forward across her bright-tinted Berlin woolwork and spoke impressively, the needle with its trailing red poised in air. "You know, I hope you will not think it indelicate of me to mention such a thing, but dear Frederick . . . your dear Ernestine would have been in every way so suitable."

"Would have been?" Aunt Emmeline's tortoise-shell shuttle ceased its swift movement among the white loops and knots of her tatting.

"Well, my dear," said the other aunt, a little shortly, "you must surely have noticed . . ."

"You don't mean to suggest Amelia . . . I thought Mr. Thesiger and Amelia . . ."

"Amelia! I really must say! No, I was alluding to Mr. Thesiger's attentions to dear Ernestine. Most marked. In dear Frederick's place I should have found some excuse for shortening Mr. Thesiger's visit. But, of course, I cannot interfere. Gentlemen must manage these things for themselves. I only hope that there will be none of that trifling with the most holy affections of others which . . ."

The less voluble aunt cut in hotly with: "Ernestine's incapable of anything so unladylike."

"Just what I was saying," the other rejoined blandly, got up and drew the blind a little lower, for the afternoon sun was glowing on the rosy wreaths of the drawing-room carpet.

Outside in the sunshine Frederick was doing his best to arrange his own affairs. He had managed to place himself beside Miss Ernestine Meutys on the stone steps of the pavilion; but then, Mr. Thesiger lay along the lower step at her feet, a very good position for looking up into her eyes. Amelia was beside him, but then it never seemed to matter whom Amelia sat beside.

They were talking about the pavilion on whose steps they sat, and Amelia who often asked uninteresting questions had wondered how old it was. It was Frederick's pavilion after all, and he felt this when his friend took the words out of his mouth and used them on his own account, even though he did give the answer in the form of an appeal.

"The foundations are Tudor, aren't they?" he said. "Wasn't it an observatory or laboratory or something of that sort in Fat Henry's time?"

"Yes," said Frederick, "there was some story about a wizard or an alchemist or something, and it was burned down, and then they rebuilt it in its present style."

"The Italian style, isn't it?" said Thesiger; "but you can hardly see what it is now, for the creeper."

"Virginia creeper, isn't it?" Amelia asked, and Frederick said: "Yes, Virginia creeper." Thesiger said it looked more like a South American plant, and Ernestine said Virginia was in South America and that was why. "I know, because of the war," she said modestly, and nobody smiled or answered. There were manners in those days.

"There's a ghost story about it surely," Thesiger began again, looking up at the dark closed doors of the pavilion.

"Not that I ever heard of," said the pavilion's owner. "I think the country people invented the tale because there have always been so many rabbits and weasels and things found dead near it. And once a dog, my uncle's favourite spaniel. But of course that's simply because they get entangled in the Virginia creeper—you see how fine and big it is—and can't get out, and die as they do in traps. But the villagers prefer to think it's ghosts."

"I thought there was a real ghost story," Thesiger persisted.

Ernestine said: "A ghost story. How delicious! Do tell it, Mr. Doricourt. This is just the place for a ghost story. Out of doors and the sun shining, so that we can't *really* be frightened."

Doricourt protested again that he knew no story.

"That's because you never read, dear boy," said Eugene Thesiger. "That library of yours. There's a delightful book—did you never notice it—brown tree calf with your arms on it; the head of the house writes the history of the house as far as he knows it. There's a lot in that book. It began in Tudor times—1515 to be exact."

"Queen Elizabeth's time." Ernestine thought that made it so much more interesting. "And was the ghost story in that?"

"It isn't exactly a ghost story," said Thesiger. "It's only that the pavilion seems to be an unlucky place to sleep in."

"Haunted?" Frederick asked, and added that he must look up that book.

"Not haunted exactly. Only several people who have slept the night there went on sleeping."

"Dead, he means," said Ernestine, and it was left for Amelia to ask: "Does the book tell anything particular about how the people died? What killed them, or anything?"

"There are suggestions," said Thesiger; "but there, it *is* a gloomy subject. I don't know why I started it. Should we have time for a game of croquet before tea, Doricourt?"

"I wish *you'd* read the book and tell me the stories," Ernestine said to Frederick, apart, over the croquet balls.

"I will," he answered fervently, "you've only to tell me what you want."

"Or perhaps Mr. Thesiger will tell us another time—in the twilight. Since people like twilight for ghosts. Will you, Mr. Thesiger?" She spoke over her blue muslin shoulder.

Frederick certainly meant to look up the book, but he delayed till after supper; the half-hour before bed when he and Thesiger put on their braided smoking-jackets and their braided smoking-caps with the long yellow tassels, and smoked the cigars which were, in those days still, more of a luxury than a necessity. Ordinarily, of course, these were smoked out of doors, or in the smoking-room, a stuffy little den littered with boots and guns and yellow-backed railway novels. But tonight Frederick left his friend in that dingy hutch, and went alone to the library, found the book and took it to the circle of light made by the colza lamp.

"I can skim through it in half an hour," he said, and wound up the lamp and lighted his second cigar. Then he opened the shutters and windows, so that the room should not smell of smoke in the morning. Those were the days of consideration for the ladies who had not yet learned that a cigarette is not exclusively a male accessory like a beard or a bass voice.

But when, his preparations complete, he opened the book, he was compelled to say "Pshaw!" Nothing short of this could relieve his feelings. (You know the expression I mean, though of course it isn't pronounced as it's spelt, any more than Featherstonehaugh or St. Maur are).

"Pshaw!" said Frederick, fluttering the pages. His remark was justified. The earlier part of the book was written in the beautiful script of the early sixteenth century, that looks so plain and is so impossible to read, and the later pages, though the handwriting was clear and Italian enough, left Frederick helpless, for the language was Latin, and Frederick's Latin was limited to the particular passages he had "been through" at his private school. He recognized a word here and there, *mors*, for instance, and *pallidus* and *pavor* and *arcanum*, just as you or I might; but to read the complicated stuff and make sense of it . . . ! Frederick said something just a shade stronger than "Pshaw!"— "Botheration!" I think it was; replaced the book on the shelf, closed the shutters and turned out the lamp. He thought he would ask Thesiger to translate the thing, but then again he thought he wouldn't. So he went to bed wishing that he had happened to remember more of the Latin so painfully beaten into the best years of his boyhood.

And the story of the pavilion was, after all, told by Thesiger.

There was a little dance at Doricourt next evening, a carpet dance, they called it. The furniture was pushed back against the walls, and the tightly stretched Axminster carpet was not so bad to dance on as you might suppose. That, you see, was before the days of polished floors and large rugs with loose edges that you can catch your feet in. A carpet was a carpet in those days, well and truly laid, conscientiously exact to the last recess and fitting the floor like a skin. And on this quite tolerable surface the young people danced very happily, some ten or twelve couples. The old people did not dance in those days, except sometimes a quadrille of state to "open the ball." They played cards in a room provided for the purpose, and in the dancing-room three or four kindly middle-aged ladies were considered to provide ample chaperonage. You were not even expected to report yourself to your chaperone at the conclusion of a dance. It was not like a real ball. And even in those far-off days there were conservatories.

It was on the steps of the conservatory, not the steps leading from the dancing-room, but the steps leading to the garden, that the story was told. The four young people were sitting together, the girls' crino-lined flounces spreading round them light huge pale roses, the young men correct in their high-shouldered coats and white cravats. Ernestine had been very kind to both the men—a little too kind, perhaps, who can tell? At any rate, there was in their eyes exactly that light which you may imagine in the eyes of rival stags in the mating season. It was Ernestine who asked Frederick for the story, and Thesiger who, at Amelia's suggestion, told it.

"It's quite a number of stories," he said, "and yet it's really all the same story. The first man to sleep in the pavilion slept there ten years after it was built. He was a friend of the alchemist or astrologer who built it. He was found dead in the morning. There seemed to have been a struggle. His arms bore the marks of cords. No; they never found any cords. He died from loss of blood. There were curious wounds. That was all the rude leeches of the day could report to the bereaved survivors of the deceased."

"How sunny you are, Mr. Thesiger," said Ernestine with that cele-brated soft low laugh of hers. When Ernestine was elderly, many people thought her stupid. When she was young, no-one seems to have been of this opinion.

"And the next?" asked Amelia.

"The next was sixty years later. It was a visitor that time, too. And he was found dead with just the same marks, and the doctors said the same thing. And so it went on. There have been eight deaths altogether—unexplained deaths. Nobody has slept in it now for over a hundred years. People seem to have a prejudice against the place as a sleeping apartment. I can't think why."

"Isn't he simply killing?" Ernestine asked Amelia, who said: "And doesn't anyone know how it happened?" No-one answered till Ernes-tine repeated the question in the form of: "I suppose it was just an accident?"

"It was a curiously recurrent accident," said Thesiger, and Frederick who throughout the conversation had said the right things at the right moment, remarked that it did not do to believe all these old legends. Most old families had them, he believed. Frederick had inherited Doricourt from an unknown great-uncle of whom in life he had not so much as heard, but he was very strong on the family tradition. "I don't attach any importance to these tales myself."

"Of course not. All the same," said Thesiger deliberately, "you wouldn't care to pass a night in that pavilion."

"No more would you," was all Frederick found on his lips.

"I admit that I shouldn't enjoy it," said Eugene, "but I'll bet you a hundred you don't *do* it."

"Done," said Frederick.

"Oh, Mr. Doricourt," breathed Ernestine, a little shocked at betting 'before ladies.'"

"Don't!" said Amelia, to whom, of course, no-one paid any attention, "don't do it."

You know how, in the midst of flower and leafage, a snake will suddenly, surprisingly rear a head that threatens? So, amid friendly talk and laughter, a sudden fierce antagonism sometimes looks out and vanishes again, surprising most of all the antagonists. This antagonism spoke in the tones of both men, and after Amelia had said, "Don't," there was a curiously breathless silence. Ernestine broke it. "Oh," she said, "I do wonder which of you will win. I should like them both to win, wouldn't you, Amelia? Only I suppose that's not always possible, is it?"

Both gentlemen assured her that in the case of bets it was very rarely possible.

"Then I wish you wouldn't," said Ernestine. "You could *both* pass the night there, couldn't you, and be company for each other? I don't think betting for such large sums is quite the thing, do you, Amelia?"

Amelia said No, she didn't, but Eugene had already begun to say, "Let the bet be off then, if Miss Meutys doesn't like it. That suggestion was invaluable. But the thing itself needn't be off. Look here, Doricourt, I'll stay in the pavilion from one to three and you from three to five. Then honour will be satisfied. How will that do?"

The snake had disappeared.

"Agreed," said Frederick, "and we can compare impressions afterwards. That will be quite interesting."

Then someone came and asked where they had all got to, and they went in and danced some more dances. Ernestine danced twice with Frederick and drank iced sherry and water and they said good-night and lighted their bedroom candles at the table in the hall.

"I do hope they won't," Amelia said as the girls sat brushing their hair at the two large white muslin frilled dressing-tables in the room they shared.

"Won't what?" said Ernestine, vigorous with the brush.

"Sleep in that hateful pavilion. I wish you'd ask them not to, Ernestine. They'd mind, if *you* asked them."

"Of course I will if you like, dear," said Ernestine cordially. She was always the soul of good nature. "But I don't think you ought to believe in ghost stories, not really."

"Why not?"

"Oh, because of the Bible and going to church and all that," said Ernestine. "Do you really think Rowland's Macassar has made any difference to my hair?"

"It's just as beautiful as it always was," said Amelia, twisting up her own little ashen-blonde handful. "What was that?"

That was a sound coming from the little dressing-room. There was no light in that room. Amelia went into the little room though Ernestine said: "Oh, don't! How can you? It might be a ghost or a rat or something," and as she went she whispered: "Hush!"

The window of the little room was open and she leaned out of it. The stone sill was cold to her elbows through her print dressing-jacket.

Ernestine went on brushing her hair. Amelia heard a movement below the window and listened. "Tonight will do," someone said.

"It's too late," said someone else.

"If you're afraid, it will always be too late or too early," said someone. And it was Thesiger.

"You know I'm not afraid," the other one, who was Doricourt, answered hotly.

"An hour for each of us will satisfy honour," said Thesiger carelessly. "The girls will expect it. I couldn't sleep. Let's do it now and get it over. Let's see. Oh, damn it!"

A faint click had sounded.

"Dropped my watch. I forgot the chain was loose. It's all right though; glass not broken even. Well, are you game?"

"Oh, yes, if you insist. Shall I go first, or you?"

"I will," said Thesiger. "That's only fair, because I suggested it. I'll stay till half-past one or a quarter to two, and then you come on. See?"

"Oh, all right. I think it's silly, though," said Frederick.

Then the voices ceased. Amelia went back to the other girl.

"They're going to do it tonight."

"Are they, dear?" Ernestine was placid as ever. "Do what?"

"Sleep in that horrible pavilion."

"How do you know?"

Amelia explained how she knew.

"Whatever can we do?" she added.

"Well, dear, suppose we go to bed," suggested Ernestine helpfully. "We shall hear all about it in the morning."

"But suppose anything happens?"

"What could happen?"

"Oh, *anything*," said Amelia. "Oh, I do wish they wouldn't! I shall go down and ask them not to."

"*Amelia!*" the other girl was at last aroused. "You *couldn't*. I shouldn't *let* you dream of doing anything so unladylike. What would the gentlemen think of you?"

The question silenced Amelia, but she began to put on her so lately discarded bodice.

"I won't go if you think I oughtn't," she said.

"Forward and fast, auntie would call it," said the other. "I am almost sure she would."

"But I'll keep dressed. I shan't disturb you. I'll sit in the dressing-room. I *can't* go to sleep while he's running into this awful danger."

"Which he?" Ernestine's voice was very sharp. "And there isn't any danger."

"Yes, there is," said Amelia sullenly, "and I mean *them*. Both of them."

Ernestine said her prayers and got into bed. She had put her hair in curl-papers which became her like a wreath of white roses.

"I don't think auntie will be pleased," she said, "when she hears that you sat up all night watching young gentlemen. Goodnight, dear!"

"Goodnight, darling," said Amelia. "I know you don't understand. It's all right."

She sat in the dark by the dressing-room window. There was no moon, but the starlight lay on the dew of the park, and the trees massed themselves in bunches of a darker grey, deepening to black at the roots of them. There was no sound to break the stillness, except the little crackling of twigs and rustlings of leaves as birds or little night wandering beasts moved in the shadows of the garden, and the sudden creakings that furniture makes if you sit alone with it and listen in the night's silence.

Amelia sat on and listened, listened. The pavilion showed in broken streaks of pale grey against the wood, that seemed to be clinging to it in dark patches. But that, she reminded herself, was only the creeper. She sat there for a very long time, not knowing how long a time it was. For anxiety is a poor chronometer, and the first ten minutes had seemed an hour. She had no watch. Ernestine had—and slept with it under her pillow. The stable clock was out of order; the man had been sent for to see it. There was nothing to measure time's flight by, and she sat there rigid, straining her ears for a footfall on the grass, straining her eyes to see a figure come out of the dark pavilion and across the dew-grey grass towards the house. And she heard nothing, saw nothing.

Slowly, imperceptibly, the grey of the sleeping trees took on faint dreams of colour. The sky turned faint above the trees, the moon perhaps was coming out. The pavilion grew more clearly visible. It seemed to Amelia that something moved along the leaves that surrounded it, and she looked to see him come out. But he did not come.

"I wish the moon would really shine," she told herself. And suddenly she knew that the sky was clear and that this growing light was not the moon's cold shiver, but the growing light of dawn.

She went quickly into the other room, put her hand under the pillow of Ernestine, and drew out the little watch with the diamond "E" on it.

"A quarter to three," she said aloud. Ernestine moved and grunted.

There was no hesitation about Amelia now. Without another thought for the ladylike and the really suitable, she lighted her candle and went quickly down the stairs, paused a moment in the hall, and so out through the front door. She passed along the terrace. The feet of Frederick protruded from the open French window of the smoking-room. She set down her candle on the terrace—it burned clearly enough in that clear air—went up to Frederick as he slept, his head between his shoulders and his hands loosely hanging, and shook him.

"Wake up," she said—"Wake up! Something's happened! It's a quarter to three and he's not come back."

"Who's not what?" Frederick said sleepily.

"Mr. Thesiger. The pavilion."

"Thesiger!—the . . . *You*, Miss Davenant? I beg your pardon. I must have dropped off."

He got up unsteadily, gazing dully at this white apparition still in evening dress with pale hair now no longer wreathed.

"What is it?" he said. "Is anybody ill?"

Briefly and very urgently Amelia told him what it was, implored him to go at once and see what had happened. If he had been fully awake, her voice and her eyes would have told him many things.

"He said he'd come back," he said. "Hadn't I better wait? You go back to bed, Miss Davenant. If he doesn't come in half an hour . . ."

"If you don't go this minute," said Amelia tensely, "I shall."

"Oh, well, if you insist," Frederick said. "He has simply fallen asleep as I did. Dear Miss Davenant, return to your room, I beg. In the morning when we are all laughing at this false alarm, you will be glad to remember that Mr. Thesiger does not know of your anxiety."

"I hate you," said Amelia gently, "and I am going to see what has happened. Come or not, as you like."

She caught up the silver candlestick and he followed its wavering gleam down the terrace steps and across the grey dewy grass.

Halfway she paused, lifted the hand that had been hidden among her muslin flounces and held it out to him with a big Indian dagger in it.

"I got it out of the hall," she said. "If there's any *real* danger. Anything living. I mean. I thought . . . But I know I couldn't use it. Will you take it?"

He took it, laughing kindly.

"How romantic you are," he said admiringly and looked at her standing there in the mingled gold and grey of dawn and candlelight. It was as though he had never seen her before.

They reached the steps of the pavilion and stumbled up them. The door was closed but not locked. And Amelia noticed that the trails of creeper had not been disturbed, they grew across the doorway, as thick as a man's finger, some of them.

"He must have got in by one of the windows," Frederick said. "Your dagger comes in handy, Miss Davenant."

He slashed at the wet sticky green stuff and put his shoulder to the door. It yielded at a touch and they went in.

The one candle lighted the pavilion hardly at all, and the dusky light that oozed in through the door and windows helped very little. And the silence was thick and heavy.

"Thesiger!" said Frederick, clearing his throat. "Thesiger! Hullo! Where are you?"

Thesiger did not say where he was. And then he saw.

There were low seats to the windows, and between the windows low stone benches ran. On one of these something dark, something dark and in places white, confused the outline of the carved stone.

"Thesiger," said Frederick again in the tone a man uses to a room that he is almost sure is empty. "Thesiger!"

But Amelia was bending over the bench. She was holding the candle crookedly so that it flared and guttered.

"Is he there?" Frederick asked, following her; "is that him? Is he asleep?"

"Take the candle," said Amelia, and he took it obediently. Amelia was touching what lay on the bench. Suddenly she screamed. Just one scream, not very loud. But Frederick remembers just how it sounded. Sometimes he hears it in dreams and wakes moaning, though he is an old man now and his old wife says: "What is it, dear?" and he says: "Nothing, my Ernestine, nothing."

Directly she had screamed: "He's dead," and fell on her knees by the bench. Frederick saw that she held something in her arms.

"Perhaps he isn't," she said. "Fetch someone from the house, brandy—send for a doctor. Oh, go, go, go!"

"I can't leave you here," said Frederick with thoughtful propriety; "suppose he revives?"

"He will not revive," said Amelia dully, "go, go, go! Do as I tell you. Go! If you don't go," she added suddenly and amazingly, "I believe I shall kill you. It's all your doing."

The astounding sharp injustice of this stung Frederick into action. "I believe he's only fainted or something," he said. "When I've roused the house and everyone has witnessed your emotion you will regret . . ."

She sprang to her feet and caught the knife from him and raised it, awkwardly, clumsily, but with keen threatening, not to be mistaken or disregarded. Frederick went.

When Frederick came back, with the groom and the gardener (he hadn't thought it well to disturb the ladies), the pavilion was filled full of white revealing daylight. On the bench lay a dead man and kneeling by him a living woman on whose warm breast his cold and heavy head lay pillowed. The dead man's hands were full of the green crushed leaves, and thick twining tendrils were about his wrists and throat. A wave of green seemed to have swept from the open window to the bench where he lay.

The groom and the gardener and the dad man's friend looked and looked.

"Looks like as if he'd got himself entangled in the creeper and lost 'is 'ead," said the groom, scratching his own.

"How'd the creeper get in, though? That's what I says," it was the gardener who said it.

"Through the window," said Doricourt, moistening his lips with his tongue.

"The window was shut, though, when I come by at five yesterday," said the gardener stubbornly. "'Ow did it get all that way since five?"

They looked at each other, voicing, silently, impossible things.

The woman never spoke. She sat there in the white ring of her crinolined dress like a broken white rose. But her arms were round Thesiger and she would not move them.

When the doctor came, he sent for Ernestine who came, flushed and sleepy-eyed and very frightened, and shocked.

"You're very upset, dear," she said to her friend, "and no wonder. How brave of you to come out with Mr. Doricourt to see what happened. But you can't do anything now, dear. Come in and I'll tell them to get you some tea."

Amelia laughed, looked down at the face on her shoulder, laid the head back on the bench among the drooping green of the creeper, stooped over it, kissed it and said quite quietly and gently: "Goodbye, dear, goodbye!"—took Ernestine's arm and went away with her.

The doctor made an examination and gave a death-certificate. "Heart failure," was his original and brilliant diagnosis. The certificate said nothing, and Frederick said nothing, of the creeper that was wound about the dead man's neck, nor of the little white wounds, like little bloodless lips half-open, that they found about the dead man's neck.

"An imaginative or uneducated person," said the doctor, "might suppose that the creeper had something to do with his death. But we mustn't encourage superstition. I will assist my man to prepare the body for its last sleep. Then we need not have any chattering woman."

"Can you read Latin?" Frederick asked. The doctor could, and, later, did.

It was the Latin of that brown book with the Doricourt arms on it that Frederick wanted read. And when he and the doctor had been together with the book between them for three hours, they closed it and looked at each other with shy and doubtful eyes.

"It can't be true," said Frederick.

"If it is," said the more cautious doctor, "you don't want it talked about. I should destroy that book if I were you. And I should root up that creeper and burn it. It is quite evident, from what you tell me, that your friend believed that this creeper was a man-eater, that it fed, just before its flowering time, as the book tells us, at dawn; and that he fully meant that the thing when it crawled into the pavilion seeking its prey should find you and not him. It would have been so, I understand, if his watch had not stopped at one o'clock."

"He dropped it, you know," said Doricourt like a man in a dream.

"All the cases in this book are the same," said the doctor, "the strangling, the white wounds. I have heard of such plants; I never believed." He shuddered. "Had your friend any spite against you? Any reason for wanting to get you out of the way?"

Frederick thought of Ernestine, of Thesiger's eyes on Ernestine, of her smile at him over her blue muslin shoulder.

"No," he said, "none. None whatever. It must have been an accident. I am sure he did not know. He could not read Latin." He lied, being, after all, a gentleman, and Ernestine's name being sacred.

"The creeper seems to have been brought here and planted in Henry the Eighth's time. And then the thing began. It seems to have been at its flowering season that it needed the . . . that, in short, it was dangerous. The little animals and birds found dead near the pavilion . . . But to move itself all that way, across the floor! The thing must have been almost conscient," he said with a sincere shudder. "One would think," he corrected himself at once, "that it knew what it was doing, if such a thing were not plainly contrary to the laws of nature."

"Yes," said Frederick, "one would. I think if I can't do anything more I'll go and rest. Somehow all this has given me a turn. Poor Thesiger!"

His last thought before he went to sleep was one of pity.

"Poor Thesiger," he said, "how violent and wicked! And what an escape for me! I must never tell Ernestine. And all the time there was Amelia . . . Ernestine would never have done *that* for *me*." And on a little pang of regret for the impossible he fell asleep.

Amelia went on living. She was not the sort that dies even of such a thing as happened to her on that night, when for the first and last time she held her love in her arms and knew him for the murderer he was. It was only the other day that she died, a very old woman. Ernestine who, beloved and surrounded by children and grand-children, survived her, spoke her epitaph: "Poor Amelia," she said, "nobody ever looked the same side of the road where she was. There was an indiscretion when she was young. Oh, nothing disgraceful, of course. She was a lady. But people talked. It was the sort of thing that stamps a girl, you know."

NOT ON THE PASSENGER LIST

Barry Pain
(1864–1928)

Barry Pain is in some ways a cautionary tale about what happens when a talented writer is forced to churn out commercial work to survive. Pain's catalogue of work—sixty novels and short story collections—is more than respectable, and his best work continues to entertain and chill readers, but one can't help but wonder what might have been, what stories he could have produced if he'd stuck to his strength—horror stories—instead of the comedic work he produced to live on.

Pain wrote romances, detective stories, and horror stories, but it was his comedies—breezy parodies and send-ups of the English middle-class—that earned him the most money. The five "Eliza" novels were his best-known work and are perhaps his best comedic work, being reprinted several times, most recently in 2002. But for the most part Pain's comic work and parodies uncomfortably show their age, lacking the technical quality that makes P.G. Wodehouse's work immortal.

Pain's horror stories, conversely, are only a little dated now, and stories like "The Moon-Slave" (1901), "Rose Rose" (1910), and "Not on the Passenger List," which first appeared in The Illustrated Sunday Magazine *(Aug. 1, 1915), retain their ability to terrify when called upon to do so.*

I HAD NOT slept. It may have been the noise which prevented me. The entire ship groaned, creaked, screamed, and sobbed. In the staterooms near mine the flooring was being torn up, and somebody was busy with a very blunt saw just over my head—at least it sounded like that. The motion, too, was not favourable for sleep. There was nothing but strong personal magnetism to keep me in my bunk. If I had relaxed it for a moment I should have fallen out.

Then the big trunk under my berth began to be busy, and I switched on the light to look at it. In a slow and portly way it began to lollop across the floor towards the door. It was trying to get out of the ship, and I never blamed it. But before it could reach the door a suit-case dashed out from under the couch and kicked it in the stomach. I switched off the light again, and let them fight it out in the dark.

I recalled that an elderly pessimist in the smoking-room the night before had expressed his belief that we were overloaded and that if the ship met any heavy weather she'd break in two for sure. And then I was playing chess with a fat negress who said she was only black when she was playing the black pieces; but in the middle of it somebody knocked and said that my bath was ready.

The last part turned out to be true. My bath was even more than ready, it was impatient; as I entered the bathroom the water jumped out to meet me and did so. Then, when the bath and I had finished with each other, my steward came slanting down the passage, at an angle of thirty degrees to the floor, without spilling my morning tea, and said that the weather was improving.

There were very few early risers at breakfast that morning, but I was not the first. Mrs. Derrison was coming out as I entered the saloon. I thought she looked ill, but it was not particularly surprising. We said good-morning, and then she hesitated for a moment.

"I want to speak to you," she said. "Do you mind? Not now. Come up on deck when you've finished breakfast."

She was not an experienced traveller, and had already consulted me about various small matters. I supposed she wanted to know what was the right tip for a stewardess or something of that kind. Accordingly, after breakfast I went up, and found her wrapped in furs—very expensive furs—in her deck-chair. I could see now that she was not in the least sea-sick, but she said she had not slept all night. I moved her chair into a better position, and chatted as I wrapped the rug round her. I confessed that with the exception of an hour's nightmare about a fat negress I also had not slept. As a rule, she would have smiled at this, for she smiled easily and readily. But now she stared out over the sea as if she had heard the words without understanding them. She was a woman of thirty-four or thirty-five, I should think, and had what is generally called an interesting face. You noticed her eyes particularly.

"Well," I said, "the wind's dropping, and we shall all sleep better tonight. Look, there's the sun coming out at last. And now, what's the trouble? What can I do for you?"

"I don't think that even you can help," she said drearily, "though you've done lots of kind things for me. Still, I've got to tell somebody. I simply can't stand it alone. Oh, if I were only the captain of this ship!"

"I don't think you'd like it! Why, what would you do?"

"Turn round and go back to New York."

"It couldn't be done. The ship doesn't carry enough coal. And we shall be at Liverpool the morning after next. But why? What's the matter?"

She held out one hand in the sunlight. It looked very small and transparent. It shook.

"The matter is that I'm frightened. I'm simply frightened out of my life."

I looked hard at her. There was no doubt about it. She was a badly frightened woman. I resisted an impulse to pat her on the shoulder.

"But really, Mrs. Derrison, if you'll forgive me for saying so, this is absolute nonsense. The boat's slower than she ought to be, and I'll admit that she rolls pretty badly, but she's as safe as a church all the same."

"Yes, I know. In any case, that is not the kind of thing that would frighten me. This is something quite different. And when I have told you it, you will probably think that I am insane."

"No," I said, "I shall not think that."

"Very well. I told you that I was a widow. I wear no mourning, and I did not tell you that Alec, my husband, died only three months ago. Nor did I tell you, which is also the truth, that I am going to England in order to marry another man."

"I understand all that. Go on."

"Alec died three months ago. But he is on this boat. I saw him last night. I think he has come for me."

She made that amazing statement quietly and without excitement. But you cannot tell a ghost story convincingly to a man who is sitting in the sun at half-past nine in the morning. I neither doubted her sincerity nor her sanity. I merely wondered how the illusion had been produced.

"Well," I said, "you know that's quite impossible, don't you?"

"Yesterday, I should have said so."

"So you will to-morrow. Tell me how it happened, and I will tell you the explanation."

"I went to my room at eleven at night. The door was a little way open—fixed by the hook arrangement—the way I generally leave it. I switched on the light and went in. He was sitting on the berth with his legs dangling, his profile towards me. The light shone on the bald place on his head. He wore blue pyjamas and red slippers—the kind that he always wore. The pocket of his coat was weighed down, and I remembered what he had told me—that when he was traveling he put his watch, money, and keys there at night. He turned his head towards me. It came round very slowly, as if with an effort. That was strange, because so far I had been startled and surprised but not frightened. When the head turned round I became really frightened. You see, it was Alec—and yet it was not."

"I don't think I understand. How do you mean?"

"Well, it was like him—a roundish face, clean-shaven, heavily lined— he was fifteen years older than I was—with his very heavy eyebrows and his ridiculously small mouth. His mouth was really abnormal. But the whole thing looked as if it had been modelled out of wax and painted. And, then, when a head turns toward you, you expect the eyes to look at you. These did not. They remained with the lids half down—very much as I remembered him after the doctors had gone. Oh, I was frightened! I fumbled with one hand behind me, trying to find the bell-push. And yet I could not help speaking out loud. I said: 'What does this mean, Alec?' Just then I got my finger on the bell-push. He knew I had rung—I could see that. His lips kept opening and shutting as if he were trying hard to speak. When the voice came at last, it was only a whisper. He said: 'I want you!' when the stewardess tapped at the door, and I did not see him any more."

"Did you tell the stewardess?"

"Oh, no! I did not mean to tell anybody then. I pretended to be nervous about the ship rolling too much, and managed to keep her with me for a long time. She offered to fetch the doctor for me, so that I could ask him for a sleeping-draught, but I wouldn't have that."

"Why not?"

"I was afraid to go to sleep. I wanted to be ready in case—in case it happened again. You see, I knew why it was."

"I don't think you did, Mrs. Derrison. But I will tell you why it was, if you like. The explanation is very simple and very prosaic."

"What is it?"

"The cause of the illusion was merely seasickness."

"But I've not felt ill at all."

"Very likely not. If you had been ill in the ordinary way, the way in which it has taken a good many of our friends, you would never have had the illusion. Brain and stomach act and react on one another. The motion of boat, too, is particularly trying to the optic nerves. In some cases, not very common perhaps, but quite well-known and recognized—it is the brain and not the other organ which is temporarily affected."

I do not know anything about it really, and had merely invented the sea-sickness theory on the spur of the moment. It was necessary to think of something plausible and very commonplace. Mrs. Derrison was suffering a good deal, and I had to stop it.

"If I could only think that," she said, "what a comfort it would be!"

"Whether you believe it or not, it's the truth," I said. I've known a similar case. It won't happen to you again, because the weather's getting better, and so you won't be ill."

She wanted to know all about the "similar case," and I made up a convincing little story about it. Gradually she began to be reassured.

"I wish I had known about it before," she said. "All last night I sat in my room, with the light turned on, getting more and more frightened. I don't think there's anything hurts one so much as fear. I can understand people being driven mad by it. You see, I had a special reason to be afraid, because Alec was jealous, very jealous. He had even, I suppose, some grounds for jealousy."

She began to tell me her story. She had married Alec Derrison nine years before. She liked him at that time, but she did not love him, and she told him so. He said that it did not matter, and that in time she would come to love him. I dare say a good many marriages that begin in that way turn out happily, but this marriage was a mistake.

He took her to his house in New York, and there they lived for a year without actual disaster. He was very kind to her, and she was touched by his kindness. She had been quite poor, and she now had plenty of money to spend, and liked it. But it became clear to her in that year not only that she did not love her husband but that she never would love him. And she was, I could believe, a rather romantic and temperamental kind of woman, by whom many men were greatly attracted. Alec Derrison began to be very jealous—at that time quite absurdly and without reason.

At the end of the year Derrison took her to Europe for a holiday. And there, in England, in her father's country rectory, she met the man whom she ought to have married—an artist of the same age as herself. The two fell desperately in love with one another. The man wanted to take her away with him and ultimately to marry her. She refused.

There is a curious mixture of conscience and temperament which is sometimes mistaken for cowardice and is often accompanied by extraordinary courage. She went to her husband and, so to speak, put her cards on the table.

"I love another man," she said. "I love him in the way in which I wished to love you but cannot. I did not want this and did not look for it, but it has happened to me. I am sorry it has happened, but I do not ask you to forgive me, for you have nothing to forgive. I want to know what you mean to do."

His answer was to take her straight back to New York. There for the eight years before he died he treated her with kindness and gave her every luxury, but all the time he had her watched. Traps were laid for her, but in vain. He had for business reasons to go to England every year, but he never took her with him.

When he was away, two of his sisters came to the house and watched for him.

And yet, because in some things a woman is cleverer than a man, and also because the feminine conscience always has its limitations, during the whole of those eight years she corresponded regularly with the other man without being found out. They never met, but she had his letters. And now she was going back to marry him.

It was, perhaps, a little curious that she should tell all this to a man whom she had known only for a few days. But intimacies grow quickly on board ship, and besides she wanted to explain her terror.

"You see how it was," she said. "If a dead man could come back again, then certainly he would come back. And when one begins to be frightened the fear grows and grows. One thinks of things. For instance, he crossed more than once in this very boat—I thought of that."

"Well, Mrs. Derrison," I said, "the dead cannot and do not come back. But a disordered interior does sometimes produce an optical illusion. That's all there is to it. However, if you like, I'll go to the purser and get your room changed for another; I can manage that all right."

It was not a very wise suggestion, and she refused it. She said that it would be like admitting that there was something in it beyond sea-sickness.

"Good!" I said. "I think you're quite right. I thought it might ease your mind not to see again the room where you were frightened, but it is much better to be firm about it. In fact, you had better take a cup of soup and then go back to your room now, and get an hour's sleep before lunch."

"I wonder if I could."

"Of course you can. You're getting your colour back, and there's much less motion on the boat. You won't have another attack. You've had a sort of suppressed form of sea-sickness, that's all. And I can quite understand that it scared you at the time, when you didn't know; but there's no reason why it should scare you now when you do know."

She took my advice. A woman will generally take advice from any man except her husband—because he's the only man she really knows. She was disproportionately grateful. Gratitude is rare, but, when found, it is in very large streaks. She had also decided to believe that I knew everything, could do everything, and had other admirable qualities. When a woman decides to believe, facts do not hamper her.

She was much better at lunch and afterwards. Next day she was apparently normal, and was taking part in the usual deck-games. I began to think that my sea-sickness theory might have been a lucky shot. I consulted the ship's doctor about it, without giving him names or details, but he was very non-committal. He was a general practitioner, of course, and I was taking him into specialist regions. Besides, naturally enough, a doctor does not care to talk his own shop with a layman. He gave me an impression that any conclusions to which I came would necessarily be wrong. But it did not worry me much. I did not see a great deal of Mrs. Derrison, but it was quite obvious that she had recovered her normal health and spirits. I believed that the trouble was over.

But it was not.

On the night before we arrived, after the smoking-room had been closed, old Bartlett asked me to come to his rooms, for a chat and a whisky and soda. The old man slept badly, and was inclined to a late sitting. We discussed various subjects, and amongst them memory for faces.

"I've got that memory," he said. "Names bother me, but not faces. For instance, I remember the faces of the seventy or eighty in the first class here."

"I thought we were more than that."

"No. People don't cross the Atlantic for fun in February. It's a pretty light list. It's a funny thing, too—we've got one man on board who's never showed up at all. I saw him for the first time this morning—to be accurate, yesterday morning—coming from the bath, and I've not seen him since. He must have been hiding in his state-room all the time."

"Ill, probably."

"No, not ill. I asked the doctor. I supposed he don't enjoy the society of his fellow-men for some reason or other."

"Well, now," I said, "let's test your memory. What was he like?"

"You've given me an easy one as it happens, for he was rather a curious chap to look at, and easy to remember in consequence. A man in the fifties, I should say; medium height; wore blue pyjamas with a gold watch-chain trickling out of the pocket, and those red slippers that you buy in Cairo. But his face was what I noticed particularly. He's got a one-inch mouth—smallest mouth I ever saw on a man. But the whole look on his face was queer, just as if it had been painted and then varnished.

"He was bald, round-faced, wrinkled, and clean-shaven. He walked very slowly, and he looked as if he were worried out of his life. There's the portrait, and you can check it when we get off the boat—you're bound to see him then."

"Yes, you've a good memory. If I had just passed the man in a passage, I shouldn't have remembered a thing about him ten minutes afterwards. By the way, have you spoken about the hermit passenger to anybody else?"

"No. Oh, yes, I did mention it to some of the ladies after dinner! Why?"

"I wondered if anybody besides yourself had seen him."

"Well, they didn't say they had. Bless you, I've known men like that. It's a sort of sulkiness. They'd sooner be alone."

A few minutes later I said good-night and left him. It was between one and two in the morning. His story had made a strong impression upon me. My theory of sea sickness had to go, and I was scared. Quite frankly, I was afraid of meeting something in blue pyjamas. But I was more afraid about Mrs. Derrison. There were very few ladies on board, and it was almost certain she was in the group to whom Bartlett had told his story. If that were so, anything might have happened. I decided to go past her state-room, listening as I did so.

But before I reached her room the door opened, and she swung out in her nightdress. She had got her mouth open and one hand at her throat. With the other hand she clutched the handle of the door, as if she was trying to hold it shut against somebody. I hurried towards her, and she turned and saw me. In an instant she was in my arms, clinging to me in sheer mad, helpless terror.

She was hysterical, of course, but fortunately did not make much noise. She kept saying: "I've got to go back to him—into the sea!" It seemed a long time before I could get her calm enough to listen to me.

"You've had a bad dream, and it has frightened you, poor child."

"No, no. Not a dream!"

"It didn't seem like one to you, but that's what it was. You're all right now. I'm going to take care of you."

"Don't let go of me for a moment. He wants me. He's in there."

"Oh, no! I'll show you that he's not there."

I opened the door. Within all was darkness. I still kept one arm round her, or she would have fallen.

"I left the light on," she whispered.

"Yes," I said, "but your sleeve caught the switch as you came out. I saw it." It was a lie, of course, but one had to lie.

I switched the light on again. The room was empty. There were the tumbled bed-clothes on the berth, and a pillow had fallen to the floor.

On the table some toilet things gleamed brightly. There was a pile of feminine garments on the couch. I drew her in and closed the door.

"I'll put you back into bed again," I said, "if you don't mind."

"If you'll promise not to go."

"Oh, I won't go!"

I picked her up and laid her on the berth, and drew the clothes over her. I put the pillow back under her head. With both her hands she clutched one of mine.

"Now, then," I said, "do you happen to have any brandy here?"

"In a flask in my dressing-bag. It's been there for years. I don't know if it's any good still."

She seemed reluctant to let go my hand, and clutched it again eagerly when I brought the brandy. She was quite docile, and drank as I told her. I have not put down half of what she said. She was muttering the whole time. The phrase "into the sea" occurred frequently. All ordinary notions of the relationship of a man and a woman had vanished. I was simply a big brother who was looking after her. That was felt by both of us. We called each other "dear" that night frequently, but there was not a trace of sex-sentimentality between us.

Gradually she became more quiet, and I was no longer afraid that she would faint. Still holding my hand, she said:

"Shall I tell you what it was?"

"Yes, dear, if you like. But you needn't. It was only a dream, you know."

"I don't think it was a dream. I went to sleep, which I had never expected to do after the thing that Mr. Bartlett told us. I couldn't have done it, only I argued that you must be right and the rest must be just a coincidence. Then I was awakened by the sound of somebody breathing close by my ear. It got further away, and I switched on the light quickly. He was standing just there—exactly as I described him to you—and he had picked up a pair of nail-scissors. He was opening and shutting them. Then he put them down open, and shook his head. (Look, they're open now, and I always close them.) And suddenly he lurched over, almost falling, and clutched the wooden edge of the berth. His red hands—they were terribly red, far redder than they used to be—came on to the wood with a slap. 'Go into the sea, Sheila,' he whispered. 'I'm waiting. I want you.' And after that I don't know what happened, but suddenly I was hanging on to you, dear. How long was it ago? Was it an hour? It doesn't matter. I'm safe while you're here."

I released her hands gently. Suddenly the paroxysm of terror returned. "You're not going?" she cried, aghast.

"Of course not." I sat down on the couch opposite her. "But what makes you think you're safe while I'm here?"

"You're stronger than he is," she said.

She said it as if it were a self-evident fact which did not admit of argument. Certainly, though no doubt unreasonably, it gave me confidence. I felt somehow that he and I were fighting for the woman's life and soul, and I had got him down. I knew that in some mysterious way I was the stronger.

"Well," I said, "the dream that one is awake is a fairly common dream. But what was the thing that Bartlett told you?"

"He saw him—in blue pyjamas and red slippers. He mentioned the mouth too."

"I'm glad you told me that," I said, and began a few useful inventions. "The man that Bartlett saw was Curwen. We've just been talking about it."

"Who's Curwen?"

"Not a bad chap—an electrical engineer, I believe. As soon as Bartlett mentioned the mole on the cheek and the little black moustache I spotted that it was Curwen."

"But he said he had never seen him before."

"Nor had he. Curwen's a bad sailor and has kept to his state-room—in fact, that was his first public appearance. But I saw Curwen when he came on board, and had a talk with him. As soon as Bartlett mentioned the mole, I knew who it was."

"Then the colour of the slippers and—"

"They were merely a coincidence, and a mighty unlucky one for you."

"I see," she said. Her muscles relaxed. She gave a little sigh of relief and sank bank on the pillow. I was glad that I had invented Curwen and the mole.

I changed the subject now, and began to talk about Liverpool—not so many miles away now. I asked her if she had changed her American money yet. I spoke about the customs, and confessed to some successful smuggling that I had once done. In fact, I talked about anything that might take her mind away from her panic.

Then I said:

"If you will give me about ten seconds start now, so that I can get back to my own room, you might ring for your stewardess to come and take care of you. It will mean an extra tip for her, and she won't mind."

"Yes," she said, "I ought not to keep you any longer. Indeed, it is very kind of you to have helped me and to have stayed so long. I'll never forget it. But even now I daren't be alone for a moment. Will you wait until she's actually here?"

I was not ready for that.

"Well," I said hesitatingly.

"Of course," she said. "I hadn't thought of it. I can't keep you. You've had no sleep at all. And yet if you go, he'll—Oh, what am I to do? What am I to do?"

I was afraid she would begin to cry.

"That's all right," I said. "I can stay for another hour or two easily enough."

She was full of gratitude. She told me to throw the things off the end of the couch so that I could lie at full length. I dozed for a while, but I do not think she slept at all. She was wide awake when I opened my eyes. I talked to her for a little, and found her much reassured and calmed. People were beginning to move about. It was necessary for me to go immediately if I was not to be seen.

She agreed at once. When I shook hands with her, and told her to try for an hour's sleep, she kissed my hand fervently in a childish sort of way. Frightened people behave rather like children.

I was not seen as I came from her room. The luck was with me. It is just possible that on the other side of the ship, a steward saw me enter my own room in evening clothes at a little after five. If he did, it did not matter.

★ ★ ★

I have had the most grateful and kindly letters from her and from her new husband—the cheery and handsome man who met her at Liverpool. In her letter she speaks of her "awful nightmare, that even now it seems sometimes as if it must have been real." She has sent me a cigarette case that I am afraid I cannot use publicly. A gold cigarette-case with a diamond push-button would give a wrong impression of my income, and the inscription inside might easily be misunderstood. But I like to have it.

Thanks to my innocent mendacity, she has a theory which covers the whole ground. But I myself have no theory at all. I know this—that I might travel to New York by that same boat to-morrow, and that I am waiting three days for another.

I have suppressed the name of the boat, and I think I have said nothing by which she could be identified. I do not want to spoil business.
Besides, it may be funk and superstition that convinces me that on
every trip she carries a passenger whose name is not on the list. But, for
all that, I *am* quite convinced!

THE LIQUEUR GLASS

Phyllis Bottome
(1884–1963)

Posterity is cruel. Once the most famous of all the writers in this anthology, Bottome is now the most obscure. But in her time she regularly appeared on the best-sellers' lists, and was famous to the degree that the arrival of a ship carrying the corrected proofs for her new novel merited mention in The New York Times. *Deservedly so, as "The Liqueur Glass" shows, for Bottome was a talented, insightful writer, even if she was ultimately ahead of her time in a number of regards.*

She wrote under her birth name, publishing her first novel (of thirty-three) when she was only twenty, and produced continuously throughout her life. During the early years of World War One she lived in London as a part of the same literary circle as Ezra Pound and May Sinclair, and her short stories appeared in the better sorts of English fiction magazines, like The Red Magazine, The Century Magazine, *and* The Smart Set. *Married at thirty-three to a man she'd known for thirteen years, she and her new husband moved to Vienna. He became a diplomat and ultimately the MI6 Head of Station for Austria, Hungary, and Yugoslavia. She met Alfred Adler, underwent analysis, and became a friend of his and a proponent of his work, ultimately writing a biography of Adler in 1939. In 1924 she opened a school in Austria designed to teach languages and apply psychology and educational theory to the benefit of students and nations. One of her prized pupils, who always remembered her fondly, was Ian Fleming.*

She became most famous for two novels: Private Worlds *(1934), which she hoped would raise public awareness about mental illness, filmed in 1935 with Charles Boyer and Claudette Colbert; and* The Mortal Storm *(1937), about the rising threat of Hitler and the Nazis to European Jews.* The Mortal Storm *was a best-seller in both the U.K. and the U.S., and was filmed in 1940 with James Stewart and Margaret Sullavan. It was the first Hollywood film to mention Hitler by name and was an influential piece of anti-German propaganda. It also earned her the label "premature anti-fascist," something the openly political Bottome embraced. Most of her works were progressive and feminist, with ideological aims beyond mere entertainment, and Bottome was successful as few men or women of her time were in combining politics and entertainment.*

"The Liqueur Glass," which originally appeared in The Smart Set's *March 1915 issue, is one of Bottome's earliest stories, written while she and her future husband were still only corresponding. It shows, perhaps, some of the attitudes of a 1910s feminist toward traditional marriage. Fortunately for Bottome, her own marriage was much healthier than the Watkins', and she was never required to contemplate the actions Mrs. Watkins takes here.*

MRS. HENRY WATKINS loved going to church. She could not have told you why she loved it. It had perhaps less to do with religious motives than most people's reasons for attending divine service; and she took no interest in other peoples' clothes.

She gazed long and fixedly at the stained glass window in which St. Peter, in a loose magenta blouse, was lading salmon-colored sardines out of a grass-green sea; but she did not really see St. Peter or notice his sleight-of-hand preoccupation with the fish. She was simply having a nice, quiet time.

She always sat where she could most easily escape seeing the back of Henry Watkins's head. She had never liked the back of his head and twenty years' married life had only deepened her distaste for it.

Hetty and Paul sat between her and their father, and once or twice it had occurred to Mrs. Watkins as strange that she should owe the life of these two beloved beings to the man she hated.

It was no use pretending at this time of the day that she didn't hate Henry Watkins. She hated him with all the slow, quiet force of a slow, quiet nature.

She had hated him for some time before she discovered that she no longer loved him.

Mrs. Watkins took a long time before she arrived at the recognition of a new truth; she would go on provisionally for years with a worn-out platitude, but when she once dropped it, she never returned to pick it up again; and she acted upon her discoveries.

The choir began to sing "O God. Our Help in Ages Past." Mrs. Watkins disliked this hymn; and she had never found God much of a help. She thought the verse that compared men's lives to the flight of leaves was nonsense. Nobody could imagine Henry Watkins flying like a leaf.

The first lesson was more attractive. Mrs. Watkins enjoyed Jael's reception of Sisera. "She brought him butter in a lordly dish," boomed the curate. Henry Watkins ate a lot of butter, though he insisted, from motives of economy, upon its being Danish. Sisera, worn out with battle, slumbered. Jael took up the nail and carried out with efficiency and dispatch her inhospitable deed. Mrs. Watkins thought the nails in those days must have been larger than they are now and probably a lot sharper at the end.

The curate cleared his throat a little over the story; it seemed to him to savor of brutality.

"Why tarry the wheels of his chariot?" cried Sisera's mother.

Mrs. Watkins leaned back in her seat and smiled. Sisera was done for, his mother would never hear the sound of those returning chariot wheels.

Jael had permanently recouped herself for the butter.

A little later on the vicar swept out of his stall and up to the pulpit covered by the prolonged "Amen" of the accompanying hymn. Henry looked at his watch and shut it with a click. Then his hard blue eyes closed suddenly—he had no eyelashes. Mrs. Watkins folded her hands in her lap and fixed her attention upon St. Peter.

This was her nice, quiet time, and she spent it in considering how she could most easily kill Henry Watkins.

She was not in the least touched by the sight of her wedding ring. Her marriage had been an accident, one of those accidents that happened frequently twenty years ago, and which happen, though more seldom, now. An unhappy blunder of ignorance, inexperience, and family pressure.

She had liked making Henry Watkins jump, and her mother had explained to her that the tendency to jump on Henry's part was an ardent, manly love, and that her own amused contemplation of the performance was deep womanly inclination.

It was then that Mrs. Watkins urged that she did not like the back of Henry's head. She had been told that it was immodest to notice it. His means were excellent and her own parents were poor. Twenty years ago Mrs. Watkins had known very little about life, and what she did know she was tempted to enjoy. She knew a good deal about it now, and she had long ago outgrown the temptation to enjoy it.

Still, that in itself wouldn't have given her any idea of killing her husband. She was a just woman and she knew that her husband had not invented the universe; if he had, she thought it would have been more unpleasant still.

Henry's idea of marriage was very direct; he knew that he had done his wife an enormous favor. She was penniless and he had the money; she was to come to him for every penny and all she had was his as a matter of course. She could do him no favors, she had no rights, and her preferences were silly.

It had occurred to Mrs. Watkins in one awful moment of early resentment that she would rather be bought by a great many men than by one. There would be more variety, and some of them, at least, wouldn't be like Henry.

Then her children came; she aged very rapidly. Nothing is so bad for the personal appearance as the complete abrogation of self-respect. Henry continually threw her birthdays in her teeth. "A woman of your age," he would say with deep contempt.

He was a man of favorite phrases. Mrs. Watkins was not constitu-
tionally averse to repetition, but the repetition of a phrase that means
to hurt can be curiously unpleasant. Still, as her mother had pointed out
to her long years ago, you can get used to the unpleasant.

She never complained, and her father and mother were gratefully
conscious of how soon she had settled down.

But there was a strange fallacy that lingered deep in Mrs. Watkins's
heart.

She had given up her rights as a woman, since presumably her marriage necessitated the sacrifice. But she believed that she would be
allowed the rights of a mother. This, of course, was where she made
her mistake.

Henry Watkins meant to be master in his own house. The house was
his own, so was his wife, so were his children.

There is no division of property where there is one master. This was
a great religious truth to Henry, so that when his son displeased him he
thrashed him, and when his daughter got in his way he bullied her.

Mrs. Watkins disputed this right not once but many times, till she
found the results were worse for the children. Then she dropped her
opposition. Henry Watkins saw that she had learnt her lesson. It taught
the children a lesson, too; they saw that it made no difference what
mother said to father.

Nothing happened to alter either her attitude or Henry's.

They went to the same church twice every Sunday, except when it
rained; and they ate roast beef afterwards.

In spite of Henry, Hetty had grown into a charming, sympathetic,
slightly nervous young woman, and in spite of Henry, Paul had become
a clever, highly strung, regrettably artistic young man.

But if Henry couldn't help their temperaments he could put his foot
down about their future.

Paul should go into the bank and learn to be a man. (By learning to
be a man, Henry meant learning to care more for money than for anything else); and Hetty should receive no assistance toward marrying an
impecunious young architect to whom she had taken a fancy.

Hetty could do as she chose; she could marry Henry's old friend
Baddeley, who had a decent income, or she could stay at home and
pretend to be ill; but she certainly shouldn't throw herself away on a
young fool who hadn't the means (rather fortunately, as it happened)
to support her.

Henry looked at his watch; the sermon had already lasted twenty minutes.

Mrs. Watkins went over once more in her mind how she had better do it. "And now to God the Father," said the vicar. The sermon had lasted twenty-seven minutes, and Henry meant to point it out to the vicar in the vestry. "Oh, what the joy and the glory must be!" sang the choir. "And if I am hanged," said Mrs. Watkins to herself, "they'll get the money just the same. I shall try not to be, because it would be so upsetting for them, poor young things; still it's wonderful what you can get over when you're young."

"Keep the beef hot!" whispered Henry, as he set off for the vestry.

At lunch Henry made Hetty cry and leave the room.

Paul flashed out in his sister's defense. "You're unbearable, sir—why can't you leave us alone?"

His mother strangely interposed.

"Never mind, Paul," she said. "Let father have his own way."

Paul looked at her in astonishment, and Henry was extremely annoyed. He was perfectly capable of taking his own way without his wife's interference, and he told her so.

It was the cook's evening out, and the house parlor-maid—a flighty creature—was upstairs in her room, trimming a new hat. There was no one downstairs in the kitchen after supper.

Paul went out to smoke in the garden, and Hetty had gone to finish her tears in her own room. That was something Mrs. Watkins hadn't got; but she needed no place for finishing her tears, because she had never yet begun them. She did not see the use of tears.

Mrs. Watkins stood and looked at her husband as he sprawled at his ease in the most comfortable of the drawing-room chairs.

"Henry," she said, "would you like some of that sloe gin your brother sent you? You haven't tried it yet."

"I don't mind trying a glass," said Henry good-naturedly, yawning in her face.

His wife paused at the door. She came back a step or two. "You've not changed your mind," she asked, "about the children's futures?"

"No! Why should I change my mind?" said Henry. "Do I ever change my mind? They can make as much fuss as they like, but the man who pays the piper calls the tune!"

"I've heard you say that before," said his wife reflectively.

"I daresay you'll hear me say it again!" said Henry with a laugh.

Mrs. Watkins's hand went toward the handle of the door; she did not think she would ever hear Henry say this favorite maxim again; but still she lingered.

"Hurry up with that liqueur!" said her husband.

Mrs. Watkins went into the pantry and took out a liqueur glass. She poured a little sloe gin into it, then she put down the bottle and left the pantry. She went into the children's dark-room—they were allowed that for their photography.

She still had the glass in her hand. There was a bottle on the highest shelf. She took it down and measured it carefully with her eye. The children's manual of photography and the medical dictionary in Henry's dressing-room had been a great help to her.

She poured out into the deep red of the sloe gin some of the contents of the bottle; it looked very white and harmless and hardly smelt at all. She wondered if it was enough, and she tipped up the bottle a little to make sure. She used a good deal more than the medical dictionary said was necessary, but the medical dictionary might have underestimated Henry's constitution. She put the bottle back where she found it, and returned to the pantry. There she filled up the liqueur-glass with more sloe gin.

She saw Paul on a garden seat through the window. "I wish you'd come out, Mother," he said impatiently.

"I will in a minute, dear," she answered quietly. Then she went back to her husband. "Here it is, Henry," she said.

"What a slow woman you are!" he grumbled. "Still I must say you have a steady hand."

She held the full glass toward him and watched him drink it in a gulp.

"It tastes damned odd," said Henry thoughtfully. "I don't think I shall take any more of it."

Mrs. Watkins did not answer; she took up the liqueur-glass and went back into the pantry.

She took out another glass, filled it with sloe gin, drank it, and put it on the pantry table.

The first glass she slipped up her long sleeve and went out into the garden.

"I thought you were never coming, Mother!" Paul exclaimed. "Oh, I do feel so sick about everything! If this kind of thing goes on, I shall do something desperate. I know I shall. I sometimes think I should like to kill father."

Mrs. Watkins drew a long breath of relief. Once or twice lately it had occurred to her while she was thinking things over in church that Paul might get desperate and attack his father. He couldn't now.

"Don't talk like that, dear," she said gently. "I sometimes think your father can't help himself. Besides, it's very natural he should want you and Hetty to have money; he values money."

"He doesn't want us to have it!" Paul exclaimed savagely. "He only wants to keep us in his power because we haven't got it, and can't get away! What money has he ever given you—or ever let us have for our own freedom?"

Mrs. Watkins looked up at the substantial house and around the well-stocked garden. Henry had gone in especially for cabbages. She looked as if she were listening for something.

"I don't like to hear you talk like that, Paul," she said at last. "I want you to go up to Hetty's room and bring her out into the garden. She ought to have some air. The evenings are beginning to draw in. It'll be church time presently."

"But if I bring her down, won't he come out and upset her?" Paul demanded.

"I don't think he is coming out again," said Mrs. Watkins. She watched her son disappear into the house, and then walked on into the thick shrubbery at the end of the garden. She slipped the liqueur-glass out of her sleeve and broke it into fragments against the garden wall, then she covered the pieces with loose earth.

She had hardly finished before she heard a cry from the house. "Mother! Mother! Oh, Mother!"

"I've done the best I can," she said suddenly, between the kitchen garden and the house.

There was an inquest the following week, and Mrs. Watkins, dressed in decent black, gave her evidence with methodical carefulness.

Her husband had been quite well before dinner, she explained. At dinner he had been a little disturbed with one of the children, but nothing out of the ordinary at all. He had merely said a few sharp words. After dinner he had gone to sit in the drawing-room, and at his request she had brought him a glass of sloe gin sent him by his brother; when he had finished it she had carried the glass back into the pantry. She did not see him again. The maids were not downstairs at the time. The glass was examined, the pantry was examined, the whole household was examined. The parlor maid had hysterics, and the cook gave notice to the coroner for asking her if she kept her pans clean. The verdict was death through misadventure, though a medical officer declared that poison was evidently the cause.

It was considered possible that Henry had privately procured it and taken it himself.

It is true he had no motive for suicide, but there was still less motive for murder. Nobody wished ardently that Henry might live, but, on the other hand, nobody benefitted by his interesting and mysterious death—that is to say, nobody but Henry's family; and it is not considered probable that well-dressed, respectable people benefit by a parent's death.

Mrs. Watkins was never tempted to confession; and she continued to gaze just as fixedly at St. Peter and the sardines every Sunday. She thought about quite different subjects now; but she still had a nice quiet time.

It was the day before Hetty's wedding to the young architect that Mrs. Watkins made her final approach to the question of her husband's death. She never referred to it afterwards.

"Do you know, Mummy darling," Hetty said, "I was sure there were a dozen liqueur-glasses in the cupboard. I always looked after them myself. Father was so particular about them; and they put back the horrid inquest one, I know, and yet I can only find eleven."

Mrs. Watkins looked at her daughter with a curious expression, then she asked abruptly, "Are you very happy, child?" Hetty assented radiantly. Her mother nodded. "And Paul," said Mrs. Watkins thoughtfully, "he seems very contented in his painting. He wants me to go with him to Paris. He always did want to go to Paris."

"Paul can't be as happy as I am," Hetty triumphantly assured her, "because he hasn't got Dick—but it does seem as if both our wildest dreams had come true in the most extraordinary way, doesn't it, Mummy?"

Mrs. Watkins did not answer her daughter at once. She turned toward the cupboard. She seemed to be counting the broken set over again.

"Well, I don't think it matters about that liqueur-glass," she said finally. "I'm not as particular as your father."

THE PIN-PRICK

May Sinclair
(1863–1946)

Mary Amelia St. Clair, who wrote under the pseudonym of "May Sinclair," was best known in her lifetime as a modernist, a literary critic (she was the first to use the phrase "stream of consciousness"), a suffragist, and the author of twenty-three novels, several short story collections, in addition to extensive poetry. Her reputation has dimmed considerably since her death, and today, when she is remembered, it is for her criticism and her mainstream work, such as The Life of Harriett Frean *(1922). That she wrote excellent supernatural fiction will likely come as a surprise to even those who know her work.*

Sinclair's life was a difficult one. Her father went bankrupt, became an alcoholic, and died before she reached adulthood, and her mother was inflexibly religious. Sinclair was only allowed one year at college before she was summoned home to act as a caretaker for her brothers, four of whom were dying of a congenital heart condition. Sinclair was forced to write professionally to support her family from 1896 and was not free of the ties of family until 1901, after the death of her mother. Literary success followed the 1904 publication of The Divine Fire, *and for the next twenty-seven years Sinclair was a highly respected member of London's literateurs. After a diagnosis of Parkinson's disease in the late 1920s, she moved to Buckinghamshire with her companion/housekeeper. After the move she only published a handful of stories and one collection,* The Intercessor and Other Stories *(1931), and the last fifteen years of her life were spent in quiet isolation. She was forgotten even by her friends when she died.*

But ars longa, vita brevis *(art is long; life is short), and while only one of her novels is still in print, many of her wonderful supernatural stories can be found online—to the great pleasure of those who find them. Classics like "The Villa Désirée" (1921), "Where Their Fire Is Not Quenched" (1922), and "The Nature of the Evidence" (1923) combine psychological realism and the supernatural to chilling effect. "The Pin-Prick" straddles the line between purely realistic and the supernatural, perhaps leaning toward realism, although no one would deny that there is horror to be found here.*

WHAT? THAT'S ONE of poor May Blissett's things, the one she used to say she'd leave me in her will, because, she said, she knew I'd be kind to it. Her reasons were always rather quaint. She spoke of it as if it were a live thing that could be hurt or made happy.

I've tried to be kind to it. I've framed it as it ought to be framed, and hung it in not too bad a light. I—I've consented to live with it.

You needn't look at it like that. Of course I know it isn't a bit alive in our sense. She couldn't draw, she could only paint a little; her inspiration was reminiscent, and she got hung more than once in the Academy. She was like so many of them. But she had a sense of beauty, of color, of decoration, and, at her best, a sort of magic queerness that was suggested irresistibly even when the things didn't quite come off.

That *this* hasn't come off—not quite—is really, to me, what makes it so poignantly alive. It's a bit of *her*, a little sensitive, palpitating shred, torn off from her and flung there—all that was left of her. It stands for her mystery, her queerness, her passionate persistence, and her pluck. To anybody who knew her the thing's excruciatingly alive.

It's so alive, so much *her*, that Frances Archdale wonders how I can bear to live with it, with the terrible reproach of it. She insisted that we—or, rather, that *she*—was responsible for what happened. But that's the sort of thing that Frances always did think.

Certainly she *was* responsible for May's coming here. She was with her when she was looking over the studio above mine, the one that Hanson had—it had been empty nearly a year—and she brought her in to me. I was to tell her whether the studio would do or not. I think, when it came to the point, Frances wanted to saddle me with the responsibility. There were no other women in the studios—never had been; they're uncomfortable enough for a man who isn't fastidious; there's no service to speak of; and May Blissett purposed to live alone.

I looked at her and decided instantly that it wouldn't do. You had only to look at her to see that it wouldn't. She was small and presented what Frances called the illusion of fragility—an exquisite little person in spite of her queerness. She had one of those broad-browed, broad-cheeked, and suddenly pointed faces, with a rather prominent and intensely obstinate chin. The queerness was in her long eyes and in the way her delicate nose broadened at the nostrils and in the width of her fine mouth, so much too wide for the slenderly pointed face, and in the tiny scale of the whole phenomenon. She was swarthy, with lots of very dark, crinkly hair. There was something subtle about her, and something that I felt, God forgive me, as mysteriously and secretly malign.

Even if we had wanted women in the studios at all, I didn't want that woman. So I told her that it wouldn't do.

She looked at me straight with her long, sad eyes, and said: "But it's just what I'm hunting for. Why won't it do?"

I could have sworn that she knew what I was thinking.

I said there would be nobody to look after her. And Frances cut in, to my horror, "There would be *you*, Roly."

It was only one of her inconsiderate impulses, but it annoyed me and I turned on her. I said, "Has your friend seen that studio next to *yours?*" I knew that it was to let, and Frances knew that I knew. I suspected her of concealing its existence from May Blissett. She didn't want her near her; she didn't like the responsibility. I wished her to know that it was her responsibility, not mine. I wasn't going to be saddled with it.

Her face—the furtive guilt of it—confirmed my suspicion as we stared at each other across the embarrassment we had created. I ought to have been sorry for Frances. She was mutely imploring me to get her out of it, to see her through. And I wasn't going to.

And then May Blissett laughed, an odd little soft laugh that suggested some gentle but diabolic appreciation of our agony.

"*That* wouldn't do."

I was remorseless and said in my turn: "Why wouldn't it? You'd be near Miss Archdale."

She said: "We don't either of us want to be so near. We should get in each other's way most horribly—just *because* we like each other. I shouldn't be in *your* way, Mr. Simpson."

She was still exquisite, but at the same time a little sinister.

I remember trying to say something about the inference not being very flattering, but Frances got in first.

"She doesn't mean that she doesn't like you, Roly. What she means is—"

"What I mean is that, as Frances knows me and likes me a little—you said you did"—(It was as if she thought that Frances was going to say she didn't. She flung her a look that was not sinister, not sinister at all—purely exquisite—exquisitely incredulous, exquisitely shy. And she went on with her explanation)—"I should be on her mind. And I couldn't be on *your* mind, you know."

I said, "Oh, *couldn't* you!"

But she took no notice. She said, "No, if I come here—and I'm coming"—(She got up to go. She was absolutely determined, absolutely final)—"we must make a compact never"—(she was most impressive)—"never to get in each other's way. It's no use for Frances and me to make a compact. We couldn't keep it for five minutes."

She had the air, under all her incredulity, of paying high tribute to their mutual affection.

"I'm coming here to work, and I want to be alone. What's more, I want to feel alone."

"And you think," I said, "I'll make you feel it?"

She said, "I hope so."

She had put herself between Frances and the door. She said: "You'd better stay and explain it if he doesn't understand. I'm going."

She went like a shot, and I gathered that her precipitance was to give me the measure of her capacity for withdrawal.

Frances stayed. I could see her stiffening herself to meet my wrath.

"Frances," I said, "how *could* you?"

Frances was humble and deprecating—for her. She said, "Roly, she really won't be in your way."

"She *will* be in it," I said, "most abominably. You know we're not supposed to have women here."

"I know; but she's not like a woman. She was trying to tell you that she wasn't. She isn't. She isn't—really—quite human. You won't have to do any of the usual things."

I asked her what she meant by the usual things, and she became instantly luminous. She said, "Well—she won't expect you to fall in love with her."

I'm afraid I said, Heaven only knew what she'd expect. But Frances walked over me with "And *you* needn't expect *her* to fall in with you."

And she put it to me, if there'd been a chance of that sort of thing happening, if May had been dangerous, would she have risked it? (We were engaged in those days.) Would she have gone out of her way to plant her up there over my head? Would she have asked me to look after her if she had—well—required looking after? And she reminded me that she wasn't a fool.

As for May, that sort of thing was beyond her.

"Is it," I said, "beyond any woman? I wouldn't put it—"

"Past her?" she snatched me up. "Perhaps not. But she's past it. Gone through it all, my dear. She's utterly beyond. Immune."

I said: "Never. A face with that expression—that half-malign subtlety. She might do things."

And Frances turned on me. You know how she can turn. Malign subtlety! Malign suffering. The malignity was not in the things she'd do, poor lamb, but in the things that had been done to her. And then she sat down and told me a few of them—told me what, in fact, May had gone through.

First of all, she had lost all her people—father, mother, brothers, and sisters. (She was the youngest of a large family.) That was years and years ago, and she was only thirty-two now, so you may judge the frantic pace of the havoc. And by way of pretty interlude her father had gone mad—mad as a hatter. May had looked after him. Then they lost all their money. (That was a mere detail.) Then she married a man who left her for another woman. Left her with a six-months'-old baby to bring up. Then the child died and she divorced him—he dragged her through horrors. Then, as if that wasn't enough, her lover—I beg her pardon, the man who loved her—was drowned before her eyes in a boating accident. Nothing, Frances said, had happened since then. What could, when everything had happened? As for doing things, there was nothing poor May wanted to do except pictures. And if she thought she could do them better here over my head, wouldn't I be a brute to try and stop her?

Of course I said I shouldn't dream of stopping her, and that it was very sad—it was, indeed, appalling. But it seemed to me that, though Frances had let out so much, she was still keeping something back. And a brutal instinct made me say to her:

"What is it, then, that you dislike so much in her?"

She took it quite simply, as if she had been prepared for it. She even smiled as she answered: "Nothing—except her obstinacy."

I asked her, "Wouldn't that be precisely what would get in my way?"

And she said, No; May's obstinacy would consist in keeping out of it. Still, I objected, obstinate people are nearly always tactless.

And Frances said, "No, not always." She said—dear Frances!—"I'm not obstinate. But I'm tactless, if you like. Look at the horrid mess I got us both into just now. And look how she got us out. She saved us."

I admitted that she had.

And Frances finished up, triumphantly: "Can't you trust her? Can't you see that she's beyond? That she really won't be there? There never was a more effaced and self-effacing person, a person more completely self-contained. I assure you none of us exist for her. So she needn't, really, be on your mind."

And she wasn't, not for a moment, from the day of her coming till the day—Though I must say, afterward—

To begin with, she chose a week-end for her installation—a Friday till Tuesday when I was away. I literally didn't know that she was there, so secret and so silent was she in her movements overhead. I couldn't have believed it possible for a woman to be so effacing and effaced. It was super-feminine; it was, as Frances said, hardly human. And yet she didn't overdo it. I had to own that the most exquisite thing about this exquisite and queer little person was her tact. By overdoing it the least bit, by insisting on her detachment, her isolation, she would have made us disagreeably aware. When you met her on the stairs (she used to run up and down them incredibly soft-footed) she smiled and nodded at you (she had really a singularly intriguing smile) as much as to say that she was in an awful hurry, life being so full of work, of a joyous activity, but still it was lucky that we could meet like this, sometimes, on the stairs.

And she used to come in to tea, sometimes, when I had a party. She took hardly any room in the studio, and hardly any part in the conversation, but she would smile prettily when you spoke to her; the implication being that it made her happy to be asked to tea, but it was not so necessary to her happiness that you would have to ask her often. She used to come a little late and go a little early—and yet not too early—on the plea (it sounded somehow preposterous) that she was busy. Even the poor art that kept her so was tactful. It had no embarrassing pretensions, it called for no criticism, you could look at it without sacrificing your sincerity to your politeness. And if it hadn't been May was too well-bred ever to refer to it. And it kept her. It got itself hung, as I've said, now and again. Supremely tactful, it spared your pity.

In short, she made no claim on us, unless, indeed, her courage called to us to admire the spectacle it was.

For, when you think of the horrible things that had happened to her, the wonder was how she ever contrived to smile at all. But that was what she had effaced more than anything—the long trail of her tragedy. Her reticence was inspired by the purest, the most delicate sense of honor. It was as if she felt that it wouldn't be playing the game, the high game of life, to appeal to us on that ground, when we couldn't have resisted. Besides, it would have hurt, and she wouldn't for the world have hurt us. Her subtlety, you see, was anything but malign. It was beneficent, tender, supernaturally lucid. It allowed for every motive, every shade. And we took her as she presented herself—detached, impersonal, and, as Frances said, immune.

I said to Frances: "We needn't have worried. You were right."

And Frances exulted: "Didn't I tell you? She's quite kind to us, but she doesn't want us."

She had made us forget that we hadn't wanted her.

She had made me forget that I had ever said she'd do things. Even now I don't know what on earth it was I thought she'd do.

She had been living up in that studio, I think, three years before it happened.

I can tell you just how it was. On the evening, rather late, Frances came to see me. She asked me if I'd seen anything of May Blissett lately.

I said: No. Had she?

And she said: Yes, May had called that afternoon.

I noticed something funny about Frances's face—something that made me say, "And you weren't very glad to see her?"

She asked me how I knew she wasn't, and I told her that her funny face betrayed her.

Then, by way of extenuation, she told me the tale of May's calling. I remember every word of it, because we went, she and I—she made me go over it again and again—afterward. She told me that she was not really at home that afternoon to anybody but Daisy Valentine. Daisy had got something on her mind that she wanted to talk about. I knew what those two were when they got together—they were as thick as thieves. And as I also knew that the something on Daisy's mind was Reggie Cotterill, I understood that their communion would be private and intimate to the last degree.

And it seemed that the servant had blundered and let May Blissett in upon the mysteries before they had well begun, and that she'd stayed interminably. There they were, the two of them, snug together on the sofa; their very attitude must have shown May what Daisy was there for. They were just waiting for tea to come before they settled down to it. Poor Daisy was quivering visibly with the things she'd got to say. Couldn't I see her? I could. I gathered that the atmosphere was fairly tingling with suppressed confidence, and that May, obtuse to these vibrations, sat there and simply wouldn't go.

I remember I suggested that she, too, might have had something on her mind and have had things to say. But Frances said: No, she never had things. She'd come for nothing—nothing in the world. She was in one of her silences, those fits which gave her so often the appearance of stupidity. (I knew them. They were formidable, exasperating; for you never could tell what she might be thinking of; and she had a way of smiling through them, a way that we knew now was all part of her high courage, of the web she had spun, that illusion of happiness she had covered herself up in, to spare us.) Frances said she wouldn't have minded May's immobility for herself. It was Daisy who sat palpitating with anxiety, wondering why on earth she didn't go.

I wondered, too. It was so unlike her. I said so.

And Frances, who seemed to understand May through and through, said it wasn't. It was most characteristic. It was just May's obstinacy. If May had made up her mind to do a thing she did it *quand meme*. Generally she made up her mind not to be a nuisance. She'd made it up that afternoon that she'd stay, and so she stayed.

"I'm afraid," Frances said, "we weren't very nice to her. We let her see we didn't want her."

"And then?" I asked.

"Oh, then, of course, she went."

I must say I marveled at the obstinacy that could override a delicacy so consummate as May Blissett's. And I thought that Frances's imagination must have been playing her tricks. It did sometimes.

That night, about nine o'clock, I ran up to May Blissett's studio. I knocked at her door three or four times. I knew she was there. I'd heard her come in an hour or two before. Then, remembering our compact, I went away, going rather slowly, in the hope that she'd relent. I can't tell you whether I really heard her open her door and come out on to the stair-head after I'd got down to my own floor; whether I really thought that she leaned out over the banister to see what was there; or whether I tortured myself with the mere possibility—afterward.

It must have been about six o'clock in the morning when they came to me, the hall porter and his son. They told me that Miss Blissett was not in her room and that they couldn't get her studio door open. It wasn't locked, they said; it had given slightly, but it seemed stuck all over, and an uncommonly queer smell was coming through. They thought it was some sort of disinfectant.

I went up with them. You could smell the disinfectant oozing steadily through a chink in the studio door. We opened the big French windows opposite, and the windows of the bedroom and the stairs outside. Then we began to get the door open with knives, cutting through the paper that sealed it up inside. The reek of the sulphur was so strong that I sent the men out to open the studio windows—they were sealed up, too—from the outside, before we finished with the door. One of them came back and told me not to go into the room.

But when the smoke cleared a little I went.

Oh, it was all quite decent. Trust her for that. She was lying on the couch which she'd dragged into the middle of the great bare studio, all ready, dressed in her nightgown, with a sheet drawn up to her chin. The whole place was dim with the fog of the sulphur still burning. She had set the candles, one on each side, one at the head, and one at the foot.

No, there's nothing stately and ceremonial about a sulphur candle. Have you ever seen one? It's a little fat yellow devil that squats in a saucer. There's a crimson ooze from it when it burns, as if the thing sweated blood before it began its work. *One* of those stinking devils would have done what she wanted, and there were four. Can't you see her going softly round the couch in her white nightgown, lighting her candles, smiling her subtle and mysterious smile? The ghost of it was still there. I am sure she was thinking how beautifully she had managed and how she had saved us all. The dear woman couldn't have had any other thought.

Even Frances saw that.

Frances nearly went off her head about it. Just as she did afterward about poor Dickinson. She declared that we, or rather she, was responsible. She'd had a letter from May Blissett written that night.

It's stuck in my head ever since (it wasn't long). "Forgive me for stopping on like that. It was very thick-skinned of me when I saw you so dear and happy there together. But somehow I couldn't help it. And you *have* forgiven me."

A perfectly sane letter. Not a word about what she meant to do. Evidently she didn't want Frances to connect it with their reception of her.

But of course she did. She insisted that if she had only sent Daisy Valentine away and kept May, May would have been living and happy now. She had shown her that they hadn't wanted her, that she was in their way, and May had just gone and taken herself, once for all, out of it. In the sight of God she—she had killed May.

I couldn't do anything with her. I couldn't make her see that the two things couldn't have had anything in the world to do with each other; that the affair of the visit, to May—after what she'd been through— would be a mere pin-prick; that you don't go through such things to be killed by a pin-prick.

But Frances would have it that you do; that it was because of what May had been through that she was so vulnerable.

Besides, she maintained that her responsibility went deeper and further back. It was that from the first she had been afraid of May Blissett—afraid of something about her. No, not her queerness: her loneliness. She had been afraid that it would cling, that it would get in her way. She had compelled her to suppress it. She had driven it in, and the thing was poisonous. I reminded her that May didn't want us, and she wailed:

"We tried to make ourselves think she didn't. But she did. She did. She wanted us most awfully all the time."

If she had only known! And so on.

I did all I could. I pointed out to her that poor May was insane. What she did proved it. In her right mind she would never have done it. She would have been incapable of that cruelty to us who cared for her. But Frances stuck to it that that was just it. She wouldn't have done it if she'd known we did care. It was the very essence of her despair that she had thought we didn't.

And sometimes I wonder whether Frances wasn't right. Whether, if I had run back that night and caught May Blissett on the staircase—

But, you see, I wasn't really sure that she was there. I mean, she may have lit her candles before that.

THIRTEEN AT TABLE

Lord Dunsany
(1878–1957)

Born Edward John Moreton Drax Plunkett, the man who would later write as "Lord Dunsany" (the title of 18th Baron of Dunsany passed to him when he was twenty-one) spent time growing up in Ireland but after marriage split his time between Dublin and London. He served in the Boer War, in the First World War (being wounded during the Easter Uprising in Dublin), and on the homefront during World War Two. He was also a keen hunter, pistol shooter, and chess player, and advocate for animal rights.

Of course, to the literary world Dunsany's considerable reputation rests upon his writings, which were extensive, across multiple media, forms, and genres. Modern fantasy fiction owes a huge debt to him, both for the example of the fantasy worlds he created and for the style in which he described them and told the tales set within them. It can fairly be said that he created the sword and sorcery genre whole in his "The Fortress Unvanquishable, Save for Sacnoth" (1908). His "Jorkens" tales are perhaps the outstanding twentieth-century examples of the club story genre.

And, of course, there are his non-series short stories, which sample equally of horror and fantasy. "Thirteen at Table," first appearing in Dunsany's collection Tales of Wonder *(1916), is both a character study and a ghost story with a twist, with a surprisingly feel-good ending. One can easily see it as a "Jorkens" story, but it works excellently as a standalone.*

IN FRONT OF a spacious fireplace of the old kind, when the logs were well alight, and men with pipes and glasses were gathered before it in great easeful chairs, and the wild weather outside and the comfort that was within, and the season of the year—for it was Christmas—and the hour of the night, all called for the weird or uncanny, then out spoke the ex-master of foxhounds and told this tale.

"I once had an odd experience too. It was when I had the Bromley and Sydenham, the year I gave them up—as a matter of fact it was the last day of the season. It was no use going on because there were no foxes left in the county, and London was sweeping down on us. You could see it from the kennels all along the skyline like a terrible army in grey, and masses of villas every year came skirmishing down our valleys. Our coverts were mostly on the hills, and as the town came down upon the valleys the foxes used to leave them and go right away out of the county and they never returned. I think they went by night and moved great distances. Well, it was early April and we had drawn blank all day, and at the last draw of all, the very last of the season, we found a fox. He left the covert with his back to London and its railways and villas and wire and slipped away towards the chalk country and open Kent. I felt as I once felt as a child on one summer's day when I found a door in a garden where I played left luckily ajar, and I pushed it open and the wide lands were before me and waving fields of corn.

"We settled down into a steady gallop and the fields began to drift by under us, and a great wind arose full of fresh breath. We left the clay lands where the bracken grows and came to a valley at the edge of the chalk. As we went down into it we saw the fox go up the other side like a shadow that crosses the evening, and glide into a wood that stood on the top. We saw a flash of primroses in the wood and we were out the other side, hounds hunting perfectly and the fox still going absolutely straight. It began to dawn on me then that we were in for a great hunt, I took a deep breath when I thought of it; the taste of the air of that perfect Spring afternoon as it came to one galloping, and the thought of a great run, were together like some old rare wine. Our faces now were to another valley, large fields led down to it, with easy hedges, at the bottom of it a bright blue stream went singing and a rambling village smoked, the sunlight on the opposite slopes danced like a fairy; and all along the top old woods were frowning, but they dreamed of Spring. The "field" had fallen off and were far behind and my only human companion was James, my old first whip, who had a hound's instinct, and a personal animosity against a fox that even embittered his speech.

"Across the valley the fox went as straight as a railway line, and again we went without a check straight through the woods at the top. I remember hearing men sing or shout as they walked home from work, and sometimes children whistled; the sounds came up from the village to the woods at the top of the valley. After that we saw no more villages, but valley after valley arose and fell before us as though we were voyaging some strange and stormy sea, and all the way before us the fox went dead up-wind like the fabulous Flying Dutchman. There was no one in sight now but my first whip and me, we had both of us got on to our second horses as we drew the last covert.

"Two or three times we checked in those great lonely valleys beyond the village, but I began to have inspirations, I felt a strange certainty within me that this fox was going on straight up-wind till he died or until night came and we could hunt no longer, so I reversed ordinary methods and only cast straight ahead and always we picked up the scent again at once. I believe that this fox was the last one left in the villa-haunted lands and that he was prepared to leave them for remote uplands far from men, that if we had come the following day he would not have been there, and that we just happened to hit off his journey.

"Evening began to descend upon the valleys, still the hounds drifted on, like the lazy but unresting shadows of clouds upon a summer's day, we heard a shepherd calling to his dog, we saw two maidens move towards a hidden farm, one of them singing softly; no other sounds, but ours, disturbed the leisure and the loneliness of haunts that seemed not yet to have known the inventions of steam and gun-powder (even as China, they say, in some of her further mountains does not yet know that she has fought Japan).

"And now the day and our horses were wearing out, but that reso-lute fox held on. I began to work out the run and to wonder where we were. The last landmark I had ever seen before must have been over five miles back and from there to the start was at least ten miles more. If only we could kill! Then the sun set. I wondered what chance we had of killing our fox. I looked at James' face as he rode beside me. He did not seem to have lost any confidence yet his horse was as tired as mine. It was a good clear twilight and the scent was as strong as ever, and the fences were easy enough, but those valleys were terribly trying and they still rolled on and on. It looked as if the light would outlast all possible endurance both of the fox and the horses, if the scent held good and he did not go to ground, otherwise night would end it. For long we had seen no houses and no roads, only chalk slopes with the twilight on them, and here and there some sheep, and scattered copses darkening in the evening. At some moment I seemed to realise all at once that the light was spent and that darkness was hovering, I looked at James, he was solemnly shaking his head. Suddenly in a little wooded valley we saw climb over the oaks the red-brown gables of a queer old house; at that instant I saw the fox scarcely heading by fifty yards. We blundered through a wood into full sight of the house, but no avenue led up to it or even a path nor were there any signs of wheel-marks anywhere. Already lights shone here and there in windows. We were in a park, and a fine park, but unkempt beyond credibility; brambles grew everywhere. It was too dark to see the fox any more but we knew he was dead beat, the hounds were just before us,—and a four-foot railing of oak. I shouldn't have tried it on a fresh horse the beginning of a run, and here was a horse near his last gasp. But what a run! an event standing out in a lifetime, and the hounds close up on their fox, slipping into the darkness as I hesitated. I decided to try it. My horse rose about eight inches and took it fair with his breast, and the oak log flew into handfuls of wet decay—it rotten with years. And then we were on a lawn and at the far end of it the hounds were tumbling over their fox. Fox, hounds and light were all done together at the twenty-mile point. We made some noise then, but nobody came out of the queer old house.

"I felt pretty stiff as I walked round to the hall door with the mask and the brush while James went with the hounds and the two horses to look for the stables. I rang a bell marvellously encrusted with rust, and after a long while the door opened a little way revealing a hall with much old armour in it and the shabbiest butler that I have ever known.

"I asked him who lived there. Sir Richard Arlen. I explained that my horse could go no further that night and that I wished to ask Sir Richard Arlen for a bed for the night.

"'O, no one ever comes here, sir,' said the butler.

"I pointed out that I had come.

"'I don't think it would be possible, sir,' he said.

"'This annoyed me and I asked to see Sir Richard, and insisted until he came. Then I apologised and explained the situation. He looked only fifty, but a Varsity oar on the wall with the date of the early seventies, made him older than that; his face had something of the shy look of the hermit; he regretted that he had not room to put me up. I was sure that this was untrue, also I had to be put up there, there was nowhere else within miles, so I almost insisted. Then to my astonishment he turned to the butler and they talked it over in an undertone. At last they seemed to think that they could manage it, though clearly with reluctance. It was by now seven o'clock and Sir Richard told me he dined at half past seven. There was no question of clothes for me other than those I stood in, as my host was shorter and broader. He showed me presently to the drawing-room and there he reappeared before half past seven in evening dress and a white waistcoat. The drawing-room was large and contained old furniture but it was rather worn than venerable, an Aubusson carpet flapped about the floor, the wind seemed momentarily to enter the room, and old draughts haunted corners; the stealthy feet of rats that were never at rest indicated the extent of the ruin that time had wrought in the wainscot; somewhere far off a shutter flapped to and fro, the guttering candles were insufficient to light so large a room. The gloom that these things suggested was quite in keeping with Sir Richard's first remark to me after he entered the room: 'I must tell you, sir, that I have led a wicked life. O, a very wicked life.'

"Such confidences from a man much older than oneself after one has known him for half an hour are so rare that any possible answer merely does not suggest itself. I said rather slowly, 'O, really,' and chiefly to forestall another such remark I said 'What a charming house you have.'

"'Yes,' he said, 'I have not left it for nearly forty years. Since I left the Varsity. One is young there, you know, and one has opportunities; but I make no excuses, no excuses.' And the door slipping its rusty latch, came drifting on the draught into the room, and the long carpet flapped and the hangings upon the walls, then the draught fell rustling away and the door slammed to again.

"'Ah, Marianne,' he said, 'we have a guest to-night. Mr. Linton. This is Marianne Gib.' And everything became clear to me. 'Mad,' I said to myself, for no one had entered the room.

"The rats ran up the length of the room behind the wainscot ceaselessly, and the wind unlatched the door again and the folds of the carpet fluttered up to our feet and stopped there, for our weight held it down.

"'Let me introduce Mr. Linton,' said my host—'Lady Mary Errinjer.'

"The door slammed back again. I bowed politely. Even had I been invited I should have humoured him, but it was the very least that an uninvited guest could do.

"This kind of thing happened eleven times, the rustling, and the fluttering of the carpet and the footsteps of the rats, and the restless door, and then the sad voice of my host introducing me to phantoms. Then for some while we waited while I struggled with the situation; conversation flowed slowly. And again the draught came trailing up the room, while the flaring candles filled it with hurrying shadows. 'Ah, late again, Cicely,' said my host in his soft, mournful way. 'Always late, Cicely.' Then I went down to dinner with that man and his mind and the twelve phantoms that haunted it. I found a long table with fine old silver on it and places laid for fourteen. The butler was now in evening dress, there were fewer draughts in the dining-room, the scene was less gloomy there. 'Will you sit next to Rosalind at the other end,' Richard said to me. 'She always takes the head of the table, I wronged her most of all.' I said, 'I shall be delighted.'

"I looked at the butler closely, but never did I see by any expression of his face or by anything that he did any suggestion that he waited upon less than fourteen people in the complete possession of all their faculties. Perhaps a dish appeared to be refused more often than taken but every glass was equally filled with champagne. At first I found little to say, but when Sir Richard speaking from the far end of the table said, 'You are tired, Mr. Linton,' I was reminded that I owed something to a host upon whom I had forced myself. It was excellent champagne and with the help of a second glass I made the effort to begin a conversation with a Miss Helen Errold for whom the place upon one side of me was laid. It came more easy to me very soon. I frequently paused in my monologue, like Mark Anthony, for a reply, and sometimes I turned and spoke to Miss Rosalind Smith. Sir Richard at the other end talked sorrowfully on. He spoke as a condemned man might speak to his judge, and yet somewhat as a judge might speak to one that he once condemned wrongly. My own mind began to turn to mournful things. I drank another glass of champagne, but I was still thirsty. I felt as if all the moisture in my body had been blown away over the downs of Kent by the wind up which we had galloped. Still I was not talking enough; my host was looking at me. I made another effort, after all I had something to talk about, a twenty-mile point is not often seen in a lifetime, especially south of the Thames. I began to describe the run to Rosalind Smith. I could see then that my host was pleased, the sad look in his face gave a kind of a flicker, like mist upon the mountains on a miserable day when a faint puff comes from the sea and the mist would lift if it could. And the butler refilled my glass very attentively. I asked her first if she hunted, and paused and began my story. I told her where we had found the fox and how fast and straight he had gone, and how I had got through the village by keeping to the road, while the little gardens and wire, and then the river, had stopped the rest of the field. I told her the kind of country that we crossed and how splendid it looked in the Spring, and how mysterious the valleys were as soon as the twilight came, and what a glorious horse I had and how wonderfully he went. I was so fearfully thirsty after the great hunt that I had to stop for a moment now and then, but I went on with my description of that famous run, for I had warmed to the subject, and after all there was nobody to tell of it but me except my old whipper-in, and 'the old fellow's probably drunk by now,' I thought. I described to her minutely the exact spot in the run at which it had come to me clearly that this was going to be the greatest hunt in the whole history of Kent. Sometimes I forgot incidents that had happened as one well may in a run of twenty miles, and then I had to fill in the gaps by inventing. I was pleased to be able to make the party go off well by means of my conversation, and besides that the lady to whom I was speaking was extremely pretty: I do not mean in a flesh and blood kind of way but there were little shadowy lines about the chair beside me that hinted at an unusually graceful figure when Miss Rosalind Smith was alive; and I began to perceive that what I first mistook for the smoke of guttering candles and a table-cloth waving in the draught was in reality an extremely animated company who listened, and not without interest, to my story of by far the greatest hunt that the world had ever known: indeed I told them that I would confidently go further and predict that never in the history of the world would there be such a run again. Only my throat was terribly dry. And then as it seemed they wanted to hear more about my horse. I had forgotten that I had come there on a horse, but when they reminded me it all came back; they looked so charming leaning over the table intent upon what I said, that I told them everything they wanted to know. Everything was going so pleasantly if only Sir Richard would cheer up. I heard his mournful voice every now and then—these were very pleasant people if only he would take them the right way. I could understand that he regretted his past, but the early seventies seemed centuries away and I felt sure that he misunderstood these ladies, they were not revengeful as he seemed to suppose. I wanted to show him how cheerful they really were, and so I made a joke and they all laughed at it, and then I chaffed them a bit, especially Rosalind, and nobody resented it in the very least. And still Sir Richard sat there with that unhappy look, like one that has ended weeping because it is vain and has not the consolation even of tears.

"We had been a long time there and many of the candles had burned out, but there was light enough. I was glad to have an audience for my exploit, and being happy myself I was determined Sir Richard should be. I made more jokes and they still laughed good-naturedly; some of the jokes were a little broad perhaps but no harm was meant. And then—I do not wish to excuse myself—but I had had a harder day than I ever had had before and without knowing it I must have been completely exhausted; in this state the champagne had found me, and what would have been harmless at any other time must somehow have got the better of me when quite tired out—anyhow I went too far, I made some joke—I cannot in the least remember what—that suddenly seemed to offend them. I felt all at once a commotion in the air. I looked up and saw that they had all arisen from the table and were sweeping towards the door: I had not time to open it but it blew open on a wind. I could scarcely see what Sir Richard was doing because only two candles were left. I think the rest blew out when the ladies suddenly rose. I sprang up to apologise, to assure them—and then fatigue overcame me as it had overcome my horse at the last fence. I clutched at the table but the cloth came away and then I fell. The fall, and the darkness on the floor and the pent up fatigue of the day overcame me all three together.

"The sun shone over glittering fields and in at a bedroom window and thousands of birds were chanting to the Spring, and there I was in an old four-poster bed in a quaint old panelled bedroom, fully dressed and wearing long muddy boots; someone had taken my spurs and that was all. For a moment I failed to realise and then it all came back, my enormity and the pressing need of an abject apology to Sir Richard. I pulled an embroidered bell rope until the butler came. He came in perfectly cheerful and indescribably shabby. I asked him if Sir Richard was up, and he said he had just gone down, and told me to my amazement that it was twelve o'clock. I asked to be shown in to Sir Richard at once. He was in his smoking-room. 'Good morning,' he said cheerfully the moment I went in. I went directly to the matter in hand. 'I fear that I insulted some ladies in your house—' I began.

"'You did indeed,' he said, 'You did indeed.' And then he burst into tears and took me by the hand. 'How can I ever thank you?' he said to me then. 'We have been thirteen at table for thirty years and I never dared to insult them because I had wronged them all, and now you have done it and I know they will never dine here again.' And for a long time he still held my hand, and then he gave it a grip and a kind of a shake which I took to mean 'Goodbye' and I drew my hand away then and left the house. And I found James in the stables with the hounds and asked him how he had fared, and James, who is a man of very few words, said he could not rightly remember, and I got my spurs from the butler and climbed on to my horse and slowly we rode away from that queer old house, and slowly we wended home, for the hounds were footsore but happy and the horses were tired still. And when we recalled that the hunting season was ended we turned our faces to Spring and thought of the new things that try to replace the old. And that very year I heard, and have often heard since, of dances and happier dinners at Sir Richard Arlen's house."

THE BIRD

Thomas Burke
(1886–1945)

Burke was born and raised in London, and lived there all his life. He wrote extensively about the city that he lived in and loved, but his expertise, that which he became known for during his lifetime and which his fading reputation still rests upon, was his knowledge of Limehouse, London's Chinatown. Burke gained renown for his first major collection, Limehouse Nights *(1916), set in Limehouse and telling stories of the Chinese immigrants living there (and, scandalously to his contemporary audience, having relationships with white women). Burke would return to Limehouse in* Twinkletoes *(1918) and* More Limehouse Nights *(1921) and later short stories, even as the real Limehouse he was fictionalizing and largely romanticizing was disappearing, its Chinese inhabitants becoming more regulated by the white police, more assimilated, and dispersing to other boroughs. Burke wrote about London and its citizens in a variety of stories and novels, even (in his 1937* For Your Convenience*) describing London's gay community, but for his readers always remained "The Laureate of Limehouse."*

However, Burke had a natural talent as a storyteller and did not limit himself to genre. Conscious of criticism that he was repeating himself in his many Limehouse stories, Burke varied his subject matter and plots (if not the environment of his stories) and began writing crime and horror stories. Perhaps his best known is "The Hands of Ottermole" (1929), voted "The Best Mystery of All Time" by critics in 1949. "The Bird," which originally appeared in Burke's Limehouse Nights *collection, has the Burkean trappings while delving into cruel depths to which Burke rarely went in his fiction.*

I T   I S   A tale that they tell softly in Pennyfields, when the curtains are drawn and the shapes of the night shut out. . . . Those who held that Captain Chudder, s.s. Peacock, owners, Peter Dubbin & Co., had a devil in him, were justified. But they were nearer the truth who held that his devil was not within him, but at his side, perching at his elbow, dropping sardonic utterance in his ear; moving with him day and night and prompting him—so it was held—to frightful excesses. His devil wore the shape of a white parrot, a bird of lusty wings and the cruellest of beaks. There were those who whispered that the old man had not always been the man that his crew knew him to be: that he had been a normal, kindly fellow until he acquired his strange companion from a native dealer in the malevolent Solomons. Certainly his maniac

moods dated from its purchase; and there was truth in the dark hints of
his men that there was something wrong with that damned bird . . . a
kind of . . . something you sort of felt when it looked at you or
answered you back. For one thing, it had a diabolical knack of mimicry, and many a chap would cry: "Yes, George!" or "Right, sir!" in
answer to a commanding voice which chuckled with glee as he came
smartly to order. They invariably referred to it as "that bloody bird,"
though actually it had done nothing to merit such opprobrium. When
they thought it over calmly, they could think of no harm that it had
done to them: nothing to arouse such loathing as every man on the
boat felt towards it. It was not spiteful; it was not bad-tempered. Mostly
it was in cheery mood and would chuckle deep in the throat, like the
Captain, and echo or answer, quite pleasantly, such remarks, usually
rude, as were addressed to it.

And yet . . . Somehow . . .

There it was. It was always there—everywhere; and in its speech
they seemed to find a sinister tone which left them guessing at the
meaning of its words. On one occasion, the cook, in the seclusion of
the fo'c'sle, had remarked that he would like to wring its neck if he
could get hold of it; but old grizzled Snorter had replied that that bird
couldn't be killed. There was a something about that bird that . . . well,
he betted no one wouldn't touch that bird without trouble. And a
moment of panic stabbed the crowd as a voice leapt from the sombre
shadows of the corner:

"That's the style, me old brown son. Don't try to come it with me—
what?" and ceased on a spasmodic flutter of wicked white wings.

That night, as the cook was ascending the companion, he was caught
by a huge sea, which swept across the boat from nowhere and dashed
him, head-on, below. For a week he was sick with a broken head, and
throughout that week the bird would thrust its beak to the berth where
he lay, and chortle to him:

"Yep, me old brown son. Wring his bleeding neck—what? Waltz
me around again, Willie, round and round and round!"

That is the seamen's story and, as the air of Limehouse is thick with
seamen's stories, it is not always good to believe them. But it is a widely
known fact that on his last voyage the Captain did have a devil with
him, the foulest of all devils that possess mortal men: not the devil of
slaughter, but the devil of cruelty. They were from Swatow to London,
and it was noted that he was drinking heavily ashore, and he continued
the game throughout the voyage. He came aboard from Swatow,

drunk, bringing with him a Chinese boy, also drunk. The greaser, being a big man, kicked him below; otherwise, the boat in his charge would have gone there; and so he sat or sprawled in his cabin, with a rum bottle before him and, on the corner of his chair, the white parrot, which conversed with him and sometimes fluttered on deck to shout orders in the frightful voice of his master and chuckle to see them momentarily obeyed.

"Yes," repeated old man Snorter, sententiously, "I'd run a hundred miles 'fore I'd try to monkey with the old man or his bloody bird. There's something about that bird. . . . I said so before. I 'eard a story once about a bird. Out in T'aip'ing I 'eard it. It'll make yeh sick if I tell it. . . ."

Now while the Captain remained drunk in his cabin, he kept with him for company the miserable, half-starved Chinky boy whom he had brought aboard. And it would make others sick if the full dark tale were told here of what the master of the Peacock did to that boy. You may read of monstrosities in police reports of cruelty cases; you may read old records of the Middle Ages; but the bestialities of Captain Chudder could not be told in words.

His orgy of drink and delicious torture lasted till they were berthed in the Thames; and the details remain sharp and clear in the memories of those who witnessed it. At all the ceremonial horrors which were wrought in that wretched cabin, the parrot was present. It jabbered to the old man; the old man jabbered back, and gave it an occasional sip of rum from his glass; and the parrot would mimic the Chink's entreaties, and wag a grave claw at him as he writhed under the ritual of punishment; and when that day's ceremony was finished it would flutter from bow to stern of the boat, its cadaverous figure stinging the shadows with shapes of fear for all aboard; perching here, perching there, simpering and whining in tune with the Chink's placid moaning.

Placid; yes, outwardly. But the old man's wickedness had lighted a flame beneath that yellow skin which nothing could quench: nothing but the floods of vengeance. Had the old man been a little more cute and a little less drunk, he might have remembered that a Chinaman does not forget. He would have read danger in the face that was so submissive under his devilries. Perhaps he did see it, but, because of the rum that was in him, felt himself secure from the hate of any outcast Chink; knew that his victim would never once get the chance to repay him, Captain Chudder, master of the Peacock, and one of the very smartest. The Chink was alone and weaponless, and dare not come aft without orders. He was master of the boat; he had a crew to help him, and knives and guns, and he had his faithful white bird to warn him. Too, as soon as they docked at Limehouse, he would sling him off or arrange quick transfer to an outward boat, since he had no further use for him.

But it happened that he made no attempt to transfer. He had forgotten that idea. He just sat below, finished his last two bottles, paid off his men, and then, after a sleep, went ashore to report. Having done that, he forgot all trivial affairs, such as business, and set himself seriously to search for amusement. He climbed St George's, planning a real good old booze-up, and the prospect that spread itself before his mind was so compelling that he did not notice a lurking yellow phantom that hung on his shadow. He visited the Baltic on the chance of finding an old pal or so, and, meeting none, he called at a shipping office at Fenchurch Street, where he picked up an acquaintance, and they two returned eastward to Poplar, and the phantom feet sup-supped after them. Through the maze and clamour of the London streets and traffic the shadow slid; it dodged and danced about the Captain's little cottage in Gill Street; and when he, and others, came out and strolled to a bar, and, later, to a music hall, it flitted, mothlike, around them.

Surely, since there is no step in the world that has just the obvious stealth of the Chinaman's, he must have heard those whispering feet? Surely his path was darkened by that shadow? But no. After the music hall he drifted to a water-side wineshop, and then, with a bunch of the others, went wandering.

It was late. Eleven notes straggled across the waters from many grey towers. Sirens were screeching their derisive song; and names of various Scotch whiskies spelt themselves in letters of yellow flame along the night. Far in the darkness a voice was giving the chanty:

"What shall we do with a drunken sailor?"

The Captain braced himself up and promised himself a real glittering night of good-fellowship, and from gin-warmed bar to gin-warmed bar he roved, meeting the lurid girls of the places and taking one of them upstairs. At the last bar his friends, too, went upstairs with their ladies, and, it being then one o'clock in the morning, he brought a pleasant evening to a close at a certain house in Poplar High Street, where he took an hour's amusement by flinging half-crowns over the fan-tan table.

But always the yellow moth was near, and when, at half-past two, he came, with uncertain step, into the sad street, now darkened and loud only with the drunken, who found unfamiliar turnings in familiar streets, and old landmarks many yards away from their rightful places, the moth buzzed closer and closer.

The Captain talked as he went. He talked of the night he had had, and the girls his hands had touched. His hard face was cracked to a meaningless smile, and he spat words at obstructive lamp-posts and kerbstones, and swears dropped like toads from his lips. But at last he found his haven in Gill Street, and his hefty brother, with whom he lived when ashore, shoved him upstairs to his bedroom. He fell across the bed, and the sleep of the swinish held him fast.

The grey towers were tolling three o'clock, and the thick darkness of the water-side covered the night like a blanket. The lamps were pale and few. The waters slucked miserably at the staples of the wharves. One heard the measured beat of a constable's boot; sometimes the rattle of chains and blocks; mournful hooters; shudders of noise as engines butted lines of trucks at the shunting station.

Captain Chudder slept, breathing stertorously, mouth open, limbs heavy and nerveless. His room was deeply dark, and so little light shone on the back reaches of the Gill Street cottages that the soft raising of the window made no visible aperture. Into this blank space something rose from below, and soon it took the shape of a flat, yellow face which hung motionless, peering into the room. Then a yellow hand came through; the aperture was widened; and swiftly and silently a lithe, yellow body hauled itself up and slipped over the sill.

It glided, with outstretched hand, from the window, and, the moment it touched the bed, its feeling fingers went here and there, and it stood still, gazing upon the sleep of drunkenness. Calmly and methodically a yellow hand moved to its waist and withdrew a creese. The same hand raised the creese and held it poised. It was long, keen and beautifully curved, but not a ray of light was in the room to fall upon it, and the yellow hand had to feel its bright blade to find whether the curve ran from or towards it.

Then, with terrific force and speed, it came down: one—two—three. The last breath rushed from the open lips. Captain Chudder was out.

The strong yellow hand withdrew the creese for the last time, wiped it on the coverlet of the bed, and replaced it in its home. The figure turned, like a wraith, for the window; turned for the window and found, in a moment of panic, that it knew not which way to turn. It hesitated a moment. It thought it heard a sound at the bed. It touched the coverlet and the boots of the Captain; all was still. Stretching a hand to the wall, Sung Dee began to creep and to feel his way along. Dark as the room was, he had found his way in, without matches or illuminant. Why could he not find his way out? Why was he afraid of something?

Blank wall was all he found at first. Then his hand touched what seemed to be a picture frame. It swung and clicked and the noise seemed to echo through the still house. He moved farther, and a sharp rattle told him that he had struck the loose handle of the door. But that was of little help. He could not use the door; he knew not what perils lay behind it. It was the window he wanted—the window.

Again he heard that sound from the bed. He stepped boldly forward and judged that he was standing in the middle of the room. Momentarily a sharp shock surged over him. He prayed for matches, and something in his throat was almost crying: "The window! The window!" He seemed like an island in a sea of darkness; one man surrounded by legions of immortal, intangible enemies. His cold Chinese heart went hot with fear.

The middle of the room, he judged, and took another step forward, a step which landed his chin sharply against the jutting edge of the mantel shelf over the fireplace. He jumped like a cat and his limbs shook; for now he had lost the door and the bed, as well as the window, and had made terrible noises which might bring disaster. All sense of direction was gone. He knew not whether to go forward or backward, to right or left.

He heard the tinkle of the shunting trains, and he heard a rich voice crying something in his own tongue. But he was lapped around by darkness and terror, and a cruel fancy came to him that he was imprisoned here for ever and for ever, and that he would never escape from this enveloping, suffocating room. He began to think that——

And then a hot iron of agony rushed down his thick back as, sharp and clear at his elbow, came the Captain's voice:

"Get forrard, you damn lousy Chink—get forrard. Lively there! Get out of my room!"

He sprang madly aside from the voice that had been the terror of his life for so many weeks, and collided with the door; realised that he had made further fearful noises; dashed away from it and crashed into the bed; fell across it and across the warm, wet body that lay there. Every nerve in every limb of him was seared with horror at the contact, and he leapt off, kicking, biting, writhing. He leapt off, and fell against a table, which tottered, and at last fell with a stupendous crash into the fender.

"Lively, you damn Chink!" said the Captain. "Lively, I tell yeh. Dance, d'yeh hear? I'll have yeh for this. I'll learn you something. I'll give you something with a sharp knife and a bit of hot iron, my cocky. I'll make yer yellow skin crackle, yeh damn lousy chopstick. I'll have yeh in a minute. And when I get yeh, orf with yeh clothes. I'll cut yeh to pieces, I will."

Sung Dee shrieked. He ran round and round, beating the wall with his hands, laughing, crying, jumping, while all manner of shapes arose in his path, lit by the grey light of fear. He realised that it was all up now. He cared not how much noise he made. He hadn't killed the old man; only wounded him. And now all he desired was to find the door and any human creatures who might save him from the Captain. He met the bed again, suddenly, and the tormentor who lay there. He met the upturned table and fell upon it, and he met the fireplace and the blank wall; but never, never the window or the door. They had vanished. There was no way out. He was caught in that dark room, and the Captain would do as he liked with him. . . . He heard footsteps in the passage and sounds of menace and alarm below. But to him they were friendly sounds, and he screamed loudly toward them.

He cried to the Captain, in his pidgin, for mercy.

"Oh, Captain—no burn me to-day, Captain. Sung Dee be heap good sailor, heap good servant, all same slave. Sung Dee heap plenty solly hurt Captain. Sung Dee be good boy. No do feller bad lings no feller more. O Captain. Let Sung Dee go lis time. Let Sung Dee go. O Captain!"

But "Oh, my Gawd!" answered the Captain. "Bless your yellow heart. Wait till I get you trussed up. Wait till I get you below. I'll learn yeh."

And now those below came upstairs, and they listened in the passage, and for the space of a minute they were hesitant. For they heard all manner of terrible noises, and by the noises there might have been half-a-dozen fellows in the Captain's room. But very soon the screaming and the pattering feet were still, and they heard nothing but low moans; and at last the bravest of them, the Captain's brother, swung the door open and flashed a large lantern.

And those who were with him fell back in dumb horror, while the brother cried harshly: "Oh! . . . my . . . God!" For the lantern shone on a Chinaman seated on the edge of the bed. Across his knees lay the dead body of the Captain, and the Chink was fondling his damp, dead face, talking baby talk to him, dancing him on his knee, and now and then making idiot moans. But what sent the crowd back in horror was that a great death-white Thing was flapping about the yellow face of the Chink, cackling: "I'll learn yeh! I'll learn yeh!" and dragging strips of flesh away with every movement of the beak.

ENOCH SOAMES

Max Beerbohm
(1872–1956)

"The Incomparable Max," as George Bernard Shaw once called him, was a multiple threat: as an essayist, as a drama critic, as a public wit, and as a parodist and caricaturist. Beerbohm met Oscar Wilde and his circle while at Oxford, and then Aubrey Beardsley and his group, and through them became well-known socially in Oxford. He gained greater fame for his articles and caricatures while still at Oxford, ultimately leaving school without gaining his degree. After publishing a collection of essays and then his first work of fiction, he succeeded George Bernard Shaw as the drama critic for the Saturday Review, *in which position he remained until 1910, after which he moved to Italy, where he stayed (with the exception of the years of World Wars One and Two) for the rest of his life, living off his caricatures and writings. In the 1930s he became famous to a new generation as an occasional radio commentator for the BBC.*

Beerbohm was good at everything he did, from prose parodies to pastiches to his numerous, instantly recognizable drawings, so it's disappointing though not surprising that he did not spend more time working on straight, non-satirical fantastic fiction. His Zuleika Dobson *(1911) is still worth reading, and "Enoch Soames," which first appeared in* Century Magazine *(May, 1916), still stands as one of the best deal-with-the-devil stories of the time.*

WHEN A BOOK about the literature of the eighteen-nineties was given by Mr. Holbrook Jackson to the world, I looked eagerly in the index for Soames, Enoch. It was as I feared: he was not there. But everybody else was. Many writers whom I had quite forgotten, or remembered but faintly, lived again for me, they and their work, in Mr. Holbrook Jackson's pages. The book was as thorough as it was brilliantly written. And thus the omission found by me was an all the deadlier record of poor Soames's failure to impress himself on his decade.

I dare say I am the only person who noticed the omission. Soames had failed so piteously as all that! Nor is there a counterpoise in the thought that if he had had some measure of success he might have passed, like those others, out of my mind, to return only at the historian's beck. It is true that had his gifts, such as they were, been acknowledged in his lifetime, he would never have made the bargain I saw him make—that strange bargain whose results have kept him always in the foreground of my memory. But it is from those very results that the full piteousness of him glares out.

Not my compassion, however, impels me to write of him. For his sake, poor fellow, I should be inclined to keep my pen out of the ink. It is ill to deride the dead. And how can I write about Enoch Soames without making him ridiculous? Or, rather, how am I to hush up the horrid fact that he WAS ridiculous? I shall not be able to do that. Yet, sooner or later, write about him I must. You will see in due course that I have no option. And I may as well get the thing done now.

In the summer term of '93 a bolt from the blue flashed down on Oxford. It drove deep; it hurtlingly embedded itself in the soil. Dons and undergraduates stood around, rather pale, discussing nothing but it. Whence came it, this meteorite? From Paris. Its name? Will Rothenstein. Its aim? To do a series of twenty-four portraits in lithograph. These were to be published from the Bodley Head, London. The matter was urgent. Already the warden of A, and the master of B, and the Regius Professor of C had meekly "sat." Dignified and doddering old men who had never consented to sit to any one could not withstand this dynamic little stranger. He did not sue; he invited: he did not invite; he commanded. He was twenty-one years old. He wore spectacles that flashed more than any other pair ever seen. He was a wit. He was brimful of ideas. He knew Whistler. He knew Daudet and the Goncourts. He knew every one in Paris. He knew them all by heart. He was Paris in Oxford. It was whispered that, so soon as he had polished off his selection of dons, he was going to include a few undergraduates. It was a proud day for me when I—I was included. I liked Rothenstein not less than I feared him; and there arose between us a friendship that has grown ever warmer, and been more and more valued by me, with every passing year.

At the end of term he settled in, or, rather, meteoritically into, London. It was to him I owed my first knowledge of that forever-enchanting little world-in-itself, Chelsea, and my first acquaintance with Walter Sickert and other August elders who dwelt there. It was Rothenstein that took me to see, in Cambridge Street, Pimlico, a young man whose drawings were already famous among the few—Aubrey Beardsley by name. With Rothenstein I paid my first visit to the Bodley Head. By him I was inducted into another haunt of intellect and daring, the domino-room of the Café Royal.

There, on that October evening—there, in that exuberant vista of gilding and crimson velvet set amidst all those opposing mirrors and upholding caryatids, with fumes of tobacco ever rising to the painted and pagan ceiling, and with the hum of presumably cynical conversation broken into so sharply now and again by the clatter of dominoes shuffled on marble tables, I drew a deep breath and, "This indeed," said I to myself, "is life!" (Forgive me that theory. Remember the waging of even the South African War was not yet.)

It was the hour before dinner. We drank vermouth. Those who knew Rothenstein were pointing him out to those who knew him only by name. Men were constantly coming in through the swing-doors and wandering slowly up and down in search of vacant tables or of tables occupied by friends. One of these rovers interested me because I was sure he wanted to catch Rothenstein's eye. He had twice passed our table, with a hesitating look; but Rothenstein, in the thick of a disquisition on Puvis de Chavannes, had not seen him. He was a stooping, shambling person, rather tall, very pale, with longish and brownish hair. He had a thin, vague beard, or, rather, he had a chin on which a large number of hairs weakly curled and clustered to cover its retreat. He was an odd-looking person; but in the nineties odd apparitions were more frequent, I think, than they are now. The young writers of that era—and I was sure this man was a writer—strove earnestly to be distinct in aspect. This man had striven unsuccessfully. He wore a soft black hat of clerical kind, but of Bohemian intention, and a gray waterproof cape which, perhaps because it was waterproof, failed to be romantic. I decided that "dim" was the mot juste for him. I had already essayed to write, and was immensely keen on the mot juste, that Holy Grail of the period.

The dim man was now again approaching our table, and this time he made up his mind to pause in front of it.

"You don't remember me," he said in a toneless voice.

Rothenstein brightly focused him.

"Yes, I do," he replied after a moment, with pride rather than effusion—pride in a retentive memory. "Edwin Soames."

"Enoch Soames," said Enoch.

"Enoch Soames," repeated Rothenstein in a tone implying that it was enough to have hit on the surname. "We met in Paris a few times when you were living there. We met at the Café Groche."

"And I came to your studio once."

"Oh, yes; I was sorry I was out."

"But you were in. You showed me some of your paintings, you know. I hear you're in Chelsea now."

"Yes."

I almost wondered that Mr. Soames did not, after this monosyllable, pass along. He stood patiently there, rather like a dumb animal, rather like a donkey looking over a gate. A sad figure, his. It occurred to me that "hungry" was perhaps the mot juste for him; but—hungry for what? He looked as if he had little appetite for anything. I was sorry for him; and Rothenstein, though he had not invited him to Chelsea, did ask him to sit down and have something to drink.

Seated, he was more self-assertive. He flung back the wings of his cape with a gesture which, had not those wings been waterproof, might have seemed to hurl defiance at things in general. And he ordered an absinthe. "Je me tiens toujours fidele," he told Rothenstein, "a la sorciere glauque."

"It is bad for you," said Rothenstein, dryly.

"Nothing is bad for one," answered Soames. "Dans ce monde il n'y a ni bien ni mal."

"Nothing good and nothing bad? How do you mean?"

"I explained it all in the preface to 'Negations.'"

"'Negations'?"

"Yes, I gave you a copy of it."

"Oh, yes, of course. But, did you explain, for instance, that there was no such thing as bad or good grammar?"

"N-no," said Soames. "Of course in art there is the good and the evil. But in life—no." He was rolling a cigarette. He had weak, white hands, not well washed, and with finger-tips much stained with nicotine. "In life there are illusions of good and evil, but"—his voice trailed away to a murmur in which the words "vieux jeu" and "rococo" were faintly audible. I think he felt he was not doing himself justice, and feared that Rothenstein was going to point out fallacies. Anyhow, he cleared his throat and said, "Parlons d'autre chose."

It occurs to you that he was a fool? It didn't to me. I was young, and had not the clarity of judgment that Rothenstein already had. Soames was quite five or six years older than either of us. Also—he had written a book. It was wonderful to have written a book.

If Rothenstein had not been there, I should have revered Soames. Even as it was, I respected him. And I was very near indeed to reverence when he said he had another book coming out soon. I asked if I might ask what kind of book it was to be.

"My poems," he answered. Rothenstein asked if this was to be the title of the book. The poet meditated on this suggestion, but said he rather thought of giving the book no title at all. "If a book is good in itself—" he murmured, and waved his cigarette.

Rothenstein objected that absence of title might be bad for the sale of a book.

"If," he urged, "I went into a bookseller's and said simply, 'Have you got?' or, 'Have you a copy of?' how would they know what I wanted?"

"Oh, of course I should have my name on the cover," Soames answered earnestly. "And I rather want," he added, looking hard at Rothenstein, "to have a drawing of myself as frontispiece." Rothenstein admitted that this was a capital idea, and mentioned that he was going into the country and would be there for some time. He then looked at his watch, exclaimed at the hour, paid the waiter, and went away with me to dinner. Soames remained at his post of fidelity to the glaucous witch.

"Why were you so determined not to draw him?" I asked.

"Draw him? Him? How can one draw a man who doesn't exist?"

"He is dim," I admitted. But my mot juste fell flat. Rothenstein repeated that Soames was non-existent.

Still, Soames had written a book. I asked if Rothenstein had read "Negations." He said he had looked into it, "but," he added crisply, "I don't profess to know anything about writing." A reservation very characteristic of the period! Painters would not then allow that any one outside their own order had a right to any opinion about painting. This law (graven on the tablets brought down by Whistler from the summit of Fuji-yama) imposed certain limitations. If other arts than painting were not utterly unintelligible to all but the men who practiced them, the law tottered—the Monroe Doctrine, as it were, did not hold good. Therefore no painter would offer an opinion of a book without warning you at any rate that his opinion was worthless. No one is a better judge of literature than Rothenstein; but it wouldn't have done to tell him so in those days, and I knew that I must form an unaided judgment of "Negations."

Not to buy a book of which I had met the author face to face would have been for me in those days an impossible act of self-denial. When I returned to Oxford for the Christmas term I had duly secured "Negations." I used to keep it lying carelessly on the table in my room, and whenever a friend took it up and asked what it was about, I would say: "Oh, it's rather a remarkable book. It's by a man whom I know." Just "what it was about" I never was able to say. Head or tail was just what I hadn't made of that slim, green volume. I found in the preface no clue to the labyrinth of contents, and in that labyrinth nothing to explain the preface.

> Lean near to life. Lean very near—
> nearer.
> Life is web and therein nor warp nor
> woof is, but web only.
> It is for this I am Catholick in church and in thought, yet do let
> swift Mood weave there what the shuttle of Mood wills.

These were the opening phrases of the preface, but those which followed were less easy to understand. Then came "Stark: A Conte," about a midinette who, so far as I could gather, murdered, or was about to murder, a mannequin. It was rather like a story by Catulle Mendes in which the translator had either skipped or cut out every alternate sentence. Next, a dialogue between Pan and St. Ursula, lacking, I rather thought, in "snap." Next, some aphorisms (entitled "Aphorismata" [spelled in Greek]). Throughout, in fact, there was a great variety of form, and the forms had evidently been wrought with much care. It was rather the substance that eluded me. Was there, I wondered, any substance at all? It did not occur to me: suppose Enoch Soames was a fool! Up cropped a rival hypothesis: suppose I was! I inclined to give Soames the benefit of the doubt. I had read "L'Apres-midi d'un faune" without extracting a glimmer of meaning; yet Mallarme, of course, was a master. How was I to know that Soames wasn't another? There was a sort of music in his prose, not indeed, arresting, but perhaps, I thought, haunting, and laden, perhaps, with meanings as deep as Mallarme's own. I awaited his poems with an open mind.

And I looked forward to them with positive impatience after I had had a second meeting with him. This was on an evening in January. Going into the aforesaid domino-room, I had passed a table at which sat a pale man with an open book before him. He had looked from his book to me, and I looked back over my shoulder with a vague sense that I ought to have recognized him. I returned to pay my respects. After exchanging a few words, I said with a glance to the open book, "I see I am interrupting you," and was about to pass on, but, "I prefer," Soames replied in his toneless voice, "to be interrupted," and I obeyed his gesture that I should sit down.

I asked him if he often read here.

"Yes; things of this kind I read here," he answered, indicating the title of his book—"The Poems of Shelley."

"Anything that you really"—and I was going to say "admire?" But I cautiously left my sentence unfinished, and was glad that I had done so, for he said with unwonted emphasis, "Anything second-rate."

I had read little of Shelley, but, "Of course," I murmured, "he's very uneven."

"I should have thought evenness was just what was wrong with him. A deadly evenness. That's why I read him here. The noise of this place breaks the rhythm. He's tolerable here." Soames took up the book and glanced through the pages. He laughed. Soames's laugh was a short, single, and mirthless sound from the throat, unaccompanied by any movement of the face or brightening of the eyes. "What a period!" he uttered, laying the book down. And, "What a country!" he added.

I asked rather nervously if he didn't think Keats had more or less held his own against the drawbacks of time and place. He admitted that there were "passages in Keats," but did not specify them. Of "the older men," as he called them, he seemed to like only Milton. "Milton," he said, "wasn't sentimental." Also, "Milton had a dark insight." And again, "I can always read Milton in the reading-room."

"The reading-room?"

"Of the British Museum. I go there every day."

"You do? I've only been there once. I'm afraid I found it rather a depressing place. It—it seemed to sap one's vitality."

"It does. That's why I go there. The lower one's vitality, the more sensitive one is to great art. I live near the museum. I have rooms in Dyott Street."

"And you go round to the reading-room to read Milton?"

"Usually Milton." He looked at me. "It was Milton," he certificatively added, "who converted me to diabolism."

"Diabolism? Oh, yes? Really?" said I, with that vague discomfort and that intense desire to be polite which one feels when a man speaks of his own religion. "You—worship the devil?"

Soames shook his head.

"It's not exactly worship," he qualified, sipping his absinthe. "It's more a matter of trusting and encouraging."

"I see, yes. I had rather gathered from the preface to 'Negations' that you were a—a Catholic."

"Je l'etais a cette epoque. In fact, I still am. I am a Catholic diabolist."

But this profession he made in an almost cursory tone. I could see that what was upmost in his mind was the fact that I had read "Negations." His pale eyes had for the first time gleamed. I felt as one who is about to be examined viva voce on the very subject in which he is shakiest. I hastily asked him how soon his poems were to be published.

"Next week," he told me.

"And are they to be published without a title?"

"No. I found a title at last. But I sha'n't tell you what it is," as though I had been so impertinent as to inquire. "I am not sure that it wholly satisfies me. But it is the best I can find. It suggests something of the quality of the poems—strange growths, natural and wild, yet exquisite," he added, "and many-hued, and full of poisons."

I asked him what he thought of Baudelaire. He uttered the snort that was his laugh, and, "Baudelaire," he said, "was a bourgeois malgre lui." France had had only one poet—Villon; "and two thirds of Villon were sheer journalism." Verlaine was "an epicier malgre lui." Altogether, rather to my surprise, he rated French literature lower than English. There were "passages" in Villiers de l'Isle-Adam. But, "I," he summed up, "owe nothing to France." He nodded at me. "You'll see," he predicted.

I did not, when the time came, quite see that. I thought the author of "Fungoids" did, unconsciously of course, owe something to the young Parisian decadents or to the young English ones who owed something to THEM. I still think so. The little book, bought by me in Oxford, lies before me as I write. Its pale-gray buckram cover and silver lettering have not worn well. Nor have its contents. Through these, with a melancholy interest, I have again been looking. They are not much. But at the time of their publication I had a vague suspicion that they MIGHT be. I suppose it is my capacity for faith, not poor Soames's work, that is weaker than it once was.

TO A YOUNG WOMAN

THOU ART, WHO HAST NOT BEEN!

Pale tunes irresolute

And traceries of old sounds

Blown from a rotted flute
Mingle with noise of cymbals rouged with rust,
Nor not strange forms and epicene
Lie bleeding in the dust,

Being wounded with wounds.

For this it is
That in thy counterpart
Of age-long mockeries
THOU HAST NOT BEEN NOR ART!

There seemed to me a certain inconsistency as between the first and
last lines of this. I tried, with bent brows, to resolve the discord. But I
did not take my failure as wholly incompatible with a meaning in
Soames's mind. Might it not rather indicate the depth of his meaning?
As for the craftsmanship, "rouged with rust" seemed to me a fine
stroke, and "nor not" instead of "and" had a curious felicity. I wondered who the "young woman" was and what she had made of it all. I
sadly suspect that Soames could not have made more of it than she. Yet
even now, if one doesn't try to make any sense at all of the poem, and
reads it just for the sound, there is a certain grace of cadence. Soames
was an artist, in so far as he was anything, poor fellow!

It seemed to me, when first I read "Fungoids," that, oddly enough,
the diabolistic side of him was the best. Diabolism seemed to be a
cheerful, even a wholesome influence in his life.

NOCTURNE

Round and round the shutter'd Square
I strolled with the Devil's arm in mine.
No sound but the scrape of his hoofs was there
And the ring of his laughter and mine.
We had drunk black wine.
I scream'd, "I will race you, Master!"
"What matter," he shriek'd, "to-night
Which of us runs the faster?
There is nothing to fear to-night
In the foul moon's light!"

> Then I look'd him in the eyes
> And I laugh'd full shrill at the lie he told
> And the gnawing fear he would fain disguise.
> It was true, what I'd time and again been told:
> He was old—old.

There was, I felt, quite a swing about that first stanza—a joyous and rollicking note of comradeship. The second was slightly hysterical, perhaps. But I liked the third, it was so bracingly unorthodox, even according to the tenets of Soames's peculiar sect in the faith. Not much "trusting and encouraging" here! Soames triumphantly exposing the devil as a liar, and laughing "full shrill," cut a quite heartening figure, I thought, then! Now, in the light of what befell, none of his other poems depresses me so much as "Nocturne."

I looked out for what the metropolitan reviewers would have to say. They seemed to fall into two classes: those who had little to say and those who had nothing. The second class was the larger, and the words of the first were cold; insomuch that

"Strikes a note of modernity. . . . These tripping numbers."—*The Preston Telegraph.*

was the only lure offered in advertisements by Soames's publisher. I had hoped that when next I met the poet I could congratulate him on having made a stir, for I fancied he was not so sure of his intrinsic greatness as he seemed. I was but able to say, rather coarsely, when next I did see him, that I hoped "Fungoids" was "selling splendidly." He looked at me across his glass of absinthe and asked if I had bought a copy. His publisher had told him that three had been sold. I laughed, as at a jest.

"You don't suppose I CARE, do you?" he said, with something like a snarl. I disclaimed the notion. He added that he was not a tradesman. I said mildly that I wasn't, either, and murmured that an artist who gave truly new and great things to the world had always to wait long for recognition. He said he cared not a sou for recognition. I agreed that the act of creation was its own reward.

His moroseness might have alienated me if I had regarded myself as a nobody. But ah! hadn't both John Lane and Aubrey Beardsley suggested that I should write an essay for the great new venture that was afoot—"The Yellow Book"? And hadn't Henry Harland, as editor, accepted my essay? And wasn't it to be in the very first number? At Oxford I was still in statu pupillari. In London I regarded myself as very much indeed a graduate now—one whom no Soames could ruffle. Partly to show off, partly in sheer good-will, I told Soames he ought to contribute to "The Yellow Book." He uttered from the throat a sound of scorn for that publication.

Nevertheless, I did, a day or two later, tentatively ask Harland if he knew anything of the work of a man called Enoch Soames. Harland paused in the midst of his characteristic stride around the room, threw up his hands toward the ceiling, and groaned aloud: he had often met "that absurd creature" in Paris, and this very morning had received some poems in manuscript from him.

"Has he NO talent?" I asked.

"He has an income. He's all right." Harland was the most joyous of men and most generous of critics, and he hated to talk of anything about which he couldn't be enthusiastic. So I dropped the subject of Soames. The news that Soames had an income did take the edge off solicitude. I learned afterward that he was the son of an unsuccessful and deceased bookseller in Preston, but had inherited an annuity of three hundred pounds from a married aunt, and had no surviving relatives of any kind. Materially, then, he was "all right." But there was still a spiritual pathos about him, sharpened for me now by the possibility that even the praises of "The Preston Telegraph" might not have been forthcoming had he not been the son of a Preston man. He had a sort of weak doggedness which I could not but admire. Neither he nor his work received the slightest encouragement; but he persisted in behaving as a personage: always he kept his dingy little flag flying. Wherever congregated the jeunes feroces of the arts, in whatever Soho restaurant they had just discovered, in whatever music-hall they were most frequently, there was Soames in the midst of them, or, rather, on the fringe of them, a dim, but inevitable, figure. He never sought to propitiate his fellow-writers, never bated a jot of his arrogance about his own work or of his contempt for theirs. To the painters he was respectful, even humble; but for the poets and prosaists of "The Yellow Book" and later of "The Savoy" he had never a word but of scorn. He wasn't resented. It didn't occur to anybody that he or his Catholic diabolism mattered. When, in the autumn of '96, he brought out (at his own expense, this time) a third book, his last book, nobody said a word for or against it. I meant, but forgot, to buy it. I never saw it, and am ashamed to say I don't even remember what it was called. But I did, at the time of its publication, say to Rothenstein that I thought poor old Soames was really a rather tragic figure, and that I believed he would literally die for want of recognition. Rothenstein scoffed. He said I was trying to get credit for a kind heart which I didn't possess; and perhaps this was so. But at the private view of the New English Art Club, a few weeks later, I beheld a pastel portrait of "Enoch Soames, Esq." It was very like him, and very like Rothenstein to have done it. Soames was standing near it, in his soft hat and his waterproof cape, all through the afternoon. Anybody who knew him would have recognized the portrait at a glance, but nobody who didn't know him would have recognized the portrait from its bystander: it "existed" so much more than he; it was bound to. Also, it had not that expression of faint happiness which on that day was discernible, yes, in Soames's countenance. Fame had breathed on him. Twice again in the course of the month I went to the New English, and on both occasions Soames himself was on view there. Looking back, I regard the close of that exhibition as having been virtually the close of his career. He had felt the breath of Fame against his cheek—so late, for such a little while; and at its withdrawal he gave in, gave up, gave out. He, who had never looked strong or well, looked ghastly now—a shadow of the shade he had once been. He still frequented the domino-room, but having lost all wish to excite curiosity, he no longer read books there. "You read only at the museum now?" I asked, with attempted cheerfulness. He said he never went there now. "No absinthe there," he muttered. It was the sort of thing that in old days he would have said for effect; but it carried conviction now. Absinthe, erst but a point in the "personality" he had striven so hard to build up, was solace and necessity now. He no longer called it "la sorciere glauque." He had shed away all his French phrases. He had become a plain, unvarnished Preston man.

Failure, if it be a plain, unvarnished, complete failure, and even though it be a squalid failure, has always a certain dignity. I avoided Soames because he made me feel rather vulgar. John Lane had published, by this time, two little books of mine, and they had had a pleasant little success of esteem. I was a—slight, but definite—"personality." Frank Harris had engaged me to kick up my heels in "The Saturday Review." Alfred Harmsworth was letting me do likewise in "The Daily Mail." I was just what Soames wasn't. And he shamed my gloss. Had I known that he really and firmly believed in the greatness of what he as an artist had achieved, I might not have shunned him. No man who hasn't lost his vanity can be held to have altogether failed. Soames's dignity was an illusion of mine. One day, in the first week of June, 1897, that illusion went. But on the evening of that day Soames went, too.

I had been out most of the morning and, as it was too late to reach home in time for luncheon, I sought the Vingtieme. This little place— Restaurant du Vingtieme Siecle, to give it its full title—had been dis- covered in '96 by the poets and prosaists, but had now been more or less abandoned in favor of some later find. I don't think it lived long enough to justify its name; but at that time there it still was, in Greek Street, a few doors from Soho Square, and almost opposite to that house where, in the first years of the century, a little girl, and with her a boy named De Quincey, made nightly encampment in darkness and hunger among dust and rats and old legal parchments. The Vingtieme was but a small whitewashed room, leading out into the street at one end and into a kitchen at the other. The proprietor and cook was a Frenchman, known to us as Monsieur Vingtieme; the waiters were his two daughters, Rose and Berthe; and the food, according to faith, was good. The tables were so narrow and were set so close together that there was space for twelve of them, six jutting from each wall.

Only the two nearest to the door, as I went in, were occupied. On one side sat a tall, flashy, rather Mephistophelian man whom I had seen from time to time in the domino-room and elsewhere. On the other side sat Soames. They made a queer contrast in that sunlit room, Soames sitting haggard in that hat and cape, which nowhere at any season had I seen him doff, and this other, this keenly vital man, at sight of whom I more than ever wondered whether he were a diamond merchant, a conjurer, or the head of a private detective agency. I was sure Soames didn't want my company; but I asked, as it would have seemed brutal not to, whether I might join him, and took the chair opposite to his. He was smoking a cigarette, with an untasted salmi of something on his plate and a half-empty bottle of Sauterne before him, and he was quite silent. I said that the preparations for the Jubilee made London impossible. (I rather liked them, really.) I professed a wish to go right away till the whole thing was over. In vain did I attune myself to his gloom. He seemed not to hear me or even to see me. I felt that his behavior made me ridiculous in the eyes of the other man. The gangway between the two rows of tables at the Vingtieme was hardly more than two feet wide (Rose and Berthe, in their ministrations, had always to edge past each other, quarreling in whispers as they did so), and any one at the table abreast of yours was virtually at yours. I thought our neighbor was amused at my failure to interest Soames, and so, as I could not explain to him that my insistence was merely chari- table, I became silent. Without turning my head, I had him well within my range of vision. I hoped I looked less vulgar than he in contrast with Soames. I was sure he was not an Englishman, but what WAS his nationality? Though his jet-black hair was en brosse, I did not think he was French. To Berthe, who waited on him, he spoke French fluently, but with a hardly native idiom and accent. I gathered that this was his first visit to the Vingtieme; but Berthe was offhand in her manner to him: he had not made a good impression. His eyes were handsome, but, like the Vingtieme's tables, too narrow and set too close together. His nose was predatory, and the points of his mustache, waxed up behind his nostrils, gave a fixity to his smile. Decidedly, he was sinister. And my sense of discomfort in his presence was intensified by the scarlet waistcoat which tightly, and so unseasonably in June, sheathed his ample chest. This waistcoat wasn't wrong merely because of the heat, either. It was somehow all wrong in itself. It wouldn't have done on Christmas morning. It would have struck a jarring note at the first night of "Hernani." I was trying to account for its wrongness when Soames suddenly and strangely broke silence. "A hundred years hence!" he murmured, as in a trance.

"We shall not be here," I briskly, but fatuously, added.

"We shall not be here. No," he droned, "but the museum will still be just where it is. And the reading-room just where it is. And people will be able to go and read there." He inhaled sharply, and a spasm as of actual pain contorted his features.

I wondered what train of thought poor Soames had been following. He did not enlighten me when he said, after a long pause, "You think I haven't minded."

"Minded what, Soames?"

"Neglect. Failure."

"FAILURE?" I said heartily. "Failure?" I repeated vaguely. "Neglect—yes, perhaps; but that's quite another matter. Of course you haven't been—appreciated. But what, then? Any artist who—who gives—" What I wanted to say was, "Any artist who gives truly new and great things to the world has always to wait long for recognition"; but the flattery would not out: in the face of his misery—a misery so genuine and so unmasked—my lips would not say the words.

And then he said them for me. I flushed. "That's what you were going to say, isn't it?" he asked.

"How did you know?"

"It's what you said to me three years ago, when 'Fungoids' was published." I flushed the more. I need not have flushed at all. "It's the only important thing I ever heard you say," he continued. "And I've never forgotten it. It's a true thing. It's a horrible truth. But—d'you remember what I answered? I said, 'I don't care a sou for recognition.' And you believed me. You've gone on believing I'm above that sort of thing. You're shallow. What should YOU know of the feelings of a man like me? You imagine that a great artist's faith in himself and in the verdict of posterity is enough to keep him happy. You've never guessed at the bitterness and loneliness, the"—his voice broke; but presently he resumed, speaking with a force that I had never known in him. "Posterity! What use is it to ME? A dead man doesn't know that people are visiting his grave, visiting his birthplace, putting up tablets to him, unveiling statues of him. A dead man can't read the books that are written about him. A hundred years hence! Think of it! If I could come back to life THEN—just for a few hours—and go to the reading-room and READ! Or, better still, if I could be projected now, at this moment, into that future, into that reading-room, just for this one afternoon! I'd sell myself body and soul to the devil for that! Think of the pages and pages in the catalogue: 'Soames, Enoch' endlessly—endless editions, commentaries, prolegomena, biographies"—But here he was interrupted by a sudden loud crack of the chair at the next table. Our neighbor had half risen from his place. He was leaning toward us, apologetically intrusive.

"Excuse—permit me," he said softly. "I have been unable not to hear. Might I take a liberty? In this little restaurant-sans-facon—might I, as the phrase is, cut in?"

I could but signify our acquiescence. Berthe had appeared at the kitchen door, thinking the stranger wanted his bill. He waved her away with his cigar, and in another moment had seated himself beside me, commanding a full view of Soames.

"Though not an Englishman," he explained, "I know my London well, Mr. Soames. Your name and fame—Mr. Beerbohm's, too—very known to me. Your point is, who am I?" He glanced quickly over his shoulder, and in a lowered voice said, "I am the devil."

I couldn't help it; I laughed. I tried not to, I knew there was nothing to laugh at, my rudeness shamed me; but—I laughed with increasing volume. The devil's quiet dignity, the surprise and disgust of his raised eyebrows, did but the more dissolve me. I rocked to and fro; I lay back aching; I behaved deplorably.

"I am a gentleman, and," he said with intense emphasis, "I thought I was in the company of GENTLEMEN."

"Don't!" I gasped faintly. "Oh, don't!"

"Curious, nicht wahr?" I heard him say to Soames. "There is a type of person to whom the very mention of my name is—oh, so awfully—funny! In your theaters the dullest comedian needs only to say 'The devil!' and right away they give him 'the loud laugh what speaks the vacant mind.' Is it not so?"

I had now just breath enough to offer my apologies. He accepted them, but coldly, and re-addressed himself to Soames.

"I am a man of business," he said, "and always I would put things through 'right now,' as they say in the States. You are a poet. Les affaires—you detest them. So be it. But with me you will deal, eh? What you have said just now gives me furiously to hope."

Soames had not moved except to light a fresh cigarette. He sat crouched forward, with his elbows squared on the table, and his head just above the level of his hands, staring up at the devil.

"Go on," he nodded. I had no remnant of laughter in me now.

"It will be the more pleasant, our little deal," the devil went on, "because you are—I mistake not?—a diabolist."

"A Catholic diabolist," said Soames.

The devil accepted the reservation genially.

"You wish," he resumed, "to visit now—this afternoon as-ever-is—the reading-room of the British Museum, yes? But of a hundred years hence, yes? Parfaitement. Time—an illusion. Past and future—they are as ever present as the present, or at any rate only what you call 'just round the corner.' I switch you on to any date. I project you—pouf! You wish to be in the reading-room just as it will be on the afternoon of June 3, 1997? You wish to find yourself standing in that room, just past the swing-doors, this very minute, yes? And to stay there till closing-time? Am I right?"

Soames nodded.

The devil looked at his watch. "Ten past two," he said. "Closing-time in summer same then as now—seven o'clock. That will give you almost five hours. At seven o'clock—pouf!—you find yourself again here, sitting at this table. I am dining to-night dans le monde—dans le high life. That concludes my present visit to your great city. I come and fetch you here, Mr. Soames, on my way home."

"Home?" I echoed.

"Be it never so humble!" said the devil, lightly.

"All right," said Soames.

"Soames!" I entreated. But my friend moved not a muscle.

The devil had made as though to stretch forth his hand across the table, but he paused in his gesture.

"A hundred years hence, as now," he smiled, "no smoking allowed in the reading-room. You would better therefore—"

Soames removed the cigarette from his mouth and dropped it into his glass of Sauterne.

"Soames!" again I cried. "Can't you"—but the devil had now stretched forth his hand across the table. He brought it slowly down on the table-cloth. Soames's chair was empty. His cigarette floated sodden in his wine-glass. There was no other trace of him.

For a few moments the devil let his hand rest where it lay, gazing at me out of the corners of his eyes, vulgarly triumphant.

A shudder shook me. With an effort I controlled myself and rose from my chair. "Very clever," I said condescendingly. "But—'The Time Machine' is a delightful book, don't you think? So entirely original!"

"You are pleased to sneer," said the devil, who had also risen, "but it is one thing to write about an impossible machine; it is a quite other thing to be a supernatural power." All the same, I had scored.

Berthe had come forth at the sound of our rising. I explained to her that Mr. Soames had been called away, and that both he and I would be dining here. It was not until I was out in the open air that I began to feel giddy. I have but the haziest recollection of what I did, where I wandered, in the glaring sunshine of that endless afternoon. I remember the sound of carpenters' hammers all along Piccadilly and the bare chaotic look of the half-erected "stands." Was it in the Green Park or in Kensington Gardens or WHERE was it that I sat on a chair beneath a tree, trying to read an evening paper? There was a phrase in the leading article that went on repeating itself in my fagged mind: "Little is hidden from this August Lady full of the garnered wisdom of sixty years of Sovereignty." I remember wildly conceiving a letter (to reach Windsor by an express messenger told to await answer): "Madam: Well knowing that your Majesty is full of the garnered wisdom of sixty years of Sovereignty, I venture to ask your advice in the following delicate matter. Mr. Enoch Soames, whose poems you may or may not know—" Was there NO way of helping him, saving him? A bargain was a bargain, and I was the last man to aid or abet any one in wriggling out of a reasonable obligation. I wouldn't have lifted a little finger to save Faust. But poor Soames! Doomed to pay without respite an eternal price for nothing but a fruitless search and a bitter disillusioning.

Odd and uncanny it seemed to me that he, Soames, in the flesh, in the waterproof cape, was at this moment living in the last decade of the next century, poring over books not yet written, and seeing and seen by men not yet born. Uncannier and odder still that to-night and ever-more he would be in hell. Assuredly, truth was stranger than fiction.

Endless that afternoon was. Almost I wished I had gone with Soames, not, indeed, to stay in the reading-room, but to sally forth for a brisk sight-seeing walk around a new London. I wandered restlessly out of the park I had sat in. Vainly I tried to imagine myself an ardent tourist from the eighteenth century. Intolerable was the strain of the slow-passing and empty minutes. Long before seven o'clock I was back at the Vingtieme.

I sat there just where I had sat for luncheon. Air came in listlessly through the open door behind me. Now and again Rose or Berthe appeared for a moment. I had told them I would not order any dinner till Mr. Soames came. A hurdy-gurdy began to play, abruptly drowning the noise of a quarrel between some Frenchmen farther up the street. Whenever the tune was changed I heard the quarrel still raging. I had bought another evening paper on my way. I unfolded it. My eyes gazed ever away from it to the clock over the kitchen door.

Five minutes now to the hour! I remembered that clocks in restau-rants are kept five minutes fast. I concentrated my eyes on the paper. I vowed I would not look away from it again. I held it upright, at its full width, close to my face, so that I had no view of anything but it. Rather a tremulous sheet? Only because of the draft, I told myself.

My arms gradually became stiff; they ached; but I could not drop them—now. I had a suspicion, I had a certainty. Well, what, then? What else had I come for? Yet I held tight that barrier of newspaper. Only the sound of Berthe's brisk footstep from the kitchen enabled me, forced me, to drop it, and to utter:

"What shall we have to eat, Soames?"

"Il est souffrant, ce pauvre Monsieur Soames?" asked Berthe.

"He's only—tired." I asked her to get some wine—Burgundy—and whatever food might be ready. Soames sat crouched forward against the table exactly as when last I had seen him. It was as though he had never moved—he who had moved so unimaginably far. Once or twice in the afternoon it had for an instant occurred to me that perhaps his journey was not to be fruitless, that perhaps we had all been wrong in our esti-mate of the works of Enoch Soames. That we had been horribly right was horribly clear from the look of him. But, "Don't be discouraged,"

I falteringly said. "Perhaps it's only that you—didn't leave enough time. Two, three centuries hence, perhaps—"

"Yes," his voice came; "I've thought of that."

"And now—now for the more immediate future! Where are you going to hide? How would it be if you caught the Paris express from Charing Cross? Almost an hour to spare. Don't go on to Paris. Stop at Calais. Live in Calais. He'd never think of looking for you in Calais."

"It's like my luck," he said, "to spend my last hours on earth with an ass." But I was not offended. "And a treacherous ass," he strangely added, tossing across to me a crumpled bit of paper which he had been holding in his hand. I glanced at the writing on it—some sort of gibberish, apparently. I laid it impatiently aside.

"Come, Soames, pull yourself together! This isn't a mere matter of life or death. It's a question of eternal torment, mind you! You don't mean to say you're going to wait limply here till the devil comes to fetch you."

"I can't do anything else. I've no choice."

"Come! This is 'trusting and encouraging' with a vengeance! This is diabolism run mad!" I filled his glass with wine. "Surely, now that you've SEEN the brute—"

"It's no good abusing him."

"You must admit there's nothing Miltonic about him, Soames."

"I don't say he's not rather different from what I expected."

"He's a vulgarian, he's a swell mobs-man, he's the sort of man who hangs about the corridors of trains going to the Riviera and steals ladies' jewel-cases. Imagine eternal torment presided over by HIM!"

"You don't suppose I look forward to it, do you?"

"Then why not slip quietly out of the way?"

Again and again I filled his glass, and always, mechanically, he emptied it; but the wine kindled no spark of enterprise in him. He did not eat, and I myself ate hardly at all. I did not in my heart believe that any dash for freedom could save him. The chase would be swift, the capture certain. But better anything than this passive, meek, miserable waiting. I told Soames that for the honor of the human race he ought to make some show of resistance. He asked what the human race had ever done for him. "Besides," he said, "can't you understand that I'm in his power? You saw him touch me, didn't you? There's an end of it. I've no will. I'm sealed."

I made a gesture of despair. He went on repeating the word "sealed." I began to realize that the wine had clouded his brain. No wonder!

Foodless he had gone into futurity, foodless he still was. I urged him to
eat, at any rate, some bread. It was maddening to think that he, who
had so much to tell, might tell nothing. "How was it all," I asked,
"yonder? Come, tell me your adventures!"

"They'd make first-rate 'copy,' wouldn't they?"

"I'm awfully sorry for you, Soames, and I make all possible allow-
ances; but what earthly right have you to insinuate that I should make
'copy,' as you call it, out of you?"

The poor fellow pressed his hands to his forehead.

"I don't know," he said. "I had some reason, I know. I'll try to
remember." He sat plunged in thought.

"That's right. Try to remember everything. Eat a little more bread.
What did the reading-room look like?"

"Much as usual," he at length muttered.

"Many people there?"

"Usual sort of number."

"What did they look like?"

Soames tried to visualize them.

"They all," he presently remembered, "looked very like one another."

My mind took a fearsome leap.

"All dressed in sanitary woolen?"

"Yes, I think so. Grayish-yellowish stuff."

"A sort of uniform?" He nodded. "With a number on it perhaps—a
number on a large disk of metal strapped round the left arm? D. K. F.
78,910—that sort of thing?" It was even so. "And all of them, men
and women alike, looking very well cared for? Very Utopian, and
smelling rather strongly of carbolic, and all of them quite hairless?" I
was right every time. Soames was only not sure whether the men and
women were hairless or shorn. "I hadn't time to look at them very
closely," he explained.

"No, of course not. But—"

"They stared at ME, I can tell you. I attracted a great deal of attention." At last he had done that! "I think I rather scared them. They
moved away whenever I came near. They followed me about, at a
distance, wherever I went. The men at the round desk in the middle
seemed to have a sort of panic whenever I went to make inquiries."

"What did you do when you arrived?"

Well, he had gone straight to the catalogue, of course,—to the S
volumes,—and had stood long before SN-SOF, unable to take this
volume out of the shelf because his heart was beating so. At first, he

said, he wasn't disappointed; he only thought there was some new arrangement. He went to the middle desk and asked where the catalogue of twentieth-century books was kept. He gathered that there was still only one catalogue. Again he looked up his name, stared at the three little pasted slips he had known so well. Then he went and sat down for a long time.

"And then," he droned, "I looked up the 'Dictionary of National Biography,' and some encyclopedias. I went back to the middle desk and asked what was the best modern book on late nineteenth-century literature. They told me Mr. T. K. Nupton's book was considered the best. I looked it up in the catalogue and filled in a form for it. It was brought to me. My name wasn't in the index, but—yes!" he said with a sudden change of tone, "that's what I'd forgotten. Where's that bit of paper? Give it me back."

I, too, had forgotten that cryptic screed. I found it fallen on the floor, and handed it to him.

He smoothed it out, nodding and smiling at me disagreeably.

"I found myself glancing through Nupton's book," he resumed. "Not very easy reading. Some sort of phonetic spelling. All the modern books I saw were phonetic."

"Then I don't want to hear any more, Soames, please."

"The proper names seemed all to be spelt in the old way. But for that I mightn't have noticed my own name."

"Your own name? Really? Soames, I'm VERY glad."

"And yours."

"No!"

"I thought I should find you waiting here to-night, so I took the trouble to copy out the passage. Read it."

I snatched the paper. Soames's handwriting was characteristically dim. It and the noisome spelling and my excitement made me all the slower to grasp what T. K. Nupton was driving at.

The document lies before me at this moment. Strange that the words I here copy out for you were copied out for me by poor Soames just eighty-two years hence!

From page 234 of "Inglish Littracher 1890-1900" bi T. K. Nupton, publishd bi th Stait, 1992.

Fr egzarmpl, a riter ov th time, naimed Max Beerbohm, hoo woz stil alive in th twentith senchri, rote a stauri in wich e pautraid an immajnari karrakter kauld "Enoch Soames"—a thurd-rait poit hoo beleevz imself a grate jeneus an maix a bargin with th Devvl in auder ter no wot posterriti thinx ov im! It iz a sumwot labud sattire, but not without vallu az showing hou seriusli the yung men ov th aiteen-ninetiz took themselvz. Nou that th littreri profeshn haz bin auganized az a departmnt of publik servis, our riters hav found their levvl an hav lernt ter doo their duti without thort ov th morro."Th laibrer iz werthi ov hiz hire" an that iz aul. Thank hevvn we hav no Enoch Soameses amung us to-dai!

I found that by murmuring the words aloud (a device which I commend to my reader) I was able to master them little by little. The clearer they became, the greater was my bewilderment, my distress and horror. The whole thing was a nightmare. Afar, the great grisly background of what was in store for the poor dear art of letters; here, at the table, fixing on me a gaze that made me hot all over, the poor fellow whom—whom evidently—but no: whatever down-grade my character might take in coming years, I should never be such a brute as to—

Again I examined the screed. "Immajnari." But here Soames was, no more imaginary, alas! than I. And "labud"—what on earth was that? (To this day I have never made out that word.) "It's all very—baffling," I at length stammered.

Soames said nothing, but cruelly did not cease to look at me.

"Are you sure," I temporized, "quite sure you copied the thing out correctly?"

"Quite."

"Well, then, it's this wretched Nupton who must have made—must be going to make—some idiotic mistake. Look here Soames, you know me better than to suppose that I—After all, the name Max Beerbohm is not at all an uncommon one, and there must be several Enoch Soameses running around, or, rather, Enoch Soames is a name that might occur to any one writing a story. And I don't write stories; I'm an essayist, an observer, a recorder. I admit that it's an extraordinary coincidence. But you must see—"

"I see the whole thing," said Soames, quietly. And he added, with a touch of his old manner, but with more dignity than I had ever known in him, "Parlons d'autre chose."

I accepted that suggestion very promptly. I returned straight to the more immediate future. I spent most of the long evening in renewed appeals to Soames to come away and seek refuge somewhere. I remember saying at last that if indeed I was destined to write about him, the supposed "stauri" had better have at least a happy ending. Soames repeated those last three words in a tone of intense scorn.

"In life and in art," he said, "all that matters is an INEVITABLE ending."

"But," I urged more hopefully than I felt, "an ending that can be avoided ISN'T inevitable."

"You aren't an artist," he rasped. "And you're so hopelessly not an artist that, so far from being able to imagine a thing and make it seem true, you're going to make even a true thing seem as if you'd made it up. You're a miserable bungler. And it's like my luck."

I protested that the miserable bungler was not I, was not going to be I, but T. K. Nupton; and we had a rather heated argument, in the thick of which it suddenly seemed to me that Soames saw he was in the wrong: he had quite physically cowered. But I wondered why—and now I guessed with a cold throb just why—he stared so past me. The bringer of that "inevitable ending" filled the doorway.

I managed to turn in my chair and to say, not without a semblance of lightness, "Aha, come in!" Dread was indeed rather blunted in me by his looking so absurdly like a villain in a melodrama. The sheen of his tilted hat and of his shirt-front, the repeated twists he was giving to his mustache, and most of all the magnificence of his sneer, gave token that he was there only to be foiled.

He was at our table in a stride. "I am sorry," he sneered witheringly, "to break up your pleasant party, but—"

"You don't; you complete it," I assured him. "Mr. Soames and I want to have a little talk with you. Won't you sit? Mr. Soames got nothing, frankly nothing, by his journey this afternoon. We don't wish to say that the whole thing was a swindle, a common swindle. On the contrary, we believe you meant well. But of course the bargain, such as it was, is off."

The devil gave no verbal answer. He merely looked at Soames and pointed with rigid forefinger to the door. Soames was wretchedly rising from his chair when, with a desperate, quick gesture, I swept together two dinner-knives that were on the table, and laid their blades across each other. The devil stepped sharp back against the table behind him, averting his face and shuddering.

"You are not superstitious!" he hissed.

"Not at all," I smiled.

"Soames," he said as to an underling, but without turning his face, "put those knives straight!"

With an inhibitive gesture to my friend, "Mr. Soames," I said emphatically to the devil, "is a Catholic diabolist"; but my poor friend did the devil's bidding, not mine; and now, with his master's eyes again fixed on him, he arose, he shuffled past me. I tried to speak. It was he that spoke. "Try," was the prayer he threw back at me as the devil pushed him roughly out through the door—"TRY to make them know that I did exist!"

In another instant I, too, was through that door. I stood staring all ways, up the street, across it, down it. There was moonlight and lamplight, but there was not Soames nor that other.

Dazed, I stood there. Dazed, I turned back at length into the little room, and I suppose I paid Berthe or Rose for my dinner and luncheon and for Soames's; I hope so, for I never went to the Vingtieme again. Ever since that night I have avoided Greek Street altogether. And for years I did not set foot even in Soho Square, because on that same night it was there that I paced and loitered, long and long, with some such dull sense of hope as a man has in not straying far from the place where he has lost something. "Round and round the shutter'd Square"—that line came back to me on my lonely beat, and with it the whole stanza, ringing in my brain and bearing in on me how tragically different from the happy scene imagined by him was the poet's actual experience of that prince in whom of all princes we should put not our trust!

But strange how the mind of an essayist, be it never so stricken, roves and ranges! I remember pausing before a wide door-step and wondering if perchance it was on this very one that the young De Quincey lay ill and faint while poor Ann flew as fast as her feet would carry her to Oxford Street, the "stony-hearted stepmother" of them both, and came back bearing that "glass of port wine and spices" but for which he might, so he thought, actually have died. Was this the very door-step that the old De Quincey used to revisit in homage? I pondered Ann's fate, the cause of her sudden vanishing from the ken of her boy friend; and presently I blamed myself for letting the past override the present. Poor vanished Soames!

And for myself, too, I began to be troubled. What had I better do? Would there be a hue and cry—"Mysterious Disappearance of an Author," and all that? He had last been seen lunching and dining in my company. Hadn't I better get a hansom and drive straight to Scotland Yard? They would think I was a lunatic. After all, I reassured myself, London was a very large place, and one very dim figure might easily drop out of it unobserved, now especially, in the blinding glare of the near Jubilee. Better say nothing at all, I thought.

AND I was right. Soames's disappearance made no stir at all. He was utterly forgotten before any one, so far as I am aware, noticed that he was no longer hanging around. Now and again some poet or prosaist may have said to another, "What has become of that man Soames?" but I never heard any such question asked. As for his landlady in Dyott Street, no doubt he had paid her weekly, and what possessions he may have had in his rooms were enough to save her from fretting. The solicitor through whom he was paid his annuity may be presumed to have made inquiries, but no echo of these resounded. There was something rather ghastly to me in the general unconsciousness that Soames had existed, and more than once I caught myself wondering whether Nupton, that babe unborn, were going to be right in thinking him a figment of my brain.

In that extract from Nupton's repulsive book there is one point which perhaps puzzles you. How is it that the author, though I have here mentioned him by name and have quoted the exact words he is going to write, is not going to grasp the obvious corollary that I have invented nothing? The answer can be only this: Nupton will not have read the later passages of this memoir. Such lack of thoroughness is a serious fault in any one who undertakes to do scholar's work. And I hope these words will meet the eye of some contemporary rival to Nupton and be the undoing of Nupton.

I like to think that some time between 1992 and 1997 somebody will have looked up this memoir, and will have forced on the world his inevitable and startling conclusions. And I have reason for believing that this will be so. You realize that the reading-room into which Soames was projected by the devil was in all respects precisely as it will be on the afternoon of June 3, 1997. You realize, therefore, that on that afternoon, when it comes round, there the selfsame crowd will be, and there Soames will be, punctually, he and they doing precisely what they did before. Recall now Soames's account of the sensation he made. You may say that the mere difference of his costume was enough to make him sensational in that uniformed crowd. You wouldn't say so if you had ever seen him, and I assure you that in no period would Soames be anything but dim. The fact that people are going to stare at him and follow him around and seem afraid of him, can be explained only on the hypothesis that they will somehow have been prepared for his ghostly visitation. They will have been awfully waiting to see

whether he really would come. And when he does come the effect will
of course be—awful.

An authentic, guaranteed, proved ghost, but; only a ghost, alas! Only
that. In his first visit Soames was a creature of flesh and blood, whereas
the creatures among whom he was projected were but ghosts, I take
it—solid, palpable, vocal, but unconscious and automatic ghosts, in a
building that was itself an illusion. Next time that building and those
creatures will be real. It is of Soames that there will be but the semblance. I wish I could think him destined to revisit the world actually,
physically, consciously. I wish he had this one brief escape, this one
small treat, to look forward to. I never forget him for long. He is where
he is and forever. The more rigid moralists among you may say he has
only himself to blame. For my part, I think he has been very hardly
used. It is well that vanity should be chastened; and Enoch Soames's
vanity was, I admit, above the average, and called for special treatment.
But there was no need for vindictiveness. You say he contracted to pay
the price he is paying. Yes; but I maintain that he was induced to do
so by fraud. Well informed in all things, the devil must have known
that my friend would gain nothing by his visit to futurity. The whole
thing was a very shabby trick. The more I think of it, the more detest-
able the devil seems to me.

Of him I have caught sight several times, here and there, since that
day at the Vingtieme. Only once, however, have I seen him at close
quarters. This was a couple of years ago, in Paris. I was walking one
afternoon along the rue d'Antin, and I saw him advancing from the
opposite direction, overdressed as ever, and swinging an ebony cane
and altogether behaving as though the whole pavement belonged to
him. At thought of Enoch Soames and the myriads of other sufferers
eternally in this brute's dominion, a great cold wrath filled me, and I
drew myself up to my full height. But—well, one is so used to nodding
and smiling in the street to anybody whom one knows that the action
becomes almost independent of oneself; to prevent it requires a very
sharp effort and great presence of mind. I was miserably aware, as I
passed the devil, that I nodded and smiled to him. And my shame was
the deeper and hotter because he, if you please, stared straight at me
with the utmost haughtiness.

To be cut, deliberately cut, by HIM! I was, I still am, furious at having had that happen to me.

THE GHOUL

Sir Hugh Clifford
(1866–1941)

History records Sir Hugh Clifford as a colonial officer and governor first and as a writer second. Clifford, the descendant of British nobility, defied family expectations and did not follow his father into the British Army, choosing instead in 1883 to join the British civil service in what was then called the Protected Malay States. For the next twenty years Clifford worked as a district administrator, then resident, then governor, learning the language, familiarizing himself with the many peoples and cultures of the Malay peninsula, and spending long periods in remote parts of the country.

It was this experience which formed the basis for the essays, eighty stories, and four novels he published; Malay culture and society, legends, and characters were the subjects that he made his own in the 1910s, as Edgar Wallace (in his "Sanders" stories) and L. Patrick Greene (in his "The Major" stories) were doing during this decade with Africa. Clifford wrote with an intimate knowledge and personal conviction in his stories and reminiscences, which show a surprising amount of sympathy for the Malays and an even more surprising doubt about the rightness of the British imperial mission. That Clifford usually wrote in a realistic vein, rather than in a supernatural one, as he does here in "The Ghoul," stands as the genre's loss.

WE HAD BEEN sitting late upon the veranda of my bungalow at Kuâla Lîpis, which, from the top of a low hill covered with coarse grass, over-looked the long, narrow reach formed by the combined waters of the Lîpis and the Jelai. The moon had risen some hours earlier, and the river ran white between the black masses of forest, which seemed to shut it in on all sides, giving to it the appearance of an isolated tarn. The roughly cleared compound, with the tennis ground which had never got beyond the stage of being dug over and weeded, and the rank growths beyond the bamboo fence, were flooded by the soft light, every tattered detail of their ugliness standing revealed as relentlessly as though it were noon. The night was very still, but the heavy, scented air was cool after the fierce heat of the day.

I had been holding forth to the handful of men who had been dining with me on the subject of Malay superstitions, while they manfully stifled their yawns. When a man has a working knowledge of anything which is not commonly known to his neighbours, he is apt to presuppose their

149

interest in it when a chance to descant upon it occurs, and in those days it was only at long intervals that I had an opportunity of forgathering with other white men. Therefore, I had made the most of it, and looking back, I fear that I had occupied the rostrum during the greater part of that evening. I had told my audience of the *penanggal*—the "Undone One"—that horrible wraith of a woman who has died in childbirth, who comes to torment and prey upon small children in the guise of a ghastly face and bust, with a comet's tail of blood-stained entrails flying in her wake; of the *mâti-ânak*, the weird little white animal which makes beast noises round the graves of children, and is supposed to have absorbed their souls; and of the *pôlong*, or familiar spirits, which men bind to their service by raising them up from the corpses of babies that have been stillborn, the tips of whose tongues they bite off and swallow after the infant has been brought to life by magic agencies. It was at this point that young Middleton began to pluck up his ears; and I, finding that one of my hearers was at last showing signs of being interested, launched out with renewed vigour, until my sorely tried companions, one by one, went off to bed, each to his own quarters.

Middleton was staying with me at the time, and he and I sat for a while in silence, after the others had gone, looking at the moonlight on the river. Middleton was the first to speak.

"That was a curious myth you were telling us about the *pôlong*," he said. "There is an incident connected with it which I have never spoken of before, and have always sworn that I would keep to myself; but I have a good mind to tell you about it, because you are the only man I know who will not write me down a liar if I do."

"That's all right. Fire away," I said.

"Well," said Middleton. "It was like this. You remember Juggins, of course? He was a naturalist, you know, dead nuts upon becoming an F.R.S. and all that sort of thing, and he came to stay with me during the close season[1] last year. He was hunting for bugs and orchids and things, and spoke of himself as an anthropologist and a botanist and a zoölogist and Heaven knows what besides; and he used to fill his bedroom with all sorts of creeping, crawling things, kept in very indifferent custody, and my veranda with all kinds of trash and rotting green trade that he brought in from the jungle. He stopped with me for about ten

---

1. "Close season," *i.e.* from the beginning of November to the end of February, during which time the rivers on the eastern seaboard of the Malay Peninsula used to be closed to traffic on account of the North East Monsoon.

days, and when he heard that duty was taking me upriver into the Sâkai country, he asked me to let him come, too. I was rather bored, for the tribesmen are mighty shy of strangers and were only just getting used to me; but he was awfully keen, and a decent beggar enough, in spite of his dirty ways, so I couldn't very well say 'No.' When we had poled upstream for about a week, and had got well up into the Sâkai country, we had to leave our boats behind at the foot of the big rapids, and leg it for the rest of the time. It was very rough going, wading up and down streams when one wasn't clambering up a hillside or sliding down the opposite slope—you know the sort of thing—and the leeches were worse than I have ever seen them—thousands of them, swarming up your back, and fastening in clusters on to your neck, even when you had defeated those which made a frontal attack. I had not enough men with me to do more than hump the camp-kit and a few clothes, so we had to live on the country, which doesn't yield much up among the Sâkai except yams and tapioca roots and a little Indian corn, and soft stuff of that sort. It was all new to Juggins, and gave him fits; but he stuck to it like a man.

"Well, one evening when the night was shutting down pretty fast and rain was beginning to fall, Juggins and I struck a fairly large Sâkai camp in the middle of a clearing. As soon as we came out of the jungle, and began tightroping along the felled timber, the Sâkai sighted us and bolted for cover *en masse*. By the time we reached the huts it was pelting in earnest, and as my men were pretty well fagged out, I decided to spend the night in the camp, and not to make them put up temporary shelters for us. Sâkai huts are uncleanly places at best, and any port has to do in a storm.

"We went into the largest of the hovels, and there we found a woman lying by the side of her dead child. She had apparently felt too sick to bolt with the rest of her tribe. The kid was as stiff as Herod, and had not been born many hours, I should say. The mother seemed pretty bad, and I went to her, thinking I might be able to do something for her; but she did not seem to see it, and bit and snarled at me like a wounded animal, clutching at the dead child the while, as though she feared I should take it from her. I therefore left her alone; and Juggins and I took up our quarters in a smaller hut nearby, which was fairly new and not so filthy dirty as most Sâkai lairs.

"Presently, when the beggars who had run away found out that I was the intruder, they began to come back again. You know their way. First a couple of men came and peeped at us, and vanished as soon as they saw they were observed. Then they came a trifle nearer, bobbed up suddenly, and peeped at us again. I called to them in Se-noi,[2] which always reassures them, and when they at last summoned up courage to approach, gave them each a handful of tobacco. Then they went back into the jungle and fetched the others, and very soon the place was crawling with Sâkai of both sexes and all ages.

"We got a meal of sorts, and settled down for the night as best we could; but it wasn't a restful business. Juggins swore with eloquence at the uneven flooring, made of very roughly trimmed boughs, which is an infernally uncomfortable thing to lie down upon, and makes one's bones ache as though they were coming out at the joints, and the Sâkai are abominably restless bedfellows as you know. I suppose one ought to realize that they have as yet only partially emerged from the animal, and that, like the beasts, they are still naturally nocturnal. Anyway, they never sleep for long at a stretch, though from time to time they snuggle down and snore among the piles of warm wood ashes round the central fireplace, and whenever you wake, you will always see half a dozen of them squatting near the blazing logs, half hidden by the smoke, and jabbering like monkeys. It is a marvel to me what they find to yarn about: food, or rather the patent impossibility of ever getting enough to eat, and the stony-heartedness of Providence and of the neighbouring Malays must furnish the principal topics, I should fancy, with an occasional respectful mention of beasts of prey and forest demons. That night they were more than ordinarily restless. The dead baby was enough to make them uneasy, and besides, they had got wet while hiding in the jungle after our arrival, and that always sets the skin disease, with which all Sâkai are smothered, itching like mad. Whenever I woke I could hear their nails going on their dirty hides; but I had had a hard day and was used to my hosts' little ways, so I contrived to sleep fairly sound. Juggins told me next morning that he had had *une nuit blanche*, and he nearly caused another stampede among the Sâkai by trying to get a specimen of the fungus or bacillus, or whatever it is, that occasions the skin disease. I do not know whether he succeeded. For my own part, I think it is probably due to chronic anæmia—the poor devils have never had more than a very occasional full meal for

---

2. *Se-noi*—one of the two main branches, into which the Sâkai are divided. The other is called *Tê-mi-au* by the *Se-noi*. All the Sâkai dialects are variants of the languages spoken by these two principal tribes, which, though they have many words in common, differ from one another almost as much as, say, Italian from Spanish.

hundreds of generations. I have seen little brats, hardly able to stand, white with it, the skin peeling off in flakes, and I used to frighten Juggins out of his senses by telling him he had contracted it when his nose was flayed by the sun.

"Next morning I woke just in time to see the stillborn baby put into a hole in the ground. They fitted its body into a piece of bark, and stuck it in the grave they had dug for it at the edge of the clearing. They buried a flint and steel and a woodknife and some food, and a few other things with it, though no living baby could have had any use for most of them, let alone a dead one. Then the old medicine man of the tribe recited the ritual over the grave. I took the trouble to translate it once. It goes something like this:

"'O Thou, who hast gone forth from among those who dwell upon the surface of the earth, and hast taken for thy dwelling-place the land which is beneath the earth, flint and steel have we given thee to kindle thy fire, raiment to clothe thy nakedness, food to fill thy belly, and a woodknife to clear thy path. Go, then, and make unto thyself friends among those who dwell beneath the earth, and come back no more to trouble or molest those who dwell upon the surface of the earth.'

"It was short and to the point; and then they trampled down the soil, while the mother, who had got upon her feet by now, whimpered about the place like a cat that had lost its kittens. A mangy, half-starved dog came and smelt hungrily about the grave, until it was sent howling away by kicks from every human animal that could reach it; and a poor little brat, who chanced to set up a piping song a few minutes later, was kicked and cuffed and knocked about by all who could conveniently get at him with foot, hand, or missile. Abstinence from song and dance for a period of nine days is the Sâkai way of mourning the dead, and any breach of this is held to give great offence to the spirit of the departed and to bring bad luck upon the tribe. It was considered necessary, therefore, to give the urchin who had done the wrong a fairly bad time of it in order to propitiate the implacable dead baby.

"Next the Sâkai set to work to pack all their household goods—not a very laborious business; and in about a half an hour the last of the laden women, who was carrying so many cooking-pots, and babies and rattan bags and carved bamboo-boxes and things, that she looked like the outside of a gipsy's cart at home, had filed out of the clearing and disappeared in the forest. The Sâkai always shift camp, like that, when a death occurs, because they think the ghost of the dead haunts the place where the body died. When an epidemic breaks out among them they are so busy changing quarters, building new hunts, and planting fresh catch crops that they have no time to procure proper food, and half those who are not used up by the disease die of semi-starvation. They are a queer lot.

"Well, Juggins and I were left alone, but my men needed a rest, so I decided to trek no farther that day, and Juggins and I spent our time trying to get a shot at a *sélâdang*,[3] but though we came upon great ploughed-up runs, which the herds had made going down to water, we saw neither hoof nor horn, and returned at night to the deserted Sâkai camp, two of my Malays fairly staggering under the piles of rubbish which Juggins called his botanical specimens. The men we had left behind had contrived to catch some fish, and with that and yams we got a pretty decent meal, and I was lying on my mat reading by the aid of a *dâmar* torch, and thinking how lucky it was that the Sâkai had cleared out, when suddenly old Juggins sat up, with his eyes fairly snapping at me through his gig-lamps in his excitement.

"'I say,' he said, 'I must have that baby. It would make a unique and invaluable ethnological specimen.'

"'Rot,' I said. 'Go to sleep, old man. I want to read.'

"'No, but I'm serious,' said Juggins. 'You do not realize the unprecedented character of the opportunity. The Sâkai have gone away, so their susceptibilities would not be outraged. The potential gain to science is immense—simply immense. It would be criminal to neglect such a chance. I regard the thing in the light of a duty which I owe to human knowledge. I tell you straight, I mean to have that baby whether you like it or not, and that is flat.'

"Juggins was forever talking about human knowledge, as though he and it were partners in a business firm.

"'It is not only the Sâkai one has to consider,' I said, 'My Malays are sensitive about body snatching, too. One has to think about the effect upon them.'

"'I can't help that,' said Juggins resolutely. 'I am going out to dig it up now.'

"He had already put his boots on, and was sorting out his botanical tools in search of a trowel. I saw that there was no holding him.

"'Juggins,' I said sharply. 'Sit down. You are a lunatic, of course, but I was another when I allowed you to come up here with me, knowing

---

3. *Sêlâdang.* The gaur or wild buffalo. It is the same as the Indian variety, but in the Malay Peninsula attains to a greater size than in any other part of Asia.

as I did that you are the particular species of crank you are. However, I've done you as well as circumstances permitted, and as a mere matter of gratitude and decency, I think you might do what I wish.'

"'I am sorry,' said Juggins stiffly. 'I am extremely sorry not to be able to oblige you. My duty as a man of science, however, compels me to avail myself of this god-sent opportunity of enlarging our ethnological knowledge of a little-known people.'

"'I thought you did not believe in God,' I said sourly; for Juggins added a militant agnosticism to his other attractive qualities.

"'I believe in my duty to human knowledge,' he replied sententiously. 'And if you will not help me to perform it, I must discharge it unaided.'

"He had found his trowel, and again rose to his feet.

"'Don't be an ass, Juggins,' I said. 'Listen to me. I have forgotten more about the people and the country here than you will ever learn if you go and dig up that dead baby, and if my Malays see you, there will be the devil to pay. They do not hold with exhumed corpses, and have no liking for or sympathy with people who go fooling about with such things. They have not yet been educated up to the pitch of interest in the secrets of science which has made of you a potential criminal, and if they could understand our talk, they would be convinced that you need the kid's body for some devilry or witchcraft business, and ten to one they would clear out and leave us in the lurch. Then who would carry your precious botanical specimens back to the boats for you, and just think how the loss of them would knock the bottom out of human knowledge for good and all.'

"'The skeleton of the child is more valuable still,' replied Juggins. 'It is well that you should understand that in this matter—which for me is a question of my duty—I am not to be moved from my purpose either by arguments or threats.'

"He was obstinate as a mule, and I was pretty sick with him; but I saw that if I left him to himself he would do the thing so clumsily that my fellows would get wind of it, and if that happened I was afraid that they might desert us. The tracks in that Sâkai country are abominably confusing, and quite apart from the fear of losing all our camp-kit, which we could not hump for ourselves, I was by no means certain that I could find my own way back to civilization unaided. Making a virtue of necessity, therefore, I decided that I would let Juggins have his beastly specimen, provided that he would consent to be guided entirely by me in all details connected with the exhumation.

"'You are a rotter of the first water,' I said frankly. 'And if I ever get you back to my station, I'll have nothing more to do with you as long as I live. All the same, I am to blame for having brought you up here, and I suppose I must see you through.'

"'You're a brick,' said Juggins quite unmoved by my insults. 'Come on.'

"'Wait,' I replied repressively. 'This thing cannot be done until my people are all asleep. Lie down on your mat and keep quiet. When it is safe, I'll give you the word.'

"Juggins groaned, and tried to persuade me to let him go at once; but I swore that nothing would induce me to move before midnight, and with that I rolled over to my side and lay reading and smoking, while Juggins fumed and fretted as he watched the slow hands of his watch creeping round the dial.

"I always take books with me into the jungle, and the more completely incongruous they are to my immediate surroundings the more refreshing I find them. That evening, I remember, I happened to be reading Miss Florence Montgomery's 'Misunderstood' with the tears running down my nose; and by the time my Malays were all asleep, this incidental wallowing in sentimentality had made me more sick with Juggins and his disgusting project than ever.

"I never felt so like a criminal as I did that night, as Juggins and I gingerly picked our way out of the hut across the prostrate forms of my sleeping Malays; nor had I realized before what a difficult job it is to walk without noise on an openwork flooring of uneven boughs. We got out of the place and down the crazy stair-ladder at last, without waking any of my fellows, and we then began to creep along the edge of the jungle that hedged the clearing about. Why did we think it necessary to creep? I don't know. Partly we did not want to be seen by the Malays, if any of them happened to walk; but besides that, the long wait and the uncanny sort of work we were after had set our nerves going a bit, I expect.

"The night was as still as most nights are in real, *pukka* jungle. That is to say, that it was as full of noises—little, quiet, half-heard beast and tree noises—as an egg is full of meat; and every occasional louder sound made me jump almost out of my skin. There was not a breath astir in the clearing, but miles up above our heads the clouds were racing across the moon, which looked as though it were scudding through them in the opposite direction at a tremendous rate, like a great white fire balloon. It was pitch dark along the edge of the clearing, for the jungle threw a heavy shadow; and Juggins kept knocking those great clumsy feet of his against the stumps, and swearing softly under his breath.

"Just as we were getting near the child's grave the clouds obscuring the moon became a trifle thinner, and the slightly increased light showed me something that caused me to clutch Juggins by the arm.

"'Hold hard!' I whispered, squatting down instinctively in the shadow, and dragging him after me. 'What's that on the grave?'

"Juggins hauled out his six-shooter with a tug, and looking at his face, I saw that he was as pale as death and more than a little shaky. He was pressing up against me, too, as he squatted, a bit closer, I fancied, than he would have thought necessary at any other time, and it seemed to me that he was trembling. I whispered to him, telling him not to shoot; and we sat there for nearly a minute, I should think, peering through the uncertain light, and trying to make out what the creature might be which was crouching above the grave and making a strange scratching noise.

"Then the moon came out suddenly into a patch of open sky, and we could see clearly at last, and what it revealed did not make me, for one, feel any better. The thing we had been looking at was kneeling on the grave, facing us. It, or rather she, was an old, old Sâkai hag. She was stark naked, and in the brilliant light of the moon I could see her long, pendulous breasts swaying about like an ox's dewlap, and the creases and wrinkles with which her withered hide was criss-crossed, and the discolored patches of foul skin disease. Her hair hung about her face in great matted locks, falling forward as she bent above the grave, and her eyes glinted through the tangle like those of some unclean and shaggy animal. Her long fingers, which had nails like claws, were tearing at the dirt of the grave, and her body was drenched with sweat, so that it glistened in the moonlight.

"'It looks as though some one else wanted your precious baby for a specimen, Juggins,' I whispered; and a spirit of emulation set him floundering on to his feet, till I pulled him back. 'Keep still, man,' I added. 'Let us see what the old hag is up to. It isn't the brat's mother, is it?'

"'No,' panted Juggins. 'This is a much older woman. Great God! What a ghoul it is!'

"Then we were silent again. Where we squatted we were hidden from the hag by a few tufts of rank *lâlang* grass, and the shadow of the jungle also covered us. Even if we had been in the open, however, I question whether the old woman would have seen us, she was so eagerly intent upon her work. For full five minutes, as near as I can guess, we squatted there watching her scrape and tear and scratch at the earth of the grave, with a sort of frenzy of energy; and all the while her lips kept going like a shivering man's teeth, though no sound that I could hear came from them.

"At length she got down to the corpse, and I saw her lift the bark wrapper out of the grave, and draw the baby's body from it. Then she sat back upon her heels, threw up her head, just like a dog, and bayed at the moon. She did this three times, and I do not know what there was about those long-drawn howls that jangled up one's nerves, but each time the sound became more insistent and intolerable, and as I listened, my hair fairly lifted. Then, very carefully, she laid the child's body down in a position that seemed to have some connection with the points of the compass, for she took a long time, and consulted the moon and the shadows repeatedly before she was satisfied with the orientation of the thing's head and feet.

"Then she got up, and began very slowly to dance round and round the grave. It was not a reassuring sight, out there in the awful loneliness of the night, miles away from every one and everything, to watch that abominable old beldam capering uncleanly in the moonlight, while those restless lips of hers called noiselessly upon all the devils in hell, with words that we could not hear. Juggins pressed up against me harder than ever, and his hand on my arm gripped tighter and tighter. He was shaking like a leaf, and I do not fancy that I was much steadier. It does not sound very terrible, as I tell it to you here in comparatively civilized surroundings; but at the time, the sight of that obscure figure dancing silently in the moonlight with its ungainly shadow scared me badly.

"She capered like that for some minutes, setting to the dead baby as though she were inviting it to join her, and the intent purposefulness of her made me feel sick. If anybody had told me that morning that I was capable of being frightened out of my wits by an old woman, I should have laughed; but I saw nothing outlandish in the idea while that grotesque dancing lasted.

"Her movements, which had been very slow at first, became gradually faster and faster, till every atom of her was in violent motion, and her body and limbs were swaying this way and that, like the boughs of a tree in a tornado. Then, all of a sudden, she collapsed on the ground, with her back toward us, and seized the baby's body. She seemed to nurse it, as a mother might nurse her child; and as she swayed from side to side, I could see first the curve of the creature's head, resting on her thin left arm, and then its feet near the crook of her right elbow. And now she was crooning to it in a cracked falsetto chant that might have been a lullaby or perhaps some incantation.

"She rocked the child slowly at first, but very rapidly the pace quickened, until her body was swaying to and fro from the hips, and from side to side, at such a rate that, to me, she looked as though she were falling all ways at once. And simultaneously her shrill chanting became faster and faster, and every instant more nerve-sawing.

"Next she suddenly changed the motion. She gripped the thing she was nursing by its arms, and began to dance it up and down, still moving with incredible agility, and crooning more damnably than ever. I could see the small, puckered face of the thing above her head every time she danced it up, and then, as she brought it down again, I lost sight of it for a second, until she danced it up once more. I kept my eyes fixed upon the thing's face every time it came into view, and I swear it was not an optical illusion—*it began to be alive*. Its eyes were open and moving, and its mouth was working, like that of a child which tries to laugh but is too young to do it properly. Its face ceased to be like that of a new-born baby at all. It was distorted by a horrible animation. It was the most unearthly sight.

"Juggins saw it, too, for I could hear him drawing his breath harder and shorter than a healthy man should.

"Then, all in a moment, the hag did something. I did not see clearly precisely what it was; but it looked to me as though she bent forward and kissed it; and at that very instant a cry went up like the wail of a lost soul. It may have been something in the jungle, but I know my Malayan forests pretty thoroughly, and I have never heard any cry like it before nor since. The next thing we knew was that the old hag had thrown the body back into the grave, and was dumping down the earth and jumping on it, while that strange cry grew fainter and fainter. It all happened so quickly that I had not had time to think or move before I was startled back into full consciousness by the sharp crack of Juggins's revolver fired close to my ear.

"'She's burying it alive!' he cried.

"It was a queer thing for a man to say, who had seen the child lying stark and dead more than thirty hours earlier; but the same thought was in my mind, too, as we both started forward at a run. The hag had vanished into the jungle as silently as a shadow. Juggins had missed her, of course. He was always a rotten bad shot. However, we had no thought for her. We just flung ourselves upon the grave, and dug at the earth with our hands, until the baby lay in my arms. It was cold and stiff, and putrefaction had already begun its work. I forced open its mouth, and saw something that I had expected. The tip of its tongue was missing. It looked as though it had been bitten off by a set of shocking bad teeth, for the edge left behind was like a saw.

"'The thing's quite dead,' I said to Juggins.

"'But it cried—it cried!' whimpered Juggins. 'I can hear it now. To think that we let that horrible creature murder it.'

"He sat down with his head in his hands. He was utterly unmanned.

"Now that the fright was over, I was beginning to be quite brave again. It is a way I have.

"'Rot,' I said. 'The thing's been dead for hours, and anyway, here's your precious specimen if you want it.'

"I had put it down, and now pointed at it from a distance. Its proximity was not pleasant. Juggins, however, only shuddered.

"'Bury it, in Heaven's name,' he said, his voice broken by sobs. 'I would not have it for the world. Besides, it *was* alive. I saw and heard it.'

"Well, I put it back in its grave, and next day we left the Sâkai country. Juggins had a whacking dose of fever, and anyway we had had about enough of the Sâkai and of all their engaging habits to last us for a bit.

"We swore one another to secrecy as Juggins, when he got his nerve back, said that the accuracy of our observations was not susceptible of scientific proof, which, I understand, was the rock his religion had gone to pieces on; and I did not fancy being told that I was drunk or that I was lying. You, however, know something of the uncanny things of the East, so to-night I have broken our vow. Now I'm going to turn in. Don't give me away."

Young Middleton died of fever and dysentery, somewhere upcountry, a year or two later. His name was not Middleton, of course; so I am not really "giving him away," as he called it, even now. As for his companion, though when I last heard of him he was still alive and a shining light in the scientific world, I have named him Juggins, and as the family is a large one, he will run no great risk of being identified.

POWERS OF THE AIR

J. D. Beresford
(1873–1947)

Beresford never quite achieved the reputation he deserved, and today is remembered primarily for two early works of science fiction, The Hampdenshire Wonder *(1911), about a superhuman child born a generation or two too early, and* Goslings *(1913), a catastrophe novel in which a plague takes nearly all of England's men but none of its women. The* Hampdenshire Wonder *interestingly anticipates later supermen novels like Philip Wylie's* Gladiator *(1930) and Olaf Stapledon's* Odd John *(1935) while being stylistically superior to either, while* Goslings *is one of the first male-written utopias to try to depict an all-female society in a sober and sympathetic fashion.*

But Beresford wrote considerably more than just those two novels. Born to a clergyman and crippled as a child by polio, Beresford began writing in his thirties and quickly produced an array of novels, short stories, criticism (particularly of his mentor, H.G. Wells), and biographies. In middle age his interest in science fiction and horror was replaced by an interest in religious and spiritual topics, and his work took on increasingly religious overtones and themes, though the fantastic element was rarely missing from them.

An unusual work of horror for Beresford, whose primary genres were scientific romance and religious fantasy, "Powers of the Air," which originally appeared in the magazine Seven Arts *(October, 1917), inverts the common trope of the wise scholar and the ignorant peasant to striking effect.*

I FORESAW THE danger that threatened him. He was so ignorant, and his sight had been almost destroyed in the city streets. A trustful ignorance is the beginning of wisdom, but these townspeople are conceited with their foolish book-learning; and reading darkens the eyes of the mind.

I began to warn him in early October when the gales roar far up in the sky. They are harmless then; they tear at the ricks and the slate roofs, and waste themselves in stripping the trees; but we are safe until the darkness comes.

I took him to the crown of the stubble land, and turned him with his back to the dark thread of the sea. I pointed to the rooks tumbling about the sky like scattered leaves that sported in a mounting wind.

"We are past the turn," I said. "The black time is coming."

He stood thoughtlessly watching the ecstatic rooks. "Is it some game they play?" he asked.

161

I shook my head. "They belong to the darkness," I told him.

He looked at me in that slightly forbearing way of his, and said, "Another of your superstitions?"

I was silent for a moment. I stared down at the texture of black fields ploughed for winter wheat, and thought of all the writing that lay before us under that wild October hill, all the clear signs that he could never be taught to read.

"Knowledge," I said. I was afraid for him, and I wished to save him. He had been penned in that little world of the town like a caged gull. He had been blinded by staring at the boards of his coop.

He smiled condescendingly. "You are charmingly primitive still," he said. "Do you worship the sun in secret, and make propitiatory offerings to the thunder?"

I sighed, knowing that if I would save him I must try to reach his mind by the ear, by the dull and clumsy means of language. That is the fetish of these townspeople. They have no wisdom, only a little recognition of those things that can be described in printed or spoken words. And I dreaded the effort of struggling with the infirmity of this obstinate blind youth.

"I came out here to warn you," I began.

"Against what?" he asked.

"The forces that have power in the black time," I said. "Even now they are beginning to gather strength. In a month it will not be safe for you to go out on the cliffs after sunset. You may not believe me, but won't you accept my warning in good faith?"

He patronized me with his smile. "What are these forces?" he asked.

That is the manner of these book-folk. They ask always for names. If they can but label a thing in a word or in a volume of description they are satisfied that they have achieved knowledge. They bandy these names of theirs as a talisman.

"Who knows?" I replied. "We have learnt their power. Call them what you will, you cannot change them by any baptism."

"Well, what do they do?" he said, still tolerant. "Have you ever seen them?" he added, as if he would trick me.

I had, but how could I describe them to him? Can one explain the colors of autumn to a man born blind? Or is there any language which will set out the play of a breaker among the rocks? How then could I talk to him of that which I had known only in the fear of my soul?

"Have you ever seen the wind?" I said.

He laughed. "Well, then, tell me your evidence," he replied.

I searched my mind for something that he might regard as evidence. "Men," I said, "used to believe that the little birds, the finches and the tits, rushed blindly at the lanterns of the light-houses, and dashed themselves to death as a moth will dash itself into the candle. But now they know that the birds only seek a refuge near the light, and that they will rest till dawn on the perches that are built for them."

"Quite true," he agreed. "And what then?"

"The little birds are prey to the powers of the air when the darkness comes," I said; "and their only chance of life is to come within the beam of the protecting light. And when they could find no place to rest, they hovered and fluttered until they were weak with the ache of flight, and fell a little into the darkness; then in panic and despair they fled back and overshot their mark."

"But gulls . . ." he began.

"A few," I interrupted him. "A few, although they also belong to the wild and the darkness. They fall in chasing the little birds who, like us, are a quarry."

"A pretty fable," he said; but I saw that the shadow of a doubt had fallen across him, and when he asked me another question I would not reply . . .

I took him to the door at ten o'clock that night and made him listen to the revels in the upper air. Below it was almost still and very dark, for the moon was near the new, and the clouds were traveling North in diligent masses that would presently bring rain.

"Do you hear them?" I asked.

He shivered slightly, and pretended that the air was cold . . .

As the nights drew in, I began to hope that he had taken my warning to heart. He did not speak of it, but he took his walks while the sun edged across its brief arc of the sky.

I took comfort in the thought that some dim sense of vision was still left to him; and one afternoon when the black time was almost come, I walked with him on the cliffs. I meant then to test him; to discover if, indeed, some feeble remnant of sight was yet his.

The wind had hidden itself that day, but I knew that it lurked in the grey depths that hung on the sea's horizon. Its outrunners streaked the falling blue of the sky with driven spirits of white cloud; and the long swell of the rising sea cried out with fear as it fled, breaking, to its death.

I said no word to him, then, of the coming peril. We walked to the cliff's edge and watched the thousand runnels of foam that laced the blackness of Trescore rock with milk-white threads, as those driven rollers cast themselves against the land and burst moon-high in their last despair.

We saw the darkness creeping toward us out of the far distance, and then we turned from the sea and I saw how the coming shadow was already quenching the hills. All the earth was hardening itself to await the night.

"God! What a lonely place!" he said.

It seemed lonely to him, but I saw the little creeping movements among the black roots of the furze. To me the place seemed over-populous. Nevertheless I took it as a good sign that he had found a sense of loneliness; it is a sense that often precedes the coming of knowledge . . .

And when the darkness of winter had come I thought he was safe. He was always back in the house by sunset and he went little to the cliffs. But now and again he would look at me with something of defiance in his face, as if he braced himself to meet an argument.

I gave him no encouragement to speak. I believed that no knowledge could come to him by that way, that no words of mind could help him. And I was right. But he forced speech upon me. He faced me one afternoon in the depths of the black time. He was stiffened to oppose me.

"It's absurd," he said, "to pretend a kind of superior wisdom. If you can't give me some reason for this superstition of yours I must go out and test it myself."

I knew my own feebleness, and I tried to prevaricate by saying: "I gave you reasons."

"They will all bear at least two explanations," he said.

"At least wait," I pleaded. "You are so young."

He was a little softened by my weakness but he was resolute. He meant to teach me, to prove that he was right. He lifted his head proudly and smiled.

"Youth is the age of courage and experiment," he boasted.

"Of recklessness and curiosity," was my amendment.

"I am going," he said.

"You will never come back," I warned him.

"But if I do come back," he said, "will you admit that I am right?"

I would not accept so foolish a challenge. "Some escape," I said.

"I will go every night until you are convinced," he returned. "Before the winter is over, you shall come with me. I will cure you of your fear."

I was angry then; and I turned my back upon him. I heard him go out and made no effort to hinder him. I sat and brooded and consoled myself with the thought that he would surely return at dusk.

I waited until sunset and he had not come back.

I went to the window and saw that a dying yellow still shone feebly in the west; and I watched it as I have watched the last flicker of a lantern when a friend makes his way home across the hill.

Already the horrified clouds were leaping up in terror from the edge of the sea, coming with outflung arms that sprawled across the hollow sky.

I went into the hall and found my hat; and I stood there in the twilight listening for the sound of a footstep. I could not believe that he would stay on the cliff after the darkness had come. I hesitated and listened while the shadows crept together in the corners of the hall.

He had taunted me with my cowardice and I knew I must go and seek him. But before I opened the door I waited again and strained my ears so eagerly for the click and shriek of the gate that I created the sound in my own mind. And yet, as I heard it, I knew it for a phantasm.

At last I went out suddenly and fiercely.

A gust of wind shook me before I had reached the gate, and the air was full of intimidating sound. I heard the cry of the driven clouds, and the awful shout of the pursuers mingled with the drumming and thudding of the endless companies that hurried across the width of heaven.

I dared not look up. I clutched my head with my arms, and ran stumbling to the foot of the path that climbs to the height of the undefended cliff.

I tried to call him, but my voice was caught in the rout of air; my shout was torn from me and dispersed among the atoms of scuttling foam that huddled a moment among the rocks before they leaped to dissolution.

I stooped to the lee of the singing furze. I dared go no further. Beyond was all riot, where the mad sport took strange shapes of soaring whirlpools and sudden draughts, and wonderful calms that suckingly enticed the unknowing to the cliff's edge.

I knew that it would be useless to seek him now. The scream of the gale had mounted unendurably; he could not be still alive up there in the midst of that reeling fury.

I crept back to the road and the shelter of the cutting, and then I fled to my house.

For a long hour I sat over the fire seeking some peace of mind. I blamed myself most bitterly that I had not hindered him. I might have given way; have pretended conviction, or, at least, some sympathy with his rash and foolish ignorance. But presently I found consolation in the thought that his fate had always been inevitable. What availed any effort of mine against the unquestionable forces that had pronounced his doom? I listened to the thudding procession that marched through the upper air, and to the shrieking of the spirits that come down to torture and destroy the things of earth; and I knew that no effort of mine could have saved him. . . .

And when the outer door banged, and I heard his footstep in the hall, I believed that he was appearing to me at the moment of his death; but when he came into the room with shining eyes and bright cheeks, laughing and tossing the hair back from his forehead, I was curiously angry.

"Where have you been?" I asked. "I went out to the cliff to find you, and thought you were dead."

"You came to the cliffs?" he said.

"To the foot of the cliff," I confessed.

"Ah! You must never go further than that in the black time," he said.

"Then you believe me now?" I asked.

He smiled. "I believe that you would be in danger up there tonight," he said, "because you believe in the powers of the air, and you are afraid."

He stood in the doorway, braced by his struggle with the wind; and his young eyes were glowing with the consciousness of discovery and new knowledge.

Yet he cannot deny that I showed him the way.

OLD FAGS

Stacy Aumonier
(1877–1928)

It's hard to say that someone who died aged 51, having produced six collections of short stories, six novels, and collections of character studies and essays died "too young" or "left too little behind," but Stacy Aumonier's death from tuberculosis in 1928 certainly robbed English letters of one of its best short story writers, and we can only wonder what he would have written had he been granted even ten more years of life.

Born in 1877 to an artistic family, Aumonier began as a painter before marrying in 1907 and switching to stage work, performing his own sketches to considerable local acclaim. In 1915 Aumonier began publishing his short work, and it is in that role, as short story writer, that he gained the most recognition, being praised by Rebecca West, John Galsworthy, and James Hilton, among others. Until his death Aumonier continued to produce high-quality work, ultimately writing 87 short stories for magazines like Argosy, The Strand, *and* The Saturday Evening Post.

"Old Fags" shows Aumonier's typical compassion for the very poor, while at the same time twisting the knife, on all concerned, with an almost dispassionate air.

THE BOYS CALLED him "Old Fags," and the reason was not hard to seek. He occupied a room in a block of tenements off Lisson Grove, bearing the somewhat grandiloquent title of Bolingbroke Buildings and, conspicuous among the many doubtful callings that occupied his time, was one in which he issued forth with a deplorable old canvas sack, which, after a day's peregrination along the gutters, he would manage to partly fill with cigar and cigarette ends. The exact means by which he managed to convert this patently gathered garbage into the wherewithal to support his disreputable body, nobody took the trouble to inquire; nor was there any further interest aroused by the disposal of the contents of the same sack when he returned with the gleanings of dustbins, distributed thoughtfully at intervals along certain thoroughfares by a maternal Borough Council.

No one had ever penetrated to the inside of his room, but the general opinion in Bolingbroke Buildings was that he managed to live in a state of comfortable filth. And Mrs. Read, who lived in the room opposite Number 477 with her four children, was of the opinion that "Old Fags 'ad 'oarded up a bit." He certainly was never behind with the payment of the weekly three and sixpence that entitled him to the sole enjoyment of Number 475; and when the door was opened, among the curious blend of odours that issued forth, that of onions and other luxuries of this sort was undeniable. Nevertheless, he was not a popular figure in the Buildings; many, in fact, looked upon him as a social blot on the Bolingbroke escutcheon. The inhabitants were mostly labourers and their wives, charwomen and lady helps, dressmakers' assistants, and mechanics. There was a vague, tentative effort among a great body of them to be a little respectable, and among some, even to be clean. No such uncomfortable considerations hampered the movements of "Old Fags." He was frankly and ostentatiously a social derelict. He had no pride and no shame. He shuffled out in the morning, his blotchy face covered with dirt and black hair, his threadbare green clothes tattered and in ranges, the toes all too visible through his forlorn-looking boots. He was rather a large man with a fat, flabby person, and a shiny face that was over-affable and bleary through a too constant attention to the gin bottle.

He had a habit of ceaseless talk. He talked and chuckled to himself all the time; he talked to every one he met in an undercurrent of jeering affability. Sometimes he would retire to his room with a gin bottle for days together and then—the walls at Bolingbroke Buildings are not very thick—he would be heard to talk and chuckle and snore alternately, until the percolating atmosphere of stewed onions heralded the fact that "Old Fags" was shortly on the war-path again.

He would meet Mrs. Read with her children on the stairs and would mutter: "Oh! Here we are again! All these dear little children. Been out for a walk, eh? Oh! These dear little children!" and he would pat one of them gaily on the head. And Mrs. Read would say: "'Ere, you, keep your filthy 'ands off my kids, you dirty swine, or I'll catch you a swipe over the mouth!" And "Old Fags" would shuffle off muttering: "Oh, dear; oh, dear; these dear little children! Oh, dear; oh, dear." And the boys would call after him and even throw orange peel and other things at him, but nothing seemed to disturb the serenity of "Old Fags." Even when young Charlie Good threw a dead mouse, that hit him on the chin, he only said: "Oh, these Boys! These BOYS!"

Quarrels, noise and bad odours were the prevailing characteristics of Bolingbroke Buildings, and "Old Fags," though contributing in some degree to the latter quality, rode serenely through the other two in spite of multiform aggression. The penetrating intensity of his onion stew had driven two lodgers already from Number 476, and was again a source of aggravation to the present holders, old Mrs. Birdle and her daughter, Minnie.

Minnie Birdle was what was known as a "tweeny" at a house in Hyde Park Square, but she lived at home. Her mistress—to whom she had never spoken, being engaged by the Housekeeper—was Mrs. Bastien-Melland, a lady who owned a valuable collection of little dogs. These little dogs somehow gave Minnie an unfathomable sense of respectability. She loved to talk about them. She told Mrs. Read that her mistress paid "'undreds and 'undreds of pahnds for each of them." They were taken out every day by a groom on two leads of five—ten highly groomed, bustling, yapping, snapping, vicious little luxuries. Some had won prizes at Dog Shows, and two men were engaged for the sole purpose of ministering to their creative comforts.

The consciousness of working in a house which furnished such an exhibition of festive cultivation brought into sharp relief the degrading social condition of her next-room neighbour. Minnie hated "Old Fags" with a bitter hatred. She even wrote to a firm of lawyers, who represented some remote landlord, and complained of the dirty habits of the old drunken wretch next door. But she never received any answer to her complaint. It was known that "Old Fags" had lived there for seven years and paid his rent regularly. Moreover, on one critical occasion, Mrs. Read, who had periods of rheumatic gout and could not work, had got into hopeless financial straits, having reached the very limit of her borrowing capacity, and being three weeks in arrears with her rent, "Old Fags" had come over and had insisted on lending her fifteen shillings! Mrs. Read eventually paid it back, and the knowledge of the transaction further accentuated her animosity toward him.

One day "Old Fags" was returning from his dubious round and was passing through Hyde Park Square with his canvas bag slung over his back, when he ran into the cortège of little dogs under the control of Meads, the groom.

"Oh, dear! Oh, dear!" muttered "Old Fags" to himself. "What dear little dogs! H'm! What dear little dogs!"

A minute later Minnie Birdle ran up the area steps and gave Meads a bright smile. "Good-night, Mr. Meads," she said.

Mr. Meads looked at her and said: "'Ullo! You off?"

"Yes!" she answered.

"Oh, well," he said, "good-night! Be good!" They both sniggered, and Minnie hurried down the street. Before she reached Lisson Grove "Old Fags" had caught her up.

"I say," he said, getting into her stride, "what dear little dogs those are! Oh, dear! What dear little dogs!"

Minnie turned, and when she saw him her face flushed, and she said: "Oh, you go to Hell!" with which unladylike expression she darted across the road and was lost to sight.

"Oh, these women!" said "Old Fags" to himself, "these WOMEN!"

It often happened, thereafter, that "Old Fags'" business carried him in the neighbourhood of Hyde Park Square, and he ran into the little dogs. One day he even ventured to address Meads and to congratulate him on the beauty of his canine protégées, an attention that elicited a very unsympathetic response; a response, in fact, that amounted to being told to "clear off."

The incident of "Old Fags" running into this society was entirely accidental. It was due, in part, to the fact that the way lay through there to a tract of land in Paddington that "Old Fags" seemed to find peculiarly attractive. It was a neglected strip of ground by the railway, that butted one end into a canal. It would have made quite a good siding, but that it seemed somehow to have been overlooked by the Railway Company, and to have become a dumping ground for tins and old refuse from the houses in the neighbourhood of Harrow Road. "Old Fags" would spend hours there alone with his canvas bag.

When the winter came on there was a great wave of what the papers would call economic unrest. There were strikes in three great industries, a political upheaval, and a severe tightening of the Money Market. All of these misfortunes reacted on Bolingbroke Buildings. The dwellers became even more impecunious, and consequently more quarrelsome, more noisy and more malodorous. Rents were all in arrears, ejections were the order of the day, and borrowing became a tradition rather than an actuality. Want and hunger brooded over the dejected Buildings. But still "Old Fags" came and went, carrying his shameless gin and permeating the passages with his onion stews.

Old Mrs. Birdle became bedridden and the support of Room Number 476 fell on the shoulders of Minnie. The wages of a "tweeny" are not excessive, and the way in which she managed to support herself and her invalid mother must have excited the wonder of the other dwellers in the building, if they had not had more pressing affairs of their own to wonder about. Minnie was a short, sallow little thing with a rather full figure, and heavy grey eyes that somehow conveyed a sense of sleeping passion. She had a certain instinct for dress, a knack of putting some trinket in the right place, and of always being neat. Mrs.

Bastien-Melland had one day asked who she was. On being informed, her curiosity did not prompt her to push the matter further, and she did not speak to her; but the incident gave Minnie a better standing in the domestic household at Hyde Park Square. It was probably this attention that caused Meads, the head dog groom, to cast an eye in her direction. It is certain that he did so, and, moreover, on a certain Thursday evening had taken her to a Cinema performance in the Edgware Road. Such attention naturally gave rise to discussion; and, alas, to jealousy; for there was an under house maid, and even a Lady's maid, who were not impervious to the attentions of the good-looking groom.

When Mrs. Bastien-Melland went to Egypt in January, she only took three of the small dogs with her, for she could not be bothered with the society of a groom, and three dogs were as many as her two maids could spare time for, after devoting their energies to Mrs. Bastien-Melland's toilette. Consequently, Meads was left behind, and was held directly responsible for seven, five Chows, and two Pekinese, or, as he expressed it, over a thousand pounds' worth of dogs. It was a position of enormous responsibility. They had to be fed on the very best food, all carefully prepared and cooked, and in small quantities. They had to be taken for regular exercise, and washed in specially prepared condiments. Moreover, at the slightest symptom of indisposition he was to telephone to Sir Andrew Fossiter, the great veterinary specialist in Hanover Square. It is not to be wondered at that Meads became a person of considerable standing and envy, and that little Minnie Birdle was intensely flattered when he occasionally condescended to look in her direction. She had been in Mrs. Bastien-Melland's service now for seven months, and the attentions of the dog groom had not only been a matter of general observation, for some time past, but had become a subject of reckless mirth and innuendo among the other servants.

One night she was hurrying home. Her mother had been rather worse than usual of late, and she was carrying a few scraps that the cook had given her. It was a wretched night and she was not feeling well herself: a mood of tired dejection possessed her. She crossed a drab street off Lisson Grove and, as she reached the curb her eye lighted on "Old Fags." He did not see her. He was walking along the gutter, patting the road occasionally with his stick. She had not spoken to him since the occasion we have mentioned. For once he was not talking— his eyes were fixed in listless apathy on the road. As he passed, she caught the angle of his chin silhouetted against the window of a shop. For the rest of her walk the haunting vision of that chin beneath the drawn cheeks, and the brooding hopelessness of those sunken eyes, kept recurring to her. Perhaps, in some remote past, he had been as good to look upon as Meads, the groom! Perhaps some one had cared for him! She tried to push this thought from her, but some chord in her nature seemed to have been awakened and to vibrate with an unaccountable sympathy toward this undesirable fellow lodger.

She hurried home, and in the night was ill. She could not go to Mrs. Melland's for three days and she wanted the money badly. When she got about again she was subject to fainting fits and sickness. On one such occasion, as she was going upstairs at the Buildings, she felt faint and leant against the wall just as "Old Fags" was going up.

He stopped and said: "Hullo, now what are we doing? Oh, dear! Oh, dear!" And she said: "It's all right, old 'un." These were the kindest words she had ever spoken to "Old Fags."

During the next month there were strange symptoms about Minnie Birdle that caused considerable comment, and there were occasions when old Mrs. Birdle pulled herself together, and became the active partner and waited on Minnie. On one such occasion, "Old Fags" came home late and, after drawing a cork, varied his usual programme of talking and snoring by singing in a maudlin key, and old Mrs. Birdle came banging at his door and shrieked out: "Stop your row, you old—. My daughter is ill. Can't you hear?"

And "Old Fags" came to his door and blinked at her and said: "Ill, is she? Oh, dear! Oh, dear! Would she like some stew, eh?"

And old Mrs. Birdle said: "No, she don't want any of your muck," and bundled back. But they did not hear any more of "Old Fags" that night, or any other night when Minnie came home queer.

Early in March Minnie got the sack from Hyde Park Square. Mrs. Melland was still away—having decided to winter in Rome—but the Housekeeper assumed the responsibility of this action, and in writing to Mrs. Melland, justified the course she had taken by saying that "she could not expect the other maids to work in the same house with an unmarried girl in that condition." Mrs. Melland, whose letter in reply was full of the serious illness of poor little Annisette, one of the Chows, that had suffered in Egypt on account of a maid giving it too much rice, with its boned chicken; and how much better it had been in Rome under the treatment of Dr. Lascati,—made no special reference to the question of Minnie Birdle, only saying that "she was *so* sorry if Mrs. Bellingham was having trouble with these tiresome servants."

The spring came, and the summer, and the two inhabitants of Room 476 eked out their miserable existence. One day Minnie would pull herself together and get a day's charring and occasionally Mrs. Birdle would struggle along to a laundry in Maida Vale, where a benevolent proprietress would pay her one shilling and threepence to do a day's ironing; for the old lady was rather neat with her hands. And once, when things were very desperate, the brother of a nephew from Walthamstow turned up. He was a small cabinet-maker by trade, and he agreed to allow them three shillings a week, "till things righted themselves a bit." But nothing was seen of Meads, the groom. One night Minnie was rather worse and the idea occurred to her that she would like to send a message to him. It was right that he should know. He had made no attempt to see her since she had left Mrs. Melland's service. She lay awake thinking of him and wondering how she could send a message, when she suddenly thought of "Old Fags." He had been quiet of late; whether the demand for cigarette ends was abating and he could not afford the luxuries that their disposal seemed to supply, or whether he was keeping quiet for any ulterior reason, she was not able to determine. In the morning she sent her mother across to ask him if he would "oblige by calling at Hyde Park Square and asking Mr. Meads if he would oblige by calling at 476 Bolingbroke Buildings, to see Miss Birdle."

There is no record of how "Old Fags" delivered this message, but it is known that same afternoon Mr. Meads did call. He left about three-thirty in a great state of perturbation, and in a very bad temper. He passed "Old Fags" on the stairs, and the only comment he made was: "I never have any luck! God help me!" And he did not return, although he had apparently promised to do so.

In a few weeks' time the position of the occupants of Room 476 became desperate. It was, in fact, a desperate time all round. Work was scarce and money scarcer. Waves of ill-temper and depression swept Bolingbroke Buildings. Mrs. Read had gone—Heaven knows where. Even "Old Fags" seemed at the end of his tether. True, he still managed to secure his inevitable bottle, but the stews became scarcer and less potent. All Mrs. Birdle's time and energy were taken up in nursing Minnie, and the two somehow existed on the money—now increased to four shillings a week—which the sympathetic cabinet-maker from Walthamstow allowed them. The question of rent was shelved. Four shillings a week for two people means ceaseless, gnawing hunger. The widow and her daughter lost pride and hope, and further messages to

Mr. Meads failed to elicit any response. The widow became so desperate that she even asked "Old Fags" one night if he could spare a little stew for her daughter who was starving. The pungent odour of the hot food was too much for her.

"Old Fags" came to the door: "Oh, dear! Oh, dear!" he said, "what trouble there is! Let's see what we can do!" He messed about for some time and then took it across to them. It was a strange concoction. Meat that it would have been difficult to know what to ask for at a butcher's, and many bones, but the onions seemed to pull it together. To any one starving it was good. After that it became a sort of established thing: whenever "Old Fags" *had* a stew, he sent some over to the widow and daughter. But apparently things were not going too well in the cigarette-end trade, for the stews became more and more intermittent, and sometimes were desperately "boney."

And then one night a climax was reached. "Old Fags" was awakened in the night by fearful screams. There was a district nurse in the next room, and also a student from a great hospital. No one knows how it all affected "Old Fags." He went out at a very unusual hour in the early morning, and seemed more garrulous and meandering in his speech. He stopped the widow in the passage and mumbled incomprehensible solicitude.

Minnie was very ill for three days, but she recovered, faced by the insoluble proposition of feeding three mouths, instead of two, and two of them requiring enormous quantities of milk. This terrible crisis brought out many good qualities in various people. The cabinet-maker sent ten shillings extra, and others came forward as though driven by some race instinct. "Old Fags" disappeared for ten days after that. It was owing to an unfortunate incident in Hyde Park, when he insisted on sleeping on a flower bed with a gin bottle under his left arm, and on account of the unreasonable attitude that he took up toward a policeman in the matter. When he returned things were assuming their normal course. Mrs. Birdle's greeting was: "Ullo, old 'un, we've missed your stoos."

"Old Fags" had undoubtedly secured a more stable position in the eyes of the Birdles, and one day he was even allowed to see the baby. He talked to it from the door.

"Oh, dear! Oh, dear!" he said. "What a beautiful little baby! What a dear little baby! Oh, dear! Oh, dear!" The baby shrieked with unrestrained terror at sight of him, but that night some more stew was sent in.

Then the autumn came on. People, whose romantic instincts had been touched at the arrival of the child, gradually lost interest and fell

away. The cabinet-maker from Walthamstow wrote a long letter, saying that after next week the payment of the four shillings would have
to stop, he hoped he had been of some help in their trouble, but that
things were going on all right now; of course he had to think of his
own family first, and so on.

The lawyers of the remote landlord, who was assiduously killing stags
in Scotland, regretted that their client could not see his way to allow
any further delay in the matter of the payment of rent due. The position of the Birdle family became once more desperate. Old Mrs. Birdle
had become frailer, and though Minnie could now get about, she
found work difficult to obtain, owing to people's demand for a character reference from the last place. Their thoughts once more reverted to
Meads, and Minnie lay in wait for him one morning as he was taking
the dogs out. There was a very trying scene ending in a very vulgar
quarrel, and Minnie came home and cried all the rest of the day and
through half the night.

"Old Fags'" stews became scarcer and less palatable. He, too, seemed
in dire straits.

We now come to an incident that, we are ashamed to say, owes its
inception to the effect of alcohol. It was a wretched morning in late
October, bleak and foggy. The blue-grey corridors of Bolingbroke
Buildings seemed to exude damp. The strident voices of the unkempt
children, quarrelling in the courtyard below, permeated the whole
Buildings. The strange odour, that was its characteristic, lay upon it like
the foul breath of some evil god. All its inhabitants seemed hungry,
wretched and vile. Their lives of constant protest seemed, for the
moment, lulled to a sullen indifference, whilst they huddled behind their
gloomy doors and listened to the raucous railings of their offspring.

The widow Birdle and her daughter sat silently in their room. The
child was asleep. It had had its milk, and it would have to have its milk,
whatever happened. The crumbs from the bread the women had had
at breakfast lay ungathered on the bare table. They were both hungry
and very desperate. There was a knock at the door. Minnie went to it,
and there stood "Old Fags." He leered at them meekly and under his
arm carried a gin bottle, three parts full.

"Oh, dear! Oh, dear!" he said. "What a dreadful day! What a dreadful day! Will you have a little drop of gin to comfort you? Now! What
do you say?"

Minnie looked at her mother—in other days the door would have
been slammed in his face, but "Old Fags" had certainly been kind in

the matter of stews. They asked him to sit down. Then old Mrs. Birdle did accept just a tiny drop of gin, and they both persuaded Minnie to have a little. Now neither of the women had had food of any worth for days, and the gin went straight to their heads. It was already in "Old Fags'" head, firmly established. The three immediately became garrulous. They all talked volubly and intimately. The women railed "Old Fags" about his dirt, but allowed that he had "a good 'eart." They talked longingly and lovingly about "his stoos" and "Old Fags" said: "Well, my dears, you shall have the finest stoo you've ever had in your lives tonight."

He repeated this nine times, only each time the whole sentence sounded like one word.

Then the conversation drifted to the child, and the hard lot of parents, and by a natural sequence to Meads, its father. Meads was discussed with considerable bitterness, and the constant reiteration of the threat by the women that they meant to 'ave the Lor on 'im all right, mingled with the jeering sophistries of "Old Fags" on the genalman's behaviour, and the impossibility of expecting a dog groom to be a sportsman, lasted a considerable time. "Old Fags" talked expansively about leaving it to him, and somehow as he stood there with his large, puffy figure, looming up in the dimly lighted room, and waving his long arms, he appeared to the women a figure of portentous significance. In the eyes of the women he typified powers they had not dreamt of. Under the veneer of his hidebound depravity Minnie seemed to detect some slow moving force trying to assert itself.

He meandered on in a vague monologue, using terms and expressions they did not know the meaning of. He gave the impression of some fettered animal, launching a fierce indictment against the fact of its life. At last he took up the gin bottle and moved to the door and then leered round the room.

"You shall have the finest stoo you've ever had in your life tonight, my dears."

He repeated this seven times again and then went heavily out.

That afternoon a very amazing fact was observed by several inhabitants of Bolingbroke Buildings. "Old Fags" washed his face! He went out about three o'clock without his sack. His face had certainly been cleaned up and his clothes seemed in some mysterious fashion to hold together. He went across Lisson Grove and made for Hyde Park Square. He hung about for nearly an hour at the corner, and then he saw a man come up the area steps of a house on the south side and walk rapidly away. "Old

Fags" followed him. He took a turning sharp to the left through a
Mews, and entered a narrow street at the end. There he entered a
deserted-looking pub, kept by an ex-butler and his wife. He passed right
through to a room at the back and called for some beer. Before it was
brought, "Old Fags" was seated at the next table ordering gin.

"Dear, oh, dear! What a wretched day!" said "Old Fags."

The groom grunted assent. But "Old Fags" was not one to be put off
by mere indifference. He broke ground on one or two subjects that
interested the groom, one subject in particular being Dog. He seemed to
have a profound knowledge of Dog, and before Mr. Meads quite realised
what was happening he was trying gin in his beer at "Old Fags'" expense.

The groom was feeling particularly morose that afternoon. His luck
seemed out. Bookmakers had appropriated several half-crowns that he
sorely begrudged, and he had other expenses. The beer-gin mixture
comforted him, and the rambling eloquence of the old fool, who
seemed disposed to be content paying for drinks and talking, fitted in
with his mood. They drank and talked for a full hour, and at length got
to a subject that all men get to sooner or later if they drink and talk
long enough—the subject of Woman.

Mr. Meads became confiding and philosophic. He talked of women
in general and what triumphs and adventures he had had among them
in particular. But what a trial and tribulation they had been to him in
spite of all! "Old Fags" winked knowingly and was splendidly compre-
hensive and tolerant of Meads' peccadillos.

"It's all a game," said Meads. "You've got to manage 'em. There
ain't much I don't know, old bird!" Then suddenly "Old Fags" leaned
forward in the dark room and said: "No, Mr. Meads, but you ought to
play the game, you know. Oh, dear, yes!"

"What do you mean, *Mister Meads?*" said that gentleman sharply.

"Minnie Birdle, eh, you haven't mentioned Minnie Birdle yet!" said
"Old Fags."

"What the Devil are you talking about?" said Meads drunkenly.

"She's starving," said "Old Fags," "starving, wretched, alone with
her old mother and your child. Oh, dear! Yes, it's terrible!"

Meads' eyes flashed with a sullen frenzy, but fear was gnawing at his
heart, and he felt more disposed to placate this mysterious old man than
to quarrel with him.

"I tell you I have no luck," he said after a pause.

"Old Fags" looked at him gloomily and ordered some more gin.
When it was brought he said, "You ought to play the game, you know,

Mr. Meads. After all—luck? Oh, dear! Oh, dear! Would you rather be the woman? Five shillings a week, you know, would—"

"No, I'm damned if I do!" cried Meads fiercely. "It's all right for all these women—Gawd! How do I know if it's true? Look here, old bird, do you know I'm already done in for two five bobs a week, eh! One up in Norfolk and the other at Enfield. Ten shillings a week of my— money goes to these blasted women. No fear, no more, I'm through with it!"

"Oh, dear! Oh, dear!" said "Old Fags," and he moved a little further into the shadow of the room and watched the groom out of the depths of his sunken eyes.

But Meads' courage was now fortified by the fumes of a large quan- tity of fiery alcohol, and he spoke witheringly of women in general and seemed disposed to quarrel if "Old Fags" disputed his right to place them in the position that Meads considered their right and natural posi- tion. But "Old Fags" gave no evidence of taking up the challenge—on the contrary he seemed to suddenly shift his ground. He grinned and leered and nodded at Meads' string of coarse sophistry, and suddenly he touched him on the arm and looked round the room and said very confidentially:

"Oh, dear! Yes, Mr. Meads. Don't take too much to heart what I said," and then he sniffed and whispered: "I could put you on to a very nice thing, Mr. Meads. I could introduce you to a lady I know would take a fancy to you, and you to her. Oh, dear, yes!"

Meads pricked up his ears like a fox-terrier and his small eyes glittered.

"Oh!" he said. "Are you one of those, eh, old bird? Who is she?"

"Old Fags" took out a piece of paper and fumbled with a pencil. He then wrote down a name and address somewhere at Shepherds Bush.

"What's a good time to call?" said Meads.

"Between six and seven," answered "Old Fags."

"Oh, Hell!" said Meads. I can't do it. I've got to get back and take the dogs out at half-past five, old bird. From half-past five to half-past six. The missus is back, she'll kick up a hell of a row."

"Oh, dear! Oh, dear!" said "Old Fags." "What a pity! The young lady is going away, too!" He thought for a moment and then an idea seemed to strike him. "Look here, would you like me to meet you and take the dogs round the Park till you return?"

"What!" said Meads, "trust you with a thousand pounds' worth of dogs! Not much."

"No, no, of course not, I hadn't thought of that!" said "Old Fags" humbly.

Meads looked at him, and it is very difficult to tell what it was about the old man that gave him a sudden feeling of complete trust. The ingenuity of his speech, the ingratiating confidence that a mixture of beer-gin gives, tempered by the knowledge that famous pedigree Pekinese would be almost impossible to dispose of, perhaps it was a combination of these motives. In any case a riotous impulse drove him to fall in with "Old Fags'" suggestion, and he made the appointment for half-past five.

★ ★ ★

Evening had fallen early, and a fine rain was driving in fitful gusts when the two met at the corner of Hyde Park. There were the ten little dogs on their lead, and Meads with a cap pulled close over his eyes.

"Oh, dear! Oh, dear!" cried "Old Fags" as he approached. "What dear little dogs! What dear little dogs!"

Meads handed the lead over to "Old Fags" and asked more precise instructions of the way to get to the address.

"What are you wearing that canvas sack inside your coat for, old bird, eh?" asked Meads when these instructions had been given.

"Oh, my dear sir," said "Old Fags," "if you had the asthma like I get it! And no underclothes on these damp days! Oh, dear! Oh, dear!" He wheezed drearily.

Meads gave him one or two more exhortations about the extreme care and tact he was to observe.

"Be very careful with that little Chow on the left lead. 'E's got his coat on, see? 'E's 'ad a chill and you must keep 'im on the move. Gently, see?"

"Oh, dear! Oh, dear! Poor little chap! What's his name?" said "Old Fags."

"Pelleas," answered Mr. Meads.

"Oh, poor little Pelleas! Poor little Pelleas! Come along, you won't be too long, Mr. Meads, will you?"

"You bet I won't," said the groom, and nodding he crossed the road rapidly and mounting a Shepherds Bush motor 'bus, he set out on his journey to an address that didn't exist.

"Old Fags" ambled slowly round the Park snuffling and talking to the dogs. He gauged the time when Meads would be somewhere about Queens Road, then he ambled slowly back to the point from which he had started. With extreme care he piloted the small army across the High Road and led them in the direction of Paddington. He drifted with leisurely confidence through a maze of small streets. Several people stopped and looked at the dogs and the boys barked and mimicked them, but nobody took the trouble to look at "Old Fags." At length he came to a district where their presence seemed more conspicuous. Rows of squalid houses and advertisement hoardings. He slightly increased his pace, and a very stout policeman standing outside a funeral furnisher's glanced at him with a vague suspicion. In strict accordance, however, with an ingrained officialism, that hates to act "without instructions," he let the cortège pass.

"Old Fags" wandered through a wretched street that seemed entirely peopled by children. Several of them came up and followed the dogs.

"Dear little dogs, aren't they? Oh my, yes, dear little dogs!" he said to the children.

At last he reached a broad, gloomy thoroughfare with low, irregular buildings on one side, and an interminable length of hoardings on the other, that screened a strip of land by the railway land that harboured a wilderness of tins and garbage. "Old Fags" led the dogs along by the hoarding. It was very dark. Three children who had been following, tired of the pastime and drifted away. He went along once more. There was a gap in a hoarding on which was notified that "Pogram's Laundaulettes could be hired for the evening at an inclusive fee of two guineas. Telephone 47901 Mayfair." The meagre light from a street lamp thirty yards away revealed a colossal coloured picture of a very beautiful young man and woman stepping out of a car and entering a gorgeous restaurant, having evidently just enjoyed the advantage of this peerless luxury.

"Old Fags" went on another forty yards and then returned. There was no one in sight.

"Oh, dear little dogs!" he said. "Oh, dear! Oh, dear! What dear little dogs! Just through here, my pretty pets. Gentle, Pelleas! Gently, very gently! There, there, there! Oh, what dear little dogs!"

He stumbled forward through the quagmire of desolation, picking his way as though familiar with every inch of ground, to the further corner where it was even darker, and where the noise of shunting freight trains drowned every other murmur of the night.

★ ★ ★

It was eight o'clock when "Old Fags" reached his room in Bolingbroke Buildings, carrying his heavily laden sack across his shoulders. The child in Room 476 had been peevish and fretful all the afternoon, and the two women were lying down, exhausted. They heard "Old Fags" come in. He seemed very busy, banging about with bottles and tins and alternately coughing and wheezing. But soon the potent aroma of onions reached their nostrils and they knew he was preparing to keep his word.

At nine o'clock he staggered across with a steaming saucepan of hot stew. In contrast to the morning's conversation, which though devoid of self-consciousness had taken on at times an air of moribund analysis, making little stabs at fundamental things, the evening passed off on a note of almost joyous levity. The stew was extremely good to the starving women, and "Old Fags" developed a vein of fantastic pleasantry. He talked unceasingly, sometimes on things they understood, sometimes on matters of which they were entirely ignorant; and sometimes he appeared to the obtuse, maudlin, and incoherent. Nevertheless, he brought to their room a certain light-hearted raillery that had never visited it before. No mention was made of Meads.

The only blemish to the serenity of this bizarre supper party was that "Old Fags" developed intervals of violent coughing, intervals when he had to walk around the room and beat his chest. These fits had the unfortunate result of waking the baby.

When this undesirable result had occurred for the fourth time, "Old Fags" said: "Oh, dear! Oh, dear! This won't do. Oh, no, this won't do. I must go back to my hotel!" A remark that caused paroxysms of mirth to old Mrs. Birdle. Nevertheless, "Old Fags" retired, and it was then just on eleven o'clock.

The women went to bed, and all through the night Minnie heard the old man coughing.

★ ★ ★

Meads jumped off the 'bus at Shepherds Bush and hurried in the direction that "Old Fags" had instructed him. He asked three people for the Pomeranian Road before an errand boy told him that he believed it was somewhere off Giles Avenue; but at Giles Avenue no one seemed to know it. He retraced his steps in a very bad temper and inquired again. Five other people had never heard of it. So he went to a post office, and a young lady in charge informed him that there was no such road in the neighbourhood. He tried other roads whose names vaguely resembled it, then he came to the conclusion that "that blamed old fool had made some silly mistake."

He took a 'bus back with a curious gnawing fear at the pit of his stomach, a fear that he kept thrusting back, he dare not allow himself to contemplate it. It was nearly seven-thirty when he got back to Hyde Park, and his eye quickly scanned the length of railing near which "Old Fags" was to be. Immediately when he saw no sign of him or the little dogs, a horrible feeling of physical sickness assailed him. The whole truth flashed through in his mind. He saw the fabric of his life crumble to dust. He was conscious of visions of past acts and misdeeds tumbling over each other in a furious kaleidoscope. The groom was terribly frightened. Mrs. Bastien-Melland would be in at eight o'clock to dinner, and the first thing she would ask for would be the little dogs. They were never supposed to go out after dark, but he had been busy that afternoon and arranged to take them out later. How was he to account for himself and their loss? He visualised himself in a dock, and all sorts of other horrid things coming up—a forged character, an affair in Norfolk, and another at Enfield, and a little trouble with a bookmaker seven years ago. For he felt convinced that the little dogs had gone forever, and "Old Fags" with them.

He cursed blindly in his soul at his foul luck and the wretched inclination that had lured him to drink "beer-gin" with the old thief. Forms of terrific vengeance passed through his mind, if he should meet the old evil again. In the meantime what should he do? He had never even thought of making "Old Fags" give him any sort of address. He dared not go back to Hyde Park Square without the dogs. He ran breathlessly up and down, peering in every direction. Eight o'clock came and there was still no sign. Suddenly he remembered Minnie Birdle. He remembered that the old ruffian had mentioned, and seemed to know, Minnie Birdle. It was a connection that he had hoped to have wiped out of his life, but the case was desperate. Curiously enough, during his desultory courtship of Minnie, he had never been to her home; the only occasion when he *had* visited it, was after the birth of the child. He had done so under the influence of three pints of beer, and he hadn't the faintest recollection now of the number or the block. He hurried there, however, in feverish trepidation.

Now Bolingbroke Buildings harbour some eight hundred people; and it is a remarkable fact that, although the Birdles had lived there

about a year, of the eleven people that Meads asked, not one happened
to know the name. People develop a profound sense of self-concentra-
tion in Bolingbroke Buildings.

Meads wandered up all the stairs and through the slate-tile passages.
Twice he passed their door without knowing it—on the first occasion,
only five minutes after "Old Fags" had carried a saucepan of steaming
stew from Number 475 to Number 476. At ten o'clock he gave it up.
He had four shillings on him, and he adjourned to a small "pub" hard
by, and ordered a tankard of ale, and as an afterthought three penny-
worth of gin which he mixed in it. Probably he thought that this mixture, which was so directly responsible for the train of tragic
circumstance that encompassed him, might continue to act in some
manner toward a more desirable conclusion.

It did, indeed, drive him to action of a sort, for he sat there drinking
and smoking Navy Cut cigarettes, and by degrees he evolved a most
engaging, but impossible, story, of being lured to the river by three
men and chloroformed; and when he came to, finding that the dogs
and the men had gone. He drank a further quantity of beer-gin, and
rehearsed his rôle in detail, and at length brought himself to the point
of facing Mrs. Melland. . . .

It was the most terrifying ordeal of his life. The servants frightened
him for a start. They almost shrieked when they saw him and drew
back. Mrs. Bastien-Melland had left word that he was to go to a small
breakfast-room in the basement directly after he came in, and she
would come and see him. There was a small dinner party on that
evening and an agitated game of bridge. Meads had not stood on the
hearth-rug of the breakfast-room two minutes before he heard the
foreboding swish of skirts, the door burst open, and Mrs. Bastien-
Melland stood before him, a thing of penetrating perfumes, high-
lights and trepidation.

She just said, "Well!" and fixed her hard, bright eyes on him.

Meads launched forth into his impossible story, but he dared not
look at her. He tried to gather together the pieces of the tale he had so
carefully rehearsed in the pub, but he felt like some helpless bark at the
mercy of a hostile battle fleet; the searchlight of Mrs. Melland's cruel
eyes was concentrated on him; while a flotilla of small diamonds on her
heaving bosom winked and glittered with a dangerous insolence.

He was stumbling over a phrase about the effects of chloroform
when he became aware that Mrs. Melland was not listening to the matter of his story, she was only concerned with the manner. Her lips were

set and her straining eyes insisted on catching his. He looked full at her
and caught his breath and stopped.

Mrs. Melland still staring at him was moving slowly to the door. A
moment of panic seized him. He mumbled something, and also moved
toward the door. Mrs. Melland was first to grip the handle. Meads
made a wild dive and seized her wrist. But Mrs. Bastien-Melland came
of a hard-riding Yorkshire family. She did not lose her head. She struck
him cross the mouth with her flat hand, and as he reeled back she
opened the door and called to the servants.

Suddenly Meads remembered that the room had a French window
onto the garden. He pushed her clumsily against the door and sprang
across the room. He clutched wildly at the bolts while Mrs. Melland's
voice was ringing out:

"Catch that man! Hold him! Catch thief!"

But before the other servants had had time to arrive he managed to
get through the door and to pull it after him. His hand was bleeding
with cuts from broken glass, but he leapt the wall and got into the
shadow of some shrubs three gardens away.

He heard whistles blowing and the dominant voice of Mrs. Melland,
directing a hue-and-cry. He rested some moments, then panic seized
him and he laboured over another wall and found the passage of a semi-
detached house. A servant opened a door and looked out and screamed.
He struck her wildly and unreasonably on the shoulder, and rushed up
some steps and got into a front garden. There was no one there, and
he darted into the street and across the road.

In a few minutes he was lost in a labyrinth of back streets and laughing hysterically to himself.

He had two shillings and eightpence on him. He spent fourpence of
this on whiskey, and then another fourpence just before the pubs
closed. He struggled vainly to formulate some definite plan of campaign. The only point that seemed terribly clear to him was that he
must get away. He knew Mrs. Melland only too well. She would spare
no trouble in hunting him down. She would exact the uttermost far-
thing. It meant gaol and ruin. The obvious impediment to getting away
was that he had no money and no friends. He had not sufficient
strength of character to face a tramp-life. He had lived too long in the
society of the pampered Pekinese. He loved comfort.

Out of the simmering tumult of his soul grew a very definite passion—
the passion of hate. He developed a vast, bitter, scorching hatred for the
person who had caused this ghastly climax to his unfortunate career—

"Old Fags." He went over the whole incidents of the day again, rapidly recalling every phase of "Old Fags'" conversation and manner. What a blind fool he was not to have seen through the filthy old swine's game! But what had he done with the dogs? Sold the lot for a pound, perhaps! The idea made Meads shiver. He slouched through the streets harbouring his pariah-like lust.

We will not attempt to record the psychologic changes that harassed the soul of Mr. Meads during the next two days and nights; the ugly passions that stirred him and beat their wings against the night; the tentative intuitions urging toward some vague new start; the various compromises he made with himself, his weakness and inconsistency that found him bereft of any quality other than the sombre shadow of some ill-conceived revenge. We will only note that on the evening of the day we mention, he turned up at Bolingbroke Buildings. His face was haggard and drawn, his eyes bloodshot and his clothes tattered and muddy. His appearance and demeanour were, unfortunately, not so alien to the general character of Bolingbroke Buildings as to attract any particular attention, and he slunk like a wolf through the dreary passages, and watched the people come and go.

It was at about a quarter to ten, when he was going along a passage in Block "F," that he suddenly saw Minnie Birdle come out of one door and go into another. His small eyes glittered and he went on tiptoe. He waited till Minnie was quite silent in her room and then he went stealthily to Room 475. He tried the handle and it gave. He opened the door and peered in. There was a cheap tin lamp guttering on a box, that dimly revealed a room of repulsive wretchedness. The furniture seemed to mostly consist of bottles and rags. But in one corner on a mattress he beheld the grinning face of his enemy—"Old Fags."

Meads shut the door silently and stood with his back to it.

"Oh," he said, "so here we are at last, old bird, eh!"

This move was apparently a supremely successful dramatic coup; for "Old Fags" lay still, paralysed with fear, no doubt.

"So this is our little 'ome, eh?" Meads continued, "where we bring little dogs and sell 'em. What have you got to say, you old—"

The groom's face blazed into a sudden accumulated fury. He thrust his chin forward and let forth a volley of frightful and blasting oaths. But "Old Fags" didn't answer, his shiny face seemed to be intensely amused with his outburst.

"We got to settle our little account, old bird, see?" and the suppressed fury of Meads' voice denoted some physical climax. "Why the

Hell don't you answer?" he suddenly shrieked; and springing forward he lashed "Old Fags" across the cheek.

A terrible horror came over him. The cheek he had struck was as cold as marble and the head fell a little impotently to one side.

Trembling as though struck with an ague the groom picked up the guttering lamp and held it close to the face of "Old Fags." It was set in an impenetrable repose, the significance of which even the groom could not misunderstand. The features were calm and childlike, lit by a half-smile of splendid tolerance, that seemed to have over-ridden the temporary buffets of a queer world.

Meads had no idea how long he stood there gazing horror-struck at the face of his enemy. He only knew that he was presently conscious that Minnie Birdle was standing by his side; and as he looked at her, her gaze was fixed on "Old Fags," and a tear was trickling down either cheek.

"'E's dead," she said, "'Old Fags' is dead. 'E died this morning of noomonyer."

She said this quite simply, as though it was a statement that explained the wonder of her presence. She did not look at Meads, or seem aware of him.

He watched the flickering light from the lamp illumining the underside of her chin and nostrils and her quivering brows.

"'E's dead," she said again, and the statement seemed to come as an edict of dismissal, as though love and hatred and revenge had no place in these fundamental things.

Meads looked from her to the tousled head, leaning slightly to one side on the mattress, and he felt himself in the presence of forces he could not comprehend. He put the lamp back quietly on the box and tiptoed from the room.

THE SEPARATE ROOM

Ethel Colburn Mayne
(1865–1941)

Ethel Colburn Mayne was of Irish descent. She grew up in Cork and attended private schools in Ireland and only began writing when she was thirty, sending "A Pen-and-Ink Effect" to The Yellow Book *in 1895. The magazine's editor, Henry Harland, invited her to become the magazine's sub-editor in 1896, a role she accepted but was forced out of later that year. She continued writing, however, and two years later published her first collection of short stories, beginning a thirty-one-year-long career as novelist, author of short stories, literary biographer (her two-volume biography of Lord Byron is her best-known work), translator of foreign novels (her 1907 translation of German writer Margarete Böhme's* The Diary of a Lost Girl *was a minor sensation), journalist, and critic.*

"The Separate Room" first appeared in her 1917 collection Come In *and was later selected by Dorothy Sayers for her* Great Short Stories of Detection, Mystery and Horror *(1928). As Sayers wrote, "In the purely human sphere of horror, spiritual cruelty now holds its place alongside with bodily cruelty, and we can place Ethel Colburn Mayne's 'The Separate Room' next door to H. G. Wells' 'The Cone' as examples of man's inhumanity to man."*

IT WAS CLEAR that Bergsma was pleased, and Marion Cameron held her breath in thrilled alarm.

"You've done it—why! you've done it rippingly," said Bergsma, in his intermittent foreign accent, which now made a *w* and *y* precede the *r* in "rippingly." He did not look up, but read on eagerly from the sheet that Marion had typed for him, this morning, before he came into the study. She had felt tired, on waking, after the late evening with its difficult job, and then the exciting sense of having done it not so badly; she had hardly slept a wink, but she was at Bergsma's house much earlier than usual, so that all should be in best array when Bergsma came, and she herself in something that might figure as composure.

"So it was interesting," Bergsma said, still reading. "Miss Grey was in good voice, and Woolley not too—woolly?" He grinned at his mild joke, but still did not look up.

"Miss Grey was splendid," Marion said, in her clear solemn tones; "and Mr. Woolley was . . ."

She stopped. She wanted to acknowledge the joke, to say that Mr. Woolley had been something textile, but the word would not present itself, and Marion gave it up. "Mr. Woolley was quite good."

"Loose?" asked Bergsma, with another grin.

"Loose—Mr. Woolley?"

He glanced at her. "The part—it's quelque peu! I thought he might have 'given' a bit for once, pulled his voice out . . . ah, peste, no more of it!" He frowned.

Marion blushed. She knew she had been slow, and knew that Bergsma hated slowness.

He laid the sheet aside. "It's all right. Send it off." Now he looked up, and at her. "You enjoyed it—the job, I mean?"

"Indeed I did," she answered with the full force of her earnestness.

He turned his thick blue eyes away.

"Like to do it again?"

"If you think I'm worthy . . ." Marion said, a shade more solemnly still. All at once a different mood seized Bergsma. "Oh, any intelligent person can turn out a notice like that. It wasn't an important production . . . You've done it very nicely." He took the morning paper; Marion knew she was dismissed to her own table in the corner.

This kind of thing had happened before—the disconcerting change of tone, when she had thought that he was really pleased beyond the ordinary limits of a secretary's "giving-of-satisfaction."

Marion did not resent, but she would have liked to understand it. Was it something in him, or in herself, that brought the quick reaction? For she knew, as she had known before, that this was not the mere return to business-manner when the moment for expansion is over. No; he was cross, and about something that was definite, to him.

She put up her article for post—the first words she had ever written for print, and they were to appear, in the foremost musical weekly, not as hers but his. She was Bergsma's "ghost!" Marion, when first she had realized that this was what she was to be, had smiled to herself with the humour of which, for all her lack of wit, she was capable. Bergsma's ghost—a ludicrously dissimilar one! He was short and squat, with a flat, smooth, white face, and thick, prominent, most heavy-lidded eyes that deadened into boredom frankly and alarmingly: "the eyes of genius," somebody had said of them to Marion. Certainly, if that power of extinguishing his eyes were proof of genius, Bergsma had it; and if the other power of lighting so excitedly that they lit up his whole face were further proof, the eyes doubly marked him. That was what made it

comic that she should be his ghost. Marion's eyes were large, but that
was the most they were. They always looked the same; their brightness
was constant—not a luminous brightness, but a mere surface glitter, just
enough to rescue them from dulness. They bored her; she despised
them heartily. Other things about herself she did not so much mind.
She was glad to have her strong white teeth, to be so very tall and not
an atom weedy; she could not help thinking, too, that she looked more
like "a lady" than most working-girls. (Marion liked to call herself a
working-girl, but it annoyed her mother.) She carried herself gallantly,
and had adopted the right manner of dress for an impoverished but
undeniable gentlewoman, glad and proud to be the hard-working secretary to a leading critic of music—the musical drama, especially. She
wore dark, well-cut coats and skirts, and broad, low stiff white collars,
and sober hats that had not "too much surface," as her friend, Mrs.
Wynne, was fond of saying. Marion didn't know what her friend
meant, yet she always contrived to get the kind of hat. It was worn
one-sidedly, "crammed" a little; that suited the frank, earnest face with
its wide brows and mouth, for it toned down what might have been
too much of earnestness. "You look almost piquante," Mrs. Wynne
had said.

"Not quite—I shouldn't countenance that; it would spoil you."

Marion laughed. "You wouldn't countenance my countenance!"

But Mrs. Wynne did not laugh, and Marion flushed, as she often did
when people didn't laugh, as they often didn't. It wasn't a good joke;
one saw that when one heard it . . . She thought of saying that; it
sounded funny; but perhaps it wouldn't be a good joke, either? At all
events, it was a good joke that she should be Bergsma's ghost. His public, this week, would read her devoutly, thinking she was he! And he
had known that this was to be so, and yet had ordered her to send it
off . . . She had not believed that she could do it, when Bergsma, harried by a crisis at the theatre where the opera in rehearsal was of his
discovery—when he had said:

"Look here, Miss Cameron, they want a notice of that Russian oper-
etta at the Yellow on Wednesday night: the International Amateurs,
you know. Do you think you could do it? I'm so bothered! It's interesting, though not important. I'd like to give them a word or two this
week, but I can't spare the time just now."

Marion had trembled. "Would they take a notice—from me?"

"They'll take what I send them," Bergsma said. "How are they to
know who wrote it? Do you feel inclined to try?"

His eyes were beginning to deaden . . . Marion hastened to say something that would show she was not thinking of the sudden evolution of her duties, or was thinking of it as an honour.

"If I only felt sure I could do it," she faltered.

"You know my point of view by this time, and it's only a short notice—anything long would be absurd . . . It's very good of you, Miss Cameron; we'll regard it as settled that you go and try your hand." He had glanced at her again, a little suspiciously, she thought; so Marion said, "I feel honoured," in her most earnest manner.

He had a shrug and a grunted word for it; she felt again that haunting sense of error . . . It made her the more ardent when the evening at the Yellow Theatre arrived. Her mind was stretched to fullest tension; the little opera was Russian of the subtlest, all accumulation and intention, expressed in a new, disconcerting scale, "that beats Schönberg," said one of the appalling experts among whom she sat, "into an egg-flip." Though she did know Bergsma's point of view, it was not an easy task for Marion, writing her first article, to utter it, and so that it would be accepted as his work. For Bergsma had a very special manner. It seemed almost impious to ape it, but what else could he expect of her? and Marion, blushing while she wrote, did ape it: the quivering, suffused attack, the adjectives and adverbs, the conviction and conversion, as in a revivalist campaign—Bergsma's patent, making each experience of the higher musical drama into a vicarious public change of heart; his heart, of course, had never been anywhere but in the right scale.

Marion, though elated, was alarmed to find that she could "do" it. Suppose he was angry? That opening—it was like . . . —But if Bergsma had noticed the mimicry, he had said nothing about it, the crossness did not refer to that, she knew. And now she had sent it off—it would appear! Even though he had said it wasn't important, she couldn't help regarding next Saturday as an epoch—she and her mother, who had sat up for her, that "Yellow" night, with cocoa and biscuits in their bedroom, and at one o'clock in the morning had heard the article, and thought it exactly like Mr. Bergsma's own.

Soon Marion was writing all the minor notices, yet the weekly did not lose prestige. It was an astonishing development. All she had had to offer, in the beginning, was her wide acquaintance (it was hardly knowledge, in the deepest sense) with some new developments in foreign music.

She had travelled, and (most useful, too) was polyglot in a degree that rivalled even Bergsma, who never used his native language—probably the one he now knew least, for it was Dutch, and Holland has

added little to the musical drama. Marion knew Dutch, but that seemed
to be one of the things in her that did not please him.

"Ah, Dutch I now speak never," he had said hurriedly, when she
told him, and she had noticed with what an unusually foreign idiom he
then spoke. Normally he used quite normal English.

However, this had not deterred him from engaging her, and she had
not again mentioned her acquaintance with Dutch. His vexation was
put away among the rest of the puzzlements, once she had thoroughly
discussed it with her mother.

Marion discussed everything with her mother. Both were younger
than their ages, but while Marion, at twenty-eight, showed merely a
retarded maturity, Mrs. Cameron was of the type that never does grow
up. She was not "well-preserved"; her hair was grey, her small pink
face was frankly though quite prettily wrinkled and withered; she was,
in short, the confessed old lady who is a little self-consciously a child.
True to her type, she held herself to be a deep diplomatist; Marion
believed this of her too—she had been nurtured in the faith. Thus they
could, with zest and a tinge of vanity on Mrs. Cameron's part, sit argu-
ing for hours and hours about other people's reasons for being or doing
this or that. They would turn an incident round and round, and up and
down; then Mrs. Cameron would bring forth an explanation which
lately, now and then, had seemed to Marion a little superannuated. She
would laugh her big, whole-hearted laugh. "Oh, mother, that's your
generation!"—and Mrs. Cameron, though offended, would laugh too,
and declare that Marion was now leading such a free life that no doubt
she must know better, but "that would have been the reason when I
was a girl."

In this way the repulse of Dutch had been explained. "He must have
been dissatisfied with a former secretary who spoke it. That was it, you
may be sure."

"Or perhaps," cried Marion the emancipate, "he was in love with a
secretary who spoke it. That could account for his nervousness, too."

"But, Marion, Mr. Bergsma is married."

"Ça n'empêche pas," Marion smiled.

Mrs. Cameron pondered the smile. Marion was growing; her
mother must grow with her.

"Will he fall in love with you, I wonder?" she said, archly.

Marion rose up from her chair. They were in their private hotel's
drawing-room, quite alone together; everybody else preferred the
lounge.

"Mother! If you ever say that again . . ."

Mrs. Cameron's little face at once took on a rosy obstinacy.

"I don't see why you fly at me, Marion. You said it first."

"I! Say such a thing about myself and . . . and Mr. Bergsma! I'm a useful servant to him, that's all."

"So would the other one have been."

Marion gasped. "The 'other one!'" For a moment she could not say any more.

Her mother became injured. "I see nothing dreadful in calling another secretary 'the other one.' And please don't speak of yourself as a servant, Marion; there's no need to do that, if you are working for a salary."

Marion sat down again. "I am a servant, and I'm not ashamed of it."

"You are an accomplished lady, who makes use of her talent to help a busy man—not of course a gentleman, but. . ."

"Not a gentleman," Marion gasped again.

"Do not repeat every word I say." Mrs. Cameron was calm, but her little fallen-in, pink mouth was closely set. "Mr. Bergsma is very clever, but you must know as well as I do that he is not a gentleman, in the way your father was, and Neil is."

"He's foreign," Marion panted. She had only just saved herself from echoing "Neil!" Neil liked Bergsma; he had said so when he met him before going out again to India.

"You are used to foreigners," continued Mrs. Cameron. "You know that the Count and M. de la Vigne and Herr von Adelbert were not a bit like Mr. Bergsma. He may be very courteous to you; I have no doubt he is, but his manners to me . . ."

And all this because Bergsma had omitted to open a door, the other day, for Mrs. Cameron! He had been talking so eagerly that he hadn't seen her get up. Marion did not speak; she could do nothing but echo if she spoke. "The Count—horrid old M. de la Vigne—manners . . ."

"It is time to go to bed," said Mrs. Cameron, cheerfully, as if nothing had happened. That was her tact, the famous tact which had carried her—and Neil and Marion—through so many difficulties. Marion wondered why she hated it, now that it was being exercised upon herself. But mother had forgotten it when she spoke of Mr. Bergsma as not being a gentleman. A cloud obscured the earnest face, as she followed Mrs. Cameron upstairs, and wished, for the first time in all her life, that they could afford to have separate bedrooms.

She said much less about her work from that time forward. It grew more and more exacting; there were few nights now on which she was not out at concerts, for Bergsma was devoting himself to musical drama: he found it more inspiring for his gifts of exposition. It was clear that Marion's efforts pleased him; and yet his crossness grew more pronounced, more constant—not rudeness, but a curious coolness and aloofness, as if it were a watchfulness. And since now she did not talk about it with her mother, it seemed the more oppressive, even sinister. Her mother did not ask the questions Marion had expected, and would perhaps have welcomed; they might have eased the dual strain. The strain was dual because Mrs. Cameron, too, was often cool now about little things—the cocoa, for example. It was always there when Marion came in late, but there with an effect of duty, not of glad excited revel, as on that first night. Marion sometimes felt a strange depression. Life seemed altered; though outwardly more exhilarating, it was inwardly less happy. Her toil was not the cause—that grew more dear and glorious every day. No one could have told her articles from Bergsma's now, and still he didn't seem to notice, or if he did, he liked it, to judge by the opportunities he gave her.

One day, Mrs. Wynne said something which infuriated Marion. "What's your salary now? I suppose it's a good deal bigger."

There fell an almost tangible silence. It was as if something they had waited for had happened.

Marion looked at her friend. Mrs. Wynne was not looking at Marion, but her eyes had just met Mrs. Cameron's, and Marion caught the gleam. She felt her own eyes flash.

"My salary remains the same."

There was another little silence; then Mrs. Wynne said, "Well done, Bergsma!"

"What do you mean?" cried Marion, choking.

Mrs. Cameron intervened at that point; she said something about "on probation."

"Rather a long probation," Mrs. Wynne observed.

Marion got up. Her voice was gone, her eyes did not flash now, but dimmed with sudden, smarting tears. She stood a moment, looking at the others, then hurried from the room.

So that was what her mother had been plotting. She had asked Mrs. Wynne to say something; the meeting of their eyes betrayed it . . . When one was being given such a chance! If Bergsma knew, he wouldn't think so highly of his lady-secretary. Rather common, a sordid rise, as if she were indeed a servant! That was just the difference it made, to be a lady. But mother was a lady too, if Mrs. Wynne was a little too shrewd to be "quite-quite . . ." However, there was no time to worry about it; she had a bigger job tonight than she had ever had before—a symphony, a Danish one, produced by a Society on their special Sunday night for the innermost circle (Bergsma was out of town). She must keep fit for that. And supper—Sunday supper here, with her mother!

Could she stand it? All the time that hateful incident would hover, of the eyes that met and parted furtively . . . No; she couldn't go through supper.

When Mrs. Cameron came up to change her dress, she found a note upon the pin-cushion.

Marion was supping at a little restaurant, "quite nice and respectable," close to the hall where her job lay; she would be home at the usual hour.

Her mother was asleep, or seemed to be asleep, when she came in. There was no cocoa.

★ ★ ★

Quite without warning it came—the letter in which Bergsma said he had decided to dispense with a secretary for the present.

Marion read it at breakfast. She managed not to cry out; if she turned white, nobody saw her, in the pre-occupation with their food which, at breakfast especially, was a source of continual unrest among the boarders. She put the letter in her belt, and blindly took a plate displaying a poached egg. Marion cut her egg mechanically; it flowed over the toast, and something in the sight made her feel sick . . . She would have to tell her mother after breakfast. It would be dreadful; her mother would gush out, like the egg. But the thing could not be hidden: better get it told as soon as possible.

"Come up to our room a moment, mother, before you read the paper," Marion said, when Mrs. Cameron had finished. She had smuggled her own streaming plate away, before it could be noticed that she had not touched the egg except to cut it.

"Are you staying in this morning, then?" Mrs. Cameron said, wondering.

"Yes," Marion answered, and a bitter wave of woe swept into her. She would be staying in all mornings now . . . She mounted the steep stairs before her mother, the distress increasing as she went, until at the last landing (for their room was at the very top) she broke down, and stood with her face hidden, trembling.

"What's the matter?" Mrs. Cameron called sharply from the flight below; she had seen through the balusters.

Without answering, Marion went into their room. When the little staring face appeared, she silently held out the letter.

Mrs. Cameron began to read. Almost as soon as she began, her daughter broke out crying—weakly, the sound muffled by her covering hands.

"What is it, mother, what can I have done? Oh, tell me, tell me!" Marion sobbed.

"Don't cry, Marion," Mrs. Cameron said quickly. "Whatever you do, don't cry."

She was feeling for a prop to clutch at—there was nothing but their pride: they must not cry.

That man, whom she had always thought so common—that man had done this to them! She dropped the letter; Bergsma's cheque fell out. Money—his . . . she could have stamped upon the cheque.

"Oh, Marion, do not cry. Remember what you are—and what he is!" she added fiercely. But the fierceness died. Soon she was crying too, because she could not bear to cry. Their sobs were audible outside, for Mrs. Cameron had forgotten to shut the door; a sloppy servant came and stared into the room. It had not been "done" yet, and the girl's face grew sulky—now they'd stop her doing it, and she was to get out so soon as she had finished upstairs.

Mrs. Cameron went to the door, and locked it. "I saw that horrid Annie staring in," she gulped.

Then she did not know what to say. Annie would be cross if they delayed her, and Annie could make a lot of difference to the boarders' comfort. But Marion would certainly not be able to come downstairs for some time yet. She had thrown herself upon her unmade bed; her sobs grew deeper every minute. Mrs. Cameron had never, since the baby-years, heard Marion cry until today.

"Oh, mother, tell me what I can have done," she kept on moaning.

Was it not an occasion for the tact?

"I believe," said Mrs. Cameron, "that you were getting to write so well that he was jealous."

But Marion only groaned. "Oh, mother!" on a different note of anguish.

"Mrs. Wynne says your articles really seem like making fun of him sometimes—they are so alike."

"Mrs. Wynne!"

"She was your idol, Marion, before . . . all this."

The tact seemed to be working, for Marion suddenly sat up. Her face was blurred, but it could show that she was cross, her mother thought—and then she saw that Marion was not cross, but desperate.

"It's no use," said Marion. "There's no good talking about it. The servant is dismissed, with a quarter's salary in lieu of notice."

Mrs. Cameron's eyes burned. "Extra salary! How dare he?"

"I'll throw his cheque back in his face," the girl said, getting off the bed.

"Not in his face, Marion—you wouldn't go there?"

"Mother!" Marion groaned again.—They were hunted from their room at last, for Annie knocked at the door violently.

Mrs. Cameron put on her hat before she yielded; she was going out to do some shopping, for she couldn't settle to the morning paper now. When she came back, in half-an-hour, Marion still was sitting at a table in the drawing-room, her face buried in her hands, as she had been when Mrs. Cameron had left her . . . It all began again, and through the whole day it went on. The letter to Bergsma must be written—a dignified, ladylike letter. Marion made draft upon draft: they were not torn up as they accumulated, for in each there was a phrase that seemed essential to her solace—one of gratitude, of meek reproach, of sad affection. But to every phrase like this, her mother objected. "No, not that, Marion—please, not that."

So it went on, and they got crosser and crosser. Tea in their bedroom—their own China tea—was the one change from the hot, dingy, saddle-backed drawing-room. The house-tea was in the lounge as usual; they rarely went down. This hotel was their poverty's consent—a place so typical of its kind as to be almost mythical; no aggravation of the cheap private hotel's horrors was absent. But tea in their room did not refresh them. They drank cups down like poison-cups; Marion could "touch nothing," though Mrs. Cameron had specially, that morning, bought some favourite and expensive cakes. Would tomorrow be as bad, the older woman wondered. At any rate, the letter would be sent by then, and Marion might pick up some courage after it had gone.

After dinner Mrs. Wynne came in. The final draft had not been written yet, and they had lingered in the lounge—each shrinking from renewal.

"Shall we tell her?" Mrs. Cameron said in a whisper, as Mrs. Wynne came towards them, threading her way among the chairs. "Just as you like," said Marion, weakly. "She'll have to know some day."

But in her heart she knew that she desired to tell. Despite that incident about the salary, Marion still liked Mrs. Wynne. With her much
wider knowledge of the world she might throw light on Bergsma's
action, and anyhow one couldn't talk or think of any other subject.
Mrs. Cameron, on her side, wanted to hear Bergsma blamed "as he
deserved"; so eagerly they welcomed Mrs. Wynne, and quickly transferred her and themselves to the drawing-room.

"You can smoke there—nobody ever enters it but ourselves," Mrs.
Cameron assured her.

Sunk in the saddle-back Chesterfield with her cigarette, Mrs. Wynne
sat listening. Her expressive monkey-face said more than she did, for at
first she only murmured sympathetically.

But Marion, watching her face, asked suddenly, "Have you ever
heard that Mr. Bergsma was . . . was given to dismissing secretaries
without notice?" She laughed—a wretched little laugh, most sadly
changed from the big note of other days.

Mrs. Wynne said, "Not exactly that."

"Then what?" said Marion.

"I may as well tell you. He is a 'woman's man,' they say; attractive
to women, I mean. I shouldn't have supposed so, but that's his reputation. And there's a Mrs. Bergsma, you see. Have you ever met her?"

"She has come into the study once or twice," said Marion coldly,
and wished she had not asked her question.

"She may be jealous."

"Jealous—of me!"

"Not of you personally. It's common enough, you know, with these
men's wives."

"But Mr. Bergsma never . . ."

Mrs. Cameron interrupted Marion. "You said it yourself."

"Said what, mother?"

"That he might have been in love with the other one who spoke
Dutch. You know he did, Marion." Marion saw a smile—at once
repressed—break on the visitor's lips. But there was no stopping Mrs.
Cameron; the Dutch episode was told, with "Marion's" explanation of
it, and in that vein the dialogue developed, while Marion sat and
writhed. There was a transition to the other theory of jealousy—
Bergsma's jealousy of the articles. Mrs. Wynne rejected it.

"A writer with . . . with his sort of style" (Marion wondered what
that meant) "would never notice."

There were no more smiles, no looks exchanged with Mrs. Cameron, yet Mrs. Wynne preserved an air of knowing something that they didn't know. Soon she went away, a little bored perhaps, for they had talked of nothing else. Then Mrs. Cameron and Marion went to bed, the letter still unwritten. Mrs. Wynne had said there was no hurry; Bergsma would anticipate a short delay. It galled Mrs. Cameron—she would have liked to finish with him; but Marion seemed relieved, and indeed neither could have faced an evening like the day. So they went up to bed, quite early.

. . . A separate room—a room in which she could have cried herself to sleep! But Marion must be quiet every night—there never would be one when she might cry.

Soon after the candle was put out, her mother spoke.

"Are you awake, Marion? Mrs. Wynne thinks you're in love with Mr. Bergsma, I am sure."

No answer from the other bed.

"You're not asleep; I heard you move the pillow—that's what she thinks. I never liked her, but she was your friend, so I said nothing. After all, I daresay it's a blessing the connection is ended."

"Anything that gives rise to gossip . . . I should have thought of that; I blame myself. However, it's all over now, and Neil need never know how it happened. We can let him think that the work had got too hard for you, as indeed I think it had. And with no rise in salary! Do you remember how Mrs. Wynne remarked on that?"

But her voice had got drowsy; soon she was asleep. Marion for a long while did not dare to move. She lay, like a dead body, stiff and straight, and thought how like she was to one, except that the dead body would be dead. It would not wake next morning, and the morning after that, nor go to bed next night and lie so still because it feared to set its mother talking of how it was believed to be in love with Mr. Bergsma, but how Neil need never know.

Miss Cameron had been working too hard, Dr. Ferguson said; she would have had to take a long rest anyhow—she could not have gone on at that rate.

Marion peered at him suspiciously, and found him peering in a similar way at her. He was a good-looking pompous man, her mother's contemporary. Marion felt that he would be on her mother's side. She could not have accounted for the feeling, nor till now would it have come to her—there had been no "sides" till now. But as he peered at her, she found herself reflecting:

"He'll call mother wonderful, too, like Colonel Morris and the Admiral." Though Dr. Ferguson had attended the Camerons for years, he knew nothing of their lives except their ailments and their poverty; he now was obviously impressed when he heard that Marion had been working with Bergsma. It was his foible to be up-to-date, as he still called it; Bergsma's work appealed to him—there had been a new Scriabin piece lately: "the Theosophical School," said Dr. Ferguson, with pride, looking at Marion more respectfully. "Exacting work, no doubt, yours must have been."

"I was only his secretary," Marion said.

"'Only!'" said Mrs. Cameron. She was standing, very upright, at the foot of the bed, gazing pathetically from the doctor's face to Marion's, like a child who knew that it was like a child.

Marion groaned. "Be quiet, mother"; and at the same instant her conviction of the doctor's partisanship changed. He was on her side! He had been peering at her still more closely, but when Mrs. Cameron spoke he turned his head and peered at her. His eyes lit up with a quick gleam; he prevented Mrs. Cameron from going on by going on himself with animation, ordaining change of air as soon as Marion was well enough ("and rich enough," said Marion, but he took no notice); in the meantime she was to see her friends, not read nor write at all, not brood, but look forward instead of backwards, make the best of life . . . Marion lay and listened. She knew what would happen when her mother and the doctor left the bedroom. He would be told about the extra work, and the not-extra salary, and her too faithful mimicry of Bergsma's style. Perhaps he would not be told of Mrs. Wynne's imputed theory, but she wasn't sure: mother was so . . . so foolish! That was the amazing word that came to her, and Marion's thoughts diverged. Her mother foolish—she who had done such marvels with her tact, who had carried her big son and her big daughter on its shoulders, as it were. "Minnie Cameron's a wonderful woman." Had there ever been a Colonel or an Admiral, among their large acquaintance in the sort, who had not at some time said that to Marion? And Neil too: he was always saying how wonderful mother was . . . was she?

Outside the door she heard them whispering. Why didn't her mother take the doctor to the ever-empty drawing-room? He couldn't know there was a place that they might, practically, call their own sitting-room, but Mrs. Cameron knew it; and wasn't whispering supposed to be the thing most fatal to a patient's nerves? "No rise in her salary": she could have sworn she caught the words. There could be no need to tell him that; the work would have been just as hard if she had had the bigger salary. But it was vain to torment one's-self; mother always did what she "thought right." And as Marion lay and strained her ears, the certainty grew stronger that Mrs. Cameron would put the other view before him—the view that Marion might have been in love with Bergsma. She would think that, also, right. Perhaps it was; perhaps a doctor should be told such things about a helpless, useless daughter who would be a burden again now, instead of a breadwinner. And she had been so proud of earning her own living! Hot tears ran down her cheeks. As a secretary pure and simple, she would not have broken down. It was the hard work, late hours, excitement, mental strain, and—and Bergsma's growing crossness and aloofness, his avoidance of her, even while he used her; the thick eyes that had not flashed for her this many a day, but always deadened, deadened more and more with each infrequent interview. How she had watched to see the eyes light up, the way they used, when she had "done" some concert more capably than usual—and the eyes never had, though still he sent her: "in case there should be something startling that I'd better do myself, and then I can write-up your article." That had meant that she must take even more pains than usual, lest Bergsma be "let down," and ignore a masterpiece. But Marion had not minded, or would not have minded, if . . . And then had come the letter.

They had not sent back the cheque. Mrs. Wynne had said it would be futile and undignified; they couldn't bandy money about—Bergsma would insist, it would be horribly uncomfortable; and the "salary in lieu of notice" was the proper thing for him to do. So a colourless letter had gone, in which the phrases of affection and reproach were all left out. It had had the effect of making Bergsma write again, holding forth vague hopes that some day he would be able to resume Miss Cameron's "invaluable services." There had been discussions on what he meant by that. Marion said, "Nothing"; Mrs. Cameron (commenting with much sarcasm on invaluable) hoped so, but was afraid he did mean something. That went on for days and nights; inspirations on what Bergsma meant would flock in the darkness. But the breakdown had mercifully come at last, and had done this for Marion—she might cry in her bed now. It was called part of her illness. Without the illness, another explanation of her melancholy had been showing itself as imminent. "I shall begin to think that your friend Mrs. Wynne was right."

Those words had been said one day, in a flurry of temper, at teatime. Marion could go out of the room then; but if they should be said and added to, at night, when the candle was extinguished . . .

Mrs. Cameron came back, brisk and brave and pathetic.

"The doctor thinks we shall have rain at last. I'm glad for your sake, Marion; this room gets so hot. The sun is cheerful, but the rain will make things fresh again."

"Did you talk about the weather all that time?" asked Marion.

"Of course we talked of you a little; he had to tell me about your diet. But, Marion, dear, you know there are other things in the world besides your trouble."

"Oh yes—the weather," Marion said.

"Invalids are never told what the doctor says about them. You must not be unreasonable, Marion."

Marion fixed her eyes upon the little face, like a ventriloquist's puppet's face. It looked back at her, and the lips drew together, with a kind of peevish patience. "You've been crying. The doctor says (as you insist on being told what he says) that I mustn't let you cry, on any account."

"Then of course you mustn't, mother. How are you going to stop me? Shall I tell you what I was crying about? It was about never being alone. I'm going to ask the doctor to order me a separate bedroom. The extra-quarter's salary will pay for it. It will do me more good than any other change."

Mrs. Cameron began to cry.

"Oh, mother, that's not tactful, is it, showing me a bad example?" Marion loathed herself, yet could not stop. It was too much for her— the triple wreck, of herself and Bergsma and her mother.

The doctor would not order the separate room. He gave all sorts of unconvincing reasons, very cheerily. Marion lay and looked at him.

"I shall torment myself till I find out the real reason," she said. "Will that be good for me?"

He laughed. "You have far too much intelligence, Miss Cameron. You won't waste your mental strength like that."

"I have no use for my intelligence," said Marion. "I have no use for my mental strength. One way of wasting them is as good as another."

"Oh, nonsense, nonsense!" laughed the doctor. "What you've got to do is to get well, and then see if you haven't a use for them. Mr. Bergsma's not the only busy man who needs a secretary."

A cunning look came in Marion's face. "And he may 'resume my invaluable services,'" she said, fixing her eyes on her mother.

Mrs. Cameron winced, but she stood bravely up to Marion's eyes. "Well, all right, darling, if he does." She smiled pathetically.

The cunning look died out. "I'm not mad, I tell you both!" cried Marion. The doctor took her wrist between his fingers. "What put that brilliant idea into your head, may I inquire?"

"You two!" Marion shrieked, and tore her wrist away. "You two think I am. That's why you won't let me have a room to myself, and that's why mother grins and pretends she wouldn't rather die than ever let me work again for Mr. Bergsma. She hated him, you know," she told the doctor in a sudden mood of confidence, "and all because he forgot to open the drawing-room door for her one day!" She sank back on the pillow. "That was why, just that"; and she began to sob and moan . . .

But as time went on, she did get better. Her strength came back, and with it, self-control. It was not often now that she sneered at, or "flew at," her mother; she only lay and watched her, with a smile. Mrs. Cameron did not like the smile, but she avoided looking—it was the most tactful thing to do. And when Marion got better and could be up, and better still could come out for little walks, the smile, though it was there sometimes, was not so frequent. It, like the crying, had been part of her illness, and that was nearly over; the smile would disappear when all the illness did, and everything would be as it had been before, except that the horrid Bergsma connection would be done with. Neil need never know that Marion had, for a while, been so—so overstrained that Dr. Ferguson had warned Mrs. Cameron not to let her be alone even for a moment. Neil need never know, and that was all that mattered . . . She looked at Marion complacently, one day in Kensington Gardens; but instantly she looked away again. Marion's eyes were fixed on her; the smile was there.

"You're a wonderful woman, mother," Marion said. "You've got me over it."

"Over what, Marion?" Mrs. Cameron faltered, off her guard.

"My passion for Mr. Bergsma."

"Don't be wicked!" the old woman exclaimed. Marion was nearly well now; there was no need to humour her to this extent.

"And my suicidal tendency, too," continued Marion. "I wonder which I ought to be most grateful for. Which do you think?"

"I am not aware that either of those things was the matter with you, I assure you, Marion, and neither is Dr. Ferguson. You exaggerate your illness absurdly."

"You and Dr. Ferguson exaggerated it too, then. I often heard you both; I was able to get out of bed, you know. I always thought you should have taken him down to the drawing-room instead of whispering outside my door, but it didn't seem to occur to you, and as it was convenient to me, I said nothing . . . Well, mother, if I can't believe in your wisdom any more, I can believe in your pluck. It's just as good; I don't know that it isn't better. But I hope you didn't tell anyone besides the doctor that I was in love with Mr. Bergsma."

The little puppet-face was convulsed in the effort not to cry. "I never could have dreamed that my daughter would listen."

"I was mad, you see."

"You were not, Marion, so don't bring that up as an excuse. You were not mad, only overstrained. You exaggerate everything. I only told the doctor what your own friend, Mrs. Wynne, had said—or what she thought, at any rate. I never thought so myself."

"You should have thought so, mother. It was true. That was why he dismissed me. He didn't want his secretary to have a passion for him."

"Don't use that wicked word! And about that man, with his flat face and horrid collars—they were never clean."

"Oh yes, they were clean, but they were lower than the men you know would wear. That's all, mother . . . I used to watch for a look from the flat face—was it flat? I suppose so. I only saw his eyes." She spoke in a deep musing tone, with no smile now; she had forgotten her mother.

Mrs. Cameron stood up. "It's nearly lunch-time."

The girl looked at her again. "Won't you let me talk about my passion, a little now and then?"

"Oh, Marion," the other moaned, returning. "How can you torment me so? It's cruel of you!"

She sat down again. "You frighten me, indeed you do." Her voice shattered into sobs.

The girl sat unmoved. "We're like two dead bodies tied together. We don't love each other any more, yet we must be for ever side by side . . . I think I won't forgive you for curing the tendency to suicide, mother. The passion's different—I can brood on that. I can think of his flat face, and wonder why a man with a flat face was not more flattered—there's a joke. But he's a woman's man, isn't he? He's tired of passionate secretaries, I suppose. That was why he snubbed my Dutch; it would have been dangerous to speak in his own language with a yearning secretary—"

Mrs. Cameron got up again, her pink cheeks glistening. "I won't listen to you. It's disgraceful—that's what it is. You ought to be ashamed."

"Haven't I been ashamed enough? Let me glory in my shame now, for a change." She got up too. "Come home to lunch, mother. Tuesday

. . . it will be mutton-hash to-day, and treacle-pudding. That will be so nice; we'll easily forget this painful scene. Yes, let's go—home."

Mrs. Cameron pointed out the beauty of the autumn tints as they went through the Gardens.

Marion looked at each example; then looked at her mother, with the smile.

★ ★ ★

That phase also passed. Marion felt abominable while it lasted; it was like daggers into a doll, and the daggers hurt this doll. They made no difference, moreover; Mrs. Cameron said the same kind of things between-times.

Mother and daughter went away together for their change of air, returned, and Marion was nearly well. The doctor still came sometimes, but now as though he were a friend, vigilant and interested. He seemed, as she had felt before, to be Marion's friend rather than her mother's; but Marion did not care; she cared for nothing. In the passage of the months her bitterness had grown beneath the outward self-control; she had one watchword now—concealment of all feeling.

"I feel nothing, but if you must feel hide it—hide everything about you, all you think and are."

It became a trial of skill. She paid visits with her mother, watching for good opportunities for lies about herself, especially the lie of being lazy, glad to cease breadwinning and be entirely dependent, hanging as it were upon her mother's arm like a spoilt child.

Mrs. Cameron's friends began to disapprove; Marion perceived it, fostered it. The plan of the Minnie party was that Marion now should teach the many languages—such work could always be procured. Marion refused to try for pupils, not saying that she liked best to be lazy—that would have spoilt the game. She let it be inferred, amid glances of concern at the sad change in her.

The glances of concern pleased Mrs. Cameron. They made her feel a wonderful woman again.

During the later Bergsma period there had been a certain obscuration—Marion had been so prominent with her "inside" knowledge of musical events, her acquaintance with the virtuosi, her own remarkable development in capacity and self-reliance. But now people saw again that Minnie was the heroine, with her bravery and cheer, her patience with the lazy daughter. She loved to take the lazy daughter out to tea, to come into a room thus followed, and display her pluck and tact. But as the months drew out and she felt firmer on the pedestal, an insidious change began. At some houses there would sound again a note of interest in Marion rather than in Minnie.

Mrs. Wynne's was one of these. The dark monkey-face would turn and dwell, observing silently but intently taking in. She would talk about music, that inhibited topic on which Marion, lamentably and surprisingly, still enjoyed to talk. Tactless of Mrs. Wynne! It brought the whole thing up again—the buried past, with all its mystery and invidiousness; and besides, "Marion would never try for pupils, while she was encouraged to remember those horrible days," said Mrs. Cameron to her friends.

Mrs. Wynne's Irish maid was another grievance. This little creature was "positively insulting" to Mrs. Cameron, one day soon after the return to London. It happened thus. Marion and her mother entered, and put down their umbrellas—Mrs. Cameron thrusting hers into the stand, Marion propping hers against the table. Bridget (she had an engaging cast in her right eye) gave swimming Irish looks at Marion, whose height and "style" she openly admired—she was far too free with both her eyes and tongue. Then she went towards the stairs, with no admiring glance for Mrs. Cameron, who had on a new grey toque. Marion, un-delayed by the small difficulty of getting an umbrella neatly into the narrow stand, had begun to ascend at Bridget's heels, conversing with her.

Suddenly Mrs. Cameron called out: "Come back here, Marion." The two on the stairs stopped short.

"Come back and put your umbrella in the proper place."

"Oh, ma'am, it doesn't matter," Bridget cried. "The mistress never—"

"Come back here, Marion." The face under the new toque was scarlet.

Marion, pale and silent, stood still on the stairs. Her eyes were dreadful. For an instant they met Bridget's.

"Do you hear what I say?" the voice below vibrated shrilly.

"For heaven's sake, mother . . ." Marion gasped, and came down from the stairs. She went by her mother, and put her umbrella into the stand.

"Oh, miss; oh, ma'am!" breathed Bridget, almost crying—but Mrs. Cameron was now on Marion's stair, and was looking at her angrily. Bridget gulped, and went on to the drawing-room door. Her voice broke as she announced them. Mrs. Cameron pushed by her haughtily; Marion . . . Bridget never knew what Marion did, except that she did not break down, nor speak to Bridget, nor look angry, but—"Oh, ma'am," said Bridget, choking, to her mistress, "it was awful! As if Mrs. Cameron wanted to shame her before me, turning her into a child like that. The umbrella—Miss Cameron went down and put it in the stand; I could hardly keep quiet when I saw her face. She'll go mad, ma'am, if she can't get away from her mother."

Bridget's agitation was so great that Mrs. Wynne, though she too thought it "awful," tried to calm the girl and herself by saying that there was really nothing in it.

"Oh yes, ma'am, there was, and you'd know if you'd seen it. The way Mrs. Cameron looked at her—you wouldn't believe the wicked-ness of it."

"Nonsense; you're fond of Miss Cameron; you exaggerate."

"It's well someone's fond of her. You are yourself, ma'am. Is there no way you could get her away from that old—"

But this was decidedly too much; Mrs. Wynne dismissed the girl. She sat thinking. She had long perceived the trouble. The mother's jealousy—innate and ineradicable—never roused by Marion till the Bergsma phase, and then appeased by the dismissal, now again was quickened by her daughter's attitude. If Marion's friends should show more interest in that than in the mother's pluck and patience, the jeal-ousy would crouch, a-stretch like a wild beast that sees its prey; and ah, that prey was visible! The daughter's pride—what a long feasting meal . . . One knew such moods in these undeveloped women, these old children, with the cruelty and blindness of a child, but not the child's inconsequence. No; the feast once begun, the wild beast would drive out the child; its prey would not be loosened till consumed. "And one can do not one least thing to save—unless indeed one should abandon Marion, and join with Mrs. Cameron! Shall I urge the poor girl to the teaching that she shrinks from? It might help; I'll try it."

When Mrs. Wynne next went to see them, in pursuance of her scheme, she found a message from the Bergsma quarter so absorbing Mrs. Cameron that even she—now almost openly cold-shouldered—was called into council.

The message had taken the shape of a visiting-card—Mrs. Bergsma's, intimating change of address. It had come to Mrs. Cameron, not to Marion.

"Now what ought we to do?"

"Take no notice," Mrs. Wynne said, at a venture. She had not yet surveyed the ground, but it seemed probable that this would please.

It did not please, and as that showed, the visitor began to see the rest. Marion sat by, silent. Not even by a look did she confess herself, but Mrs. Wynne's nerves shuddered for her.

"There's nothing in it," Mrs. Wynne continued. "Mrs. Bergsma just went through her address-book, or someone else did for her, more likely. They'll not expect a call."

The argument began, went on; and Mrs. Wynne knew horror. All cruelty seemed in it, all base vengeance, all that once meant woman; each word seemed chosen to retaliate for that brief spell of bliss and glory; yet as the listener looked into the little face, she told herself that she, like Bridget, was imputing that which was not in its owner's competence. This could be only sheer stupidity; the worst evil was not there. But then again some glance, some word, abominable, would upset the milder judgment.

"What does Marion say?" her friend broke out at last, unable longer to fight single-handed. She turned to the dumb girl and saw her quiver momentarily, then constrain herself to sit impassive as before. But it were kindlier to force her speech, and Mrs. Wynne persisted.

"Tell me, Marion," she entreated, casting aside caution, putting all her friendship into the low tone. It was as if she challenged the fell mother for the daughter's voice. No answer came. The girl's eyes met hers for an instant, and she caught her breath. What a look—what weary wastes of suffering . . . And yet admitted the thing was trivial— almost certainly, a mere card-leaving: they would not be admitted, no one ever was home on chance, in London. But Mrs. Wynne could understand the girl's repugnance.

"I can't see why Marion should be with you, if you wish to go," she repeated, for this had been of course the first thing she had said.

"It is only through her that I ever knew these people"—yes, the tone, the look . . . "It is for her sake that I wish to go."

"But if she doesn't want it? Such morbid nonsense! 'Hanging round the house,' she calls it. I think it is we who confer the favour by calling."

But as if this, in its absurdity, were the breaking point, Marion spoke at last.

"Mother has never consented to recognize Mr. Bergsma as a social being. He's only a common little man with a crushed collar to her. 'No one' goes to his house; 'no one' knows the Bergsma."

She smiled—the old smile which had frightened Mrs. Cameron, but now had lost its power.

"I don't profess to understand the society in which people like the Bergsmas move. I leave that to you . . . and your friends."

There was a silence.

"Could you, Marion?" Mrs. Wynne then murmured. "Could you go, I mean. It wouldn't be a case of getting in, I'm sure." Marion, having spoken at all, seemed to have abandoned wholly her new attitude, for she gave her friend an overwhelming answer. "I could go, but I won't. I won't be dragged there at mother's chariot-wheels." She stood up. "Now you know, mother. I dare say you'll say you don't understand, but I'll explain another time. Don't drag Mrs. Wynne into a scene like this morning's. She wouldn't like it. Let her off the rest."

But the teeth were firm in the flesh now, and Mrs. Wynne heard all the rest. She heard that Marion was still absurdly 'sorry for herself' and that her friends encouraged her, while Mrs. Cameron's were more and more disgusted every day; that "that man" would imagine, if no one else did, all that their omission to call might signify; that indeed his wife could not be blamed if she had been suspicious, and her card was intended for a delicate hint that, having nipped the thing in the bud, she was prepared to resume a friendly acquaintance. "Anything more disgusting, more indecent, than Marion's whole behaviour since that man cast her off . . ."

And Marion stood and heard, without the smile, and said at last in a pause:

"The most devoted and most tactful mother, you can see—and Mrs. Bergsma is to see. How do you know I haven't been 'hanging round the house' in secret, mother? Mr. Bergsma cast me off, as you say, but men do that and women hang about them, still. Perhaps that's why I stick at going to call—how do you know it isn't?"

But this was a bad slip.

"I know," said Mrs. Cameron, "because I've never let you out of my sight for a single instant, and never intend to."

Mrs. Wynne saw Marion pale at that. She exclaimed after a moment: "But Dr. Ferguson said yesterday that I'm to have a room to myself, in future. They're getting it ready now; you know they are." Her voice was harsh with fear.

"They're not getting it ready. I countermanded it, after this morning's 'scene,' as you call it."

The girl sank on a chair. Her face was terrible to see, but Mrs. Wynne did not see it—she had hidden her own. She sat, crumpled into a heap, in her corner of the sofa. Marion looked at her, then at her mother. Mrs. Cameron was by the tea-table; she was picking biscuits from a plate and nibbling at them, and then dropping them; her face was red and angry, but exultant.

"Look at Mrs. Wynne, mother," Marion said at last, in the old languid tone. "She seems distressed. It's not a pretty scene. We ought to let her go."

Mrs. Wynne sprang up. "I'm going. I can't stand it. You two should be entirely apart—it's monstrous. Is there no one who could take you, Marion, for a while? I will, if you like. I can't stand by and let this be—it's not safe; I feel responsible . . . Let her come to me!" She turned to the mother, speaking gently now: she had regained her self-control.

Mrs. Cameron, a biscuit at her lips, laughed slightingly. Her voice took a vile note as she replied: "I'll keep my unfortunate daughter, thank you."

"Then some day you'll have to keep her in a mad-house," Mrs. Wynne exclaimed, once more forgetting prudence.

"That's no worse than the kind of house you'd keep her in."

Mrs. Wynne did not hear; she was looking at Marion, who had got up again.

"Stop!" she cried.

But Marion laughed, and threw the biscuit-plate—now empty—in her mother's face.

It grazed the skin, that was all. Mrs. Cameron wept, Marion stood and laughed. Mrs. Wynne took out her handkerchief to stop the blood. The plate lay whole upon the floor some distance off; it had fallen into a thick woolly rug. The blood soon ceased—it was the merest graze. Marion stopped laughing; and Mrs. Wynne escaped. There was nothing she could do, except go to Dr. Ferguson. He must insist upon the separate room, at any rate.

She went, straight from the hotel—she found him in and told her tale, and Dr. Ferguson confessed that he was anxious. He would see the Camerons tomorrow. As a measure of precaution—"you understand me?"—he had at first refused the separate bedroom; now he, too, considered it essential.

"There can be no doubt that the mother's constant presence is injurious to Miss Cameron."

"But what should make her so inhuman to the girl? It has been a strain for both, of course; but what happened to-day was more than nerves. I assure you, Dr. Ferguson, it looked like intentional persecution. Yet surely such things cannot be?"

The doctor thought awhile; then said, "Persecution, yes; intentional persecution (in your sense), no. Do you happen to have read what is now being published here about Freud, a German scientist, and his theory of the 'suppressed wish'?"

Mrs. Wynne had not. He set it forth, rudimentarily—a subconscious motive, usually sexual in origin and sinister in aim, underlying the conscious will, and secretly inspiring the action. In certain conditions, it became the dominant impulse, potent above all others.

"That amiable old lady," he continued, and as Mrs. Wynne exclaimed, he sagely smiled. "As she appears, or appeared, to us to be, and in her own view still is. She knows nothing of the 'wish,' you must consider, either as a psychological theory or in herself—the wish in her case being to dominate, nay, humiliate, her daughter. You have perceived this in her, and may even, being a woman" (he bowed), "have diagnosed it correctly as jealousy: no rare thing, as doubtless you are aware, in a mother towards her daughter, though here it takes a somewhat unusual form. It was awakened, as I early saw, in Mrs. Cameron by her daughter's prominence during the Bergsma period."

"It sounds more devilish than ever," Mrs. Wynne exclaimed.

"You must remember that the state is pathological. To inhibit the 'wish' is not within the victim's competence, did she even know that it exists. A pitiable condition—and the more because it engenders dislike in all who witness its effects."

But Mrs. Wynne could feel no sense of mitigation; rather, the "Freudian wish," in its gaunt determinism, seemed to add despair to all the other ills.

"And the unhappy girl!" she cried. "Is she to be condemned to this, because a German scientist has an interesting psychological theory?"

He had an indulgent smile for her feminine unreason. "Most natural—in a woman, most natural . . . But reflect that if the daughter's martyrdom can be explained, it is not thereby increased."

She groaned. "Explanations have a way of paralysing us, I think! What are you going to do?"

Dr. Ferguson stiffened a little. "What can be done, you may rest assured. The separate room, for example."

His tone annoyed her. "Is that the certain panacea?"

"We are struggling against an occult force in human nature, Mrs. Wynne," he said, more stiffly still.

"But we're not sure it's there; we have only this man's word for it!" And as he shrugged, she exclaimed, "I want to take Marion away from her."

"Do so, by all means, if you can compass it," Dr. Ferguson more cordially rejoined.

"Meanwhile, I will ordain the lesser separation." His gesture was dismissive, and she rose.

At the door she turned. "To-morrow?"

"Without delay," the doctor promised, again somewhat stiffly.

But with the morning of the next day, very early, came the secretary of the Camerons' hotel to Mrs. Wynne, who, going out, met her upon the doorstep, and when she learnt who it was, drew her at once into the dining-room. The woman, with a horrible detached annoyance in her manner, told her news. Mrs. Cameron had found her daughter dead in bed at six o'clock that morning—in the same room with herself.

"In the same room, Mrs. Wynne, lying in streams of blood." The faded, worried eyes traversed Mrs. Wynne's room curiously, as she talked on. "Miss Cameron had cut open a vein in her arm, and bled to death. Such a state as everything was in—I needn't tell you!"

"It must have been," Mrs. Wynne heard herself inanely answer. She looked at the secretary; there was a kind of pity in her horror at the woman's callousness. She was so much the creature of her job that her blank face, if it could be said to wear any expression, wore only that of anger at the "state" of Marion's bedclothes and the carpet by the bed.

"And the talk and annoyance in the hotel—it's been bad enough without that; people leaving because of the old lady and her tempers. We all thought Miss Cameron would go out of her mind, three months ago, but she seemed better."

"We were getting a separate bedroom ready for her yesterday, but Mrs. Cameron countermanded it. Well, she might have spared herself something, if she hadn't—not that it would have made much difference, I suppose. And of course there's any amount of trouble and annoyance before us—the inquest, and all the unpleasantness."

The inquest . . . of course there would have to be one . . . How much could be kept back? Mrs. Wynne controlled her face and voice.

"I'll come over at once and see Mrs. Cameron," she said, though her soul fainted at thought of that interview.

"You won't find her. You wouldn't suppose that she'd be in and out of the house every minute, but that's what she is, and looking so queer with that cut on her face"—the secretary glanced at Mrs. Wynne as she said this—"that she got at tea-time yesterday."

The biscuit-plate—had either of the Camerons remembered to pick it up, or had a servant found it on the floor, so far from the tea-table? . . . Mrs. Wynne again controlled herself.

"That cut was nothing, I fancy; I remember noticing it yesterday afternoon. You say Mrs. Cameron won't be in?"

"She was out when I left, at Dr. Ferguson's; at least that's where she told the taxi to go—she had a taxi, that time. He was at the house this morning, of course; but she said she must see him again. Goodness knows why."

Even the gleam of curiosity was listless. Mrs. Wynne felt, with shuddering reassurance, that you could never fathom London's indifference.

"I'll wait, then; I won't go back with you to the hotel," she said.

"Mrs. Cameron spoke of you, this morning," the woman apathetically remarked.

"And said what?"

"It's not very pleasant to repeat, but perhaps I'd better. She said on no account to let you in."

"I was more Miss Cameron's friend than hers. It's odd, though," Mrs. Wynne returned, and hoped that she seemed only ordinarily troubled. "At such a time, however, one can't wonder at anything . . . Is there nothing I can do to help in any way?"

"I don't think so." But the woman still sat, looking round the room, and Mrs. Wynne grew fidgety. She wanted her to go at once, that she herself might get to Dr. Ferguson's before Mrs. Cameron should leave him. No place could be so good to meet, and they would have to speak together, let her knowledge be resented as it might.

The secretary seemed to feel at last that they had finished. She rose, but then she paused, and spoke with eyes averted.

"I found the plate myself," she said, as impassively as before. "I happened to go into the drawing-room. I haven't mentioned it." She waited.

"The plate?" said Mrs. Wynne, in a strained voice of questioning.

The faded eyes met hers. "The biscuit-plate. It wasn't broken, fortunately. We may as well leave it out, if we have anything to say at the inquest. It would be a nuisance, if . . ." She drifted to the door. "You see, I have to think of my employers. People hate a scandal about a private hotel; it ruins business. You won't speak of it?"

"I don't know what you mean," Mrs. Wynne lied bravely.

The secretary looked at her again. "Something happened in the drawing-room," she went on, unmoved. "Any fool could see that—and you were there at the time. But it's just as well for me to know nothing about it, so don't tell me if I'm right."

With that, she opened the door at last; Mrs. Wynne went with her to the steps in a stunned silence.

As she drove to Dr. Ferguson's, Mrs. Wynne reflected on his theory. It, like the biscuit-plate, would have to be kept dark! Even in her grief, she smiled at a quick thought. The Freudian Wish—and the Bergsma visiting-card . . . but such ironic fellowships would be the very core, no doubt, of speculations in this kind. Was it another Wish that put the silly strip of pasteboard in its halfpenny envelope? And had Marion had one too—did she "wish" Bergsma to know what had been done? For, without the card, she would have had her separate room; those words would not have sounded: "I've never left you alone for a single instant, and I never intend to . . ." Never alone from Mrs. Cameron, ridden by the Freudian Wish! A new burden had been bound upon humanity, if that frightful theory were true.

She was at once admitted at the doctor's, for she sent in her card. As she drew it from the case, she wondered if she ever should do that again without a shudder—and knew that she would, that this would pass as all things pass . . . She entered the consulting-room—yes, Mrs. Cameron was there. Instantly the old woman sprang up, and stood defiant of her. But the doctor put his hand upon her arm.

"Keep quiet, Mrs. Cameron," he said, with stern decision. "Sit down, Mrs. Wynne."

Mrs. Wynne sat down. She felt horribly unpitying. Mrs. Cameron looked as usual—the pink face was a little pinker for the sticking-plaster on the cheek, which gave her a weird air of coquetry. Her mouth was quivering, but it looked more peevish than distressed . . . And she had seen that sight, not many hours ago!

"Go on with what you were telling me," Dr. Ferguson said.

Still standing, with one hand on the table and her angry eyes on Mrs. Wynne, Mrs. Cameron obeyed eagerly, as if she trusted the man to be her friend against the woman.

She had evidently been telling him about the visiting-card.

"I thought it seemed unnecessary, but my opinion was that Marion and I should call. I considered it my duty to uphold Marion's dignity."

She stopped, still fixing Mrs. Wynne with her malignant eyes.

Mrs. Wynne dropped hers before them. A coroner's jury would not have heard of Freud.

"Yes—your daughter's dignity?" Dr. Ferguson said, smoothly. His eyes met Mrs. Wynne's when she lifted her head again.

THE KING WAITS

Clemence Dane
(1888–1965)

"Clemence Dane" was the pseudonym of Winifred Ashton, who started adult life as an artist and actress before deteriorating health during World War One led her to begin writing. "The King Waits" was one of her first published stories, following Dane's first novel, Regiment of Women *(1917), notorious in its time for its portrayal of a lesbian school-teacher at an all-girl's school. "The King Waits" did not attract the attention that* Regiment of Women *did, or that Dane's second novel,* Legend *(1919), did. (*Legend *also has a lesbian theme, leading to persistent speculation that Dane, who never married and had a "secretary-companion" of many years, was gay.) Dane began writing plays and found success in that medium, with her* A Bill of Divorcement *(1921) becoming a hit and eventually a 1932 film starring Katherine Hepburn and John Barrymore. Dane continued to write plays but added screenplays and mystery and fantasy novels to her résumé. In 1946 she won an Academy Award for* Vacation From Marriage; *among the literary set, she gained fame as one of Noel Coward's "muses." Later in life she edited a series of science fiction novels for a British publisher, publishing John Christopher and C.M. Kornbluth among others.*

Dane was largely a mainstream writer—and, obviously, a successful one—but the super-natural can be found in some of her stories and novels, whether overtly, as in Legend *and* The Babylons *(1927) and "Frau Holde" (1935), or more subtly, as in "The King Waits," which is also notable for its portrayal of Anne Boleyn, who in Dane's hands is neither evangelizing, religious, or remorseful, but proud and not a little frightening.*

THE MORNING WAS a Friday, the month was May; it was the twenty-eighth year of the Eighth Henry's reign over England, and it needed five minutes to be noon. On Richmond Hill, under the great spring-leaved oak, stood Henry the King. His outstretched hand commanded silence, and his huntsmen stilled the restless coupled hounds in dumb show, with furtive, sidelong glances, fearing that outstretched jewel-laden hand, that arrogant glance. Who will disobey Henry the King, calling in that furious voice for silence? Even the midday sun, as a little cloud slipped from its face, poured down such an answering concentra-tion of heat upon the green hill-side that the noon hush seemed an act of grace from one royalty to another. There was instantly no sound at all save the panting of the half-throttled hounds and the dry whisper of innumerable caterpillars hissing in innumerable leaves; for there was a blight that spring in the oak-woods.

For one minute—two—three—the silence endured; then a burst of wind broke it: and all the trees in Richmond Park began once more to strain, creak, rustle, and the scent of the May drifted by again in gusts, and high overhead the clouds too renewed their voyage eastward through the heavenly blue. Over the Tower of London, as the wind lulled once more, they banked together again, a white tower of the sky.

Far below the scent of the white May drifted over the town and in through the windows, doorways, and courtyards of the Tower, and over the Tower green. Through slits in the wall the river sparkled in the noon sunshine; but still it lacked four minutes to be noon.

Across the green to the new scaffold came Anne the Queen, dressed in black damask with a white cape, and her hat was in the fashion. The Lieutenant of the Tower helped her to mount the steps. She had her glance and her nod for the waiting swordsman; then she looked down upon her friends and upon her enemies gathered close about her harsh death-bed; said to them that which was in her mind to say; adjusted her dress and freed the small neck; then knelt. But she would not let friend or enemy cover her eyes, and though she knelt she did not bow her head, but looked again keenly upon the silenced crowd: and for the last time called upon the ready blood to flush her cheeks.

She had always been able to redden thus into beauty when she chose; and now the hot blood did not fail her. It was at its old trick, brightening her black eyes: and this was ever the sign of crisis with her. With that sudden flush she had won her game—how often?—with this king and husband who had now beaten her. She felt a strange pang of longing to remember, to finger once again her glorious victories over time, absence, malice, envy, a queen, a cardinal, a king—and her own resentful heart.

She was not used to deny herself any wish; so, lifting her head, she let the spell work for the last time: and her executioner, meeting that full glance, hesitated and turned aside, as if his part were not yet ready to be played. Again he advanced: again she looked at him, and had the last triumph of her beauty as she won her respite. He would wait her pleasure for a minute, no more than a minute; but she knew now that the tales they had told of drowning men were true. The dying see their lives in a minute: she, dying, would see again her life.

She turned her eyes away from the frightened faces of her women, from faithful Mary Wyatt's weeping agony: she looked in turn upon her gaoler Kingston, on courteous Gwynn clutching in his hand her last gift, on thankless Cromwell, on Suffolk's exultant face. But here her glance checked, her very heart checked on its beat, for beside Suffolk, her enemy, stood a nearer enemy; it seemed to her that her husband's eyes glittered at her, set in a younger, comelier countenance. So Henry had sent his bastard to watch her die! She smiled to herself as she thought that it was like him, like her fool and tyrant, her Henry, husband, king! She thought that he himself would have been glad to watch her die: he could not for his dignity, so he sent his left-hand son, young Richmond. Yes, to act thus was like Henry, and young Richmond, watching her, was very like Henry: she had seen on many a May morning that eager parting of the full, pinched mouth, that glistening of small, hard eyes.

Suddenly her thirty-odd years of life began to speed across her eyeballs, quickly and softy, like the scudding clouds above her speeding over the Tower in the spring wind. Childhood and youth at Hever Castle—in a flash she saw those spring years pass, and herself journeying to France in the train of Henry's sister. Little thought fifteen-year-old Anne Boleyn that she would ever call the Queen of France sister! But she saw herself, nevertheless, all unconscious, dancing, dressing, laughing, learning, learning always to be a queen. And so home again to England, to the Court at Windsor Castle, like that last lone small cloud above her scudding across the sky to join the massed castles of the air. And there she saw herself for a little while serving the good dull Katharine; but she had no memory of Katharine's lord, Henry King of England. Another face and form flitted across her eyeballs, of another Henry—Henry Percy, heir to the dukedom of Northumberland.

A high wind drove in upon the clouds as she watched, and scattered them all ways, while the executioner whispered with his underling. Thus boisterously, she thought, had Henry the King driven in upon love and lovers. Henry Percy is rated by the butcher's son, Wolsey, the hated cardinal; and his father summoned; and shamed Anne is dismissed the Court.

Home again goes Anne to Hever, her marriage and her heart broken, and never knows, so innocent is this earlier Anne, why misfortune cut off her happiness at a blow, like a skilled swordsman striking off a queen's head. But when a guest arrived at Hever Castle—then Anne knows!

Henry the King comes to Hever very sure of his welcome. And indeed her father and her stepmother may scour the county for fish, flesh, fowl and fruits in their season; and summon country gentlemen

and ladies, and handsome boys and pleasant girls, to make feasts and
plan pleasures for the King. But Maîtresse Anne keeps her chamber.
Henry is master of Hever, not of Anne. Anne knows now who has
parted her, with Wolsey's help, from Henry Percy, true love, first love,
and she will teach that greedy mouth, those glistening eyes, a lesson.
Henry the King is the singular good lord and favourable prince of Sir
Thomas and Lady Boleyn; but Maîtresse Anne Boleyn keeps her chamber. Let the King learn what it means to part lovers! Let him wait and
chafe and learn!

She watched him in memory once more as he rode away from
Hever, an angry, hungry king, spurring his horse. She watched him and
his train dwindling in the distance to such ant-like folk and swallowed
up by young green and pure white May hedges, under just such a blue
sky in just such windy weather. What a wind! There's no sound at all
in the world but the hurry of the royal wind. When will it strike
twelve? Is it a minute or a lifetime since she knelt?

More clouds scud across the sky, more years scud across her dying
eyes. She saw again her father, and smiled as she remembered that he,
too, had been among those who condemned her. Strange father! Coward father! But he had liked his new title, all those years ago—Viscount
Rochford sounded well; and her sister's husband was glad enough to
be Gentleman of the Privy Chamber; and for herself there was a place
at Court again, and jewels! (But Henry Percy is exiled to Northumberland!) Once more she saw that greedy mouth; once more she fell very
humbly on her knees, summoned the lovely blood to her cheek, and
said her say to Henry the King:

"Your wife I cannot be, both in respect of mine own unworthiness,
and also because you have a queen already. Your mistress I will not be."

And so home again to Hever in just such soft blue weather, to read
humble letters from a once blustering king, who knows now what it
means to be a lover parted from his love. How did his letter go?

"I beseech you earnestly to let me know your real mind as to the
love between us. . . . If it does not please you to answer me in writing,
let me know some place where I may have it by word of mouth; and
I will go thither with all my heart. No more for fear of tiring you."

But he tires her none the less, and she will not go to meet him. Let
him wait! Let him wait his four years!

They scud by like clouds, as her cheek burns with a new memory of
hate and reckoning. What of Wolsey? How shall Wolsey be paid if
Anne pines at Hever while the King waits unsatisfied?

So Anne Boleyn comes to town again and serves the Queen again, and takes her place at last as King's bliss: queens it at Hampton, at Windsor, and at Greenwich, and holds her state in the Cardinal's own York House. How else should Wolsey be taught what it is to part lovers? (But Henry Percy has married a wife and will not come again!) Let Wolsey learn what he has to pay for crossing "the foolish girl yonder in the Court."

She saw herself again, while Katharine, her mistress, sat weeping and praying and sewing with her dull maids, reigning at the feasts the shaken Cardinal prepared for her; saw herself May Queen on May mornings and Lady of the Revels on Christmas Eves; till, at the Greenwich midnight masque, the French ambassador watching, she danced (mark it, butcher's son!) in public with the King, the flush upon her cheek, and listened afterwards to Henry's own song:—

> The eagle force subdues each bird that flies:
> What metal can resist the flaming fire?
> Doth not the sun dazzle the clearest eyes,
> And melt the ice and make the frost retire?

The ice, indeed, is melting. Lord Cardinal! You were not wise to go to France; less wise when you returned to dissuade a king from changing old queens for new. Anne Boleyn has other weapons than her brilliant eyes, her burning cheek, her dancing feet, and quick tongue. Henry has been jealous once; he shall be jealous again! King Henry is not the only lover who sings to Anne his own verses. Besides, Tom Wyatt has a look of Henry Percy (married, out of sight, never out of mind!), and is a bolder man than Percy.

She lived again through the day when Henry stole a ring from her finger and swaggered out to play at bowls with Wyatt. Again she watched all from her window, and heard all—King Henry crying out that he wins: and Wyatt telling him that, by his leave, it is not so!—and Henry's chuckle as he points with his new-ringed finger, crying:

"Wyatt, I tell thee, it is mine!"

But Wyatt, too, wears a keepsake under his Court suit over his heart. What can a poet and a lover do but draw from that hiding place the jewel swinging on its chain.

"Give me leave to measure the cast with this, and I have good hopes yet it will be mine!"

Once again she saw him stoop, measure, and prove winner; and rise to face the Tudor thunderstorm.

"It may be so, but then I am deceived." And away storms Henry to her chamber crying "What is Wyatt to you?"

She remembered how easily then she dealt with him and his jealousies: how she struck her bargain: and how, five years later, while she, the new-made Marchioness of Pembroke, sat on the King's knee, and he kissed her, not caring who saw, she heard Wyatt's voice singing to her new ladies-in-waiting his farewell song—

> *Forget not yet thine own approved,*
> *The which so constant hath thee loved.*
> *Whose steadfast faith has never moved;*
> *Forget not yet!*

Poor Tom Wyatt! The scent of the May drifts across the scaffold like the scent of the rose-water that it was his office to pour upon her hands on her coronation day. And there was another May morning to remember—the best to remember!

The flush on her cheek deepened, and her head sank as she saw herself three years ago, only three years ago, journeying to the Tower, this same Tower that now witnessed her last journey's end. She saw the press of cheering folk at Greenwich, the branches of the oaks cracking under the weight of citizens, the may-bushes clambered over, with gaping faces thrust out, scratched and red and laughable between the pure clots of bloom. She saw again the Lord Mayor and his scarlet haberdashers, and felt the jewels on his glove dent her fingers as she put her hand in his that he might lead her to the State barge.

It waited for her on the breast of the sparkling river, the same sparkling river sparkling now through slits in her prison walls. But then the river was alive with pageantry, and instead of black damask she wore cloth of gold; and the world was full of noise where now was deadly silence and the executioner's foot behind her, breaking the silence.

But her mind rejected utterly that stealthy sound: it was filled with memories of the glorious noises—the cries of all the people and the tinkling of the fluttering, bell-sewn flags as the barge poled out into mid-stream with fifty lesser barges following. All London moved that May morning with her towards the Tower, so that her progress turned the very Thames back upon its course. (Why not when she, Anne Boleyn, had already turned back history, shaken Spain, defeated Rome, killed a cardinal, and wrecked a queen?) The great fiery dragon spat fire from the foist, and from the bachelor barge came trumpet-calls once more, and, from the maiden's barge, unceasing high-pitched singing, sweet as the singing of the waking birds had been when she met Henry Percy, not Henry of England, by stealth under the Greenwich hawthorn trees. Well, she had avenged that lost sweetness! Wolsey had parted her from Henry Percy, and where was Wolsey now? fallen, as she was falling: dead, as she in another instant must lie dead! But Henry Percy had been gaoler to the great cardinal before the end, had led the cardinal, his legs bound beneath his horse's belly like any other felon, to his prison and his grave. She had taught the greatest man in England what it cost to part lovers.

A smile lit up her face as she remembered that lesson, and the watchers saw it and wondered, and weeping Mary Wyatt called her in her heart "saint" and "innocent"; and young Richmond thought of his father, awaiting on Richmond Hill for the boom of the cannon, and wondered if he should report that inexplicable, triumphant smile. How slowly the man from Calais goes about his business! Look, he swings his sword! Does the kneeling creature know that the French executioner is swinging his sword?

But Anne did not see the present. She was smiling at her achieved past. She saw that she had done what she set out to do unafraid. She could say, when her sins rose up and looked at her, that she had never, in life or death, been made afraid. She had been fit mother for kings and queens: and—who knows? Wheels turn!—her Elizabeth might yet rule England, like her mother, unafraid! She saw again so clearly, lying open before her, the book of prophecies found once in her room, hidden there to frighten her by friends of Katharine. There had been a picture of Henry and weeping Katharine, and herself between them, kneeling at the block even as she knelt now. But when her frightened maid called out, "If this were prophesied of me, I would not have him, were he emperor!" she had answered—

"I am resolved to have him, that my issue may be royal, whatever may become of me."

She murmured the words again half aloud, and heard Mary's gasp from the scaffold foot—"She prays!" and saw the sudden upward flash of faces, watching a movement that she heard behind her but could not see. What? had so many years, had her whole life flashed before her eyes in so brief a minute? Yet the minute was too long, it seemed, for these watchers! They grew impatient and would hurry her into death. Let them know that the Queen dies at her own minute, not at theirs! Not thus had they hurried her two years ago from Greenwich landing to the Tower. They had led her slowly to the Tower then, that all the town might see her beauty. And Henry, her king and husband, had met her in the gateway and welcomed her most joyfully. She felt again upon her lips his loving kiss, and his great arm flung about her neck.

It fell upon her neck again like an all-ending blow; and there was a booming in her ears. . . .

The echoes of the gun went rolling round and out over the Tower walls, went rolling over the City and its suburbs, went rolling with the river up to Richmond Hill. Henry the King, motionless beneath the oak, like a painted monarch, like a card king of hearts, heard the heavy voice and understood the awaited, welcome message.

He started joyfully from his trance and, stripping a little ring from his finger, flung it into a bloom-laden may-thorn bush ten yards away.

"The deed is done!" cried Henry. "Uncouple the hounds and away!"

He clambered to his saddle while the statues of his huntsmen, his horses, and his hounds came to life about him, and, spurring his eager beast, led the hunt westward, ever westward, towards Wiltshire and Jane Seymour, and his wedding morrow.

A CATALOG OF SELECTED
DOVER BOOKS
IN ALL FIELDS OF INTEREST

A CATALOG OF SELECTED DOVER
BOOKS IN ALL FIELDS OF INTEREST

100 BEST-LOVED POEMS, Edited by Philip Smith. "The Passionate Shepherd to His Love," "Shall I compare thee to a summer's day?" "Death, be not proud," "The Raven," "The Road Not Taken," plus works by Blake, Wordsworth, Byron, Shelley, Keats, many others. Includes 13 selections from the Common Core State Standards Initiative. 112pp. 0-486-28553-7

ABC BOOK OF EARLY AMERICANA, Eric Sloane. Artist and historian Eric Sloane presents a wondrous A-to-Z collection of American innovations, including hex signs, ear trumpets, popcorn, and rocking chairs. Illustrated, hand-lettered pages feature brief captions explaining objects' origins and uses. 64pp. 0-486-49808-5

ADVENTURES OF HUCKLEBERRY FINN, Mark Twain. Join Huck and Jim as their boyhood adventures along the Mississippi River lead them into a world of excitement, danger, and self-discovery. Humorous narrative, lyrical descriptions of the Mississippi valley, and memorable characters. 224pp. 0-486-28061-6

ALICE STARMORE'S BOOK OF FAIR ISLE KNITTING, Alice Starmore. A noted designer from the region of Scotland's Fair Isle explores the history and techniques of this distinctive, stranded-color knitting style and provides copious illustrated instructions for 14 original knitwear designs. 208pp. 0-486-47218-3

ALICE'S ADVENTURES IN WONDERLAND, Lewis Carroll. Beloved classic about a little girl lost in a topsy-turvy land and her encounters with the White Rabbit, March Hare, Mad Hatter, Cheshire Cat, and other delightfully improbable characters. 42 illustrations by Sir John Tenniel. A selection of the Common Core State Standards Initiative. 96pp. 0-486-27543-4

THE ARTHUR RACKHAM TREASURY: 86 Full-Color Illustrations, Arthur Rackham. Selected and Edited by Jeff A. Menges. A stunning treasury of 86 full-page plates span the famed English artist's career, from *Rip Van Winkle* (1905) to masterworks such as *Undine, A Midsummer Night's Dream,* and *Wind in the Willows* (1939). 96pp. 0-486-44685-9

THE AWAKENING, Kate Chopin. First published in 1899, this controversial novel of a New Orleans wife's search for love outside a stifling marriage shocked readers. Today, it remains a first-rate narrative with superb characterization. New introductory note. 128pp. 0-486-27786-0

BASEBALL IS . . .: Defining the National Pastime, Edited by Paul Dickson. Wisecracking, philosophical, nostalgic, and entertaining, these hundreds of quips and observations by players, their wives, managers, authors, and others cover every aspect of our national pastime. It's a great any-occasion gift for fans! 256pp. 0-486-48209-X

THE CALL OF THE WILD, Jack London. A classic novel of adventure, drawn from London's own experiences as a Klondike adventurer, relating the story of a heroic dog caught in the brutal life of the Alaska Gold Rush. Note. 64pp. 0-486-26472-6

CANDIDE, Voltaire. Edited by Francois-Marie Arouet. One of the world's great satires since its first publication in 1759. Witty, caustic skewering of romance, science, philosophy, religion, government — nearly all human ideals and institutions. A selection of the Common Core State Standards Initiative. 112pp. 0-486-26689-3

THE CARTOON HISTORY OF TIME, Kate Charlesworth and John Gribbin. Cartoon characters explain cosmology, quantum physics, and other concepts covered by Stephen Hawking's *A Brief History of Time.* Humorous graphic novel–style treatment, perfect for young readers and curious folk of all ages. 64pp. 0-486-49097-1

THE CHERRY ORCHARD, Anton Chekhov. Classic of world drama concerns passing of semifeudal order in turn-of-the-century Russia, symbolized in the sale of the cherry orchard owned by Madame Ranevskaya. Showcases Chekhov's rich sensitivities as an observer of human nature. 64pp. 0-486-26682-6

A CHRISTMAS CAROL, Charles Dickens. This engrossing tale relates Ebenezer Scrooge's ghostly journeys through Christmases past, present, and future and his ultimate transformation from a harsh and grasping old miser to a charitable and compassionate human being. 80pp. 0-486-26865-9

CRIME AND PUNISHMENT, Fyodor Dostoyevsky. Translated by Constance Garnett. Supreme masterpiece tells the story of Raskolnikov, a student tormented by his own thoughts after he murders an old woman. Overwhelmed by guilt and terror, he confesses and goes to prison. A selection of the Common Core State Standards Initiative. 448pp. 0-486-41587-2

CYRANO DE BERGERAC, Edmond Rostand. A quarrelsome, hot-tempered, and unattractive swordsman falls hopelessly in love with a beautiful woman and woos her for a handsome but slow-witted suitor. A witty and eloquent drama. 144pp. 0-486-41119-2

A DOLL'S HOUSE, Henrik Ibsen. Ibsen's best-known play displays his genius for realistic prose drama. An expression of women's rights, the play climaxes when the central character, Nora, rejects a smothering marriage and life in "a doll's house." A selection of the Common Core State Standards Initiative. 80pp. 0-486-27062-9

DOOMED SHIPS: Great Ocean Liner Disasters, William H. Miller, Jr. Nearly 200 photographs, many from private collections, highlight tales of some of the vessels whose pleasure cruises ended in catastrophe: the *Morro Castle, Normandie, Andrea Doria, Europa*, and many others. 128pp. 0-486-45366-9

DUBLINERS, James Joyce. A fine and accessible introduction to the work of one of the 20th century's most influential writers, this collection features 15 tales, including a masterpiece of the short-story genre, "The Dead." 160pp. 0-486-26870-5

THE EARLY SCIENCE FICTION OF PHILIP K. DICK, Philip K. Dick. This anthology presents short stories and novellas that originally appeared in pulp magazines of the early 1950s, including "The Variable Man," "Second Variety," "Beyond the Door," "The Defenders," and more. 272pp. 0-486-49733-X

THE EARLY SHORT STORIES OF F. SCOTT FITZGERALD, F. Scott Fitzgerald. These tales offer insights into many themes, characters, and techniques that emerged in Fitzgerald's later works. Selections include "The Curious Case of Benjamin Button," "Babes in the Woods," and a dozen others. 256pp. 0-486-79465-2

ETHAN FROME, Edith Wharton. Classic story of wasted lives, set against a bleak New England background. Superbly delineated characters in a hauntingly grim tale of thwarted love. Considered by many to be Wharton's masterpiece. 96pp. 0-486-26690-7

FLATLAND: A Romance of Many Dimensions, Edwin A. Abbott. Classic of science (and mathematical) fiction — charmingly illustrated by the author — describes the adventures of A. Square, a resident of Flatland, in Spaceland (three dimensions), Lineland (one dimension), and Pointland (no dimensions). 96pp. 0-486-27263-X

FRANKENSTEIN, Mary Shelley. The story of Victor Frankenstein's monstrous creation and the havoc it caused has enthralled generations of readers and inspired countless writers of horror and suspense. With the author's own 1831 introduction. 176pp. 0-486-28211-2

THE GARGOYLE BOOK: 572 Examples from Gothic Architecture, Lester Burbank Bridaham. Dispelling the conventional wisdom that French Gothic architectural flourishes were born of despair or gloom, Bridaham reveals the whimsical nature of these creations and the ingenious artisans who made them. 572 illustrations. 224pp. 0-486-44754-5

THE GIFT OF THE MAGI AND OTHER SHORT STORIES, O. Henry. Sixteen captivating stories by one of America's most popular storytellers. Included are such classics as "The Gift of the Magi," "The Last Leaf," and "The Ransom of Red Chief." Publisher's Note. A selection of the Common Core State Standards Initiative. 96pp. 0-486-27061-0

THE GOETHE TREASURY: Selected Prose and Poetry, Johann Wolfgang von Goethe. Edited, Selected, and with an Introduction by Thomas Mann. In addition to his lyric poetry, Goethe wrote travel sketches, autobiographical studies, essays, letters, and proverbs in rhyme and prose. This collection presents outstanding examples from each genre. 368pp. 0-486-44780-4

GREAT ILLUSTRATIONS BY N. C. WYETH, N. C. Wyeth. Edited and with an Introduction by Jeff A. Menges. This full-color collection focuses on the artist's early and most popular illustrations, featuring more than 100 images from *The Mysterious Stranger, Robin Hood, Robinson Crusoe, The Boy's King Arthur,* and other classics. 128pp. 0-486-47295-7

HAMLET, William Shakespeare. The quintessential Shakespearean tragedy, whose highly charged confrontations and anguished soliloquies probe depths of human feeling rarely sounded in any art. Reprinted from an authoritative British edition complete with illuminating footnotes. A selection of the Common Core State Standards Initiative. 128pp. 0-486-27278-8

THE HAUNTED HOUSE, Charles Dickens. A Yuletide gathering in an eerie country retreat provides the backdrop for Dickens and his friends — including Elizabeth Gaskell and Wilkie Collins — who take turns spinning supernatural yarns. 144pp. 0-486-46309-5

HEART OF DARKNESS, Joseph Conrad. Dark allegory of a journey up the Congo River and the narrator's encounter with the mysterious Mr. Kurtz. Masterly blend of adventure, character study, psychological penetration. For many, Conrad's finest, most enigmatic story. 80pp. 0-486-26464-5

THE HOUND OF THE BASKERVILLES, Sir Arthur Conan Doyle. A deadly curse in the form of a legendary ferocious beast continues to claim its victims from the Baskerville family until Holmes and Watson intervene. Often called the best detective story ever written. 128pp. 0-486-28214-7

THE HOUSE BEHIND THE CEDARS, Charles W. Chesnutt. Originally published in 1900, this groundbreaking novel by a distinguished African-American author recounts the drama of a brother and sister who "pass for white" during the dangerous days of Reconstruction. 208pp. 0-486-46144-0

HOW TO DRAW NEARLY EVERYTHING, Victor Perard. Beginners of all ages can learn to draw figures, faces, landscapes, trees, flowers, and animals of all kinds. Well-illustrated guide offers suggestions for pencil, pen, and brush techniques plus composition, shading, and perspective. 160pp. 0-486-49848-4

HOW TO MAKE SUPER POP-UPS, Joan Irvine. Illustrated by Linda Hendry. Super pop-ups extend the element of surprise with three-dimensional designs that slide, turn, spring, and snap. More than 30 patterns and 475 illustrations include cards, stage props, and school projects. 96pp. 0-486-46589-6

THE IMITATION OF CHRIST, Thomas à Kempis. Translated by Aloysius Croft and Harold Bolton. This religious classic has brought understanding and comfort to millions for centuries. Written in a candid and conversational style, the topics include liberation from worldly inclinations, preparation and consolations of prayer, and eucharistic communion. 160pp. 0-486-43185-1

THE IMPORTANCE OF BEING EARNEST, Oscar Wilde. Wilde's witty and buoyant comedy of manners, filled with some of literature's most famous epigrams, reprinted from an authoritative British edition. Considered Wilde's most perfect work. A selection of the Common Core State Standards Initiative. 64pp. 0-486-26478-5

JANE EYRE, Charlotte Brontë. Written in 1847, *Jane Eyre* tells the tale of an orphan girl's progress from the custody of cruel relatives to an oppressive boarding school and its culmination in a troubled career as a governess. A selection of the Common Core State Standards Initiative. 448pp. 0-486-42449-9

JUST WHAT THE DOCTOR DISORDERED: Early Writings and Cartoons of Dr. Seuss, Dr. Seuss. Edited and with an Introduction by Rick Marschall. The Doctor's visual hilarity, nonsense language, and offbeat sense of humor illuminate this compilation of items from his early career, created for periodicals such as *Judge, Life, College Humor,* and *Liberty.* 144pp. 0-486-49846-8

KING LEAR, William Shakespeare. Powerful tragedy of an aging king, betrayed by his daughters, robbed of his kingdom, descending into madness. Perhaps the bleakest of Shakespeare's tragic dramas, complete with explanatory footnotes. 144pp. 0-486-28058-6

THE LADY OR THE TIGER?: and Other Logic Puzzles, Raymond M. Smullyan. Created by a renowned puzzle master, these whimsically themed challenges involve paradoxes about probability, time, and change; metapuzzles; and self-referentiality. Nineteen chapters advance in difficulty from relatively simple to highly complex. 1982 edition. 240pp.
0-486-47027-X

LEAVES OF GRASS: The Original 1855 Edition, Walt Whitman. Whitman's immortal collection includes some of the greatest poems of modern times, including his masterpiece, "Song of Myself." Shattering standard conventions, it stands as an unabashed celebration of body and nature. 128pp. 0-486-45676-5

LES MISÉRABLES, Victor Hugo. Translated by Charles E. Wilbour. Abridged by James K. Robinson. A convict's heroic struggle for justice and redemption plays out against a fiery backdrop of the Napoleonic wars. This edition features the excellent original translation and a sensitive abridgment. 304pp. 0-486-45789-3

LIGHT FOR THE ARTIST, Ted Seth Jacobs. Intermediate and advanced art students receive a broad vocabulary of effects with this in-depth study of light. Diagrams and paintings illustrate applications of principles to figure, still life, and landscape paintings. 144pp. 0-486-49304-0

LILITH: A Romance, George MacDonald. In this novel by the father of fantasy literature, a man travels through time to meet Adam and Eve and to explore humanity's fall from grace and ultimate redemption. 240pp. 0-486-46818-6

LINE: An Art Study, Edmund J. Sullivan. Written by a noted artist and teacher, this well-illustrated guide introduces the basics of line drawing. Topics include third and fourth dimensions, formal perspective, shade and shadow, figure drawing, and other essentials. 208pp. 0-486-79484-9

THE LODGER, Marie Belloc Lowndes. Acclaimed by *The New York Times* as "one of the best suspense novels ever written," this novel recounts an English couple's doubts about their boarder, whom they suspect of being a serial killer. 240pp. 0-486-78809-1

MACBETH, William Shakespeare. A Scottish nobleman murders the king in order to succeed to the throne. Tortured by his conscience and fearful of discovery, he becomes tangled in a web of treachery and deceit that ultimately spells his doom. A selection of the Common Core State Standards Initiative. 96pp. 0-486-27802-6

MANHATTAN IN MAPS 1527–2014, Paul E. Cohen and Robert T. Augustyn. This handsome volume features 65 full-color maps charting Manhattan's development from the first Dutch settlement to the present. Each map is placed in context by an accompanying essay. 176pp. 0-486-77991-2

MEDEA, Euripides. One of the most powerful and enduring of Greek tragedies, masterfully portraying the fierce motives driving Medea's pursuit of vengeance for her husband's insult and betrayal. Authoritative Rex Warner translation. 64pp. 0-486-27548-5

THE METAMORPHOSIS AND OTHER STORIES, Franz Kafka. Excellent new English translations of title story (considered by many critics Kafka's most perfect work), plus "The Judgment," "In the Penal Colony," "A Country Doctor," and "A Report to an Academy." A selection of the Common Core State Standards Initiative. 96pp. 0-486-29030-1

METROPOLIS, Thea von Harbou. This Weimar-era novel of a futuristic society, written by the screenwriter for the iconic 1927 film, was hailed by noted science-fiction authority Forrest J. Ackerman as "a work of genius." 224pp. 0-486-79567-5

THE MYSTERIOUS MICKEY FINN, Elliot Paul. A multimillionaire's disappearance incites a maelstrom of kidnapping, murder, and a plot to restore the French monarchy. "One of the funniest books we've read in a long time." — *The New York Times.* 256pp. 0-486-24751-1

NARRATIVE OF THE LIFE OF FREDERICK DOUGLASS, Frederick Douglass. The impassioned abolitionist and eloquent orator provides graphic descriptions of his childhood and horrifying experiences as a slave as well as a harrowing record of his dramatic escape to the North and eventual freedom. A selection of the Common Core State Standards Initiative. 96pp. 0-486-28499-9

OBELISTS FLY HIGH, C. Daly King. Masterpiece of detective fiction portrays murder aboard a 1935 transcontinental flight. Combining an intricate plot and "locked room" scenario, the mystery was praised by *The New York Times* as "a very thrilling story." 288pp. 0-486-25036-9

THE ODYSSEY, Homer. Excellent prose translation of ancient epic recounts adventures of the homeward-bound Odysseus. Fantastic cast of gods, giants, cannibals, sirens, other supernatural creatures — true classic of Western literature. A selection of the Common Core State Standards Initiative. 256pp. 0-486-40654-7

OEDIPUS REX, Sophocles. Landmark of Western drama concerns the catastrophe that ensues when King Oedipus discovers he has inadvertently killed his father and married his mother. Masterly construction, dramatic irony. A selection of the Common Core State Standards Initiative. 64pp. 0-486-26877-2

OTHELLO, William Shakespeare. Towering tragedy tells the story of a Moorish general who earns the enmity of his ensign Iago when he passes him over for a promotion. Masterly portrait of an archvillain. Explanatory footnotes. 112pp. 0-486-29097-2

THE PICTURE OF DORIAN GRAY, Oscar Wilde. Celebrated novel involves a handsome young Londoner who sinks into a life of depravity. His body retains perfect youth and vigor while his recent portrait reflects the ravages of his crime and sensuality. 176pp. 0-486-27807-7

A PLACE CALLED PECULIAR: Stories About Unusual American Place-Names, Frank K. Gallant. From Smut Eye, Alabama, to Tie Siding, Wyoming, this pop-culture history offers a well-written and highly entertaining survey of America's most unusual place-names and their often-humorous origins. 256pp. 0-486-48360-6

PRIDE AND PREJUDICE, Jane Austen. One of the most universally loved and admired English novels, an effervescent tale of rural romance transformed by Jane Austen's art into a witty, shrewdly observed satire of English country life. A selection of the Common Core State Standards Initiative. 272pp. 0-486-28473-5

Browse over 10,000 books at www.doverpublications.com